LOKI'S WAGER

Ian Stuart Sharpe

LOKI'S WAGER
Copyright © 2019 Ian Stuart Sharpe. All rights reserved.

Published by Outland Entertainment LLC
3119 Gillham Road
Kansas City, MO 64109

Founder/Creative Director: Jeremy D. Mohler
Editor-in-Chief: Alana Joli Abbott
Senior Editor: Gwendolyn Nix

ISBN: 978-1-947659-82-7 (print)
ISBN: 978-1-947659-67-4 (ebook)
Worldwide Rights
Created in the United States of America

Developmental editor: Shannon Page
Copy editor: Alana Abbott
Cover Illustration & Design: Jeremy D. Mohler
Interior Layout: Mikael Brodu

The characters and events portrayed in this book are fictitious or fictitious recreations of actual historical persons. Any similarity to real persons, living or dead, is coincidental and not intended by the authors unless otherwise specified. This book or any portion thereof may not be reproduced or used in any manner whatsoever without the express written permission of the publisher except for the use of brief quotations in a book review.

Printed and bound in the United States of America.

Visit **outlandentertainment.com** to see more, or follow us on our Facebook Page facebook.com/outlandentertainment/

*To Beatrice and Benjamin,
and all the saviours of Mother Jörð*

*The gods in Ithavoll meet together,
Of the terrible girdler of earth they talk,
And the mighty past they call to mind,
And the ancient runes of the Ruler of Gods.*
Völuspá 60

BOOK ONE: TIME IS

— TRUMBA'S LAMENT —

Ormr inn Langi, **Imperial Yacht in orbit above Midgard**
1969

"How peaceful she looks."
The Empress stared down on the world below, her face as blank and remorseless as the sun. She rested her head against the hollow and traced her finger around the vacuum seal—the membrane flinched, then recoiled more slowly, adjusting to the momentary change in pressure.

Iðunn Lind watched the woman intently, a mere slip of a girl, her face half hidden by a delicate linen veil, her sing-song voice incongruent in its innocence.

"The first time I saw her, I was amazed. That tiny jewel, wispy and blue, was Mother Jörð. I held out my fingers as if to pluck her from the sky. I thought I'd feel like a god, but I didn't. I felt very, very small."

The waif drifted from hollow to hollow, trailing her long, red woolen dress in solemn procession across the prow of the ship.

Iðunn felt sick to the pit of her stomach. She knew this going to be gruesome, but even so, she felt compelled to join the young woman at the viewpoint. She had seen the transmissions, of course. Everyone had. But this was different. This was gazing into the abyss. Perhaps she had ventured all this way to bear witness. *Where were you when the world ended?* It wasn't a question anyone thought to ask, because it shouldn't be answerable.

The hollow loomed from floor to ceiling, affording a dizzying view. She had no choice but to look out.

The pea-green pearl was gone. A violent red smog roiled from pole to pole, and beneath it the glaciers had already begun their deadly march. The planet was inside out, wet with guts and bone. The scale of destruction was immense, unimaginable. Iðunn thought she knew grief, but her long years of loss were nothing compared to this.

"Do they understand why this happened?" The question caught in her throat. She struggled to turn her head away, to regain her composure.

Beneath the walls of her skin, her mind echoed with anguish, floundering in the darkest of depressions. Who hadn't drowned in the madness of it all? she thought, as the tears tumbled down her face. Who was there left to fathom?

Dómhild Trumba didn't answer. There was no need. Midgard had fallen, her Empire of the Heavens reduced to dust and viscera. Explanations wouldn't change anything.

Only the poetry of myth and legend could capture the catastrophe, the skalds would say. It was Ægir's daughters who rose that night, pitching and surging and grasping at the cities of man. Hálogi had burst from the earth, seething with wildfire, a procession of Eldjötnar at his heels.

Fierce grows the steam and the life-feeding flame,
Till fire leaps high about heaven itself.

But no lay could truly describe the collapse of Gulrstein Caldera, or the clouds of splintered rock and ash that blanketed the West, choking crops and livestock. No wordsmiths could convey the horror of flash-flooded cities, ripped in two by boiling seas.

If only it had ended there. Mankind had been humbled, Mother Jörð broken, but together they might have fought on, out of desperation or defiance. Across the planet there were survivors, of course: in the forests of Markland, in the mountains of the Rus, in the vain citadels of Aztland. Even in the seas off Furðustrandir, where a hundred thousand vessels struggled against the blood-dimmed tide. The relief efforts were quickly underway, the fleet flitting to and from the Hinterworlds. The rich, the noble, the powerful: they were ferried to safety.

But that was just the beginning.

Those who witnessed the bayonet of light say it outshone the moon. Like the flash of the sun on snow, it was dazzling for an instant—then the bloom faded, leaving a tear in the ash-dark clouds. It wasn't a solar flare, the seiðrmenn said. They could have predicted that, prepared for it. No, this was something much more powerful.

A collision.

A black hole, a wanderer, a vagrant that decided to settle down in the heart of a distant sun. The immense gravity ripped it to pieces, shredding it to vapor, then announced its presence with twin beams of unstoppable fury. Surtr's sword had cleaved the heavens. Hours later, the rains came. Scalding, boiling rains, each droplet a deceit, a disguise for the radiation that fell from the cosmos. Across Trankebar, Frederiksnagore, and Ny Danmǫrk, across the whole of Asaland, people dropped and died where they stood. Hindoo, Norse, or Chitai, it made no difference: a third of the globe cooked, bubbling into a soup of glue and protein.

Götterdämmerung, Ragnarök, the doom of the gods, the meistari called it, trying to protect the survivors with dreamlike tales, ringing their fading horizons with forts of the imagination. The destruction was preordained, they cried. In time, the earth would emerge out of the sea, and be green and fair again. The gods would return to their golden tables amid the grass.

But Iðunn Lind no longer traded in fiction. Her job was to speak truth to power. Even after all the horrors of the Jötunn War, she was still a Verðandi, the head of an ancient order of diviners and healers, tied to the warp and the weft of humanity.

She'd heard the Tree scream even before the first bulletins from Midgard. Iðunn had sent her mind thrashing through the greenways in a blind panic, driven by instinct, drawn to the carnage by duty and by desperation. And here she was, in orbit, above a world lying in state, with a Head of State who was considerably more alive than the rumours had suggested.

She knew enough to call it what it was.

Obliteration. The word meant to remove from existence, to purge from memory. That implied orchestration. The crime was immense.

Fuckers, she thought. Someone would have to pay.

The *Ormr inn Langi* hung above the troposphere like a shroud. The crown of the ship was a fly's eye dome, a geodesic bubble with hollows all around, cradling the stars. There was ample room for the two women to stand vigil.

The old warship was riven with fungus. Iðunn could smell the decay, sweet and sickly. She wrinkled her nose. At least the dull hum of the GEM field was reassuring. Very... grounding, she deadpanned. With the world hung, drawn, and quartered, gallows humour was the only thing she could trust. She felt utterly flat—like a fragmentary tapestry rather than a living, breathing creature.

There was some comfort in holding tight to the ship's bulkhead, in proving she maintained a grip on reality, however tenuous. The symmetry always struck her as beautiful. The Norse believed the first man and woman were born of trees, and that the universe was rooted around the great World Tree, Yggdrasil. Their warriors took to the seas in clinker-built vessels of oak and pine, shattering empires and claiming soil with blood. And when there were no more lands to conquer, the ancient forests delivered still more bounty. Iðunn's own oh-so-illustrious great-grandfather had unlocked the greenways, gateways to the supposed realms of gods—other planets, flung across the heavens. It was inevitable that when the Norse sought out the cosmos, they did so in living, breathing ships, grown from the same stock as Yggdrasil. During her rehabilitation, she'd been proud to play shipwright, merging tradition with technology.

Trees were life.

And death. The *Ormr inn Langi* was a hulk, long since designated as the imperial tomb, preserved just to be blasted off into the Gap. It was easy to imagine the blue sphere of flames engulfing the ship's crown, flickering in the vacuum, a votive offering to a silent void.

She wondered whether the Empress was aware of the irony of having survived an extinction-level event in her own mausoleum.

Odin himself had decreed all dead men should be burned, and their belongings laid with them upon the pile, and for the ashes to be cast into the sea or buried in the earth. Everyone would come to Valhöll with the riches he or she had gathered about them. A woman of consequence like Trumba would have a mound raised to her memory, and for each of her distinguished warriors, a standing stone, a custom older than the Empire itself. Until now, Iðunn reflected. There were so many dead down below, it would take a whole new Stone Age to carve the memorials.

"And the heavens departed as a scroll when it is rolled together. If you look closely, there, do you see? That. That was my Winter Palace."

Iðunn glanced over at Trumba, mouthing her prayers in the dark. She'd seen the Empress on sightbands before, been lectured by her lawspeakers in the Criminal Courts, but she'd never seen her in the flesh. The volcanic glow of the planet played about her face, the contrast of the veil making a harlequin's mask, her quizzically arched eyebrows accentuated by the wrinkled material. The effect was of catlike sensuality and slyness.

"Difficult to tell..." the Empress continued. "Every mountain and island moved out of their places. The Board of Ordnance won't be amused."

Iðunn's own body was shapeless and drab by comparison. Her dress looked funereal in the twilight. It was unadorned, with a heavier veil than that which the Empress wore—a handmaiden's, no doubt. She'd need a new vehicle, given time. This one was a thin disguise, but it had been the only occipital lobe available to hijack onboard. Iðunn was amazed she had gotten so close, so quickly, but in truth it was a mixed blessing. A servant would only see so much. She'd need to follow a Varangian to circumvent security. Come to think of it, where were the guards?

"I could never stand Miklagard, you know. All those stinking Serkir, effete Grikkir, and greedy Gyðingar," the Empress said, now focused on the fragments of the Imperial capital. "Still, melting pot never seemed a more apt description..." she cackled. She didn't really seem to care whether her handmaiden was listening or not. Like a child, she should be seen and not heard.

Iðunn didn't know what was worse, the cataclysm below or the off-hand callousness the Empress displayed. Trumba had never been popular, either as an entitled heir or a savage and brutal ruler. In fact, her reign had been so imperiled, so fraught with difficulty, people openly referred to her as the Mayfly Queen. The rumours of the assassination—the military coup out on Mímisbrunnr, Trumba deposed just months into her reign—had seemed like wish fulfillment to many of her subjects, Iðunn included. But like it or loathe it, the Verðandi had mouths to feed and the Empress was her meal ticket.

The worlds were still full of robber barons and corrupt jarls—the drengskapr set, drunk on plunder and war-stories. And her children were gone, torn from her, scattered, hiding in sooty fens and rime-jewelled caves—or else on display in macabre mobile zoos, rolled between townships, jeered at by the very fools they had hoped to save. Iðunn knew the punishment never matched the crime. Her revolution had failed.

She knew she'd got off lightly and she knew exactly why. True, she was the head of her order, but that meant little—Trumba had decapitated the Urðr sisterhood twice before. Being directly related to the great Karl Lind, the Leaf King himself, had provided her with some protection.

But most of all, she was free because she held the secret of the Apples. Iðunn could not only create, shape, and restore life. She could

LOKI'S WAGER • 11

extend it, far beyond a normal mortal span. One sweet, tantalizing bite of her apples was tantamount to immortality. Figuratively, of course. In reality, telomerase was delivered in tablet form, twice daily, but she did at least administer it with Fructone, a synthetic aroma compound with the requisite fruity smell.

Trumba had been all too ready to pardon her crimes, to redeem the Verðandi order, in return for what they knew. It was obvious she had no scruples of any kind. Iðunn stopped feeling sorry for herself, at least long enough check that Trumba was still happily extemporizing.

"The morning dews for meat shall they have, such food shall men then find.... Thence are gendered the generations..." The Empress was getting whimsical. She must have swallowed whole texts from the Ministry of Propagation.

Perhaps this wasn't a good idea. Iðunn imagined she could slip away, unnoticed. Her feet were cold, literally and figuratively—handmaids weren't given regulation footwear, it seemed. To where? she reminded herself, quickly. Dump the follow and return to her own body in Helheim? What was the point? Months had passed since her sentencing. Her new laboratory was always cold, even though buried deep in the glacier. They'd been set to work on the graving docks, little more than chattel, birthing miracles at the behest of Imperial logisticians. The new biohaven, Elvidnir, wasn't so much a place as a state of misery. She'd heard depression described as being like viewing the world through a sheet of plate glass; on Helheim, it would be more accurate to say a sheet of thick, semi-opaque ice. The effects were the same. She was irritable, clumsy, prone to accidents. The work was stultifying, demeaning, and every day was a chore. All the promise of mankind distilled into cheap DNA splices and spiteful tortures.

No wonder her mind wandered. Literally, in the case of a Verðandi.

Following had always been her strong suit, leaping behind the mind of some unwitting stooge, nestling behind their consciousness, watching the world through their eyes. The younger Vǫlur had augmented the spell-songs with technology, visors linked to all-seeing machines. Iðunn had forgotten more about the galdrar than she'd care to admit, but she still didn't need those kinds of crutches. She used the follows to look for her children, scouring the oblasts of Vanaheimr through the eyes of a Gael banjaxer, or swooping through the hoodoos of the Niðavellir Badlands aboard a Langobard air yacht pilot. She couldn't help them, her children, but it was reassuring to know they were out there. Surviving.

"Líf and Lífthrasir, lurking, hidden, in the wood of Hoddmímir; do you think the ancient seeress meant us?" Two survivors, high in the boughs," the Empress asked. It took a moment before Iðunn realized that Trumba was addressing her directly this time. She turned the body to meet her gaze. Trumba was radiant, arraigned gracefully on the adjacent bulkhead, still looking out on Midgard. Iðunn wanted to stare, to drink in that porcelain skin, to bask in the pale fire of her hair, the taut chains of muscle that coiled under her loose woolen dress.

She checked herself. Clever... an aphrodisiac, the Empress toying with her through chemical signals. Trumba was a woman determined to have her way, and clearly had an arsenal of means to do so. The Verðandi realized that the Norse had come a long way during the war. While her Apples might give them longevity, all the other tinkering and shaping had turned even a simple conversation into a battle. Like an ancient holmgang, a duel to the first blood between rival combatants.

"So, Lector, how long have you been watching me?" Trumba purred, still staring down at the broken planet. Iðunn startled. The truth was, she had no idea. Those pheromones really were the best that money could buy.

"Oh, don't worry, you're not my type. I frown on necrophilia. It wasn't just the staring that gave you away. Augmented Majesty has that effect on most people. But a word to the wise—thralls don't often question their Empress, especially thralls who were recently ritually sacrificed. *Do they understand why this happened?*" the Empress said, mimicking her earlier question. "Please," she scoffed.

Iðunn cursed, and glanced down at her hands, hoisting her sleeves in the darkness. Severed radial arteries. That would explain the challenges with animating the host—and the sickly aroma clogging the air. It was blood. Her blood. She must follow more carefully in the future, she chided herself. Check for a stronger pulse.

The Empress looked directly into *her*, beyond the vessel.

"I'm touched by your concern. For coming all this way. How long do you plan to have me under surveillance?"

"Until I understand why this all happened," Iðunn replied tartly. The handmaiden's body rattled and wheezed with the effort. She flirted momentarily with letting the body slump to the floor. She only needed its eyes and vocal chords—her cover revealed, maintaining good posture for the sake of decorum was a waste of effort.

"This? This was an Act of the Gods." Trumba laughed mirthlessly. "Unless you think I have something to confess? This isn't my handiwork, impressive though it is."

"I don't know what to think. I don't even know if there is a point to thinking. First the Jötunn War, now this."

"You clearly don't think enough to address me appropriately. The correct form is 'Your Majesty,' Iðunn."

"You know who I am then?"

Iðunn stayed motionless, resisting the urge to punch the wall in frustration or flee from the follow. No wonder it had been easy! She kicked herself mentally. She hadn't just arrived on the *Ormr inn Langi*, she'd been diverted, fished from the greenways to flop around on deck like some gullible halibut. Summoned. She hated being summoned. Still, Iðunn refused to bow and scrape. Trumba, despite all her tricks, would never be more than a girl to her. She simply stared back, indignant, until the silence grew suffocating.

Trumba turned back to the hollow, clearly amused. "You plan to play Skirlock Holmr? The Adventure of the Final Problem perhaps? What is the protocol for a death scene investigation on a planetary scale?"

There was no answer to that.

"Tell me, what would you have done down there? If I hadn't fetched you to safety? Inhabited a thrall's cinder instead of a handmaiden's corpse? Fat lot of good that would have done your search for answers. And what you hope to retrieve from the ruins of mankind? The fingerprints of vengeful gods?"

She laughed, bitterly this time, choking back a sob. Perhaps there was feeling in there after all. Her next comment was much softer.

"Will she heal?"

"Who? Mother Jörð?" Iðunn paused. "In time. But I doubt there will be a good harvest for a few hundred years. Ash clouds, nitric acid…"

The insight proved a prelude to more tears, that welled again in protest at the absurdity of it all.

Trumba tutted, clearly irritated. "That long? The islands of Aceh and Samudra, the southeastern oceans—there is an arc of volcanoes that have erupted before. Countless times. I imagined a quicker convalescence. And the stars—I see they can erupt, too?"

"Yggdrasil records it all in her rings. As to the stars, I have no idea, I am no Skuld." Iðunn shrugged.

"The Skuld are gone, most of them anyway. Traitors. Did you know they left me to die?"

"Your Majesty. Rumours of your demise are clearly much exaggerated." Iðunn hadn't been part of any conspiracy, hadn't been asked. She didn't understand why—to her mind, it would have been the obvious move, to at least try and rekindle her rebellious spirit. Perhaps she carried the stench of failure. Perhaps Helheim was simply too remote. After all, a cleaved head never plots.

"No, not overly exaggerated. Have you ever been poisoned? Circles appear before your eyes: red and orange. A ringing in the ears, it caught my breath. And such sense of fear! Poison is an unmanly weapon, but even so, those rassagr bungled the attempt on my life. And so here I am, watching the mourners become the mourned."

"They prepared a state funeral?" Iðunn was impressed by the attention to detail. It was the act of meticulous minds.

"Down to the choice of traditional burial dress. I woke up here, in the middle of the end. Ringside seat. Death makes for a good alibi, I trust?" Trumba sighed.

"Then did the Skuld engineer this?" Iðunn pointed to the devastation below. The third order of Vǫlur, all military engineers, trying to bend the universe to their will. If anyone could collapse the Earth's crust and blow up a star at the same time, it was them. "A mistake maybe? A failed experiment, crashing out of control?"

"No. The Skuld were closely watched. Besides, they rarely left their wedded bliss on Mímisbrunnr. One scant consolation for all this... harrowing." She gestured to the chaos below. "All those deceitful, conniving, backstabbing—arse-stabbing—mathematicians winked out of existence in an instant." Trumba looked up slyly. "Along with your Roarer," she added.

Iðunn's rebuttal was fierce. "He was never *my* Roarer. We were fighting for freedom, for opportunity. None of the Children would have done this. They wouldn't be capable of such..." She drifted off. She had wanted to say malice, but the word didn't do the damage justice.

Mikjáll Hofgard had been her partner in the Jötunn War, a philosopher, a rabble rouser, and a Kristin to boot. He'd been Father to her Mother, siring whole vats of vipers in the Ironwoods of Jötunheim. It had been a marriage of convenience, though, at least at the end. Desire you could synthesize, passion could be mass-produced—but love, love required nurturing. Mikjáll had been too entangled in his work to realize that.

Dead then, on Mímisbrunnr. She felt her mind heave. She wanted to vomit but she had no physical connection to a mouth.

"'Nothing is as heady as the wine of possibility.' One of the last things he said to me. I had him tortured. His mind cracked like an egg, oozing all kids of nonsense. It sounded like a threat. Was it?" Trumba continued, idly. "The war was over, our networks broken," Iðunn described. "And, despite his showmanship, the Roarer was just one man. I don't see how he could be in two places at once. Once you eliminate the impossible, whatever remains, no matter how improbable, must be the truth."

"Bravo, very droll," Trumba said, recognizing the quote.

Iðunn was stung into retaliation. "I don't mean to be funny. This must be traumatic, even for a narcissist like you."

"Which part? The murder attempts? Or the end of *my* Empire?" Trumba suddenly tore the veil from her dress, her face contorted in murderous rage. The harlequin's mask turned from farce to tragedy: it was clear that she'd been badly beaten, her face swollen with shades of purple and blue.

Iðunn's borrowed face remained a mask of impassivity, but underneath she was shocked to the core.

"How dare they?" Trumba screamed. "I see my face and feel nothing but loathing. I am a half-living ghost, imprisoned for days in my own sepulchre. You think you are the only one to have lost? I've lost children too!"

In that moment, there was something feral about her. Trumba coiled upwards like a snake, poised to strike. Iðunn wondered at the extent of her enhancements, at what kind of corruptions supreme power would twist into its DNA.

And then the Empress relaxed, a lone tear trickling down her broken cheek. "They even slaughtered my old horse, although it was well past its prime. Poor creature was bled out, until it was as white as a Helhest, then left at my feet. Now, I need a gin. I've had nothing but water. I could drink the sea dry."

She turned back to Iðunn, calmer now, her temper in check.

"Still, that's one of the benefits of being dressed for Valhöll. Servants entombed with you. It afforded us this opportunity for a nice fireside chat." The Empress unstoppered a clear glass bottle and sluiced its contents into a golden goblet. "Can I count on your loyalty? There are so few of us left."

"There must be survivors, among our sisters," Iðunn said, ignoring the request and the distinct lack of hospitality. On the far side of the planet, no doubt some of the adept had escaped, fleeing through the thinning branches of Yggdrasil and staggering through the storm to one of the Hinterworlds. The millennia-old galdr had been their salvation. Perhaps some of the imprisoned Jötnar had made it too. She'd taught her children well.

"Perhaps, but nothing can be done for them now. I am sure the military have them... contained."

"It can't be coincidence."

"I completely agree. There is no blind chance. Even Blind Höðr's aim was guided by Loki. Our gods don't play dice, they plan moves on a board."

It was Iðunn's turn to laugh. "There are no gods. This can't be laid at their door."

"You've never believed?" Trumba asked incredulously.

"Oh, once. When I was young." Iðunn had always heard the whisper of her ancestors about the family farm and called to the spirits watching from the monolithic trees. But as she grew older and her calling became clear to her, she had almost single-handedly changed the way the Empire understood its heritage. The World Tree, Yggdrasil, was the sentient, harmonious core of existence, not some spiteful reclusive god, lurking in the backs of minds and the depths of forests.

"You've grown out of it?" Trumba smiled, nodding her assent. "Regardless, there is a natural order to mankind. I rule by divine right."

The people get the gods they deserve, Iðunn thought, keeping the sentiment to herself. Man was god to man. Man was wolf to man.

"After the earthquakes and tidal waves, I think my subjects will be docile. More tractable. After all, these *events* have all been written. Long ago. The Völuspá, the prophecy of the seeress. And did Gylfi not return from Asgard, with these warnings? Did Óðinn not tell Vafþrúðnir how the world ended?"

Trumba seemed discorporate, glowing in the vespertine light of the hollow.

"And was reborn."

Iðunn started to interrupt but was swept away by the Empress's enthusiasm. "I used to envy the father of our race, dwelling as he did in the new-made fields of Asgard; but no more. People think the end is upon us, a punishment from whatever gods they cry to, but they are wrong. We live in creation's dawn.

'The Elfin-beam | shall bear a daughter,
Ere Fenris drags her forth;
That maid shall go, | when the great gods die,
To ride her mother's road.'"

"What do you mean?" Iðunn asked with a sigh, never one for esoterica or scripture. She didn't intend to go down a mystical rabbit-hole with Trumba playing Aðaliz, trying to become the Empress of Hearts as well as the Heavens. But she could feel Trumba's energy; she admired it even. It felt so alive, when she felt so dead. Mentally and physically.

"That depends. The World Tree? Can it be saved? Will your Verðandi help?"

Iðunn shook her head. "The tree is damaged. The greenways have decayed; the connections barely work, if at all."

She knew Trumba was probing to find out more. The Empress had once optimised her empire using a brilliant machine, MIM. Her supercomputer and Yggdrasil were one and the same, at root.

"But they work?"

Trumba drew herself up to her full height and thrust out her arms, grabbing the hollow at both edges. Perhaps this was what it meant to rule—taking the slenderest of hopes and weaving a future.

She turned and grinned wolfishly. "Iðunn, it is time to rebuild. Forget about why this happened, only relish that it has happened. All the Empire's problems, eradicated. The Hindoo slums are swept clean, the Skuld ants boiled alive. The faithless jarls must be quaking in their jackboots. It is time to build anew. A golden age. We are the gods now."

THE RISALA OF
— ṢĀḤIB AL-MUNAYQILLA —

Imārat Qurṭuba
November 844

— I —

I was just a boy when the Khalīfah presented his clock to the Emperor of the Franj. Many still remember the grandiose gift of the elephant, the mighty Abul-Abbas. But I was not so impressed by that. Anyone can rustle up an old bull in Ifriqiya.

It was the timepiece that was *truly* magnificent.

The Horologium from the House of Wisdom. A mechanical marvel, a contraption that could rouse the whole world to arms. Imagine the scene at noon: a weight would drop, bells sound, and twelve brass horsemen would emerge from twelve windows, riding in precise procession around the dial. Even at such a young age, it seemed to me that here was the universe in miniature. A conglomerate of connections, all pre-determined and meticulously planned in God's timeless knowledge.

To my teachers, I could talk of nothing else. I pored over translations from al-Yūnān and al-Hind, drinking my fill of a dozen books at a time. Whenever a new scholar arrived from the East, I would accost them after prayer, showering them with questions, regardless of whether they were mathematician, philosopher, or physician. Water clocks, automata, astronomical instruments—when I became a man, these things became not only my passion but my trade. In time, they became my very name.

Ṣāḥib al-Munayqilla, or, in your tongue, "the man with the little clock."

Read that again to be sure. Just in case you get any smart ideas.

It was not a unique calling. You see, scholars across Dār al-Islām were obsessed by time. In the great palaces of Qurṭuba and Madīnat

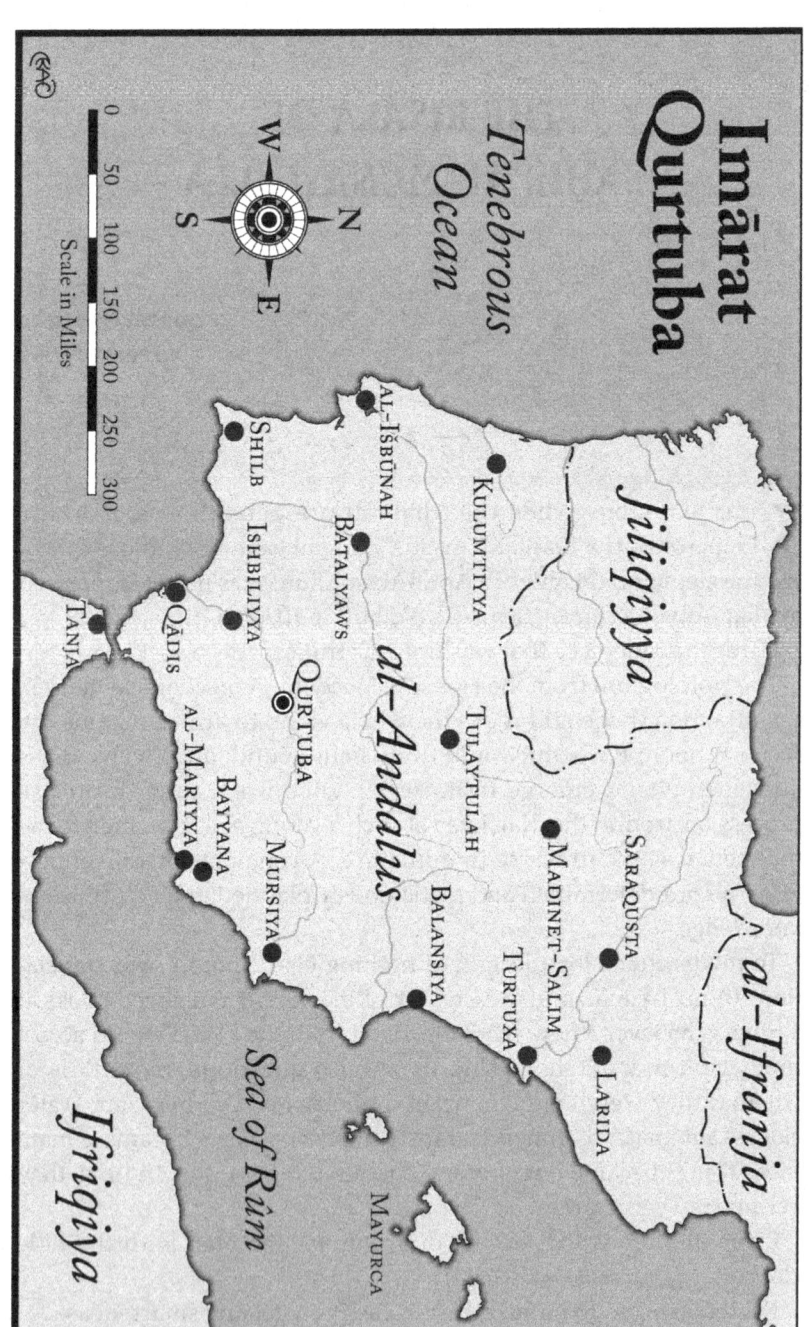

as-Salām alike, they used the astrolabe by day and then the waterclocks by night, striving to understand the world beyond their fingertips. They designed huge clocks, sometimes reaching six meters high—towers, mosques, even whole streets, were turned into clocks. But these white elephants had a crucial flaw—you couldn't measure the sun's disc or the waning crescent moon beyond the confines of the Alcázar or the observatory. You certainly couldn't travel with them. You couldn't *explore*.

My design, on the other hand, was a masterpiece of the minuscule. Not even the Banū Mūsa had dreamed of so deliberate a device as my little clock. What was my secret, you might wonder? More than just accurate calibration and intricate design, I was the first to think of a mercury escapement! How I should love to tell you of the perfection of her engineering, the beauty of her gears...

But I digress. This is not a story about my clock—how I wish it were! But my speciality does explain why I was chosen to accompany the illustrious al-Djayani—may God bless him and grant him salvation!—on his embassy to the land of the Majūs.

The journey is what matters. That is the real test of time.

— 2 —

We first heard of the cruel Majūs from the Franj.

They were a people who possessed a strength without equal for navigating the sea. To hear it told, they lived beyond the al-Baḥr al-Muzhl, the Tenebrous Ocean that girds the world like a green sash. The Franj remarked that only the Majūs could survive in the total darkness of the northern oceans—they described men of robust limbs and iron hands, who advanced like an unstoppable wall of ice. To our ambassadors, they seemed the Dār al-ḥarb—the house of war—made flesh.

I was informed by the wazīr that, in the space of that one black year, the Majūs had raided lands from al-Shaklıshunsh to al-Ifranja. It was said the great Franj tyrant, Qarlush bin Ludhwig, had been attacked in his very throne room.

It wasn't long before they arrived off our coast, filling the seas with their wooden stallions and filling the hearts of men with fear and trembling. Back and forth they sailed, back and forth, for days.

Then, they fell, whipping through the streets like a desert simoom, first at al-Išbūnah, then Qādis, then to Ishbiliyya, where the poison dust finally settled. There the Majūs remained for seven days and nights, while our people drank the dregs of the cup of bitterness.

As soon as Abd ar-Rahman, Amir of Qurṭuba, Servant of the Merciful, had news of this, he gave the command of the cavalry to the Chief Minister. The Faithful hastened to gather under the banner of the general and joined him as closely as the eyelid to the eye.

On the eighth day, the guard made known that a host of many thousands of Majūs was marching past Moron. The Hājib let them pass, cutting them off from Ishbiliyya, before signalling the charge. The cavalry hacked down our enemy in droves; the few prisoners they hanged from the palm-trees of Talyata. The Majūs who remained with their ships heard of the disaster and suddenly embarked for home.

Whether that was to be the end of their depredation, none could tell. My people have a saying: "Time is like a sword. If you do not cut it, it will cut you." And so, with the aid of God—Might and Majesty be His—the amir was spurred to measures of safety. He renewed the arsenal in Ishbiliyya, ordered ships to be built, and provided them all with war engines and naphtha.

My little clock was young then, and as brave as a lion, there among his brethren at the madrasah. Together, they would marshal the time—mechanical figurines, beasts and birds marching through the hours. *We will be safe*, he said, spinning with delight at each cymbal ring. *The amir has gathered sailors and mercenaries to all the coasts of al-Andalus. Time is on our side!*

— 3 —

The Majūs proposal of peace both surprised and delighted everyone at court. Except the ulama, of course; as far as the clerics were concerned, unbelievers had three choices: either Islam, the Jizyah tax, or the sword. Had the Moslem not been triumphant? they demanded. But with Ziryab singing in his ear, the amir was adamant that we entertain the treaty.

Ziryab—the master of song, the wonder of al-Andalus—was, at that time, elevated above all others at court. His name meant Blackbird, given to him by the people of his homeland, far in the northernmost Mashriq, because of his dark skin, his eloquent tongue, and the beauty of his features. The amir granted him privileges far beyond those of the closest, most trusted wazīr. It may surprise you to learn that such a devout man as the amir could be an admirer of singing. It was not yet one hundred years since the falcon of Quraysh sought his fortune in these lands and claimed them from the enemies of God, but, in that time, the articles of our faith had changed immeasurably. Even as a boy, I remembered the Muhatasibs breaking into houses and smashing instruments. The great judge Malik (May God have mercy on him!) had forbidden singing outright. But the Falcon had long since surrendered his nest to the Blackbird.

In fact, the amir so was enamored of music, he placed it above all his other pleasures, filling the palace and his private orchestra with the most excellent singing slave women.

And so, it was arranged, All Praises be to the Lord of All the Worlds. The great al-Djayani was summoned to bear a reply to the king of the Majūs, to deliver a gift of friendship—though whether his mission was genuine, to buy time for the new defenses, or simply to acquire more songstresses, only the amir knew. His full name was Yahya ibn-Hakam el Bekri al-Djayani, although you may know the emissary better as al-Ghazal, the Gazelle, a name given for his extraordinary good looks and fleet wit. In Qurṭuba—the dome of Islam, the garden of the fruit of ideas—the streets were paved and lit, there were bookshops, libraries and schools of music, and hardly a district lacked a skilled writer or a compelling poet, but none possessed greater keenness of mind or skill in repartee than al-Ghazal, save perhaps his great rival, the Blackbird himself.

I was at prayer at the madrasah when the emissary found me. I was delighted to see him—it was five years since our success in the country of the Rûm, where he had stood tall in the Great Hall of the Magnaura and bargained with the tyrant there. He wore one of the new short hairstyles that were the fashion—perfumed and oiled, leaving the neck, ears and eyebrows free—and the flowing white silks of summer. He was striking even in old age, full of vigour, straight of body and handsome of aspect.

"As-Salāmu 'Alaykum," al-Ghazal said, simply. Peace be upon you. He smiled serenely, utterly confident of his place in this world and the next.

"And on you be the Peace and Mercy of God and His Blessing," I cried and rushed to embrace him.

We had known each other, recreationally at least, for many years but the embassy to the East had sealed our friendship. The Rûm, who had of late been greatly harassed by the sons of al-Abbas, had asked the amir to join forces with him against their common enemy, tempting him with the conquest of the empire which his ancestors had possessed in the East. Al-Ghazal had travelled on, in the guise of a merchant, ever the amir's eyes and ears. He had been in the Bilād Fāris, the lands of the usurper, ever since.

"You did not think to send word that you had returned?" I admonished.

"Few men know. And besides, I cannot stay," he said, matter-of-factly. Now in his sixtieth year, the poet was, like me, a man who weighed time. He confided his mission to me; such were our dealings, his heart clearly full of trepidation.

"Some say that al-Ghazal is so clever that, despite his enjoying the evening of his life, he was the one selected to meet the Majūs. Yet that was not the reason. We courtiers know well that a bite from a lion is better than the look of envy." He sighed. "I will go—I have no choice—I only wish it to be God's plan that I return whether the Blackbird likes it or not. And so, to the reason for my visit. Sailing the Sea of the Rûm is one thing, but who would be so blind as to sail into the northern seas, where no-one has dared to venture? I wish for you, Ṣāḥib al-Munayqilla, to accompany me. We can keep watch together."

My little clock couldn't contain his chimes of laughter. Here was a marvellous adventure, a test worthy of his ornate apparatus. I too, could not believe my good fortune. If a touch of rivalry and politicking had played its part in paving my progress, then so be it, I reasoned. After all, there is no single event in this world that is not determined by God's will.

"May God reward you with good, O great scholar!" I exclaimed, eager to be heard above the din.

"And may Allah bless you, my devoted friend," he said with a warmth that affirmed the ritual. "Which reminds me, where are my manners? I would not wish to be thought so ungracious as to have arrived empty-handed!"

He clapped, commanding his servants to appear as if from thin air, then a second time to send them scuttling to fetch gifts and refreshments. They returned in an instant with all manner of treats— marzipan balls, candied pumpkin, iced sharbats—but my eyes were fixed on the heavy tome they handed with immense delicacy to al-Ghazal. The emissary unwrapped the book carefully, revealing pages of thick paper, sewn with silk and bound with leather-covered boards.

"I bring you a torch to light our way," he said, grinning.

In truth, all learned men knew the Sea of Darkness had been illuminated centuries ago—the Rûm had made measure of the world all the way to Northuagia, Cimbria, and the Scandian islands. There was known to be a book, Baṭlumyus's *Geography*, a compendium containing over two thousand coordinates of cities, rivers, and seas. But who among the muya-hidīn might have laid eyes on it? We had sailed to al-Rûm and had no such good fortune. Yet, something about the poet's demeanor caused me to hope against hope. If ever there was a man for miracles, it was al-Ghazal.

I watched his face carefully for clues, but the poet was as unblinking as the sand wazaghah, greedily hunting insects from dusk till dawn. Then, with a final flourish, the emissary extended this most prized possession.

"This is the *Kitāb Ṣūrat al-Arḍ*, the *Book of the Image of the Earth*. The usurper ordered seventy astronomers to attend to the maps within, led by al-Khwārizmī, the master of the House of Wisdom himself," he said, in his richest tone, as if I were a visiting dignitary.

"Glory to God!" I stammered. My dismay must have been obvious. It was a clearly a Persian text, not the fabled *Geography* after all. Even the best Moslem cartographers were barely credible compared to the Rûm. They drew their maps according to tradition, as the head, two wings, breast, and tail of a bird. The world's head was always al-Ṣīn, bordered by the Encircling Sea. Behind al-Ṣīn was a place called al-Waqwaq, which was said to be so rich in gold that the inhabitants make the chains for their dogs and the collars for their monkeys of this metal. This ridiculous fancy continued all the way to the tail, that depicted the land from the Maghreb all the way to al-Andalus.

The great scholar laughed away my frown.

"Ah, but wait! My tale is not yet told. In his determination to fashion a picture of the world worthy of the Faithful, the Khalīfah had sent his wisest uluma to the Qays'r al-Rûm, to beg for favour. Together, the great sages translated hundreds of ancient texts from the great libraries of Qusṭanṭīniyya—the *Geography* included."

I leafed through the book. It seemed to consist of inexhaustible lists of Hindu numerals—tables of latitudes and longitudes.

"This is a copy of Baṭlumyus?" I said, puzzled.

"Better. A correction. Al-Khwārizmī has improved on the original, I'm told," the great poet replied.

"If this were my treasure, I wouldn't let it leave my sight," I whispered, overcome with awe. The emissary gleaned my meaning and answered my unspoken question.

"The amir cares little for it. His propensity is for more... worldly pleasures."

My little clock was unimpressed. It was all very well for the House of Wisdom to regurgitate al-jabr and sindhind reckoning, but if you wanted to know where you are or where you were going, you needed a reliable timepiece.

— 4 —

We set out from Qurṭuba, the Ornament of the World, on the eleventh day of the month of Safar. Al-Ghazal led us first to the port of Shilb, where a fine, well-equipped ship was waiting. The envoy of the Majūs king was there too—embarked on the same vessel on which he had come, a square-sailed qarāqīr that displayed complete mastery of the waves. He planned to sail at the same time as our ship, as guide and as escort.

And so it was that I had my first measure of unbelievers. I have never seen men more intimidating than the Majūs—God be merciful! The idol worshippers are as tall as date palms and yet as prickly as cacti. They wore neither tunics nor caftans but went around barechested. From the napes of their necks down, each one of them was crisscrossed with tattoos of verdant trees, grotesque dragons and horned beasts. More glaring still, the captains among them wore an artificial eye makeup—to enhance their beauty, the envoy said, fixing me with an unholy stare. Each of their warriors carried both an axe and a sword—with furrowed blades in the manner of the Franj—and he was never far from them.

The poet could converse in many languages, but we nevertheless took with us three muwalladan converts to ease his burden—including a nobleman called al-Quti from Saraqusṭa, whose people who could converse freely with the Majūs in their tongue—and a full complement of Ṣaqāliba, infidel slaves who acted as both our servants and our guards. Alliances are wise, but a chameleon does not leave one tree until he is sure of another.

They were handsome creatures, the slave-boys. It is said all the Ṣaqāliba eunuchs on the surface of the earth are come from al-Andalus, castrated here with great skill by Yahūd merchants. We called them the al-hamra, the "reddish ones" on account of their white and rosy skin.

That very night, we planned to take our leave from the Cities of Light and plunge into shadow. The muwalladan looked most unhappy with their conscription.

"No ship ever sailed north from here. It is the Sea of Darkness... neither its extent nor its end is known," al-Quti said. "The Majūs told me that three weeks sail to the north, the duration of the night is less than an hour. A man can put a pot on the fire at the time of the sunset prayer, then perform the evening prayer without its having had time to boil."

"Then prepare three weeks of provisions," scoffed al-Ghazal, "and ensure we have plenty for breakfast!" The emissary clearly had a renewed sense of purpose and prowled the deck with a hunger in his eyes.

Al-Quti was not one to surrender so easily. "Did the Prophet, peace and blessings be upon him, not say 'When three things appear, faith will not do any good to a person who has not believed before or earned good through his faith: the rising of the sun in its place of setting, the coming of ad-Dajjal, and the beast of the earth'? Turn in repentance to the Lord!" he cried in a frenzy. The truest believers were often found among the newest converts.

The Last Hour has drawn near, and the moon has been cleft asunder, shuddered the little clock, fearing the worst.

Perhaps the muwalladan had a right to be afraid. There can be no comparison between one who lingers among kinsmen, satisfied with his part of the world, and another who spends a lifetime in travelling, carried to and fro by his journeys, extracting every morsel of knowledge.

Certainly, the journey began most perilously. When we were at the westernmost limit of al-Andalus, opposite the great cape that juts out into the sea and in sight still of the mountain known as Aluwiyah, the sea grew fearsome and a mighty storm blew upon us, more dreadful than the greatest haboob. I have never encountered more thunderbolts than in that infernal hour!

Al-Ghazal was clinging to the mast, and next to him was the Majūs steersman, who was speaking to him in growls. The poet laughed and translated: "This Majūs says to you, 'What is it that your God wants from us? Here He is hammering us with rain; why does he not make it stop?'"

And I said to him: "Tell him, 'God wants you to say: La ilaha illa Allah. There is no God but Allah.' It is He who ordained the stars for you that you may be guided thereby in the darkness of the land and the sea."

"La ilaha illa Thórr," the Majūs yelled back, but I had stopped my ears against the unbeliever.

We passed between waves like mountains—the two sails were rent, and the cable-loops were cut. The Majūs use wind-vanes on their prow, with weighted pendants hanging from the edge to measure the wind. These inconstant instruments leapt and danced and whirled like a darwīsh. The angel of death, Azrail, reached for us, and even al-Ghazal quaked in terror. But my little clock—praise be to God!—kept steady, defying the storm to do its worst. *You have come early, Azrail*, it said, as little brass gears divided out the hours. Faced with such certainty, the winds abated, and the seas calmed.

When we were saved from the terror and dangers of those seas, I enquired further of the mariners and their navigational aids. The great emissary was only too happy to assist me.

"The Majūs are expert sailors indeed, to chart a steady course when nowhere can be seen a clear sky," I said. He asked the steersman about his capabilities and received the reply that the Majūs mastered but one skill: to discern the motion of heavenly bodies, and to know the stars which mark the hours, so that they would know the length of day and night even when the sky was overcast.

To prove his point, the steersman gave a clear assertion as to the location of the sun, that he then verified by holding up a rhombus-shaped crystal that instantly radiated light. It was evidently a crude asturlāb, a star-taker, as many devout Moslem used to find Makkah.

Al-Ghazal and I looked at each other with wild surmise. The poet asked the steersman what the mineral was called.

"Sólarsteinn," he said, evidently pleased to have confounded our expectations. He crouched, tucking the crystal safely into one of the bone-mounted caskets he kept near his station, before returning with another marvel—a necklace of rock crystal, each bead mounted in filigree silver, yet highly polished and cut, so as to be almost clear. Strings of seashells and multi-coloured glass were common decoration among the idolaters, but it was obvious these jewels had an altogether different level of craftsmanship.

"Reading stones?" I asked al-Ghazal, who duly translated. The steersman tapped the side of his nose with a thick, calloused forefinger, then he lifted the chain to his eye, which instantly bulged like a swollen grape.

"Scrying tools perhaps, to peer across all the seven heavens," al-Ghazal wondered out loud.

Seeing our surprise, the Majūs started to laugh uncontrollably. Holding the crystal to his face, he strutted up and down the deck, honking like a peacock, his tattoos doubling as iridescent plumage. For a moment, I feared a malevolent jinn inhabited the talisman and had taken hold of the unbeliever's mind.

A lesser scholar might have let panic take hold and leapt overboard, lest he be turned into an ape. But in an instant, the little clock had the measure of the man. This was no Ifrit.... The Majūs knew the science of optics!

"Do not be perplexed, great emissary," I said. "My little clock has divined the purpose of the jewels. The crystals are lenses!"

But how? The Maumtahan Observatory was scarcely twenty years old. True, al-Kindi had written much on the subject, but to find such knowledge so far from the House of Wisdom was mystifying. Had these mushrikun also translated Baṭlumyus and learned the secrets of rays and refraction? And not just tables and observations, but practical applications: lenses, ground on a turning lathe. How had they escaped their abode of delusions and arrived at the vicinity of God?

Al-Ghazal was as dumbfounded as I and pressed the Majūs for answers.

The steersman gave no further answer but a wide grin, revealing deep horizontal grooves across his teeth, yet more decoration. My little clock grew uneasy—the grid of ivory and charcoal squares reminded him of the board the grandees used to play shatranj. Was the game over or had it just begun?

— 5 —

In a matter of days, we arrived at the first of the many lands of the Majūs, at one of their islands, where we repaired the ship and rested. These countries being bathed on the west by the Sea of Darkness, there came continually from that direction mists and rain, and the sky was always overcast. The waters were covered with cloud and the waves were enormous, the winds still violent.

The envoy's ship sailed on to their king to inform him of al-Ghazal's safe arrival. We were to follow to his royal residence—three days' sail, that is, three hundred miles, from our landing, hugging the coastline.

To hear the Majūs describe it, the palace was situated on a great island in the ocean, with flowing streams and gardens. I was excited, despite the inclement weather.

I remembered the porphyrized streets of the Rūmiyyat al-kubra, the Great City of the Rûm, and wondered what great fastness these Majūs must own, stretching across brilliant green hills that sloped to the sea. I pictured great coastal citadels, calling the seafarers home like the Alexandrine lighthouse on a stormy night. How else might one avoid crumbling to pieces, eroded by the winds and rain?

The Majūs appointed a man to take care of our needs and to comply with our requests in whatever we desired. Our helpmeet was a lone soul of ugly countenance, shabby appearance and mean looks, but it turned out that he had an extensive household nearby. He drove some sheep to us, that we might slaughter them in the Moslem manner, and had linen tents pitched that we settled into just as we were overtaken by a heavy rain.

We invited the islander to eat with us, but he declined, somewhat brusquely. Al-Ghazal insisted, saying to him: "We are friends of your king."

But the man only laughed: "Who is the king here? I shit on the beard of the Turgesius the Devil."

"Who is this devil he speaks of?" I asked al-Ghazal, confused.

"Ad-Dajjal, the deceiver. Perhaps the Day of Judgment is upon us?" he joked, the wind flapping the tent flaps as if in monstrous applause.

"Do not be afeared, great emissary," I said. "My little clock knows God's will. We will not die today." I tried to share in his good humour, despite the insult from our host.

We watched a while as the man and his household instead put to sea, to hunt the young of the whale, which they described as a great delicacy, with meat white like snow, and skin black as ink. We had evidently inconvenienced them already, for the hunters hurriedly assembled in their ships, having with them a great iron blade with sharp spikes, which they hauled out to sea. After some miserable hours, they came back into sight, each ship taking turns to drag a carcass to the shore. Once there, they instantly cut up the meat of the calf and salted it, preparing for the rigours of winter.

Next day, we dressed to ward off the damp and resumed our passage. Every one of us had his tunic, on top of which was a caftan, a sheepskin overcoat and a hooded cloak, so you could see nothing but our eyes.

"The Prophet, peace and blessing be upon him, warned us! Ad-Dajjal will command the sky to rain, and it will rain. If ever there was a land more accursed than this, I would like to know!" al-Quti raged, dampening all our spirits with his fervour.

My clock was nervous. His walnut heart beat faster. The change was slight, almost imperceptible, but worrying nonetheless: a simple water clock might lose its tale to condensation, or be disturbed by the motion of the ship, but my creation's ventricles flowed with mercury. Its apparatus was impervious to changes in temperature or humidity by design.

We have sailed farther than the Pleiades. Do you see that the moon does not occupy the centre of the sky? Do you see how quickly the sun sets? he said.

Seeing my concern, al-Ghazal came to me, worried whether the little clock might expire.

"He is afraid of the dark," I said, scowling, "nothing more."

I should have listened to the reckoning of my device. On the third evening, the Majūs envoy hove into sight once more, to lead us into harbour. Where I had dreamed of lamplit gardens there was only a black pool where the tide leeched into a murky, peat-filled basin. There was no oasis, no Great City or guiding Pharos. The Majūs ruled from nothing more than a fortified camp on top of a gravel ridge. It occurred to me then that the magnificent lenses we witnessed must be stolen, the sunstone a counterfeit.

As we docked, a second bastion could be seen upriver, where a fleet of some fifty ships lined the shore like a wooden wall, out of reach of the tempestuous seas. These twin outposts were like fangs, fixed in a snarl, set in the mouth of two drooling rivers.

The king sent out a party to greet the great al-Ghazal. These mushriks thronged to look at us and clearly wondered at our appearance and our garb. All at once it came to me that the Majūs were visitors too, a great sea-cast flood of foreigners to this land.

They were invaders, and we were witnesses to conquest.

— 6 —

That night, al-Ghazal entered my tent with the object of conversing. He asked me, "What do you think of this land of the Majūs?"

I told him that it was my belief that it was not their land at all.

I noted that the town was poor in goods and blessings; however, God—Exalted is He—had been benevolent in the matter of firewood

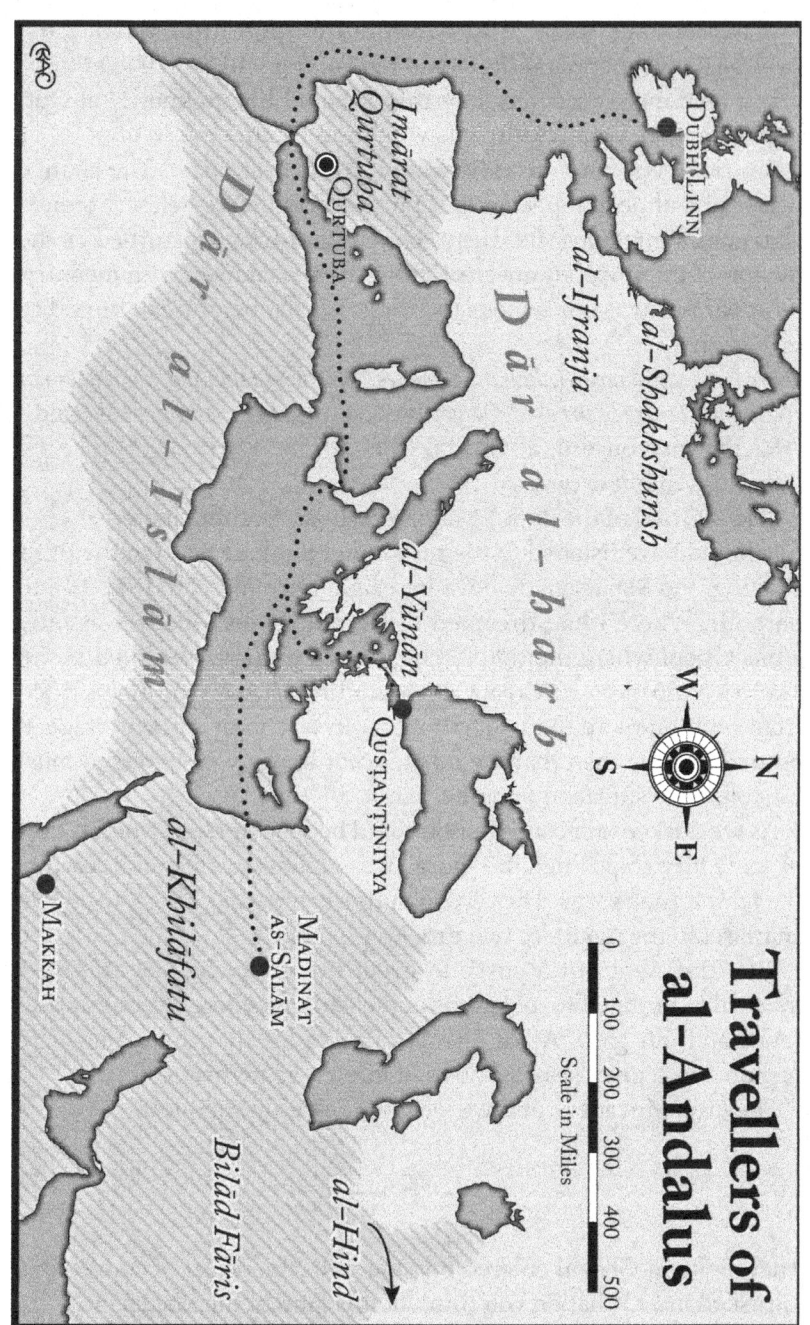

and materials for their ships through the dense forests nearby. The spot the Majūs had chosen, at the confluence of the rivers, was both defensible and close enough to the sea to be quickly reinforced.

He said, "It is as you fear. There has been an astonishing and great incursion over all these islands. Praise the Amir—peace be upon him!—that al-Andalus did not succumb to the same fate."

I asked him how he came to be so certain, and he replied, "I walked by a crossing upriver, where the Majūs take the men and women who are the true owners of this land. Fifteen or twenty of them, more or less, were gathered, slaves intended for the merchants. I spoke to them under the guise of inspection. They are People of the Book."

Truly the poet is blessed with an ear for language. He lives by the maxim 'God created nations to know each other and not to be separated,' but to me the northern speech is, of all things, most like the snarling of dogs.

"Nasrani? Christians?" I cried with dismay. "Then, truly, this is not the land of the Majūs—may God curse them! Wherever can we be?"

"The slaves called it Erinn," the emissary said. "As to your question, I was hoping you could tell me, Ṣāḥib al-Munayqilla." He gestured at the book he had provided.

I saw the plan entrusted to him by the amir at once—if we survived, we were to bring back a map to this heart of darkness, for only then could we pierce it.

He smiled, encouragingly. "If it helps, the Majūs fort is called Dubh Linn, and acts as a base for their raiding fleets. The adjoining mainland, Albu, is also theirs for a distance of many days' journey. The Danar—that's what the slaves call the Majūs—have taken the spoils of the sea between Erinn and Albu for two or three generations now."

"And they are not afforded the protection of the Majūs king?" I asked.

"The Majūs follow their own path. They have no notion of sharia and certainly no dhimma contract," the poet lamented in reply. "You have seen the fangs of these lions; do not think they are smiling."

I resolved to do my best to discover our location. It was simple enough, I explained. If you wished to know the latitude of any given town, then, first of all, one must measure the altitude of the sun at noon, when it crosses the meridian. When you know the altitude, then you must find the declination of the sun at that time—if it is north, then deduct it from the altitude, and if it is south, add it. This gives the altitude of Aries or Libra at that town. Subtract this from nine hundred; the remainder will be the latitude of the town.

Whatever this country was called, I could not but think that some celestial sluices had been opened, exposing us to a constant deluge. That night I slept poorly, covered up with garments and furs, and was soaked through come morning.

The next night, my deliberations completed, we talked for the amount of time it takes a man to read the half the Qur'an.

"Al-Khwārizmī and my little clock both agree," I offered. "Iouerníā and Albion are the Greek names for these islands. The translations use the place name from the maps of Batlamyus."

"Erinn and Albu. There you have it! The Persians ruled for a thousand years and did not need us Arabs even for a day. We have been ruling them for one or two centuries and cannot do without them for an hour."

"I wonder, what do the Nasrani call us?" I asked.

"Saracens," he said, smirking. "'A tribe of thieves.' Perhaps the time will come when we can steal them away? Like your little clock."

"What do you mean, my friend?" I said, taken aback.

"A play on words, nothing more. The Greek word *clepsydra*. It means water thief. Your device is based on a Greek design, no?" the poet said.

My little clock grumbled. *I have progressed the art of horology far further than even Arshimīdis. In any case, you cannot steal time from God. He knows all in His Eternity.*

— 7 —

After two days, the Majūs king summoned us into his presence. We clothed ourselves in white and donned our turbans as befitted the emissaries of the Prince of True Believers.

The muwalladan unfurled our two standards and marched to his hall with as much dignity as the weather would allow. The Ṣaqāliba stumbled along behind them, trying their best to keep their lances aloft.

"Remember, my friend," whispered al-Ghazal, ever the ambassador, "your tongue is like a horse—if you take care of it, it takes care of you. Many wars have been caused by a single word."

Al-Ghazal had stipulated to the envoy that he would not be made to kneel to the Majūs, neither would he be required to do anything contrary to our customs. It was not the practice for a high dignitary to kiss the ground when he entered the presence of the amir, let alone a mushrak.

But when we came to the king's hall, I was horrified to find we had been tricked. The king had prepared himself for us, with a display of arms and great pomp, but also cunning. His warriors had contrived to make the doorway so low that we could only enter by kneeling or crawling through the dirt. We would not be made to kneel, but neither could we avoid it.

Al-Ghazal was not overawed by this, nor did it frighten him.

"Khanzir," I whispered. Pigs.

"This Turgesius is called ad-Dajjal for a reason," he said with a wink.

Without pausing, he simply sat on the ground, stretched forth his legs, and dragged himself through on his rear. When he had passed through the offending doorway, he stood erect and spoke as if his means of entry were an everyday occurrence.

"Peace be with you, O auspicious king, and with those whom your assembly hall contains, and respectful greetings to you! May you not cease to enjoy power, long life, and the nobility which leads you to the greatness of this world and the next, which becomes enduring under the protection of the living and Eternal One, other than whom all things perish, to whom is the dominion and to whom we return."

It fell to al-Quti to explain what had been said, which he did commendably, his people in the north of Isbania not being immeasurably different from the infidels.

The king was also a man of striking appearance, stout and broad, who sounded as though he were speaking from inside a large barrel. His right eye was scarred and swollen, his left eye sparkled like a star. He sat quietly through the address, then spoke admiringly to the whole assembly: "This is one of the wise and clever ones of his people. We sought to humiliate him, and he greeted us with the soles of his shoes!"

The whole hall roared with laughter.

Al-Ghazal remained motionless. He waited for the hubbub to quieten and then drew out the amir's letter. He began the preamble: "Peace be upon you! I address myself to you in rendering praise unto God, other than whom there is no deity."

The interpreter continued to translate for him word for word. When they had finished reading it, I then took out the gifts of perfume, clothing, and pearls intended for the king and his honour guard. I continued to display the gifts before them, item by item, until we were done.

My last task was to offer his wife, seated by his side, a silk robe of honour. I stepped slowly toward her, only too aware that the gift jarred with her otherwise martial attire. She wore a rounded container fastened over her breasts, encircled with gold in a manner to demonstrate the magnitude of her husband's wealth. Around her neck she wore bands of gold and silver and ceramic beads strung into a necklace. As I stepped in front of her, she looked straight past me, and then said to the interpreter, "Ask this Serkir: Does his God have a wife?"

Al-Quti was rightly horrified at this, and we both implored His forgiveness, mouthing confused prayers. "Khanzir!" I cried again, confirmed in my belief that here was the enemy of God. A handmaiden snatched the silk from my unresisting grasp. Again, al-Ghazal remained unmoved, as high and white as the full moon.

The Majūs king then bid us be seated on his left-hand side, his sons sitting in front of him, while he sat alone upon the throne covered with ivory and furs. He called for a table and it was brought, piled high with roast meat. When we had eaten, he called again, this time for a beverage made from honey which they call *mead*. He drank a cup, then rose to his feet and said: "This is an expression of my pleasure with your master, the Commander of the Faithful—may Óðinn prolong his life."

The king and his sons stood up when he stood, as did we, and we drank. He did that repeatedly, until I had to overturn my bowl for fear of being judged deserving of the lash.

Al-Ghazal was in his element. He sat directly opposite the king and his envoy, drinking from his own heavy crystal glass, both a precautionary measure against poison and a subtle reminder of his status.

As the evening wore on, the Devil King called for music. For a moment I imagined a cacophony of bone flutes, drums and rattles would issue forth, but to my surprise, one of the king's men handed him an oblong instrument, with six strings, that he proceeded to pluck gently. A great hush descended in the room.

The melody was haunting, speaking of lost love and betrayal. At its close, the whole room stood with bowed heads, some men moved to silent tears. I had never imagined I would see such a display.

The emissary nodded his appreciation, at which the Majūs offered up his instrument. Al-Ghazal politely declined. "I have brought my own *harpa*," he said, using the Majūs' word, "which my people call an ūd. I made it myself, stripping the wood and working it, and no other instrument satisfies me. I left it with our ship, and, with your permission, I'll send for it."

A slave was sent running to fetch it, but before he began to play, the Majūs king asked to inspect the foreign device. "Tell me how it is made," the Lord of Infidels said.

"My strings are made of silk, although not that which has been spun with hot water, for that weakens them. The bass and third strings are made of lion gut, which is softer and more sonorous than that of any other animal. These strings are stronger than any others, and they can better withstand the striking of the pick."

The emissary used a sharpened eagle's claw, rather than the usual piece of carved wood, after the fashion of the Blackbird. The two old men then began to play, as equals, with a fire and energy that grew and grew, as if in defiance of their waning years, until they were perspiring like bedfellows. I grew quite envious of their exertions.

When their laments were over, the Majūs king called again, and this time his men brought out a horn-rimmed cup, a dhira in length, which he solemnly presented to the emissary.

Al-Quti explained. "The king is says it is fashioned from a very fierce animal called the einhyrningr—one horn—which has the head of the stag, the feet of the elephant, and the tail of the boar, and had this single black horn, which projects from the middle of its forehead. He is happy to say the horn's magical and medicinal properties are intact. Drink from this and you need never fear poison under any roof."

I was perplexed. Had the king had captured a karkadann? I had heard its horn can relieve constipation, and cure epilepsy and lameness, but al-Quti had not heard of such a creature, being altogether ignorant of the Book of the Animals.

The emissary received the gift with solemn oaths and blessings to God.

After this, the Majūs permitted us to withdraw to our dwelling, and treated us generously.

But no ships were offered to return us to al-Andalus.

— 8 —

Time doesn't fly.
Time flees.
That might seem a minor contrivance. Perhaps I should tell you how my little clock works after all?

The little clock's walnut drum was divided into twelve compartments, with small holes in each through which mercury flowed—enough mercury to fill just half. The drum filled, tipped and a weight-drive twisted the gears—thirty-six oaken teeth gritted and grimaced and heaved—and the dial revolved.

Virgil almost had it right. *Fugit inreparabile tempus:* "it escapes, irretrievable time." A good clock is a cage, with a key tantalizingly out of reach.

For a thousand years, no foreign host had settled in Erinn. But the times of peace were ended. Within days of our arrival, three more great royal fleets appeared, almost simultaneously. Seen up close, I saw they were not stallions at all, but winged serpents, dashing through the spray and foam.

They soon sailed again, one headed north and two south, each breathing fire and destruction. The Majūs sailed up every creek, and, shouldering their boats, marched from river to river and lake to lake, covering the country with their forts. Their heavy iron swords, their armour, their discipline of war, all gave them an overwhelming advantage against the native Irlandi whose bodies and necks and gentle heads were defended only by fine linen.

Time rolled on steadily, stealing past me by degrees. I admit, I was a poor custodian and neglected my charge. I sometimes saw the horizon turn redder than cinnabar, and I heard powerful noises and a loud hum coming from the clouds. Other times I would ride out, only to hear the clash of swords and spears more distinctly and be forced to steal quickly back to the coast.

Time does not change, the little clock said, *time reveals.* The Irlandi slaves were sanguine. They said the horrors were prophesied: the Danar would three times conquer their homeland. But surely no-one could have foreseen these tribulations?

I later learned that the greater part of the churches of Erinn were burned. The strange names meant nothing to me, but I noted them all the same as the Majūs demolished Dun Dermuighe, devastated Leas Mor, and burned Cenn Slebhi. The Majūs king attacked Armagh, three times in as many weeks, sacking the town before usurping the abbacy, breaking the shrine of Patrick and setting up the worship of Thórr. The few monks and scholars that survived gathered up their manuscripts and holy ornaments and fled away for refuge to the court of Qarlush al-Efranj, only to find him besieged in Bārīs, half his army hung in sacrifice to the butcher god, Óðinn. The whole Nasrani world, reduced to cinders.

Throughout it all, the poet simply said, "Hush. Do not be the wasp that brings about the destruction of its own nest through its buzzing," and returned to playing the ūd with the Majūs king. Or he'd say, "Where wolf's ears are, wolf's teeth are near," and ride out to contend with their champions. Al-Ghazal was clear: the nature of our embassy was to watch, to listen and take the measure of the Majūs. This was not our war. What could we hope to achieve by intervening in it?

Yet something was amiss. When I closed my eyes, I saw the Grand Mosque aflame; I could smell the charred orange trees, see the ruined arcades and broken minarets, their colourful mosaics scorched beyond recognition, their windows of coloured glass smashed to atoms. There was no refuge in sleep, for sleep does not help if your soul is tired.

In my dreams, it seemed to me that al-Quti was right: ad-Dajjal, whom the Prophet, peace and blessing be upon him, said will be the biggest test of the Faithful, was truly here. It was said he would go swiftly into the land like a cloud driven by the wind and that there would be no town he would not enter.

What is past is gone, what is hoped for is absent, the little clock said, mocking my imprisonment.

— 9 —

Over the course of the next three months, our slave-soldiers melted into the night, at first one by one, two by two, and then in their droves, unclean beasts returning to the wild. The muwalladan were no better, proving themselves converts of convenience, all too willing to give up their faith if it meant survival.

Al-Ghazal dismissed my concerns, long since having moved on to other delights. He now rode with the king of the Majūs daily, under his protection. All would be well, he said, given time. I was to trust him, as I had trusted him a hundred times before. No crowd ever waited at the gates of patience.

Al-Quti remained my sole companion. After each and every prayer, he would ask the whereabouts of the emissary. "Where could the Gazelle be grazing at this hour?" he would cry. "Why is he not here, standing devout and obedient before God?—highly praised and glorified is He! Has he lost sight of the duty of the muya-hidīn?"

Soon, he began to speculate openly and loudly, until one night he came to my tent, weeping in desperation.

"Do you want to know what I think, Ṣāḥib al-Munayqilla? I think we are wasting our time on the errand of a fool," he said.

"Please do not speak of my friend that way," I implored him. "We must ask God to grant us patience. In haste there is regret, but in patience and care there is peace and safety. The amir has given the emissary clear instructions. He is to create a lasting friendship with the Majūs."

"You forget, I speak their tongue. My people share a common past with them; we once worshipped the same mushrik gods. No one here talks of anything but the spoils of war and the glory of battle," he groaned, wiping his brow feverishly.

"Perhaps he means to conclude a treaty, for the amir is the chosen one, whose right it is to rule the al-Khilāfatu. The East longs for his rule and looks to the West with jealousy. The Rûm put the idea in his head, years ago, but the throne of Solomon is much diminished, barely able to hold onto their own lands, let alone restore ours. The Majūs fleets, on the other hand, would come as a surprise to the usurper." I was speculating myself now, but the thought had long occurred to me, and I now had a chance to give it air.

"Why? Because the enemy of my enemy is my friend?" al-Quti raged, incredulously.

"Strong animals cannot escape being devoured by other animals stronger than they. These khanzir sued for peace after we bested them in battle," I said.

"Victory isn't our preserve alone. Rudhmīr and his counts in Jiliqiyya bloodied the nose of the Majūs just as swiftly as the Faithful. The Majūs can overreach, just like any man. If you are so certain of your new allies, why does the Gazelle have you fashioning him a map?"

I couldn't answer directly. The little clock and I had been so excited by the enormity of the challenge, we hadn't thought to question it.

"I will tell you why. He wants the quickest, safest route home. This Thorgestr," he said, using the northern king's mushrik name, "is a veritable King of the Saqāliba, this island a reservoir of potential slaves. As to the Gazelle, he is as good as banished after his last verse implied the amir had intercourse with his harem in daytime during Ramadan. His goal is to bring so many slaves back to Qurtaba that all is forgiven. Nothing more laudable than to be showered once more with golden dinars. To upstage his great rivals. A new source of harem concubines, eunuchs, craftsmen, soldiers. And who do you think sings when the faith abhors it so?" al-Quti rasped, striking the ground in frustration. "How can you not see the truth before your very eyes?"

I was appalled. My companion had taken leave of his senses, hooting endlessly like a death-owl over a grave. Yet, there was something undeniably plausible about his insights. Buried in the minutiae of my little clock, I might have missed something. I had neither the poet's aptitude nor appetites, both of which had caused him trouble before.

"I need time to think," I said, ushering him out of my tent and into the night. "May God have mercy on you!" I added reflexively, a mere afterthought.

Hurry, hurry, the little clock urged. *Time is of the essence. Only a coward waits to be taken like a lamb from the fold.*

— 10 —

The very next day, I received word from the Majūs queen, inviting the great poet to a private audience. She had recently been installed in the famed monastery of Cluain Mhic Nóis, a full day's ride inland, where she now gave oracles from the high altar. Wherever he might be, it occurred to me that the emissary would have received the same summons. I left al-Quti to languish in our camp and rode out to find al-Ghazal alone, supposing that I might warn him of the accusations laid against him and determine the truth of them. In the cool light of day, I could almost hear him scolding me: "Believe what you see and lay aside what you hear" was a maxim he lived by.

Cluain Mhic Nóis straddled the ancient crossroads of kings, on a lazy bend of the Sēnou. A whole town, once a thriving centre of learning and art, was now a blackened waste, crops and ricks burnt to the door of the main church. Soot and charred straw matted the sodden road, staining the boots of anyone foolish enough to dismount. Only the stockade and timbers of the river port had been spared the torch—the Majūs clearly planned to use this as a new forward command.

As I suspected, the emissary was already there, sitting in contemplation on his borrowed charger. It was a fine horse, no doubt stolen from the Franj, as most of the Majūs fought on foot.

"All this waste, for little more than a cattle raid," he said, when I came alongside him. "What does your little clock say now, my friend?" Al-Ghazal had a hunted look, and his trembling hands belied his calm voice. "Is the Last Hour upon us?"

"Do not be concerned, great emissary," I said, hoping to reassure him. "My little clock knows God's will. We will not die today."

"Is that so? For I see death stealing life from the most elusive deer. And, like birds, catching them despite their flight."

And with that, he spurred his horse on, riding ahead through the blistered oratories and broken kilns, ignoring the Majūs guards who called to him. It was true—there was all manner of mischief at this place, for Shayāṭīn were created from the smoke of fire, and jinn were born from its bright blaze.

I caught up with him in the ruined church, open to the sky. The queen sat on the great altar, the stone stripped bare of its Nasrani trappings. To my horror, she, too, was as naked as a worm. It had long been clear to me that these northern women do not veil themselves before their men nor before others, but I was surprised to find the queen did not conceal any part of her body from us whatsoever.

Al-Ghazal dismounted and then, without any uttering formal greeting or acknowledgement, proceeded to stare at the woman as if struck with wonderment. In order to better avert my gaze from her immodesty, I kept looking directly at the emissary.

The pig-queen pretended not to notice at first, then feigned indifference as we skulked through the rubble. Long minutes passed like this until eventually, she said to her guard, "Ask him why he stares at me so. Is it because he finds me very beautiful, or the just the opposite?"

Al-Ghazal had no need of an interpreter, and answered directly, "It is indeed because I did not imagine that there was so beautiful a spectacle in the world. I have seen, in the palaces of our amir, chosen women from among all the nations, but never have I seen beauty such as this."

The queen was clearly puzzled, speaking again to her guardsman, "Ask him; is he serious, or does he jest?"

Al-Ghazal stepped forward, well-practised in flattery, and used to extemporising in the service of the mighty. "Serious indeed," he said. "You have to resist, O my heart, a love that troubles thee, and against which you defend yourself as a lion. You are in love with a majūsiyya, who never lets the sun of beauty set, and who lives at the rarely visited extremity of the world."

I almost laughed for joy. Even when sensing peril, his nerves fraught, the emissary was able to summon pure compositions at will. Even the little clock applauded.

The king's wife asked him his age, and he replied wryly, "Twenty."

"What youth of twenty has such grey hair?" She laughed, unable to conceal her amusement at his insolence. The hostility drained from the air.

"What is so unlikely about that? Have you never seen a foal dropped that is grey-haired at birth?" the great poet boasted. While he was talking, the queen uncrossed her legs and scratched her pudendum.

I covered my face and muttered prayers of forgiveness, suddenly annoyed that she evidently thought little of the amir's silken gown. Seeing my embarrassment, her mirth knew no bounds. She spoke quickly, and al-Ghazal hemmed and hawed before choosing his words: "What her Majesty uncovers in your presence is safeguarded and is not attainable. This is better than if her Majesty were to cover it, while making it accessible."

No doubt this exchange ingratiated him further with the queen, who sat back on her haunches as al-Ghazal returned his oratory to her.

"Noble majūsiyya, I see grey hair and the dye upon it as a sun that is swathed in mist. It is hidden for a while, and then the wind uncovers it, and the covering begins to fade away. Do not despise the gleam of white hair; it is the flower of understanding and intelligence. I have that which you lust for in the youth as well as elegance of manner, culture, and breeding."

"Given that your locks have turned white," she said, grinning. "There is plenty of ash outside to dye it."

It was clearly not a suggestion. There was malice in her voice.

Al-Ghazal thanked her and made a small bow to signal his departure from her presence. Suddenly regaining my presence of mind, I rushed to his side and hissed, "Why did you say such things?"

"By your father, do you think she had no charm? I spoke as any ambassador might to a queen as I hoped to win her good graces. It might be our only way to return home," he said ominously.

On impulse, I reached for the little clock. His axle was frozen in fear, the drum refusing to mark the intervals, defying gravity itself. Something was dreadfully wrong.

The queen had crawled to the altar, clutching in her hand a thin iron rod, ornamented on one end, that she used to caress her intimate parts.

"Great poet, many a fair skin hides a foul mind. That woman is a sahir. I can feel the black magic in the air. There is nothing uglier than magic," I said, pulling at his sleeve in my haste to leave. I might have had better luck hefting an elephant—like the little clock, the emissary was stuck fast. He looked as surprised as I was, his body contorting violently as he wrestled with an unseen snare.

Behind us the queen began to intone: *"Is acher ingaíth innocht, Fufúasna fairggæ findfholt, Ní ágor réimm mora minn, Dondláechraid lainn ua Lothlind."*

"A spell!" I cried, tugging hard at the old man. "These are the whisperings of Shayāṭīn!"

"No," said al-Ghazal, suddenly ceasing to struggle. "A poem." He slumped, hanging his head, still held upright by the grasp of the jinn's noose.

Bitter is the wind tonight, it tosses the ocean's white hair, I fear not the coursing of a clear sea, By the fierce heroes from Laithlind.

"A poem? Why is she reciting a poem?" I asked, without understanding. I knew that the Majūs had their own rude recitals and had heard them yelp and yowl through a hundred tales of glorious battle. To compare the drivel of infidels with the exquisite compilations of Qurtuba was to name a fish as a whale.

"Because her husband is dead," the emissary whispered.

I retched loudly, and tottered like a thawee, a weak camel that can't even stand on its feet. The enormity of our situation was now obvious, even to me. No wonder the poet had been cautious. How much had he known before setting foot in the chapel?

The queen called: "I have not finished with you yet, al-Sinjab!"

Al-Ghazal did not look up, but he still managed to summon enough pride to answer with conviction. "O queen, I am known as the Gazelle, not the squirrel."

"Have you not run, chattering like Ratatoskr, between the ends of the great Ash, plotting our downfall? The Frakkar, the Grikkir, the Vestmenn." The queen was elated, cavorting with delight atop the Nasrani altar. "I have a gift for you," she growled.

Al-Ghazal was resolute and refused to accept it. He winced and twisted in pain, the jinn's grip closing like a vice.

"What did you do?!" I called to him, but whether he heard me or not, he made no reply.

The queen spoke again, saying to her guard: "Ask him why he does not accept my gift. Does he dislike my gift, or me?"

The emissary haltingly wheezed his reply: "Indeed, her gift may be magnificent... and to receive it from her is... a great honour... for she is a queen and... the daughter of a king.... But it is gift enough for me to see her... and to be received by her.... This is the only gift I want."

I kept my eyes to the ground and tried to avoid looking at the naked majūsiyya, but it proved impossible. She began to yawn, gaping her mouth unnaturally wide. For all the world, she looked like one of the qiyān, the singing slave-girls of the amir, a piece of wood forced into their jaw to train it to stay open.

"Yes, my husband is dead. Ragnar is dead, slain by Niall Caille in battle. Ragnar is dead, drowned by Máel Sechnaill, cast into a pit of snakes by Aelle. Ragnar is dead, ridden with dysentery outside Parisaborg. Time and time again. Time and time again."

The house of a tyrant is indeed a ruin. Her mind is broken with grief, I thought. Al-Ghazal's head lolled backward, drooling like a man asleep in the afternoon sun—God have mercy on him!

"At Cippanhamme, the elf-counselled will fall on the twelfth night, and with him England," she sang from somewhere else, at once on the altar and buried deep in the stone. There was something old here, something in the very soil, and she was a conduit to the bogs and peat and what lay beneath.

"Over the sea from Hlymrek sails a fleet, with the dark and the fair. At the helm stands the Iron Bear, to take the maidenhood of the Red Lady—would you yet know more?" she said, her words reverberating through the splintered beams and burnt rafters. I tried to stop my ears and plucked again at the emissary's white-hemmed robe.

"Eochaid Ollathair is with me! The Lord of the Hanged is here! To the head of Mim does my Lord give heed, a hall I see, roofed with wisdom, a gift from the gods; a city of ships saved by the house of war."

The witch had been prophesying still, cavorting with demons and jinn in a wild gyre, but she stopped abruptly at the end of her sentence.

"Is there no end to the wonders of your people? I've seen your great chemists and their al-kîmiya, the art of transmutation. I have watched you distill white naft to light whole cities. I have witnessed a man leap from a minaret on a machine of silk and eagles' feathers and fly. I should like to try an experiment of my own. I plan to change quicksilver to smouldering sulphur."

"Ya Sharmouta," I cursed, scrabbling to get purchase on my unconscious friend. "I seek refuge in the Lord of the dawn. From the evil of what He has created. And from the evil of the utterly dark night when it comes. And from the evil of those who blow on knots. And from the evil of the envious when he envies," I prayed, my camel knees collapsing underneath me.

There was no divine intervention. Her guards rendered me unconscious as the Gazelle was taken away.

— II —

The letter was brief and without answers. His penmanship was unmistakable, his letters at once rigid and flowery, lines straight and orderly like the man himself. My anguish knew no such bounds.

"My friend, Allah is done with me. Every sun must set. I have lived sixty years and some more, the first third part of them flirting, the second part living in sin, and the third part deep in an abyss, where my pity and faith are lacking. Perhaps meeting death is better than escaping from it."

I had my freedom, for what it was worth, and for how long it lasted. When the day came when the Gazelle was to be burned alongside their king, I went to the river where a great ship lay. It had already been taken out of the water, supported by four wooden pillars and wooden scaffolding, separate from the main stockade in case the fire caught the wind and spread. The stream meandered over much of the ground outside, roiled by the inevitable winds, turning the entire area into viscous marshland.

My little clock and I watched from the rampart as Majūs began to walk back and forth, wading through the mud, uttering oaths which I still did not fully understand. They arranged their king solemnly, still wearing the mail in which he had died, the corpse already turned black from the cold of that country.

They dressed him in trousers, leggings, a tunic, and a brocaded long coat with gold buttons. On his head they placed a cap made of sable fur, and then they carried him into the middle of the ship. They seated him on a quilted mattress and propped him up with the cushions. They then brought mead, fruit, and aromatic herbs and placed them with him. Servants came with bread, meat, and onions and threw them in front of him, and also a dog, oddly subdued, which they cleft in two and threw into the boat. Then his warriors brought all his weapons and laid them at his side. Lastly, they took two horses, ran them until they broke out in a sweat, then they dashed them to pieces with their swords and threw their meat into the ship.

When it was the time of the afternoon prayer, they brought the queen to something they had set up around the king, similar to the frame of a door or a tent. Three times she was lifted, peeping over the frame in search of her ancestors. The last time she cried "There! I see my lord sitting in Valhöll, and paradise is beautiful and green, and with him are men and slaves, and he is calling to us."

They handed her a chicken that clucked and squawked, oblivious to its fate until she twisted its neck and flung it inside the ship.

Men came carrying shields and wooden staves and began beating the shields with their shafts, covering the frame with canvas. For the briefest of moments, I saw the emissary through their ranks, tall and unbowed, his white turban pristine and gleaming. Then al-Ghazal went into the tent, bound by the men... and I closed my eyes. Minutes later, the warriors stepped out, one by one. But the poet did not.

The queen took a piece of wood and set it alight. She then set fire to the wood that was stacked under the ship. The people then came forward with sticks and firewood. Each one of them had with him a piece of wood, the end of which he had set on fire, and which he now threw upon the wood packed beneath the ship. This spread to the firewood, then to the ship, then to the tent, and finally to everything therein. There then began to blow a mighty and frightful wind, and the flames of the fire were intensified, and its blaze flared up.

From within the ship came a strident prayer. "O Allah! We seek refuge in You from the torment of Hellfire, from the torment of the grave, from the trials of life and death, and from the trials and tribulations of al-Masih ad-Dajjal."

There was a shriek of agony, and then only the dim reply of crackling wood. I was too distraught to call out, and so whispered my goodbyes.

"May Allah have mercy on you, Yahya ibn-Hakam el Bekri al-Djayani. What you have now is far better than what you had in life, for you are now with Allah. You were honored in life and content in death." I wept like the stream, my tears tortuous and uncontained.

The little clock cried too, his walnut heart broken, his gears undone, the mercury rolling in rivulets to the floor.

At my side, a Majūs sentry began to laugh.

"You Serkir are foolish," he guffawed.

"How so?" I asked, too stupefied to be offended.

"You take the person who is the most beloved to you and leave him in the ground, for the insects and the worms to consume. It is better like this, to be burned with fire in an instant, to rejoin our ancestors in that very moment. Because of the great love that the Ancient One has for him, the Báleygr sent the wind to carry the king off within the space of an hour."

And truly, an hour did not pass before the boat, the wood, the poet and the king had become ash dust.

I watched in horrified silence. This was the Last Hour indeed. I reached for the little clock, once so full of possibility, his cracked and empty shell now bereft of purpose or bearing. I meant to hurl it into the fire, but the Majūs guard reached out and stayed my hand.

The creature spoke softly, almost sympathetically. "Shall I tell you what your little clock is saying? He says, 'Fear not death, for the hour of your doom is set and none may escape it.'"

I stared at him, mouth agape.

"As-Salamu `Alaykum, Ṣāḥib al-Munayqilla," the Majūs said, in almost flawless Arabic. I could not see the ghūul beneath the helmet, but I could sense his trickery. And then it hit me, he had been speaking Arabic all along. I staggered backwards, shocked from my torpor, my chest heaving as if kicked by a bolting jamal.

Now alerted, I recognised the infidel at once. Close up, the man seemed huge, his broad forehead tousled with a mane of thick, curly hair, one of his eyes protuberant and blind. Al-Masīḥ ad-Dajjal, the False Messiah, the Devil-King of the Majūs. He was alive and watching his own funeral from afar.

"Who—what—are you?" I rasped, hoarse from weeping and indignant because of it. The aḥādīth were clear: whoever hears of ad-Dajjal should flee from him, for a man may end up following him due to the doubts that the Deceiver will cast into his heart.

"I have many names—there being so many branches of tongues in the world, all peoples call me something different, so they might the better entreat me on their own behalf. I have forgotten many and will forget still more," he said, wistfully.

"But why kill my friend, the Gazelle? I thought he was your firm favourite," I said.

"Did you know one of the trials of ad-Dajjal will be to seize a man by his feet and hands and cast him into the fire—to kill a man and then bring him back to life by Allah's permission? Your own Prophet says that. It seemed... fitting to send him to Valhöll," the corpse king said.

"That doesn't answer my question," I insisted.

"He uncovered my secret while we were riding. It would have been better for him if he hadn't. He was a greedy man, and I knew he would try to profit from it. You see, I cannot die," he said matter-of-factly.

I gulped, following the revelation to its natural conclusion. "You possess the al-Ikseer of life?" The Persians told stories of how al-Iskandar, fresh from his conquests, had searched the Lands of Darkness for the secret of immortality, with a mystical guide known only as al-Khidr, the Green One. Arabic alchemists across Dar el Islam had searched for the fabled formula since time immemorial, mixing mercury, sulfur, and arsenic in their desperation for "drinkable gold." If al-Ghazal had discovered these secrets among the Majūs, he would be rich beyond his wildest dreams. He could rightfully claim to be Khalīfah himself!

"After a fashion," he said, without further explanation.

"Then who is that in the fire with the emissary?" I hissed, knowing the answer in my heart before the question left my lips. Al-Quti. The poor, benighted fool.

"Now we must hurry away unseen," said the king. "It is not fitting for a dead man to linger over his own grave. Resurrection confuses the Nazarenes. Auðr's vengeance will drive the conquest now."

I struggled against the horror, hoping prayer would save me, but he held my arm in an iron grip. If I must go into the dark night, I would denounce him first.

"You are not the Lord of the Worlds. You are nothing but a false prophet, a test of my faith. I will not follow you."

"Do not worry, Ṣāḥib al-Munayqilla, you who hold infinity in the palm of your hand, and eternity in an hour," the king said. "You, above all men, I can trust. We have work ahead of us."

— IÐUNN'S HEL-RIDE —

The Grove of Thórr
Írland 1970

The whirler began its precipitous descent, a dark spinning, like a sycamore key come spiralling out of the murk, turning the locks of the future.

Iðunn felt herself flinch, startled by the suddenness of the evacuation. She groped distractedly through the dark for a knee to squeeze, a reassuring hand to hold, more out of habit than hope, but of course, there was nothing. Whirlers didn't even merit a pilot to yell at—the Imperials just strapped you in and hurled you into the ionosphere. *Stupid fuckers.* Only an empire born of pirates would make walking the plank a principle of design. Still, with the greenways in collapse, there was no safer way of conveying her thread-riders to the surface.

She pushed the small of her back firmly into the seat, trying to find reassurance in the contours of her airborne cauldron as it gyred through the heavens. Her cabin had sixteen round, reinforced hollows, positioned to provide a view of the horizon at all stages of flight. They were small compared to the gaps between them, and some were fuzzed with a sheen of ochrous mold, but she could patch together a moderately good view when she dared to open her eyes.

Her eyes. That was some consolation. Her garlanded body had been delivered like a bouquet of fresh flowers by Imperial courier, a brocade of Verðandi by way of cortege. The þráðriða had sewn her mind back into familiar muscles and membranes, healing the overlong decoherence—and now here she was, clenching her refugee organs for dear life. She tapped her feet anxiously, much preferring when they were firmly attached to the ground.

Nine more whirlers dropped alongside her, sailing the solar wind: her companions, each pod paired in symmetrical clusters like partners in a folk dance. She half expected the Imperials to blare "Ride of the Valkyrja," just as they did when they brought their revenges over Gastropnir, but they remained blissfully silent. Perhaps

Trumba felt her little mercy dash didn't deserve the fanfare, or that the upcoming fireworks needed no accompaniment.

Sprites arced briefly across the pods' Mímameiðr limbs, and then vanished, leaving only luminous red haloes in the backscatter of sunlight. She winced again—and then upbraided herself for the foolishness. The Skuld might have been decimated by the explosion at Mímisbrunnr, but their ingenuity lived on. Nanotech, the Grikkir might have called it. Dvergr-tækni claimed the purists. Either way, the infusion of heartwood and white copper was nigh on indestructible. Mjölnir itself couldn't have made a dent.

More Sprites flocked around the crown, the dissonant dance of their tendrils suggesting a thunderstorm below. The name was a whimsical acronym for Stratospheric Perturbations Resulting from Intense Thunderstorm Electrification. Ljósalfar as beautiful as the sun, or the excitation of nitrogen molecules due to electron collisions—it made no difference whether you were a skald or a vísdómsmaðr, the effect was the same: sheer, jaw-dropping majesty. Iðunn opened her eyes wide in wonder, keenly aware that, despite their beauty, these alfar were just outriders, heralds for the celestial pageant to come.

They plummeted on, the world revolving brighter still, forcing Iðunn to fumble for her sun-goggles. The main event was said to be nothing short of miraculous, and she didn't want to blink and miss it. Imperial propagandists once contrived that lights in the night sky were the reflections of Valkyrjur armour as they led the fallen past the doorpost of Gjöll—a fetishistic vision, the carnal discipline of a metal bodice designed to motivate the soldiery.

That was before the Skuld roused the Western Dawn. With the temerity of idle children, the maestari had redrawn the world, compelling a new horizon to stir—and Óðinn's Wish Maids were trampled in the rush to congratulate them.

Seen close up, the Svalinn shield was little more elaborate than a copper wire, a receiver, and a sail, snatching elf beams and funnelling them to the ground below—a satellite capable of generating billions upon billions of gigawatts of energy—but that was to ignore the bobbing, dancing, weaving bands of aurorae it created, as the flow of solar particles fluctuated around its magnetic boss, the sky igniting in bands of colours where the great sunshield faced his shining god. The Skuld's flamboyance was so large and virile, the people of Midgard nicknamed it the dayspring.

Once, when their campaign was young, Father had told her a fanciful tale, no doubt to ease her abiding fear of leaping into the dark. It was one she still cherished. He said the aurorae were caused by firefoxes, creatures so fleet of foot that they sprinted through the sky. When their large, furry tails brushed against the mountains, they created sparks that lit up the world. Of course, it was childish, they both knew that, but it was so much brighter, so much more alive with possibility, than the compulsive need most Norse felt to romanticise the dead. Iðunn often wondered whether that one story had inspired her to devise her Apples. Telomerase not only kept the Læknir away, it halted the conversation around death through the simple expedient of removing the full stop from the end of the sentence.

There had once been a hundred other tales, the ethereal lights woven into the fabric of a thousand vanquished cultures, a magnet for reminiscence. For the peoples of Markland, the lights had been the spirits of the dead playing ball with a walrus head or lost children who danced round and round twisting streamers in the sky; fires over which the great medicine men simmered their dead enemies in enormous pots, or torches used by a tribe of dvergr, half the length of a canoe paddle in height and yet so strong they caught whales with their hands.

But that was then, in the days when she had worn her laughter lines like a veil, before the decades of war had bound her every flight of fancy, before the relentless march of Norsification trampled away any vestiges of foreign thinking. These days, the inconstant polar lights were eclipsed, a mere sideshow compared to the ingenuity of the truculent ringmasters. Like all trusted shields, Svalinn was part sentinel, part canvas, richly decorated with a myriad of patterns and poems. The Vesturljós were the crowning glory of an Empire, and the false dawns of faded kingdoms were buried with their ghosts.

She tumbled through a burst of carmine, a great bloom of green, then iridescent purple fronds. The scientist in her knew the colours corresponded to different quantum transitions, excited oxygen and vibrant nitrogen atoms, but it was still wondrous to behold—like falling through a rainbow or being shrunk down and placed in a neon sign. Or being caressed by a firefox tail, nuzzled by an old flame.

Then... no sooner had the light show begun than it was over. Iðunn was dumped back into her decrepit and mildew-powdered pod, the reverie cut short. She fought for focus against a welling tear, then blinked it away, redshifting back to the darkness with practiced efficiency. This was where she lived now, with nothing to offer the cosmos but bitter determination and mordant drudgery.

Her companions were moving slower now, she noticed, snared in the downdraft of the onrushing storm, turning with the vorticity of new winds. She adjusted her own craft's fluidics and felt the whirler stiffen, then sweep past the turbulence, affording her an excellent, if bumpy view of the thunderclouds, silver-grey anvils waiting to spark. The other ships did the same, adjusting for the syncopated rhythm, before resuming their silent reel.

They were still dizzyingly high, but not so far that she couldn't make out the receptor complex glistening on the ground, surrounded by a misty, brooding forest, with ash and pine trees over a hundred ells tall, their huge canopies shading a tangled understory of hornbeams, ferns, and fungi the size of tables. From Ilbláland to Morguneyjar, half the world had been wiped clean, yet here life had survived, an emerald redoubt in a sea of chaos. The skjaldborg had clearly absorbed the worst of the blow, leaving the land untouched by Surtr's scathe of branches. Such was the caprice of heaven.

Iðunn kept her eyes firmly on the ground as it shuttled towards her—just in case there were any last-minute surprises—but her landing was feathered, with very little sideslip considering the wind. The drone chamber automatically depressurised and opened, releasing the Verðandi like a carefully nurtured seed. Now safely planted, she couldn't begrudge the Imperials their due—they had always had a way with ergonomics, with getting people from Fehu to Othala as quickly as possible. She made a mental note to punch in the schematics prior to the return, and then unwound herself from her seat, wiping herself free of a film of protective webbing. She walked down the bow ramp to heave her pack onto a waiting vagn, quickly assizing the rest of the advance preparations.

The air was thick and cool, draped with a silence that parted only briefly—for a hrafn's croak, a barn ugla's screech, or an úlfr's wail—before returning to stillness. She took a moment to rummage through her pack, to reassure herself that she had everything she needed. Trumba had been generous. There was plenty in the way of rations, sampling dredges, sounding leads and liming tools, plus extra layers of útsól protective clothing.

The other whirlers landed, accompanied by a static squall from the Imperial loudhailers. There was no further bulletin or reprimand, so Iðunn ignored the noise, chalking it up to the usual Imperial incompetence. An aborted announcement perhaps, because no sooner had Iðunn turned back to her work than her companions duly emerged in solemn procession, taking it in turns to stow their own gear.

The Grandmother of Dawn stepped out first, as befitted her seniority. She swayed as she descended, the tassels of her headdress bobbing and weaving, her back bending like an ear of corn in a piteraq. Her face was painted white with ground shells and gypsum, a mask of mourning. Ulfrun Barkfoot had always been the first to heed any summons—the Women of the First Light always greeted a challenge head on—although her brightest days were behind her and her eyes were rheumy with fatigue. The byname Barkfoot was a twisted joke—Ulfrun had lost her leg during the war, and now sported a neuro-prosthetic grown from ironwood. Alterations were common enough practice across the whole Empire, but Skræling midew were known for growing artificial limbs that were better than new.

"That was quite the ride. You know, I realize now why I never warmed to ballet as a girl."

The old woman fussed the last few steps, shifting her distress to her native tongue. When she reached the forest floor, she knelt and pressed her temple to the half-frozen soil, mingling her hair with the dirt.

"All that pirouetting. They teach you to keep the head still but never mention the stomach..." she lamented. Iðunn placed an affectionate hand on her shoulder, glad of all the help she knew the woman would provide in the hours ahead. Ulfrun, she knew, was strong and uncompromising, used to the hard scrabble of reclamation.

"More incentive for us to make sure our graft takes," Iðunn said. "I'll tell you, though: if we don't manage to fix the greenways, I'll strap on hel-shoes and we'll walk back to Elvidnir together."

Ulfrun smiled queasily and sat upright. "Smells like rain." She sniffed, wrinkling her nose, pockmarking her makeup with fresh crescents.

"You do *know* where we are?" asked another voice, waspishly. A shock of searing scarlet hair burst from one of the pods, so vivid it might have belonged to the Lady of the Isles herself, were it not for the pallet jigger trundling behind her. "The Írar invented fecking rain," the woman said. "Who would have laid odds on a fecking slave-port being the only safe harbour left? That there is the Norns pissing themselves with laughter."

Angeyja Dufgall was an initiate, not that rank counted for much within the sisterhood. She fairly buzzed out of the landing craft, stumbling and raging with a mountain of equipment.

"The patterns are holding, that's all I meant, sweetling," said the midew with a shrug, burying her discomfort in her medicine bag. Angeyja aimed a swift kick at the jigger, which rolled to a halt. "Fair enough. Well, heim again, heim again, jiggety-jig. Welcome to the Grove of Thórr."

The skalds called it the Isle of Ørlög—the land of destiny, the well of a hundred lays and laments. Had it not been here, the poets cried, that Thórr's divine hammer had first forged the spirit of Empire, irrepressible and relentless? The great slave-port of Dyflinn was described in courtly metre, likened to a furnace fuelled by the whip and the wage, its riven timber dragons spewing molten fire across the length and breadth of Midgard.

Even as eulogies went, it was bull-scutter. The skalds had always been full of shit. That was the only thing you could be sure about with destiny: nobody ever saw it coming.

For over nine hundred years the Írar were shackled to the fate of the Norse, their native land a grove of fetters. They were a devout people, and when their stone monasteries and basilicas were swept away by northern tides, they fashioned new chapels deep in the forests. In time, they came to call their home *Caill Tomair*, the Grove of Thórr.

But the hammer meant something different to them. It was not just a tool, or a symbol of destruction and protection, of the making of oaths and the imparting of fertility. In the hands of the vengeful, it represented something stronger. The hammer was justice.

The land itself seemed to call upon its sons to strike for freedom, inciting every generation from Brján Bóruma onwards to continue the struggle. Then, at the beginning of the Time of Travels, the Írar thralls finally found their voice. Almost overnight, they melted into the trees, disappearing from the destitute fields and black Óðinnic mills with patient discipline. The only trace that they'd ever existed: countless shattered chains, left to rust in the rain.

To hear the exiles tell it—the only skalds worth listening to in Iðunn's book—Thórr had decided enough was enough. So much for feckin' örlög, they sang, for one drunken, celebratory decade after another. They named the whole affair the Rupture, because they were funny bastards as well as devout ones. Dyflinn itself was recollected back into the memory of the trees, its spinning mules and pudding furnaces lost to the friction of time; the Írar diaspora took the steppingstones of the Fomhóraigh to Jötunheim.

The Skuld, never ones to respect virginity or abide a vacuum, were the next inhabitants of the forest, shaping its potential to act as a reservoir for the great electrick shield they planned to build above. Seiðrmenn like Giselbjartr and Frankeleyn had long plotted to harness the bright bride of the heavens. Overnight, their mechanical dvergr turned the Grove near Dyflinn to embers, illuminated the Black Pool with wreaths of fire. In its stead, they erected Brísingamen, a glowing city of steel pylons, toroidal cores, and porcelain bushings dedicated to Freyja, whose pale gold potency now flowed freely through the Empire—and to her twin, Freyr, whose alfar swirled and fluxed around the shield, delivering the vitality of Álfröðull.

The amber river never ceased, never subsided. Thórr could only rail, flashing his impotent anger from the sky, his thunder stolen, his people scattered. The price of penance, the Fylkir had said, for a god of sound and fury, who dealt in petty revenge. An outmoded god, without the wit to move with the times, the cult of the loud rider fell from grace. Odin had other sons.

But not everyone had broken faith with the Thunderer. Iðunn fervently hoped he was watching over them. This was the eye of his storm—there was no better place to get his attention. Jörð was his fucking mother, after all.

There was a glacial rumble in the air. Just as the Skræling had predicted, the first rains began to tumble out of the heavens, great baubles that burst on the hardened soil, dissolving the hoarfrost into muddy streaks. The odor of the forest immediately changed, a redolent combination of plant oils, bacterial spores, and errant ozone. An earthy, musty scent, the perfume of the primeval mother Jörð. All three women stooped, fishing great handfuls of soil that they smeared across their faces and clothes, a ritual connecting body and land.

"So, here we are," Iðunn said, with a grim certitude. She pulled her shawl tight to fend off the downpour and deaden the patter of leafy drumskins. "It's the weather of weapons all right…"

"Thórr's pretty PO'd with someone," said Angeyja. Iðunn had always been drawn to a defiant spirit, and there was no shortage of them among the Muintir Tomar—Thórr's exiles had thronged to

Father's rebellion. None of them had Angeyja's talents, though—when roused, the young woman boasted the voice of a valkyrja.

"Not much damage, though. Considering," Ulfrun said, scanning the treeline. She held her frame oddly, lopsided, as if she were knitting her bones together through sheer force of will.

"Svalinn took the brunt of the blow, I expect," Iðunn said, already feeling the rain seeping through her outer layers. "There is clearly some remanence at the shield."

"Oh, you mean those lights. I was awhirl in a sluagh's tresses." The Írar swooned theatrically. "I thought I'd died and gone to Sessrúmnir."

"Hush, girl. You might as well book passage if you keep hollering like that. Don't you know to whisper under the dance of the alfar?" Ulfrun said, fretfully.

"What? In case they take offence and reach down to slice off my head? You've been too long among the Finnar, Grandma Dawn. Besides—" She gestured grandly above them. "—clouds. They can't see a thing." Angeyja chuckled conspiratorially. They all knew that, alarming as it was, there was some truth to the folklore. When the Institute of Northern Industrial Ecology in Kønugarðr reported that geomagnetic activity caused an increased incidence of anxiety, depression, and suicide in Brísingamen, there had been a crackle of outrage. Father had been quick to convert it into a current of crisis. A single spark that led to conflagration.

"Bit dark for a power station, isn't it?" the novice asked.

"If it was working, believe me, you'd notice. This place used to turn night into day. The particles that were captured by the shield above, they were directed down here, towards Brísingamen, by a huge leysir. That's what made the place so... combustible," Iðunn explained.

"The explosion heard round the worlds, that was here?" Angeyja asked, incredulous. The young greenseer had been birthed in Patreksfjörður, on a reserve far from the frontlines. The Termagant there must have presumed what she didn't know couldn't hurt her. Least said, soonest mended. Still, Iðunn felt it a little disconcerting that the younger generations were oblivious to the origins of the struggle.

Ulfrun looked skyward, to where the clouds writhed with agitation. "I can scarcely remember how they got it working in the first place. Such a shadow it cast, stealing our tomorrows," she murmured.

"The challenge was always down to the technological constraints, devising a lens powerful enough to direct the leysir towards the surface without it being diffracted," Iðunn said. "The Skuld turned to ancient solarsteinn to solve that problem. We tried for years to disrupt their shipments, as well as the mining efforts. They eventually pulled the plug after the Fenrian Uprising back in '40." She'd had the dubious benefit of the show trials to jog her memory.

"So long ago! I've got some old cigarette cards and hieroglyphics somewhere," Angeyja said, a sprite of insouciance—until the moment she was startled by an unexpected voice inside her head.

I'll be delighted to give you a firsthand account, to see if it matches your imagination.

The last of Iðunn's félagi sloughed onto his gangplank, the sound echoing across the airdock until the ship's morphic cells yielded, sighing in pliant protest. Last but not least; Iðunn smiled.

The jötunn Grábakr had been Father's pride and joy—a ten-foot-tall serpent-savant, maned with the grey fur that gave him his name, his genetic circuits, computational organs, and recombinant plasmids specifically designed to make him one of the greatest minds in the Níu Heimar. Even after all this time, Iðunn found it hard not to look at him in awe and wonder: he was a true child of the Ash, as pallid as the lignin infused in his scales.

Ljósmóðir, he beamed, his mind touching hers. His brood had been hand-reared, borrowing polite, unassuming tones from the sisterhood. Grábakr had held onto them through his long confinement. She was delighted to see him, though, the prodigal son returned at last.

Welcome! You have been well treated?

The linnorm was flanked by a constable of six Varangians, their Valravn masks snapped closed. Trumba had demanded the escort, to do what all ravens did: watch and listen. It must have taken them a while to charm the linnorm out of his cage. They were already reporting back, if the incessant clacking of their visors was anything to go by.

As might be expected. And you've grown your hair?

They clinched hurriedly; the embrace starved of affection by the Imperial presence. Letting Grábakr slide freely on Midgard was controversial, to say the least. For her Order, science and art weren't mechanistic, they were as natural and wild as creation. Grábakr was the mightiest of their galdrkind, the living embodiment of life's songs, a creature weaned on the roots of Yggdrasil. For the Empire, he was a beast from beyond. At her arraignment, the Verðandi had been accused of falling out of Nature into a pool of artifice. Iðunn had—personally, singlehandedly—misshapen the beauteous form of things. Arranging his place on the expedition had involved more than pulling a few strings.

The dreki scanned his surroundings, his eyes bright with enthusiasm. "Ah, the Empire's sylvan larder. And why, might I enquire, are we here? Am I to presume second helpings?"

"We're here for Thórr's Oak," Iðunn explained. The great oak was a knútr, a doorway between realms. During the war, Father had smuggled rebels through here, right under Imperial noses, a campaign of terror that tipped the balance for emancipation.

"I see. A fishing expedition. I distinctly remember Father calling it the Skuld's Back Passage. The Jörmunsûl let us get up to all kinds of shenanigans. Speaking of which, my brothers...?"

"Heroes all. Their deeds eclipse those of even your father."

"I am gladdened to hear. Perhaps we will meet again in the Opheim.... I hope the price for my release was tolerable."

"Thórr's Oak is old growth, older than the Ages of Ice. It will answer all our questions."

And that was all she needed. Answers. There was no tactical advantage to be gained in preserving the Oak, not anymore. No price was too high for her children, she thought, least of all a secret passage and a defunct murder hole.

"And if it is occluded too? Like Uppsala?" asked Angeyja. The novice was all nerves and anticipation.

"There are other doors. Gaismar. Nametvik." In truth, Iðunn didn't know the exact extent of the damage to the greenways, but Angeyja would be key to finding out. There were precious few seiðr-workers left now that Surtr's fire was slaked, and *belonging* helped when reaching out to the ancestors. The Muintir Tomar were known to be hostile to strangers, even among the Verðandi.

The soldiers took up a perimeter around the vagn, no doubt expecting the jötunn to shoulder the burden. It occurred to Iðunn that none of her Verðandi had seen their faces: gods alone knew what brittle men hid under the armour.

"The harvester pilot is hailing," the troop leader said, his voice detached and mechanical.

"We've come this far. No sense in turning back now," Iðunn said, answering for them all.

The larger ship would collect the whirlers—they were designed for entry only. It brushed down alongside them, lobed blades scooping up each pod, before moving on to the next one. The Varangian paused to brush aside some of the bloated, viscous droplets of liquid that had begun beading on its crown, then tapped a friendly salute on the hull, signalling the all-clear.

Iðunn turned to the task at hand, already feeling stretched and weary. Angeyja was the only one buoyed by the rain. What she might give for a snippet of that DNA, the inheritance of the indefatigable Írar.

"I need you attuned to Manheimr quickly please, Grá."

"Of course; where to start, where to begin. Ozone depletion is localised but averages at 65 percent," the jötunn said, evidently needing no reminders, his own outsized visor making his calibrations visible to his immediate custodians, and probably to a kvaðrilljón more unseen Urðr watching in orbit. "There will be constant genetic damage from irradiance here on the surface, for you at least."

"Nothing that can't be easily repaired," said Ulfrun, a sly smile playing round her lips. "Dawnland has been mending the Old World since the ravens first croaked ruin."

"Let's not make work for ourselves. Masks on," Iðunn instructed, now recognising the sharp smell in the air. Each of them wore a thin reed respirator and sun-goggles—the Verðandi stored large reserves of oxygen in their blood and muscle thanks to enhanced levels of hemoglobin and myoglobin, but without a mask, the ground-level ozone would ultimately damage their lungs beyond repair. Their clothing was otherwise as identical as it was practical—unassuming beige suits, tightly woven from jute fiber with Val-hemp for extra protection from the ultraviolet light now cascading through the atmosphere.

"The Grove has been fortunate," Iðunn said. "That will change. Suffocating blankets of volcanic ash. Walls of impregnable of ice grinding from the north. Years without summer. Ague-stricken survivors. Hailstorms and sea floods. The polar jet stream will follow, and the cycle will repeat."

"Balor Béimnech bedamned. I need a drink," sighed Angeyja.

"There won't be enough wine to fill a nutshell," mourned Ulfrun. "The vineyards of the Wonderstrands are stilled, the sun above my home is nothing more than a suggestion." The Dawnlanders had been among the first peoples to treat with Snorri Thorfinnsson and the men of Leifsbuðir, and the last to leave their shores when the Guldrstein turned their home to a wasteland. It was small wonder they all felt charred and shrivelled.

"Forget the fucking Fringes," said a trooper in a menacing rash of static. He paused, shaking his head, then snapped the seal on his helmet. Iðunn hesitated, waiting for the big reveal. The Varangian didn't disappoint: his cheek muscles shivered with rage, curling his upper lip into an ascetic's sneer, demonstrating why he merited a mask in the first place. He was obviously monitoring everything they said and didn't feel obliged to pretend any different. "I don't have an ôrtug of sympathy for the bloody colonies. What about the heartlands? What about the Doggerland reclamation? The Langahaf dam crumbled, all the new—Loyalist—colonies are under thirty fathoms of saltwater."

Her companions did their best to stifle their sniggers. The huge jötunn spread his arms guilelessly wide, framing the whole treeline. "The race of man flies far in dread; his work and dwelling vanish," he crooned to his disbelieving guards, his poetry repaid with a stipend of snarling rifle muzzles.

Grábakr was nonplussed, and simply continued his soil analysis. "Go ahead. I hear divinity helps those who dare. Unless you think this flame-food"—he gestured to the still-standing forest—"is going to be saved by the luck of the Írar?" He grinned; his needle teeth embroidered with venom.

Iðunn was amused by the comment, admiring even. The Jötnar had been born of desperation and defiance, an imitation of Norse nightmares, designed to despise the mythos of Empire. She'd often debated with herself, asking if her creations had agency in shaping what they became. Grábakr had transcended her wildest dreams—even now, he exuded reason rather than rancour, despite his long captivity.

She bustled between her ward and the Varangians, hurriedly extending her arm by way of both introduction and injection. Diplomacy wasn't her strong suit, but she had little choice but to leaven the mood with whatever charm she could muster. "Sorry, I haven't had the pleasure?" she lied, addressing the bare-faced captain.

"No, you haven't," the soldier answered with practiced contempt, his rifle remaining locked in place. "Fucking trolls. You people couldn't just roll over and die. You had to take the whole Nine Worlds with you." His voice crackled with hatred.

"We are on the same side. We always were. My friends here are simple grœðari," she said, using the old word for a healer. Pleading with a Varangian was beneath her, but she didn't have time for his kind of maladaptive thinking. Iðunn shifted her weight, leaning against the ruminating giant for support. The other two Vǫlur stepped nimbly to her side in a show of solidarity.

"Tell that to the poor bastards your knucker slaughtered in their beds at Austmannatún." Strands of spittle gummed the soldier's words together like projectiles, joining the snap and spatter of the rain. His eyes were targeted malevolence; his rifle barrel was etched with a running tally of enemies he had dispatched.

Iðunn noted that Ulfrun had cycled her releasers, flushing enough messengers to flood the soldier's normal endocrine response. It was a standard tactic for cognitive diffusion. The appeasement was coded, designed to be imperceptible, but the Varangian's eyes widened in recognition.

"Don't try and play your mind tricks on me, seidrkona. Pick up the cart and move out," he said, touching the totems round his neck, a medley of Finnar wards and talismans. "Let's not keep the Empress waiting."

The implication was obvious—in all likelihood, and despite all her feigned indifference, Trumba was following one of the Varangians directly. This was a high-stakes game, after all. Secret doors, hidey-holes, and skulduggery were the Empress's stock in trade. Iðunn tilted her head, letting the torrent of rain disguise her admission of defeat just in case—the confrontation was pointless, and tensions were unnecessarily inflamed. Still, she'd be damned if she was going to fetch and carry like an ironed gang from a prison hulk.

Forget these Chenoo, Ulfrun whispered with the wind. *We should begin, before Lox puts more thorns on our plants.*

Grandmother Dawn was right, but then she always was.

"We'll travel light. Make better time. Grá has all the instrumentation we need. How far to the Back Door?" Iðunn asked, shouldering a daypack and starting out before the Varangian could register any complaint. She just hoped she was going in the right direction—she had never ventured through the Grove from this direction and didn't have her bearings.

Angeyja looked especially relieved. "Not far," she said, pointing into the forest, and then curling her finger to the right by way of course correction. She shoved her dolly with both hands and a satisfied grunt, launching it into the undergrowth.

The initiate led them along a stony ridge, presumably what passed for a path. They were soon surrounded by the hues of northern forests: blue-green shades of fir needles, flashes of bright silver birch, broad crowns of Wych elms, somber oaks. There were gaps in the canopy over the stunted trees of bogs, and thickets of young evergreens where wind had leveled older stands, but in some places, the growth was so dense that the Varangians were obliged to move ahead and cut their way through. Birds rummaged among the branches, their incessant hammering calling to their flocks, spreading word of abundant seed, the last before the unexpected frosts. Occasionally, the travellers saw the fleet hooves of a goat, bleating reminders that the ancestral spirits would suffer no trespassers in Thrúdheim.

Iðunn kept a stiff pace, accustomed to the more punishing gravity of Útgarð, and only belatedly realized that it might be grueling for the other exiles. Ulfrun, especially, took to loitering in clearings, listening to the percussion of the rain and catching her breath.

The Lector backtracked, detouring to the other side of the thicket to disguise her approach and spare the Grandmother her blushes.

"Kind of you. But no need to go out of your way," the Skræling called, sensing the nature of the deception. "It's the damn damp. Gets into the joints."

Ulfrun ran her hands along the river of leaves, feeling their tensile thoughts. "Good craftmanship. Hard to believe they aren't all real. They turned the whole Grove over to this?" she asked.

"Most of it," Iðunn said. "I seem to recall a naval base in the north, but the rest of the island is what you might call trammelled wilderness. One big energy park."

Most of what surrounded them was a living battery. The Verðandi had discovered that plants could generate, leaf by leaf, enough voltage to light up a street. The grove was full of hybrid trees, comprised of both natural and artificial leaves, the latter acting as electrical generators converting wind into electricity, the plant tissue acting like a cable. The Urðr had purloined the technology early in the war; before the schism took root. By simply connecting a "plug" to the plant stem, they harvested enough energy to power the whole home front.

"I can attest to the former nature of the naval base," Grábakr said. He was lying unblinking in the corroded foliage, invisible amongst the wisps and specks of the forest, digesting a catch. "I did give them fair warning."

Iðunn could only hope it wasn't one of his guards. A cursory scan quickly accounted for all of them, two in close proximity, the others giving the linnorm a wider berth—enough rope to hang himself with poor taste in jokes. He had clearly inherited Father's more imbrued sensibilities.

She walked on, turning her ear to the trees. Much of their song dwelt under the acoustic surface. Listening to them was like touching a stethoscope to the skin of a landscape, hearing what stirred below.

She knew Mother Jörð got fucked, she just didn't know why. She wanted a diagnosis. But beyond the all-pervasive rain and touches of tar spot, there was nothing in the tenebrous tangle that seemed... fatal.

"Grá, any predictive models?" she asked.

"I'm still ingesting," the hybrid said, uncoiling his tongue for emphasis. "Suffice to say, a reduction of only 0.35 percent in solar flux caused the Little Ice Age, and who doesn't like to ice skate to Spann? What else? Mortality for marine-based microorganisms will be significant. Lots and lots of dead fish. Caustic rains, biting wit. Trophic cascades through the food web. Standard doomsday fare."

"Then we are all gone to Rán and ruination," Angeyja lamented, with mock horror. She covered her breast with both hands and began to keen. "*Oh Danr boy, the pipes, the pipes are calling.*"

"It will rain out eventually. It's one of the primary ways the atmosphere heals, especially in this godsforsaken bog," Grábakr continued, immune to the allure of the ballad. "The forest will help wash the wound."

They muttered thanks to the greenseer, their appreciation muted by the enormity of the ordeal. Trumba had warned her—there was nothing here but windblown mementos of a bygone age.

The whole setting felt out of time. They joined a timber trackway, constructed of long ash planks, with lime and hazel posts spaced at intervals, half swallowed by the soil. Iðunn could readily imagine that a congregation might have passed through here, Kristins envisioning some kind of harmony between the old and new, their faiths intertwining like the foliage. Or Ostmen warriors on horseback, bringing cattle with them for a feast, having forded the river near Dyflinn.

Now it was just her ragtag band of healers, first into the breach; a forlorn hope, desperate to find a salve for the dying.

After an hour, they reached their destination: a lone oak, shrouded with a half millennium of moss. It jutted from a clover-covered mound, like a huge, twisted spear. The tree marked an ancient burial site, drawing its nourishment from the ashes of long-dead warriors entombed below. Here and there, scattered at the base of the tree were granite runestones, worn so smooth, and half-tumbled by roots, they'd begun to resemble the stacked pebbles left by mourning relatives. The spreading frosts had clamped windblown seeds onto the bare soil revealing what might germinate if spring ever returned.

There were carvings, of course, on the Great Oak itself. Rune-staves and glyphs, the greenways beckoning them all home, as well as marks of shielding, keeping the door from prying eyes.

"This is it?" Ulfrun asked.

Iðunn nodded and smiled, happy to find the portal intact. The Dawnlander drew in a great quantity of smog and blew it slowly into her hands, which she kept rubbing together. Suddenly she spread her arms in a broad, sweeping motion and, reaching over, picked up her medicine bag and hung it there on the mist. "Then I will prepare the ancestors for our arrival."

"Not bad for someone born in a canoe," Iðunn teased, grinning.

Nearby, there were nine postholes, each bearing a heavy log angled inward. The winds had unmasked any weaknesses in whatever structure had once been here, and the forest had exploited it without mercy, toppling it to the ground. The remaining beams were ore-pine, the heartwood of old growth; the trees had their branches removed and had been left to stand, so that their resins bled upward and out through the cut branches making the pillar more resinous. She imagined thralls, lined up in order of size, tied to the beams and whipped with a stinging branch to test their mettle. Not just Írar, but Serkir, Skrælingar, and Blamenn. Dyflinn had been an equal opportunity enslaver. She knew from bitter experience that those who did not cry—or faint—fetched a higher price at market.

"We've all seen better days," mused the old woman. "Ironic, isn't it? After all, we have been through in the name of freedom, we are right back here, where it all began."

"And we even brought our own shackles," Iðunn growled, glancing at her escort. The soldiers had fanned out, forming a perimeter where a woodhenge formed a rudimentary ward against the encroaching forest.

"Could have been worse. They've been quite circumspect for tittle-tales," Ulfrun said. "Ah, can you hear that?" She cupped her hand to a bedizened ear. "The Wa-Wa-Ba-Nal. The voice of dawn."

There was a low whistling that faltered through the opening clouds. Svalinn was aflame in the sky, waging his cosmic war, the battle manifest not just in his green gown, but the sudden clangs and cracks that popped and penetrated the air. In the still of twilight, the world wavered, becoming as transparent as the sky.

Iðunn turned her attention to the initiate, hoping to impart some words of wisdom, but the young woman was already scaling the mound, headed for the oak.

Remember, be polite. We must always whisper to the trees.

"I know the drill," Angeyja shouted over her shoulder. She was obviously enjoying herself, singing to Symeon and Glorfinkel playing in her earpods, blatantly ignoring what she had just been told. Nearby saplings seemed to bow as they guttered in the rising wind, offering leafy hands to their new dance partner.

Iðunn raised an eyebrow in concern.

You are getting old, Ljósmóðir. It's not all fimbulsongs, runes, and incantations.

Grábakr winked, a slither behind her on the ascent.

I've always been old, Iðunn thought. *Old and scared and tired.* Grábakr was the only connection she had to feeling, to being alive. The dreki was all sinew, his moonlit mane a mercurial torrent along his spine.

"He's a handsome boy. I hope you are proud of what you have accomplished," Ulfrun said behind her, intuiting the maternal impulse. "And the revolution is over. I would have given up the knot too. We're too old for games now."

"Thank you, my friend. I used to think he was Father's last laugh, but now…" She trailed off, unable to bring herself to finish the sentence. She started after them, eager not to be separated…

And ran straight into the back of a bedraggled trooper, his plasteel carapace puddling moisture like a leaking hulk. The two of them slipped and slid, grappling for purchase on each other and the muddy hill, before spilling into a heap.

"Watch where you are going, why don't you?" the Varangian cursed, his tongue flickering under his lancing beak. Iðunn wondered who was really in there, clinging to the cortex of the trooper as he trudged through the Grove. She felt like rapping on the helmet to call them out.

The troop-leader sauntered over to see what the commotion was, receiving an attentive salute for his troubles. There was a silent exchange through their visors, then without further comment, the muddy Varangian sloped off.

"Hardly a pleasure garden, is it?" the captain said. "Does your mighty oak meet expectation?"

"Tell the Empress—all in good time."

"I'm sure she'll watch the replays avidly," the captain purred, as sweet as pollen. "Catch up on anything she misses firsthand."

"You're transmitting?" Iðunn asked, aghast. She could have kicked herself for her mulishness. It wasn't just Trumba watching, it was the full Nine Worlds. The whole empire was obsessed with legacy, with achieving interlaced, high-definition immortality through their navel-gazing broadcasts. Ragnarök was little more than a snuff movie for the sightbands, encoded for maximum retention. You didn't need to rewrite history if you could annex the hippocampus.

"Of course. For posterity. It's not every day we save the world." That made it sound official. An Imperial network then. So much for lack of fanfare. She scanned his uniform for signs of rank, or any insignia that might give her some insight as to his unit, but the vargdropi was cloaked in anonymity.

He began probing the roots with his rifle to better glimpse the bones interred underneath. The incessant wind and rain had forced Mother Jörð to disgorge her secrets. "Shallow..." he mused. "The profusion of life owes much to that which is dead."

"Who is buried here?"

"Does it matter?"

She wanted to tell him that, in the forests, there were no heroes, no great men around whom history pivots. Instead, the trees shared their memories, manifest in their songs, telling of life's community, its net of relations. But she doubted she would make any converts today—the only way to change a Varangian mind was by hitting it with a rock. Instead, she pushed aside some briars and knelt by the nearest stone, hoping his viewers might learn something.

"Freði raised this stone in memory of Ólafr, his kinsman-by-marriage, a very valiant man, who fought the Mamlukar. He died in Egiptaland," she read, puzzling together the fragments that remained into a coherent whole. "Maybe one of Botulfr the Black's warriors... Did you know the Fylkir himself would travel here? He'd be crowned on the Meadows of Mora, then sail here to place his feet on the Singing Stone. It would roar with joy if the ancestors thought he was worthy." She pointed to where his men had formed the perimeter. "If you look closely, you can make out the shape of a longship. Symbolic, of course. Part of the rite of passage."

The henge stones were small and nondescript, more like rough concrete than natural stone, but if you squinted, the intent was clear. The troop-leader looked distinctly unimpressed. "I didn't ask for a bedtime story."

"As you wish," she said, distantly, waiting for the Varangian to get bored and track back the way he came.

"So, how old is all this? A thousand years—and it's never been excavated?"

Iðunn fixed him with a stare like a bayonet. "Older than that, much older. The bandruí tended this oak long before even the Kristins came. Eochaid Ollathair and his sister-brides, the three Morrígna, ruled over life and death. It was said that, when the Norse took the world above, the Tuath Dé took to the world below and entered the sídhe, the burial mounds that dotted the ancient Laithlind."

The Varangian scratched at his bristled chin with a heavy gloved hand, clearly weighing his options. It didn't take a mind reader to see what plans he was hatching.

"I wouldn't touch his treasure if I were you," she warned. "Ollathair is an aspect of Odin himself. He is said to own a magic staff which can kill with one end and bring to life with the other, an hourglass which never runs empty, not to mention a magic harp which can control men's emotions and change the seasons."

"More of your Verðandi demons," the Varangian said, dismissively. "I'm not afraid of haugbui and kattakyn." He paused, as if convincing himself of the fact, then decided discretion was the better part of valour. "Runestones. What use are they? You can barely read them," he grumbled, stalking back to the perimeter.

And who needs fairy tales when there are real wolves nearby? Iðunn thought.

She watched him go, glad that she had dissuaded the uppity vámr. The whole empire needed an enema, to remove clogged arseholes like that.

Ljósmóði.

An interruption to her train of thought. There was something in Grábakr's tone that suggested urgency. Ulfrun sensed it too and quickly put away her charms, then the two women climbed the hill together. It wasn't far or steep, little more than a stone's throw, but the climb felt interminable in the haze of rain. The cold had become suddenly animate, no longer a mere sensation but a presence. The grip strengthened, the grasp of a boreal wrestler.

Grábakr and Angeyja were standing just aside from the tree.

"What's wrong?" Iðunn called up to them, her heart pounding in her ears. The answer became immediately obvious. The great oak had called the Vesturljós. Lights rose from the branches like a coronal flare, an inexorable lure for the shoals of the sky, cajoling the aurora earthward.

Grábakr held out his hand and pulled her toward him, then did the same for Ulfrun. "Mundilferi is he who began the moon, And fathered the flaming sun; The round of heaven each day they run, To tell the time for men," he said portentously. Then he added in a more normal tone, "The tree is a clock of sorts. Its rings count the days, its betrothal to the stars."

The linnorm caressed the furrowed bark, motioning for them both to listen.

Kolefni. Carbon. Star-stuff. Seized by the wood and stored for a reckoning. Ever since they installed Svalinn, the Jörmunsûl has been marking time...

Iðunn touched the Great Oak in the same way, dissolved her sense of self for a moment, feeling the cooperation and conflict, the struggle that permeated the Grove. She reached into the crevice and ravel of wood, calling the birds, who looped their own song through the mazed branches. The winged thrum of insects joined them; percussionists as loud as a hive. The tree of life surrounded by the clamour of the world. She had been worried that the scathe had frayed, rewired, or even severed Yggdrasil's connections, but here was only recognition and welcome. She felt the delight of the womb, the immediacy of life.

And then it was gone. The door slammed shut in her face.

She watched in horror as the greenways bent in on themselves, occulted, making it impossible to tell up from down, to orient yourself for travel. It was as if the continuum was looping back on itself, a transformation worthy of Lector Möbius.

There was something else. Death was always part of a tree, genetically pre-programmed, like an unpickable embroiderer's knot. But this was new: the weave tightened, a thousand microbial interactions forming a pattern. Níðhöggr, the eater of the dead, the devourer of corpses, and countless other serpents writhed in the wound, twisting into the shape of a hangman's noose.

"It's a warning," Grábakr said. "Our guard, I can taste his name—Perfect Váli Heidumhær. You might have seen some of his earlier work from the Chancellery at Nornborg."

Iðunn returned a rictus grin, trying to keep her composure. Heidumhær was the Maestari of Propagation himself. She'd heard of him during the war, they all had. The ancient Rómverjar had once posted prefects as overseers, and praetorians as elite guards—that mutt bitch Trumba had taken her latest toga fetish and wrapped it around a group of fanatics. Perfects regarded themselves as a kind of invasive surgery, scissoring out the gene tainted. The Wicked Witch of What-the-Fuck had really done it this time!

It was only then that she saw the truth. The Perfect's resentment was more than skin-deep. As far as he was concerned, the Verðandi were heretics, impure of thought and body. The men were a death squad.

"What does it mean?" Angeyja hissed, not understanding the panic. The young woman grabbed at Iðunn's arm, reaching for reassurance she could not provide.

They are coming.

It was too late to answer. Heidumhær strode stepped right up to quartet, belching righteousness, thudding his fist onto the bark skin behind them. Iðunn made a point of ignoring the Varangian; she was trying to think, to second-guess the machinations of state, to find a way out. She exchanged apprehensive glances with Ulfrun. They were both old enough to know full well that none outlive the night when the Norns have spoken. Fucking destiny, she fumed.

"So?" The captain was nothing if not persistent.

"We can't open it. There is a binding. A seal I don't know how to break," Iðunn said, stalling. It wasn't far from the truth. She hadn't seen such galdarcraft before. Rather than being bartered away, the knot had willed itself shut, Thórr's stern rebuke.

"I'm not sure you are hearing me," the soldier screeched. He balled up his fist and, this time, slammed it into her chin. Iðunn rocked backward, the trees suddenly at all the wrong angles.

Before she fell, a choke of grey loomed into view. Grábakr seized her in his uplifted limbs and set her down in the crook of the oak.

"I always forget your meat minds have expiration dates." The jötunn rose to his full height, towering over the Ministry troopers, his skin growing darker, sclerotized with ironwood.

The Varangian didn't budge a thumb-ell. "What did you say, thurse? I don't speak fucking knucker," he spat.

If Iðunn ever saw what happened, she only recollected fragments. Grábakr springing forward, his hands like battering rams, scattering the ravens before they could take wing. His tail swiping left, a trooper falling to his knees, his preening finery tattered and abraded.

But it was never an even fight, and the Varangyar had long since learned to fell their nightmares.

"Stop this!" Ulfrun cried, but the rifles had already stuttered their reply. Grábakr lurched to the ground, shuddering with each bullet.

A harsh silence followed, perforated only by the wheezing alfar, whistling in their abandon.

"Now, open the door so we can all go home," the Perfect yelled, reinforcing his threat with bare teeth and gunmetal. "Honestly, I deserve a fucking medal for babysitting you lot. I think I'll ask for the bantling as a bed-thrall. Fair compensation, wouldn't you say?" The Perfect eyed Angeyja with a lascivious grin. "Luck of the Írar and all," he spat, scuffing his soles on the jötunn's dimming finery. "Get your pecker up, does it, Valravn?" the girl hissed in retort, running to the far side of the tree.

Iðunn felt nothing. Was nothing. An automaton, a childless mother, beyond the limits of desperation, her breath cascading from her body in one long, low ululation. Grief chewed into her breast like a canker.

"From place to place the homeless Verðandi wander, in ever-shifting exile, outlaws since the time when they were torn from their Father's abode, stained with the blood of the Norsemen they betrayed." The Perfect strutted forward, leering his monologue while his squadron circled, their beady red eyes recording the carnage. One began a perfunctory search of the jötunn's body, perhaps trying to siphon some of his exquisite DNA.

"How do you explain such profanity, on a holy site? Is that what passes for glory now, among the blood swans?" Ulfrun howled, swaddling her demolished friend in her gnarled hands. "Gunning down women and children in cold blood?"

"You know why we are here? We're the fucking Ítreksjóð, the sons of Óðinn. We carried the Blood Banner, drank the raven's wine at Utangard. We survived all the shit you whore-cunts have ever thrown at us and spat it right back in your faces. And this—this is a ratings winner! Shutting down a secret terrorist cell, slaying fucking dragons. It's election time, after all, although, when isn't it? Go on quicker, you old hag! Go on quicker! Why are you loitering? Proud men of the Ash? Children of the fucking ashes more like!"

"Thórr will have something to say," Angeyja said, twisting away from his grasping hands.

"Thórr will have something to say," he whined, his voice an imbecilic imitation. "You are sinners in the hands of a peasant god. Talk back to me again, woman, and I'll have your Dawnland bitch shot where she shits."

Iðunn sat back on her haunches and clawed for a response, disoriented by both the force of the blow and the sheer savagery that impelled it. She pulled at the fog with her hands, fighting for consciousness. Trumba had arranged all of this—who knew how long in advance. *As flies to wanton girls are we to the gods; They kill us for their sport.*

"Angeyja, you should try," Ulfrun said, answering for her. "The Thunderer might listen to you. That was always the hope."

"If you think I am ready."

"Æfingin skapar meistarann," Iðunn said, her voice hoarse. *Practice makes perfect.* She said that to all her children.

Angeyja made a long exhalation, then began the chant, its melody accenting the dusk. The sound was like silver, pure tones that melted into the lingering dark, until she was wholly suffused, wearing the raiment of the grace-shine.

Practice makes perfect. All of them, shaped from nothing. Plaiting tendons and arteries, lashing bone and skin, in sure and certain hope of growing life. All that forged promise, all that stolen hope. It was gone forever.

Angeyja yawned into the chasma, her breathing snagged, the alfar whistling around her in penetrating bursts. Iðunn watched her distantly, too dazed and absent to add anything to the chorus.

It didn't appear to matter. The initiate was rattling her ancestral rights, channeling the anger of the Írar.

"I see Glasir, before the doors of the hall of Valhalla, all of its foliage red-gold, the most beautiful tree among gods and men. Glasir's glowing foliage. Twelve women riding from the wood. All in red, on red horses, all their trappings glittering with gold."

"What the actual fuck?" one of the troopers barked. The alfar were incandescent now, soaring between branches, as if the dead had dooms to give. Angeyja stood amongst them all, her hips swaying as she fought for balance. The air around the tree coagulated with the song, calling, climbing, reaching.

"It is bright... so very bright. The Asbrú burns all with flames. Now do I see the earth anew, rise all green from the waves again; the cataracts fall, and the eagle flies, And fish he catches beneath the cliffs."

For a moment, she was embalmed in plasma, soaring on the stellar winds. And then she was gone, sunk down into the earth. There was no hedge magician's puff of smoke, no broken shackles, just the lambent orbs of the aurora, flickering lanterns held aloft by dusky shadows.

"Where has she gone? The greenways are meant to be on lock down!" The Perfect squawked in his rage, his surprise only matched by his petulance.

"Not on my watch! Not with the Empress watching!" he ranted, thrashing his arms. "This is preposterous. Shoot the rest and send for the Urðr. Shut this shit down."

Ljósmóði. You must follow. Take my hand.

Grábakr's mind was harsh with iron and decay, but still active. *There is no time for the galdr. The door is shut to me, the greenways are tangled.*

"What do you mean, looped? What are we broadcasting, fucking colour bars?" The Perfect was too busy castigating his men and gesticulating at the auroral disturbance to notice. The Varangians hadn't registered the thoughtspeak.

There is another path, where only the alfar travel. You must take the Raven road.

Iðunn looked across to where Grábakr lay, his blood pooling in the bowl of roots, a limp grin lolling on his ruined face, then up at Ulfrun. Grandmother Dawn gazed back fondly, then stood, slowly, elegantly, demanding her migrant limbs to obey her and ignore the tide of damp.

"Go. I shall stand and rest awhile."

She smiled ruefully, like a wasted morning, then walked over and tapped Heidumhær on the shoulder with an arthritic forefinger. "Let me tell you a story, Maestari."

"What is it with these tree-huggers? They are bursting with bedtime rhymes," he said, playing to his gallery of rogues.

"Humour me, before my long goodnight. You might learn something of value. I mean to tell you about the squirrel. Meeko, he was called. When the world was young, Meeko was as large and ferocious as a wolf. He killed right and left, from pure lust for blood. So it was decided to save the woods-people, Meeko would have to be cut down to size."

The Grandmother of Dawn told a compelling story, especially when she jacked the feed and commandeered the Varangian visors.

"Except, we all forgot Meeko's disposition; that remained as big and as bad as before. So now the squirrel goes about the woods with a small body and a big temper, barking, scolding, quarrelling and, since he cannot destroy and rage as before, he sets other animals by the ears to destroy each other."

The Varangians cast off their helmets like they were filled with fire ants, rasping their heads against the great oak.

"Seems to me like you Ministrymen are not ravens at all, just angry squirrels, making all this noise. It's just plain disrespectful. Didn't anyone teach you to whisper when the spirits are near?"

One by one their minds burst, leaving shattered skulls and hollowed-out eyes, and shells of armour wreathed in foxfire. The Perfect Ulfrun saved for last, dizzying him into a rainswept grave, unmarked and unmentioned in dispatches to come. Hidden from eternity.

The old woman wandered to the foot of the hill and rested her bones on the Singing Stone. The relief crews would arrive soon and finish what Surtr started. Trumba wasn't one to delay gratification.

Iðunn watched her go.

Goodbye, old friend. May the sunshine warm upon your face and the rain fall softly on your fields.

Then she leapt through the whorl and went out of memory.

THE SAGA OF
— YNGVAR THE TRAVELLER —

Jomsborg, the pirate emporium
Autumn, 1038

The army arrived on their tall ships. The sails were striped, blue, red, or green, woven from wool and magical songs, held taut by ropes of hvalros hide. Some had at the prow figures of lions, bulls, dolphins, gods in gilt copper; others were coiled and spiralled like serpents.

The dragon led them on, spreading its wings and turning. It was carved and painted from stem to stern, beautifully overlaid with gold, its gunwales gleaming with shields of polished steel, overlapping oak planks secured with silver rivets, tapering to an arching tail.

Yngvar stood on the lofting and punched the air with exhilaration. He was, in that moment at least, glad to be home. With the north-westerly wind rippling through the sail, the dragon almost flew. The spotters on the great lighthouse would have seen them on the horizon a dozen miles away, but his crew could sail her straight onto the shore and have boots on the ground within forty minutes of the hue and cry. Ten minutes, for those watching, unguarded, from the beach. If you were going to run from a Viking raid, you had better show swift heels. If only the northern tribes had learned that lesson, he wouldn't have to go splashing after them through the marsh flats every summer.

On days like these, it often seemed like the whole town had come to greet them, women and children running the long, crested ridges that overlooked the shoreline. The afternoon was bright, the sea breeze stiff but bracing, and Yngvar grew wistful. It wasn't so long ago that he'd been a boy, cheering from those bluffs, watching the fleet surge along the bay, mast after mast. The memory stirred something within him, a sullen, resentful pride perhaps. He was hoarse from shouting against the wind and the spray, so he raised both his arms by way

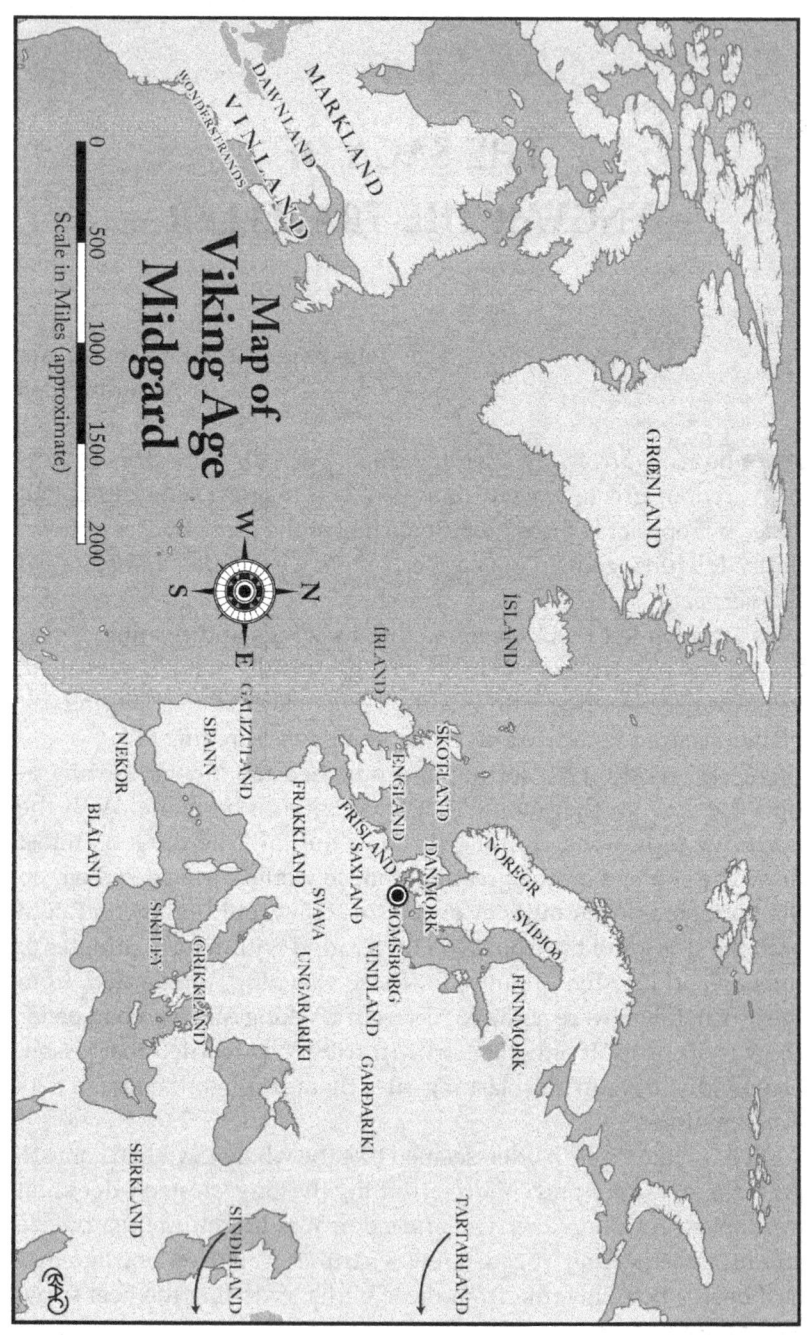

of salutation. The rest of his floating menagerie took the signal as permission to start barking, braying, whooping, and hollering. The Jomsvikings weren't known for their restraint.

The dragon approached the narrow channel at the head of the estuary, beyond the barrier spit. Yngvar was grateful Ægir's dread daughters were calm today, rolling and breaking gently on the sand.

The sea jötunn had made this land into a briny labyrinth, a morass of ponds, marshes and fields, and then the jarls of Jomsburg had conspired to make it even more impregnable. A wooden stockade stretched along the coast for miles, and the passage inland was dominated by a stone tower, bristling with catapults. Ingeniously, they'd built an arch that spanned the river mouth, with an iron gate to close the channel at will. The gate was barred, of course, as was always the case when the fleet had sailed. Hundreds of ships passed to and fro, north, east, and west into the Eystrasalt—but none without the consent of the Norse.

Yngvar motioned to his steersman to signal their arrival and the dragon duly slowed. The Keeper of the Coast would question them, sound his consent with the winding horn, and then the gates would open. Yngvar had never questioned the theatrics—his people had a ritual urge, undiminished in all the long years of conquest, exaggerated, even, by each easy victory. His crew were no different. They were mostly high born, sons of chieftains or councillors, and often the third or fourth generation to serve—they were steeped in talismans and totems. Yngvar watched as the coxswain, Soti Vagnson, kissed the amber thorrshammar around his neck, before tucking it safely back under his bright russet beard, comforted by the thought that his god was watching over them. Yngvar instinctively checked his own fetish, the Serkir timepiece he kept in the same place. The single hand pointed directly at the middle of the afternoon.

After a few moments, a figure duly emerged on the tower above, a silhouette against the sun. He shouted to the men holding water below, his voice booming across the sound. "Who commands your ship, and where did you lie up last night?"

Yngvar grinned wide in recognition. "The Jarl of Jomsborg has returned," he called. "We were with the Seimgalir this summer, sailing up the Dýna river to remind them to pay the tribute they owed my brother. Last night, we laid up at Refrnes and sailed home today with this fair wind."

The man on the tower called back, "And did Viesthard the Seimgalir fuck you?"

"Not yet."

"But he is planning to?"

"No, he is waiting for a nobler man than myself before he lowers his trousers. I told him the fylkir himself is on his way," Yngvar shouted back.

The man on the tower guffawed with delight, the golden band around his forehead catching the light. "Well said, brother. You have done me a great service with the taxes. I return your city to you." Yngvar's crews cheered in unison, now also recognising the glint of gold and flash of scarlet as belonging to Thormund, the lord of Miðgarðr's earth and kingdoms. Yngvar was genuinely delighted—and thoroughly surprised—to see his older cousin.

"Thormund! Why are you here? Are you afraid I'll keep your weregild for myself?"

Unseen hands began to winch the gate, which rose swiftly, dripping water and great clumps of bladderwrack onto the deck.

"Of course not, Yngvar. It is good to see you!"

"And you, my lord. This is an unexpected pleasure. I'll come ashore." Yngvar snapped his fingers, summoning his men to help him, but the dragon's oars were already drawing through the water, sweeping them forward through the gate. Within moments, the fylkir was out of sight, and Yngvar had to wait until his voice met them on the other side.

"No need, tonight we feast! Come to my camp then. We have lots to discuss."

Yngvar could only rasp in agreement, his voice oddly deep and broken. He reached for a water skin and drank what little was left, thumping his sternum as it cleared his throat, then sat down heavily, wracked with a coughing fit.

The steersman reached out a burly arm, passing him a wooden cup. Yngvar gulped down the water it contained, then croaked his thanks. Gard-Ketill was an Íslendingr, twice the age of the Jarl of Jomsburg and four times as obstinate. He'd fought so many campaigns in Garðariki, he'd gone native—he shaved his blond head and beard but wore a bushy moustache and a sidelock in the Rus style, with a single large gold earring.

"Overexcited, are we? Drink. Anyone would think that trolls had been moving your tongue," he said. "I'm all for fucking whatever we fancy, but don't make me your mare."

"That's the same foul mouth that kissed your wife," shot back Yngvar. "She seemed to like it. Besides, my cousin likes to banter."

Ketill ignored him and rubbed the back of his neck in thought. "And that was the All-Glorious King of the Storm-Hall? I thought he'd be taller."

Yngvar looked up at his steersman, incredulous. "He was standing on the tower! How could you possibly tell how tall he was?"

"I suppose every man is a king so long as he has someone to look down on," Ketill mused, blithely ignoring his lord. Yngvar knew better than to take the bait. The Íslandingar were a stubborn, proud people, preferring exile on a desolate outcrop to any covenant with kings—he suspected Ketill only fought in the fylkir's armies because it gave him an opportunity to insult men above his station. That same defiance made him an excellent steersman though, a wave-rider, impervious to the vagaries of the northern seas.

Not one to give up, the steersman continued prodding. "They say that kings are made in the image of the gods. If that is what he looks like, I feel sorry for Óðinn."

The dragon's skipper Valdimarr, an actual Garðar, was the only one to laugh, although it was with his usual menaces. He was a man with the mentality of a permanent sentry—gruff, guarded and suspicious, with a sneer of cold command—and had clearly been eavesdropping.

"What I want to know is, why is the king *here*?" he said, hissing the last word insistently.

"How am I supposed to know? Ask him yourself, you heard him—tonight, we're dining with the fylkir," Yngvar said, using the Overking's formal, Norse, title. Some men called it the norrænt mál, others in his crew the dönsk tunga, but all of them broadly understood the Northern speech.

Yngvar hauled himself up and drummed his hands gleefully along the saxboard. "Hear that, Ketill! That is the sound of my ancestors knocking at last. We must wear our best clothes for the feast." He instinctively checked his Serkir timepiece again, anxious about having enough time to make proper preparations.

"Woah, hurry slowly. We've not yet seen our beds. And put that thing away," the steersman complained, still preferring daymarks and dead reckoning to new-fangled klokkaverk.

"I've told you before, a good soldier has only three things to think about: the empire, the gods, and nothing else besides. So, shut up and stop ruining my good mood."

It was probably too late for that. The jarl stiffened, trying to hide his growing temper by passing the cup back to the steersman, who swilled then spat over the side of the ship. Íslandingar took their oaths seriously, although which gods Ketill kept these days was hard to tell—the Northern Empire, the Himinríki, had more cults than Yngvar could count. Each of the Vindr tribes who sought protection from the White Christ had brought their own gods, each seeking sanctuary behind the Great Shield Wall. Ásgarð must have been full to bursting.

It used to be that mariners would give thanks to Njörðr, the Old Man of the Winds, but even the augurs had changed. Just a day's journey up the coast was a holy isle, where the chief priest made his oracles while watching a white stallion prance and casting dice in his great purple-roofed temple. The island also boasted a great oaken statue of Svantevit, a god that owned a face for every season, two heads looking forward and two looking back. The northern face of this vast totem was white, the western, red, the southern, black, and the eastern, green: it had become so famous a signpost that it adorned almost every nautical chart made in the past decade. Even the fylkir would sometimes pay his respects.

Yngvar wondered how long it had been since he last saw his cousin. Eight winters, maybe, when he'd been gifted his rings and a horse of his own. What louts they'd been, riding right up to the high seat. "Ranglefants!" the old Kanceler had cried, clearly dreading the day Thormund was taken as king. "Rogues! Rascals!" He could still hear the old bear berating them now, hurling pots and stools—anything that came to hand. His cousin, his foster-brother, loved to hunt, a new gold-plumed falcon jessed and tethered to the glove. Yngvar's coronation gift, a haukr fit for a king. He'd been proud of that. Perhaps now he'd repay the favour.

He looked expectantly down the ship at each of his chosen men. He'd rewarded them all well, and they said luck followed the generous. Soti Vagnson was hollering at the oarsmen to keep time, the Dane's choleric fury worth a dozen rowers. Ordulf, the ship's hand, was wrestling with the halyard, lowering the sail—a warrior as tightly wound as the ropes he worked with. The middleman and the lookout, the tallest warriors on the ship, were the brothers, Haraldr and Haakon Thorkellson. Strong and unbending, they seemed to him more masts than men. There were fifty or sixty men on each of the Jomsviking ships, but where the lions, bulls and serpents merely snorted and snarled, the dragon's crew raged. On a good day, there were no better men in the empire. On a bad day, no worse. "I wonder which today is?" Yngvar asked the autumn air, half-hoping a portent from some benign spirit.

The dragon swept down the western channel, past small herds of visundur, browsing contentedly on lyme grass and buckthorn. Clouds of plovers rose from their shingle nests, wheeling out into the bay, crying plaintively to the skies. Yngvar felt a pang of envy, the restless race of his traveller's heart. He often wondered if he had felt so imprisoned before he was awarded the clock-pendant, its incessant demands more of a curse than a privilege of rank.

"Glad to be home?" Ketill asked, perhaps sensing some disquiet.

"Delighted. The only crown I wear is called Content, a crown that kings and jarls seldom enjoy," Yngvar deadpanned in reply.

"Well, at least you are poetic in your misery," Ketill said, turning back to focus on his steering board.

The river here was studded with islands and mudflats and dotted with fisherman's huts and small boats. It was wide enough that you would have to take half a dozen of the longest ships in the fleet, laid stern to prow, to bridge it. Set between the coastal cliffs, the great sea gate and the wide strait, Jomsborg held an ancient ford a few miles upstream. The town proper stretched along the riverbank, looping like a necklace between Silver Hill to the north and Hangman's Hill to the south, perhaps three miles when all was told.

The western side was protected by a wooden palisade, made from split tree trunks, a rampart and a retaining wall. By the main gate, poultry and sheep wandered freely, keeping to the shade afforded by the low-built cottages, whose roof rafters reached all the way to the ground. Most of the houses were, at most, decades old, simple wattle and daub structures with a turf roof, smoke-ovens keeping them nice and warm during the cool Vindr nights.

"On the bright side, no fires. Looks like the Norðanfrith has held while we were away," Soti said, striking a note somewhere between dejection and sarcasm. The Peace of the North. It was galling to men bred for war, but the dull reality was that peace was best for trade.

Measured alongside the splendour of Kristindómr, Jomsburg was little more than a pile of logs and moss. Even compared to the rest of the freshly painted empire, it was a parvenu, an upstart. It had none of the ancient sanctity of Uppsala or the rich history of Jórvík. But the town was no less vital—it commanded all trade up and down the Odra, a lynchpin, halfway between the walled cities of the Rus and the warden ports of the West. Silver from the mines of Kornbretaland, coins from the mint at Heiðabý, even the white gold from saltworks at Lunenburg, everything flowed through here. Quiet Bay, then, was always anything but—the harbour was full of bobbing, creaking ships, dozens of them, from the great imperial busse and skeide, designed for war, to the ocean-going knarr and the small rowing boats ferrying goods ashore. Many travels, many fortunes, Yngvar thought, fervently praying that his wasn't here. It was even busier on the shoreline, amongst the booths where the merchant ships drew up. He watched one Sviar crew unload a cargo of osmund iron, carefully rolling the great metal balls ashore for hammering, until they crunched onto the gravel at the foot of the wharves. Dressmakers haggled over bolts of vaðmál with Imperial factors. Fisherman cursed the shrill terns and grunting cormorants that flapped overhead, looking to steal their dinner, undeterred by the powerful white gyrfalcons lined up by the dozen on poles nearby. On the far side of the inlet, grain was unloaded under the watchful eye of the garrison, while weighmasters and tax collectors argued over duties paid, storage space, and dockage fees.

Yngvar yawned to mask his frustration. It used to be that, each summer, Viking raids would fill the imperial coffers with Serkir dirhams, Grikk miliaresia, and Frakkar deniers. Trade didn't interest him in the slightest; he left all the administration to the Kontor. The real value of his fleet wasn't protecting merchants, it was managing extortion. Even allies weren't exempt—the jarl's men exacted an annual tribute from the Vindr tribes, imposed "for the preservation of peace," reckoning it was preferable to Kristin tithes. As to the Norsemen—the Sons of Ragnar weren't meant to take arms against each other, but if they did, they found a Riksjarl, loyal to the emperor, a spear's throw from their throne, a clear reminder that Óðinn a ydyr alla—Óðinn owns you all. Yngvar has always been a relentless hunter—Thormund had chosen well.

It was all the more vexing that the homecoming prince was forced to sail to the southernmost end to beach his vessel. Ordulf starting yelling orders, and soon the sail was furled, the sail and yard were stored on uprights, and the mast unstopped. The men leapt overboard and waded ashore, carrying weapons and armour, leaving a small watch to stand guard and another to drag newly captured thralls up to the market.

Yngvar fumed; there was nothing worse than sodden boots. He coughed again, his eyes smarting as he fumbled for his clock-pendant. The hand hadn't moved, so he tapped it, once, twice, then a third time with a feeling verging on despair, before stowing it disconsolately back under his shirt. Time clearly wasn't on his side.

There was a welcome party waiting for the jarl's men on the shore—local people, grateful for his safe return. Chief among them was the town's hofgoði, Hjálmvígi, both temple guardian and lawspeaker. Yngvar was almost glad to see the flinty Saxon, his long stony-face looming above the crowd. The jarl had thought to summon him but knew that would have been a waste of breath: seiðrmenn always knew exactly when and where to arrive. Yngvar feigned enthusiasm for the rest, clasping a few well-meaning arms, but kept his thanks terse to show he was a busy man. He needn't have bothered with the pretence. Hjálmvígi rapped his walking-staff on the ground and the townsfolk quickly dispersed.

"Jarl Yngvar, I saw you were unwell? I have prepared some remedies. Libbsticka, ground in wine, and mirra incense." The old priest dithered in a leather sack, then shouted at the two Finnar who followed him like lap dogs. At last, he produced a vial and forced it into the jarl's hands. "Hold it under the roots of your tongue and the cough will subside."

He rapped the staff again and mumbled into his beard to drive away the spirit of sickness, which carried with it the added benefit of hurrying the last stragglers back up the path.

Yngvar swigged the flask of wine and tucked the mirra into a belt pouch for later, eyeing the lawspeaker's staff warily. It was carved with runes and rhomboids, so the wood resembled a snake more than a stick. A common enough tool of seiðr, but Yngvar preferred steel to sorcery.

"If you saw I was getting sick..." Yngvar started.

"...did I not divine the arrival of the fylkir? Who is to say I did not? His hirð have been here for weeks. What would you have me do? Send ravens?" The priest tutted.

The jarl paused, not wanting to antagonise the priest, but if anyone was going to send spirits to run far into the night, it was this sorcerer and his henchmen. Yngvar considered himself a devout man, and regularly led the rites of sacrifice on Hangman's Hill, but the fulltrúi of Óðinn unnerved him. They were all neatly dressed and well-groomed, at least up to a point. One of the Finnar wore a coat into which a raven-corpse had been sewn, and both wore belts dripping with knives, brass rings, bird claws, and sealed leather bags whose contents were best left unknown. It occurred to him that he couldn't be certain if that was their real form. Old Hjálmvígi had escaped so many skirmishes, the townsfolk quietly conjectured on whether he could take the shape of a horse.

The Jomsvikings at his back were unperturbed, of course. His crew ate Kvænir necromancers for day-meal, washing down their victories with the blood-wine of Kristin bishops. After the long voyage, they were in no mood for a lengthy dockside debate.

"The last ship on the left has your raf," Haakon said, using the Norse word rather than the Serkir *amber* that was in vogue. There had been all kinds of linguistic alchemy since the conquest of Lizibon, but whatever they called them, magicians the world over valued the golden stones, either to burn as incense or for their medicinal properties. To hear the witch-wives tell it, the gemstones were the tears of Freya, who wandered the world weeping for her lost husband. The fylkir duly held the monopoly, as was the case with anything that stemmed from the divine, and his Jomsvikings enforced it, punishing thieves with hanging. The raf was cast inelegantly onto beaches all over the Eystrasalt, which meant it was Loki's own job to stop every Tómi, Rik, and Haraldr from simply picking it up.

"Bane of our bloody existence," Haraldr muttered, whetting his short sword.

"Blessings to the Lady," the old sorcerer intoned, nodding his thanks, but the trite phrase only served to inflame the passions of the butescarls.

"Well, the next time you seiðmaðr have a love-in, tell her it's high time she got over herself. She should go back to shagging her way round Svartalfheimr and stop making work for the rest of us," Haraldr said, thrusting his groin towards the priest with every other word.

"Fucking dvergar... disgusting," Soti added, hawking phlegm by way of punctuation. Yngvar tried hard not to laugh, so the lawspeaker could leave with some dignity.

"Was there something else?" the jarl asked, walking ahead, conscious of the squelching sound he made as he moved. First the cough, now chilblains. He groaned inwardly, debating whether to send a boy ahead to get him fresh boots. He quickly gave some orders, and Soti raced off ahead. The rest of his chosen men formed up in a square, protecting the jarl from threats as yet unseen.

Hjálmvígi waited patiently, then simply stated, "The question isn't what *I* want; it is what you want."

"I haven't time for riddles, old man," Yngvar snapped, losing what little patience he had left. He decided the only thing more irritating than damp legs and stopped clocks was a fusty priest.

"Your plan, to ask your cousin for a crown."

Yngvar stopped mid-step and winced. Rather than turn back to face Hjálmvígi, he corrected his stride and carried on walking. He had barely admitted that thought to himself, let alone anyone else. Yet here it was, his ambition laid bare, plucked from his thoughts like falcon finding prey. Was it any wonder seiðr was feared and despised?

"The first I have heard of it," he bluffed.

"Now you are only fooling yourself. There is no trickery involved; your impatience is plain to see. Who put the idea into your head? These mordvargr?" The priest pointed at the surly crew, still spilling from the ships. "The counsel of fools is more misguided the more of them there are."

Yngvar sloshed some wine around the back of his throat, weighing his options as he walked. The lawspeaker was accomplished—to hear the skalds tell it, he'd once officiated over the Thing at Marklo. He could be a powerful ally in the days to come. He paused long enough for Hjálmvígi to catch up, still flanked by his two Finnar fetches.

"Well, if there were such a plan—and I'm not saying that there is—wouldn't I be within my rights? Wiser men than you have likened my accomplishments to those of my kinsman Styrbjorn. My grandmother was daughter of Eirik the Victorious."

"Yes, yes. I know all that. You grew up as a brother to Thormund. And that's why the fylkir named you Jarl of Jomsburg. What greater prize..."

Yngvar opened his mouth to say more, but seeing the depth of Hjálmvígi's scowl, thought better of it. The priest clearly wasn't impressed, looking for all the world like an angry hvalros, all beady eyes and twitching whiskers.

"No one is doubting your loyalty or your noble birth. But kinship of the gods is patrilineal. It passes down through male heirs."

Yngvar swore loudly, knowing full well that it was a custom more honoured in the breach than in the observance.

Nightfall was still a few hours away, but Yngvar's black mood drove him, striding back toward the harbour, clattering along the weathered planks that paved the shore path. The street was too crowded; he crossed down an alleyway to take the Army Road instead. It was only then that Yngvar noticed that the landward wall—ten feet thick, made from a mountain of stones—was lined with lookouts. Far more men than he would have posted. It was obvious why. The fylkir liked to say that fragrance of spices was financed by a debt of dust and blood. The price of peace was becoming extortionate. What was worse, it occurred to him in that moment that his Semgalir sailing wasn't a hunt at all. It was a collection, and he was not a jarl but a taxman. Incensed, his anger boiled over again. He tore off his wet boots, one by one, and hurled them into the grass. He'd had entirely enough of the ridiculous noise they made. He'd rather catch splinters from the boards than suffer yet more indignity. Let the world conspire against him, he railed. He'd stand up and be counted. Only the wounded coward lies low.

"See this, Hjálmvígi?" The jarl jabbed his finger at the men stationed on the wall. "The jarl of Jomsburg is no more than a glorified guard dog, another of my cousin's blessed moosehounds, taught to fetch, carry, and beg. Although, considerably less loved, I might add. He gave me this... trinket, because he doesn't trust anyone else to watch over his silver." He spat contemptuously.

"That's a matter of opinion," Hjálmvígi responded mildly. "Rebuilding the great fortress of Rurik on the Salt Road, marshalling the Southern March against the Kristin, keeping the peace between the King of the Danar and the King of the Vindr. These are vital tasks."

"A goatherd then, tending the flock."

"You'd rather be a freebooter?" The hofgoði was calm, despite the jarl's tantrum.

"When I was a boy, I heard nothing but glorious tales of the sons of Ragnar. They were despoilers. They were conquerors. And Jomsburg—it was a name to conjure with. The great pirate emporium, the envy of the North. When did we lose sight of what made us great?"

"You misunderstand the lessons of the past. Ragnar made it clear to his sons, the fylkir is first a servant to his people. A king is a tool, a thing of straw; but if he serves to frighten our enemies and secure our lands, it is well enough: a scarecrow is a thing of straw, but it protects the corn. You think the Jarl of Jomsburg so mundane? Are you bored? I assure you a crown is no cure for a headache."

Some of the Jomsvikings had heard the argument as they kept the flanks, and each of them shot barbs as they passed their jarl, creasing with laughter.

"A new crown? Fried sparrows just fly into your mouth, don't they? I'd like to borrow some of that luck!" Valdimarr said, deadpan.

"At least King Sparrow-Mouth might chirp less," quipped Ketill.

Silver Hill was to the north of the town, overlooking the entrance to the market. A causeway had been raised with stone, sand, and gravel to intersect with the Army Road, itself far from complete. In some places it comprised closely laid logs and well-worked timbers; in others it consisted only of brushwood and branches spread out to create a stable surface in the marsh. The settlement here was different: timber frames, with walls of vertical planks, plugged with grasswrack. But it was the pace of construction that really stood out. The hilltop was unrecognisable from just two months ago. Blacksmiths, bakers, weavers, and tanners had sprung up seemingly overnight, to be within spitting distance of the imperial retinue.

"How long is he planning on staying?" wondered Haraldr Thorkellson. He was the first to take in all the changes, on account of his height.

"Silver Hill will be Silver Mountain at this rate," laughed his brother Haakon. There was a spring in the step of most of the men, despite the long day's sailing—with the exception of Valdimarr, who was clearly annoyed at having to dash the length and breadth of town.

"I keep asking—why is the King here?" the skipper said.

"Something to hide?" Ordulf winked. "He's not looking for anyone in particular. If he was, those men would have been at the docks." He pointed at a group of men, drilling with heavy swords and weighty shields on the riverbank.

Some of the fylkir's men had clearly taken lodgings here. Many men who came to the Overking's court were considered of little consequence, simple farmers or fishermen; Thormund gave high honours to such men in return for their service. They served as spies and scouts, a sort of secret police, and were known as "gests," because they made little visits throughout the king's domain, and not always with friendly intent. The Jomsvikings were professional soldiers, lithesmen and butescarls, paid a full eight marks a year for their oars and swords, not part-time amateurs and thugs. They made no secret of their disdain as they passed and might have come to more than jeers and insults if the hofgoði hadn't have been there.

They'd not gone far when a stone arced overhead, clattering on the gravel banks by the river. A second group of gests had arrived and were clearly trying to provoke a reaction now they had numbers on their side.

"If it isn't the Sækonungrs," their leader mocked. "I see you flounder on dry land." He was a spry, wiry man, with a flat nose and grin of daggers. His ring of companions was as mirthless as they were deplorable.

"Take a walk," growled Yngvar, "or be the worse for it."

"Why do you look as though you are at death's door?" the man said. "Exhausted from cavorting with that rassagr of a priest? Did you get a little prick from Wōden's mighty spear?"

Hjálmvígi didn't so much as bat an eyelid. Instead, one of his Finnar servants barked on his behalf. "You will bow before the king's cousin, the Jarl of Jomsborg, the Lord of the Southern March."

The man said that the trolls would take him before he would bend the knee. The sky had darkened considerably—Yngvar knew witches' weather when he saw it. Not that he was worried by some braggart bumpkins; he just abhorred the inconvenience of dealing with them. He exchanged glances with his men, and they fanned out slowly, imperceptibly almost. He saw Haakon slowly unsling his shield. The rest of the men, too, inched toward their weapons.

Only Ketill remained unarmed, drifting toward the centre of the group, his hands held above his top-knot. All eyes turned to the Íslendingar. Yngvar didn't envy them the lesson they were about to be taught. "Where are you from, boy?" the steersman asked the leader of the gestir.

"I am an Englismaðr. Here on behalf of the son of the Storm King."

"Ah, that explains the squalling. Then I have a story for you Englar. See how you like it. A Dane, a Sviar, and a Vestman, much like yourself, made a wager on who could remain inside a goat pen the longest. First out was the Dane, who came out quickly yelling 'Damn! The goat stinks!' After him the Sviar went in. He lasted an hour before he came out yelling, 'Damn! The goat stinks!' Finally, the Englismaðr went in. A tough man, like you. After two hours the goat came rushing out yelling 'Damn! That Vestman skítkarl stinks!'"

The gest curled his lip in derision. "Is that what passes for a joke amongst you ladies?"

"What do you think about dying?" Ketill whispered, coming ever closer.

"I am well content to die: I shall suffer the same fate as my father." The gest tapped his spear, clearly confident of his skills with it, and the reach it granted him.

"I am glad to hear it." Ketill smiled, keeping his hands where everyone could see them. Suddenly he ducked, and the Englismaðr fell backwards, grasping at a sucking wound in his chest. Valdimarr's spear reverberated in the wall, ten yards behind him, its tip and shaft glistening with gore.

"Throw him in the river and do the goats a favour," Ketill ordered, although most of the farmers and fishermen had already scattered, disappearing into the horse paddocks beyond the peat roofs. The Jomsvikings roared their approval, clattering their shields and stamping their feet. The skirmish was over before it had begun.

Yngvar patted Ketill on the shoulder, acknowledging his showmanship. Then, keen to march his men on and away from the temptation of further trouble, he called them to order. The lawspeaker seemed reluctant to move, though, his two assistants circling the dead man like carrion crows.

"Hjálmvígi? You neglected to mention Eirik of Jórvík is here. Who else? You must have spoken to the fylkir these past few weeks," Yngvar asked.

"I blessed his court and no more. I find I have little talent for interrogating princes," he said reproachfully. "I'll say my farewells before I become more burdensome. Watch your back, Jarl Yngvar; the Kristin Lords have long arms, and I can smell their stench. Remember, it is not titles that honor men, but men that honor titles." With that, the hofgoði turned back and walked down the hill, his two companions dragging the dead man behind them.

The hirðmenn of the royal household proper had made camp on the other side of the river, a discreet distance from the town, near the appropriately named Imperial Boulder, a huge glacial rock, half submerged in the riverbed. Legend had it that the Kings of the Vindr used to stand on it and welcome mariners home, in the long years before the Northmen arrived and offered frith.

Nearby, the newly thatched Tinghöll had been repaired with oak, rather than the local beech and pine, which surely meant shipping in the necessary materials. More expense, Yngvar groaned. Soti was waiting, now with servants and a change of clothes for each of the butescarls. They bathed in the river, washing away the grime and salt, although only Ordulf looked immediately presentable—the Saxon keep a short beard and a small moustache, even going so far as to shave his cheeks. The others took time to braid their beards, then dressed on the banks. As instructed, they wore their best clothes— black fur trousers and sable hats, bright linen shirts and elaborate kaftans in the Rus style, with high embroidered collars and delicately stitched cuffs. There were no cloaks or mantles, so there could be no hidden perils or concealed weapons. Those were the simple rules of court.

Growing up together, Thormund had often expressed his embarrassment concerning the behaviour of his northerners, describing his future subjects as quarrelsome, querulous, and vindictive. His own father had been constantly plagued by his hirð's indiscipline, violence, and drinking—when just nine years old, Thormund was returning by ship to the royal seat in Uppsala, his hirðmenn still intoxicated from having "drunk hard" that evening. Their carelessness led to the ship losing its direction in harsh weather—its rudder damaged, it took an extra week to find their way to safe harbour. As fylkir, he actively strove to "educate" his men by promoting cultivated behaviour and introducing rules of etiquette—or so Yngvar had heard. He imagined it was a futile effort. Adopting good conduct at court would be incomprehensible to the Jomsvikings.

Yngvar led his men up to the Tinghöll. He strode through the doors and bowed low. "Heilir ok Sælir, my lords!"

"Here you are at last!" Thormund cried. "What kept you?"

The meal was well underway, and the room was full. Yngvar's mind went unerringly to unkind thoughts about Eirik's men, but he brightened when the whole royal household rose from their tables to greet him and gave a cheer. Festivities were being led by a midget, no taller than a toddler, an oddity the jarl dimly remembered being rescued from captivity in Frísland. Thormund had ordered the fellow to be dressed in a coat of mail, and then placed a helmet on his head, so that the tiny man trundled and tripped around the hall, moosehounds barking wildly at his every step. The noise was obviously very off-putting for the court skald, who had composed a drapa for the occasion but was having a hard time being heard in all the ruckus.

"Quite the welcome," Ketill muttered, behind him.

"The jarl returning home to unexpected house guests. It's his mead they are drinking; the least they can do it is toast him with it," said Soti.

Across the room, the fylkir took one last swig from a great bronze beaker, banded opulently with gold and silver, then set it aside and sprang from the high seat. He forged through the hall, deliberately adding to the chaos by tossing scraps to his dogs.

"Let me look at you!" he exclaimed as they clasped arms, then warmly embraced.

"No, let me look at *you!*" Yngvar replied, looking up and down at his cousin's elegant suit of silk brocade, almost as fiery as the regal side-whiskers he wore. "You used to hunt peacock, now you are dressed as one!"

"As impudent as ever. Tell me, do you still wet the bed for fear of huldufólk and lyktgubbar, or have you grown a spine?"

"Now my eye-teeth and molars have come in, I find myself much braver," Yngvar said, laughing. He'd not quite been a babe in arms when they first met, but Thormund was considerably older.

"It's been too long. Four years?"

"Twice that, at least. Your youngest was still a bantling."

"Long overdue then!" Thormund harrumphed. "I'm glad I waited for you. Ýmir's eistna! And to think, the young lords have been complaining they can't remember the last time they saw their wives. Ha! They'll learn soon enough. I'll sail north again within the week."

"So where have you been?" Yngvar was genuinely puzzled that he hadn't heard—or been informed—of any troop movements.

"I escorted our sister to old Jarizleifr Valdamarsson. He is the chosen king now. The union is long overdue. It might bring peace to the Garðaríki."

"Ingegerd won't bring anyone peace," Yngvar scoffed.

The fylkir laughed. "Least of all Jarizleifr. He's seen sixty winters if he's seen a day. But a promise is a promise, and the empire will be stronger for the marriage. You're wondering why I didn't send for you?"

Yngvar waved the concern away. It was a long journey to the Golden Gates of Kœnugarðr, and he had his duties here. He took in the room. Whenever kings met, the best men in the realm assembled, goði, jarls, and eldermen seemingly drawn from the breadth of the empire. The great Sigvat sat next to the high seat, cutting thin slices of meat. He was both skald and stallari—poet and marshall—people joked that he couldn't decide whether the pen was mightier than the sword, so chose to excel at both. He nodded at Yngvar and raised his cup when their eyes met.

He sat between two other men that Yngvar knew well. On one side sat Knutr, King of the Danar and the Nordmenn. Knutr was exceptionally tall and strong and might have been handsome but for his thin, high-set, and rather hooked nose. He was a mean bastard—to hear his men tell it, he'd once been playing chess with his brother-in-law at a banquet in Roskilde, when an argument ensued over an errant piece. The brother-in-law wasn't seen again.

On the other side was Kazimir, King of the Vindr and Laesir, sitting with wrinkled nose and pouting lips, his brows knitted, fiercely arguing with Kanceler Thurgaut. Most likely there were yet more Kristin rebellions in the south of his lands, and he needed soldiers. The Vindr always needed more soldiers.

All around them, the hirðmenn spoke in hushed low tones. It was an assembly of legends.

Beorn Estrithson, the Imperial Merkismaðr or standard bearer, was rumoured to have been sired by a polar bear. He was given his raven banner by Óðinn himself. He was drinking with the King of the Northern Isles, Sigurðr, who once caught an attacking dragon by the tail and hacked it in two behind the wings. He wore its impervious bronze scales even at night and made a game of men trying and failing to set him alight.

The fylkir sat, waving away some of his retainers from a nearby table to make room. Yngvar introduced his own men, one by one, and the fylkir thanked them. Table-men stirred up the fire, put out washing basins and fine linen cloth, then poured even finer drink into large glass goblets. Thormund asked his cousin to sit and gestured to the rest of his companions too. Haakon and Haraldr, suddenly pained, asked his leave to join their father, the jarl of Aust Englar, who sat quietly near the back of the hall. Despite his famed height, no-one had noticed Thorkell the Tall until now, but it was immediately obvious why: his glory days long since passed into shrunken dotage, he sat, spiritless and obtuse, a brittle reed barely able to eat.

"A sad end," Yngvar said after the brothers departed, unable to take his eyes off the venerable Viking.

"He was a Jomsviking once," Thormund reminisced. "One of the first, he and his brother. My father sent him to England and gave him the stewardship there when I was a boy. My own son sends him back to me, bitter and broken. I hope his lads are better than mine?"

"They'll make Thorkell proud," Yngvar said. It seemed the Jórvík King wasn't here, after all, just his messengers. That was something—Eirik was a tempest of a man, and Yngvar hadn't relished the thought of explaining the fracas across the river. Both cousins watched the slow and steady family reunion that unfurled in silence. Yngvar found it unsettling. He wasn't used to contemplating his own mortality. He prompted with a new subject. "So, the East is settled then? I can send Ketill and Valdimarr home at last?"

The fylkir missed his meaning. "Perhaps. It was easier for our foes to ditch their banners than lose their lives—I'm told they escaped to Tyrkland over the winter. Now they mean to lead another army against Jarizleifr, with Tyrkir, Blökumen, and a good many other odious people."

Yngvar's heart skipped a beat, realizing what that might mean for his sister and for his tax collections. The fylkir saw his alarm and quickly assuaged him. "I'm not so short-sighted as to put Inge in harm's way. Aldeigjuborg and the lakelands were her bride price, so I took her there, no further. I've set our cousin Ragnvald Ulfsson to hold the south, just in case."

"My home is cursed, ever since Hrøríkr bequeathed it to Helgi the Seer," said Valdimarr, listening in again. The comment ignited other opinions.

"It's the nature of the land, endless plains will drive a man mad," said Ordulf. "The Rus have been murdering each other for as long as anyone can remember."

Ketill agreed. "Always have, always will, since they butchered Asleik Bjornson. Ragnar's own blood, no less! If you can disagree with kings, are gods so far above?"

The fylkir grimaced. "I am as old as the Behmer Vald and have never seen such a brewing. Why will it stop now, you might ask? You see that boy." Thormund pointed a stubby finger at a young candleman, loafing unceremoniously by the fire. "That coal-biter is Vissivald, Jarizleifr's youngest son. There's no fight if our enemy can't rally around a pretender of the blood."

Yngvar appreciated the cunning—his cousin had learnt more from the counting house and the whorehouse than he ever did on the field of battle. He deftly took away people's reasons to fight rather than obliging them. While the men were distracted by the hostage, Thormund leaned into his cousin and beckoned him to do the same.

"I'll confess, I didn't expect you to choose an Íslandingar to command a ship," the king whispered. "I gave those people a lot, including a good bell for Thingvellir. Sent four knorrs loaded with flour, one to each quarter, during the famine. And how do they repay me?"

"His family in Snaeland are no worse than ours. Honourable men. It is not so long ago that they lived as Nordmenn. You're making a chicken out of a feather," Yngvar said dismissively. "Which reminds me, I owe you compensation. One of your son's household met with an impaling accident."

"Eirik's hirð is a ragtag bunch of fools. Forget it happened." Thormund shrugged with indifference, then muttered darkly, "I'm glad to see you, cousin. In the days ahead, I'll need loyal men at my side."

There was a long silence that persisted until Yngvar shifted the subject again. "The Queen is with you, and your sons?" He immediately wished he hadn't. The fylkir went pale and trembled slightly, an unnerving sight in so great a statesman. His eyes wandered off and found a home in the fire.

"I have bad news. I'm told Eymund took ill in the winter and passed."

Yngvar reached for his glass goblet, forcing his hand to keep from shaking. *Farðírass! Helvítismaðr!* He began to swear, but his voice ripped loose again, like a sail in storm. His father had been fighting with Jarizleifr, off and on over the years, as the rulers of the Rus marched against each other. All at once, that distant conflict was made horrifyingly real.

"I'm sorry for it. His body?" he whispered.

"He was burnt near the White Tower of Tengri-Thórr. A sickness took him, and his commanders gave him to the god of the open sky." The fylkir stretched out an arm and patted his cousin. Eymund had been close to him too, perhaps closer than his own father could have been, given the burdens of state. It reminded them both of how distant they'd grown over the years. They sat silently reminiscing for a while, half-listening to the terrible rhymes of the skald, an unlikely eulogy for an unfitting death.

"To your father." The men raised their glasses again and drank. Yngvar managed to maintain his composure, but his throat felt like rust and spikes. Each time he swallowed, he gulped down grief.

"Let's not dwell on the dead. To the living. To our sister, for Thórr's sake. Til árs ok friðar," the jarl blurted. He dimly heard Thormund offer to manage the estate, but Yngvar had reached his limit. The quarrels of the court grew louder and louder, the din driving him to distraction.

"The river," he said, by way of explanation as he stood and walked from the hall, almost tripping over the spinning midget. He looked straight ahead, conscious that he was still the Jarl of Jomsborg.

The fylkir followed, at a discreet distance, waving away his guards. "He's my foster-brother, not an assassin," he growled.

Yngvar had waded knee-deep in the river before Thormund reached the bank, the sounds of merriment far behind them. Despite his cousin's shouts of concern, he pressed on, sucking through the mud, a second pair of boots ruined. It was dusk now, the river a satin ribbon, reflecting the flames dancing in the lighthouse.

"Völundr's Lamp, they call it, as if the great smith had set it alight himself. Sometimes I think they are the true beacons in the darkness: the stories we tell our people, guiding them home." Thormund took off his boots and breeches and slipped into the water, intent on following.

Yngvar gazed at the brooding shape of the Imperial boulder ahead of them. "There is a story about that too. Local legend said that Loki, banished—and rightly so—from a dwelling nearby, came across a jötunn named Fornjótr near the river. He promises to find a suitable mate for the lovesick creature, if he, in turn, would use his might to destroy said dwelling. The mistrustful giant, of course, wants to see his future partner first, and so Loki obliges. From the depth of the waters emerges a beautiful spirit, a vision. Fornjótr reaches out his gnarled, monstrous hand, tantalisingly close to ending his years of loneliness. But in that exact moment, a rooster crows and dispels what was a trickster's illusion. The furious jötunn hurls this massive boulder at Loki, who uses more magic to speed his flight, turning into a toad. But it was too late: the boulder crashed down on him and confines him beneath it to this day."

Thormund had hitched up his trousers, and now rippled past his cousin, clambering up on the rock, hooting like a Groenland loon. "If only that were true, and there was no more mischief in the world!" he said, grinning.

Yngvar was dumbfounded. The King of the Storm Hall playing truant—years seemed to roll off him. The moosehounds suddenly splashed into view, running headlong into the river to catch up to their stray master. It completed the scene perfectly. Servants followed after them, thrashing and flailing, soaked from head to toe in seconds. Thormund was beside himself, roaring with great peals of laughter, and suddenly they were boys again, hunting and riding. The fylkir was obviously relishing the freedom because he called, uncharacteristically, for more mead.

"Hail to the Æsir! Hail to the Asyniur!" Thormund cheered, and then announced unceremoniously that he needed to piss. Once the dogs and servants had gone back to the safety of the shore, they sat on the great rock and watched as black Nótt rode across the land. The darkness was as intoxicating as the drink. Soon both men were slurring and stumbling their way through stories of their youth, one minute shamefully cowering from the huldufólk, the next famously charging down a wild boar. Each deep draught was more redolent than the last, and Yngvar soon found himself gulping down maudlin thoughts and memories, before they emerged, full formed, like in Loki's vision.

"So, what will we drink to next?" he asked, suddenly fearful of the silent waters.

"A proper funeral feast for Eymund," Thormund said, turning serious. Norsemen cemented pacts and swore allegiance to the gods and king over their cups, the drink formalizing their vows and strengthening their bond—an heir could not sit in his father's seat or claim his full inheritance without them. "After this year's Reginthing."

Vows made on the king's cup were sacred, even more so during the Great Council, where they were assiduously attended by their divine forebears. Kings vowed to expand their domains, and warriors vowed to increase their renown, whether by heroic deeds or claiming wives.

"In that case, to the king of kings and his kin," chortled Yngvar, relishing the prospect of his sovereign being tongue-tied as much as the chance to honour the memory of his father. Not to mention, it would be his chance to request the title of king and all the dignity that entailed. Perhaps his father had amassed a great store of luck, and now the hamingja had passed to him. Either that or the mead had emboldened him. True is the saying that no man shapes his own fortune, he grinned.

"When we were boys, you promised me a crown," he said, daring his guardian spirit to deny him now.

The king was taken aback. "We were boys! I cannot be held to the oath of a fourteen-year-old. Come now, Yngvar, you did me a great service with the Seimgalir—can't you be happy with that?"

Yngvar bridled. "If you think for a moment that I have served you well these past ten years, then you'll consider my request."

"Sometimes I wish we were all Íslandingar, living in a country that's out of kings. Anything else you ask, wealth or honours, I will give. But a crown is not mine to give. I am no wiser than my forbears, and kings must be taken by the people, not given by the fylkir."

"Taken by the people!" the jarl scoffed, standing now, as obstreperous as the king was pained. "Five generations have passed since the Store Hær, the Great Army, seized England, and we still pander to Ragnar's whelps."

Thormund exhaled heavily, with regretful care. "Ah, but such sons. Ragnar's greatest gift to the empire he forged. Bound together by blood and steel. The Boneless, Snake-in-the-eye, Ironside, and Whiteshirt—gods amongst men. Look at what Karl the Kristin left his

Empire with in comparison: the Frakkar birthed the Bald, the Simple, the Stammerer, the Blind, and the Fat. Mules and mares all."

"I don't need you to recite the damn bloodline. You set Eirik to rule across the Western Isles. Speak to the other jarls, the lawspeakers, the gods themselves if you have to. Command them to attend you at the Reginthing."

The fylkir was now much more subdued, his face hardening into a frozen mask. "Our most bitter enemies are our own kith and kin. Kings have no brothers, king have no sons," he said, quietly at first, his voice rising to a crescendo. Then, all at once, a long, bitter cry erupted from him, perhaps from anger, perhaps from anguish, Yngvar couldn't tell. He flung the dregs of his drink into the river. "You know, Yngvar, what I like about you? No mealy-mouthed diffidence, no walking like a cat around hot porridge. My guts are torn from me, my family is carried off—the young prince Gudmudr, dead, a babe in arms; Oysteinn asleep in the dust, and their most unhappy mother irremediably tormented by the memory of the dead."

"I didn't know..."

"You didn't ask! Why have I come to this ignominy? Thormund, ruler of a dozen lands? The two sons who remain survive only to punish me. Botulfr is like a deildegast, haunting the palace, rattling chains of misery. His brother, Eirik, depletes his kingdom with iron and lays it waste with fire, ignoring my emissaries. In all things, Óðinn has turned cruel and attacked me with the harshness of his hand. My brothers in the East fight amongst themselves, adding sorrow to sorrow, and now you undertake to usurp our laws—for what? Good Thórr, hide me until the Alföðr's fury passes, until the spears hurled at me cease."

The king was clearly deeply grieved, his face ashen and despairing. He rose unsteadily to his feet. "But what are kings, when the armies have gone, but perfect shadows in the sun?" he whispered, tears rolling down his cheeks and tumbling from his whiskers. He turned slowly to his cousin and glowered. "Vargdropi, out of my sight."

Yngvar opened his mouth to protest, to explain himself and if need be, to offer his groveling apologies. He saw now: the extra guards, the great cavalcade, it was all for protection. But his luck had deserted him. He slipped, scrabbling for purchase on the great boulder.

There was a moment then, a split second, where Yngvar saw all his futures flash before his eyes. For that moment, the Imperial Boulder seemed like Hliðskjálf, the high seat of Óðinn, offering the chastened jarl tantalising glimpses of all the wide realms of man. He saw the

LOKI'S WAGER • 97

Frakkar fortress-kingdoms, every river blocked with fortified bridges, every hilltop garrisoned with cavalrymen. He saw elite Excubitors billeted in the Great City, protecting all the mummery of Kristindómr. And he spied farther still, past endless canopies of strangler figs and mangrove swamps, where huge alpandill trampled and trumpeted. And then, he saw something else: a beautiful land, lush and bright as satin, with sweet scents and tall flowers, and streams of honey ran all over the land, in every direction. Then just as suddenly as the vision had begun, it vanished.

His chin collided with the cold, wet rock. By the time his men dragged him, sodden and squelching, to the Tinghöll, the fires had long gone out.

The Jarl of Jomsborg awoke in his own bed. Half-opening his eyes, he saw his clothes strewn across the floor and smiled slyly—the unruly path of garments promised a morning of furtive fumbling and easy desire. He groped across the silken quilts and down pillows, wondering who the lucky lady was this time. He felt woozy, but he could sleep that off later. Homecomings really did offer an abundance of delights.

"I hope you had sweet dreams," said a man's voice from one of the nearby benches. Soti, the Dane, stroking his red rooster of a beard and crowing with the dawn. It wasn't wholly unexpected: the longhouse was scarcely a place for privacy. In fact, Yngvar's life on land wasn't very different to that at sea: the entire company did everything together, eating, cooking, dressing, and sleeping. The close quarters left little room for modesty.

Yngvar was about to cluck a retort before he dived under his blankets, but his left knee gave way the instant he rolled onto it. He prodded at it, puzzled—it had blown up like a sheep's bladder. His jaw felt swollen and tender.

"Looks like you wet yourself." Haakon hoved into view, aiming some desultory kicks at the discarded clothes. Yngvar suddenly spied his clock pendant, dented and cracked on the floor, and recollection came flooding back. He groaned inwardly, swamped by a wave of shame and nausea.

"Look, it's all coming back to him now. You can tell from the maggot dangling between his legs," Ketill joked. It seemed like half the Jomsvikings were lining the hall, waiting for him to wake up.

Yngvar's once-proud manhood was now entirely and abruptly flaccid.

"He's as soft as his bedding," said Valdimarr, ridicule for Yngvar's reðr mixed with contempt for his luxurious bed closet. It was a sign of status to some, but not for the hard-bitten butescarls. "Call for the ship's hand. The mast needs some attention." The jokes were coming thick and fast now—the hooting and braying was ungodly. Yngvar had little choice than to nurse his wounds. He gave a slight bow, to acknowledge his self-immolation, then waved them all away.

He wasn't overly concerned about Thormund's wrath. Men quarrelled, and lords got drunk—they'd bandied plenty of heated words in the past and always reconciled quickly. But other memories began to surface, and he closed his eyes, trying to picture the Imperial Boulder. He needed to concentrate, to try to recall the fleeting glimpses he had seen, the visions of far-away places. He could almost…

"Yngvar the Far-Fetched! Did I not warn you about asking for a kingdom? You are a child of a man, a cautionary tale for moppets and bantlings. Hjúki and Bil! You fell down and broke your crown, and now here I am, mending your head with vinegar and brown parchment."

The vituperative voice penetrated to the dark recesses of his head, hammering around his skull. Hjálmvígi had returned, doubtless summoned to wag a calloused finger and dispense antique remedies. The old lawspeaker grasped Yngvar's head and stared deep into his eyes, as if searching a well; his laboured breath smelt of pine and iron. Then he stood and clasped Yngvar's head to his chest, first prodding and probing the jarl's teeth as if he was strumming a lyre, then slathered a foul-smelling unguent around his jawline. The jarl might have taken issue with being manhandled but didn't have the energy to protest. While the odd examination persisted, he stared at an elaborate necklace of carnelian and amber beads, from which hung several pendants—among them a silver miniature chair. The chair of the nornir, a seat of sorcery.

Hjálmvígi tapped the top of his head, signalling that that he was finished. "It doesn't take a soothsayer to know there will be no trip to the high seat this year," he said, jangling the necklace. "But you are well enough. No fractures, no concussion."

The hofgoði stood up and clattered his staff across the table to command the hall's attention.

"The rest of you would be wise to prepare your lord's ships."

"I knew it!" hissed Valdimarr. "Strive not with him who is drunk with drink and witless, for often only ill and doom come out of such things."

There was a general commotion, but the old priest only thumped his stave more insistently. "Calm yourselves. There is no need to panic. You have had good things from the Lord of the Spear, and he has not broken friendship with you. Now, you Jomsvikings will listen to me, and listen well. Each you of men is the sum of many things: his breaths and thoughts, the soil that fed him and his forebears, echoes of long-silenced battles and the much-contested laws of his land, of the smiles of girls and the slow utterance of old women. Yet, he is also this—a single flame, which can be lit and put out from one moment to the next."

He looked round expectantly at the hushed faces, grizzled warriors in rapt attention.

"It was once the custom of powerful men, kings or jarls, that they went off raiding, and won riches and renown for themselves. And even if their sons inherited the lands, they had to win wealth and fame themselves, each in his turn, or be as nothing. And now? The fylkir has given the merchants so much power, the Englandshaf and the Eystrasalt are like Norse lakes, and you his errand boys. The Kristins laugh at us across the lands of Páfadómr. They laugh at our 'Pax Nordica.' How have we forgotten that Wōden incites the princes never to make peace!"

"You Saxar... always waging holy war!" heckled Soti.

The priest continued, ignoring the interruption. "My father could well remember the Uppsala King Eirik and used to say of him that when he was in his best years, he enlarged the Norse dominion. Yngvar's father fell in the East, defending it manfully while Thormund lets his tribute-lands to go from him through laziness and weakness, starting at his own shadow. And you—what do you great sons of the North do? You spend your whole lives jesting and laughing as though at a permanent feast. Is it not worthy of your tears that with all the nine worlds at our fingertips, we have not yet become lords of one?"

Yngvar was taken aback. The Saxon had become a freewheeling demagogue. "What trickery is this? Just minutes ago, you told me that I shouldn't ask for a kingdom."

"You are a perverse mulish man, Yngvar," Hjálmvígi chided. "Sometimes you need to be goaded into action. You'd have never uttered the thought if I hadn't coaxed it from you and wouldn't have asked if you hadn't been shamed by your men or deeply drunk. Just as now, when you'd rather creep back into bed than pursue your destiny."

Yngvar was chastened, but knew it to be true.

"So, what then? If I can't be granted a crown, I'll carve myself a kingdom."

"Jarl Ulfr said the exact same thing. We took Galizuland and set up his throne in the Tower of Hercules," Ketill chimed in.

"That was ten years ago, while the fylkir was beyond the Vargsea. He wasn't happy to find his peace disturbed," Yngvar replied, testily. He couldn't abandon his cousin.

"Do you not long for a land where livestock feed themselves during the winters, that there are fish in every river and lake, and great forests, and that men are free from the assaults of kings and criminals? How many times does the fylkir mention peace? There has to be more to life than raids in Spánn and reminding Longbeards of their heritage. Soti, bring me the charts," commanded the lawspeaker, suddenly master of the house.

Soti reached up, high on the wall, beyond the shield and spears and trophies of battle, and plucked several oak frames from their resting places. Nautical charts, with bearing lines emanating from compass roses located at various points on the map, surrounded by tangled ink illustrations of black, gold, green, and blue, bought long ago from a captive Gyðingr in Manork. The Serkir were excellent cartographers, if you could get your hands on their state secrets. The priest beckoned his men to the table, where he had arranged the vellum leaves in order.

This was the skjöldr iordrīke, "Shield of the World." The human world of men, cities and seas, but also entire bestiaries of horrifying mythical creatures and the strange cultures of distant lands. It was not for use as a navigational tool, but instead was an artistic compendium of people, parables, and places. It stretched all the way from Vinland to Sindhland.

The northern quadrant was blue; the western isles, red; the southern Grikklands, green.

"Do we get to choose?" The men started to squabble, excitedly.

Yngvar scanned the map.

He had never been to Frakkarland but started to recall fragments of his vision and match them with the images on the shield. As far as he was concerned, it was all a land of Popes and pomp, one great trelleborg, every river blocked with fortified bridges, every hilltop garrisoned with cavalrymen—all to prevent the depredations of the Norse. The Frakkar were so fearful, they'd set down laws against trade with the North—the penalty for selling horses to the Vikings was death. The days of lightning raids ravaging the Frakkar coastlands—or seizing a city by stealth of night, raiding along the continent's numerous navigable rivers—were long gone. You could see the Frakkar border forts all along the Sax-elfr rivers all the way to the Ore Mountains. No, the Norse had been feasting on Frakklarand for years. Rögnvaldr's sons had ruled Namsborg for a century, along with their neighbour, the Jarls of Rúðu and Parisborg. There wasn't a tasty morsel left, at least, not one beyond the point of a riddar's lance.

"Let's rule out invading Kristindómr," Yngvar decided. "I'd rather not sail up a Frakkar's back passage, and that means forgetting Beiaraland and Sváva."

Other lands were offered up in a brawl of avarice and abandon, the warriors tumbling over each other to be heard. The Ungarariki? Sometime allies. The Kingdom of Nekor? No one relished fighting against the Veiled Ones on their bad-tempered úlfaldar.

"The west then. Snorri Thorfinnsson has claimed two colonies: Straumfjörð and Hóp. He claims descent from Ragnar."

"Everyone claims to be descended from Ragnar. The Book of Settlements is just social climbing."

"I heard he was killed by a man with one leg!"

"That was Thorvald Eiriksson, Leif the Lucky's brother. The Nordmenn who don't take to Knutr or Eirik are sailing to the Wonderstrands. We could be there within two months. Take ourselves a Skræling bride or ten."

"No, we don't want to sail north with winter on the wind."

"I agree. There is nothing for us in the west. More peace. Mere crumbs, when the real banquet is here."

Yngvar had seen where he needed to go. Farther than any Norseman. He jabbed his finger somewhere north of Khitai.

"I had a vision last night, on the rock. The god Frey once sat down on the mighty Óðinn's chair and was immediately able to look into all the worlds. Here. We sail for Ódáinsakr, beyond the lands of Guðmundr. Fialler, the governor of Skaane, went into exile there."

"The Undying Lands? You mean to make your hall on the glittering plains? That is further than Alexander himself fared," said Valdimarr, clearly awe-struck.

The old lawspeaker was delighted by the suggestion.

"Had I thought you might live forever, I'd have reared you in my wool-basket," Hjálmvígi said. "But lifetimes are shaped by what will be, not by where you are. Now, take this device. I've made it for you with all the skill I have, and my belief is this: it will bring safe passage to the ship that carries it."

The men all gathered, speaking in hushed tones, only to see little more than a diviner's bowl of water.

"How does it work?" Ketill asked, eager to augment his skills of navigation.

"When you sailors can no longer profit by the light of the sun, or when the world is wrapped up in the shades of night, look to this device. Its iron needle, after contact with the leiðsteinn, will turn itself always toward the northern star, which, like the axis of the firmament, remains immoveable."

Yngvar watched as the iron whirled round in a circle until, when its motion ceased, its point looked directly to the north.

"Pathways in the darkness, Hjálmvígi, will your wonders never cease? And the roadstone, where did it come from?"

"Call it a gift from the gods. The rock is found where thunderbolts have stricken the earth with their fury."

"Then we shall pray to Tengri-Thórr and trust that the sky god gives us safe passage. What say you men? We sail at dawn!"

— IÐUNN'S HEL-RIDE —

The Raven Road

Helvítis fokking fokk.
Iðunn Lind sucked in her breath, reflecting on her newfound isolation.

The Lakeland was much as she remembered it—a continuous ridge of russet hills, encircling the small holdings of the dalesmen. In the distance, the sunrise kissed the peak of Skalli Fjall. She had staggered here often when she was younger, leaving Uppsala for holidays with friends of the family. The birdwatching was always good in winter, with great migrant flocks descending from Svíþjóð and the East to bolster the resident population. Ordinarily, she might have heard raucous þrǫstr, quarreling over the hawthorn berries that speckled the hedge, or watched great flocks of stari twist and turn overhead, in their mesmerizing dance. But not today. Her protective echo was set at exactly the wrong frequency—it would have disoriented them.

The sun was much more penetrating. Its languid warmth came spilling over the kirkja, firing the red sandstone and glazing the retreating snow. The tombstones, capped with frost, reminded her of rows of ruddy-faced children wearing delicate lace bonnets, waiting patiently for their baptism. The old Cork Oak rose above them, leaning inwards over glistening iron railings, shepherding the throng to service with its swirling green arms.

Dellingr's doors had opened, Hrímfaxi returned to his stable, and it seemed that Kristindómr owned the bright day ahead. The church was, to say the least, unexpected. Iðunn had seen all kinds of worshipful constructions over the years, but most northern basilica translated into wood, twigs cut from the tree of life. Stone-strewn temples like this often had to be tickled from the ribs of Mother Jǫrð. It had no right to be here, but then, perhaps, neither did she. Such were the perils of hitching a ride on the Raven Road: only the Urðr discoursed with the dead; the life-wise were ordained to focus on greener pastures.

Still, it was good to be back on Midgard and feel the sun on her face. Even if it was a simulacrum.

It had taken her an age to realize. The Hel-road hadn't deposited her far from the Grove, in terms of distance. Not much more than one hundred miles, as the raven flew. The journey had been both idle and endless, like grubbing around in a summer garden, exhuming memories of childhood, tugging at the roots of remembrance. There was none of the displacement of the greenways; she was simply there, saturated by her past, like the more elegant version of the Thought and Memory concatenation the Imperials used in the war.

The cries of tawny uglur reverberated around the bowl of darkening fells. She had paused, feeling for old growth nearby, a familiar door rather than a passing acquaintance. And there it was: The Four Brothers—one of the great Knútr, used extensively by one of her grandfather's cohorts, Vilhjálmr Waddasworþ, a pioneer of the Travels. She had fond memories of the jocund old poet, of picnics among the wild daffodils and lopsided dances above Gressaer.

The Brothers were a short hike to the northwest, past Vatnsá lake, Skalli Fjall, and Borgar Dalr—a matter of hours given her enhancements. If there was better hope of safe passage, she couldn't imagine it: the yews were seedlings when Hengist first came to these shores, when Myrddin the Wild was young and the Gotar ruled in far off Árheimar.

She crossed the fells at a clip, mercifully devoid of winter travellers who might waylay her. Skalli Fjall was a rugged knuckle of rock, the highest mountain in England, sitting aloof, connected to the massif only by the slender gangway of Mikladyrr and guarded by fearsome cliffs. The northern and eastern crags were among the Lakeland's most impressive—although some might say forbidding, especially given the blustering winter winds. The paths were clearly laid out, but extremely rocky, which was no great impediment when ascending, but made for a moderately challenging descent for the uninitiated.

It was a trifle for Iðunn. The Verðandi were used to the precipices of Jötunheim: the pilgrimage along Gillingr's Way to Hnitbjǫrg was a favourite, along the bluffs of the Vimur. It was painful to think it had all gone. The mountains of Jötunheim were blasted beyond recognition now, the citadel lashed with black rains. Marshall Thunder had made her home a funeral pyre, his storm of bunker busters and thermobarics reducing their rebellion to rubble. She ran her fingers through her hair. She'd worn it shorter in those days. Out of solidarity with the slain. *Well, wasn't this a trip down memory lane?* Iðunn was enjoying the escape, the thrill of cartwheeling through the night, outrunning her thoughts.

Minutes later, she sank in to the Borgar Dalr, the valley of the fortress. There was a great military base on the far side: Breiðablik, the bright-gleaming beacon in the rain-swept hills, with a garrison of the King's Own Húskarls that protected the whole area from incursions. They might have remained at their posts. The King of England was no fan of his bellicose cousin; he might offer clemency just to spite Trumba. Baldr's Head to the north was considered a holy site, a huge lava boulder toppled from the mountain when the glaciers retreated and no longer buttressed the steep side of the valley. The stone had an uncannily well-defined chin and lips, the smiling visage of the shining god. Iðunn considered paying her respects but didn't want to risk capture so close to her goal.

She found the ancient yews exactly as they'd left them. They projected from the flank of heather and curly-tipped bracken at strange angles, more shell-torn turret than tree, their trunks bleached white and ghostly. Waddasworþ famously described the trees as "intertwisted fibres, serpentine, up-coiling and inveterately convolved," his diction perfectly matching the siblings' growth. England had been shielded from the solar blast, being in the "safe" hemisphere—if they had been damaged by radiation, the yews masked it well. They were a frame for all her yesterdays. She felt certain of her interrogation, of the validation of these eternal witnesses to mankind's folly in this, her hour of trial.

And then she saw. Only three of the "Fraternal Four" remained. A signpost, in the Latin script, from the "National Trust," explained that one sibling had succumbed to storm a century ago. She had been absent for a long time, consumed with her work at Hvergelmir, but even so, the Verðandi would have sensed the rupture, or been alerted if their protections had somehow failed. The clues came thick and fast after that: the road to Ámelsætr lined with pollards of ash and oak, their upper branches desecrated for fodder and fuel. The valley sides pocked with the old surface remains of mines. No sign of smog. The lights of farms sparking on the horizon. Life, in a place where none was possible. Survivors in the afterglow of Ragnarök? Preposterous, at least, on the scale she had witnessed. The evacuation had been mandatory, and the skies were empty—there was no sign of the Imperial Fleet returning for stragglers.

She rested on a fallen piece of heartwood for balance. The lost brother, flowing like storm sea's waves, frozen into permanence. His root cells no longer sent signals to the swarms of bacteria, his leaves had ceased their chemical chatter with insects, and fungi would receive no more messages from their gracious host. But the dead logs, collapsed branches, and upended roots had become something else, focal points for thousands of new relationships. The yew was decentered, its connections tapered but still extant. The felled sibling corroborated her wildest suspicions. There was barely a trace of Sætumálmur-10.

Sunlight might be the best disinfectant, but you couldn't wipe clean radioactive fingerprints. And if there was no radiation, there was no Ragnarök... this wasn't the Midgard she knew. The complete and total absence of Breiðablik was further proof, if she needed it. A military-industrial complex didn't just up and leave.

She began her rune-song nonetheless, hoping for the answers that escaped her in Thórr's Grove. Amongst the distorted, inflated limbs of the yews there came a serenity, an unexpected silence like a hidden lacuna in the squall of composition. As she had done countless times before, she began to walk into the perspective. The trees were so low to the ground, she seemed to be in deep conversation, face to gnarled face. Then all at once, the way was barred with fizzing cascades of foliage, the boughs suddenly twisting into life. Perhaps the eigenvalues had been wrong, or the göndul's breath dissipated; whatever it was, her incantation died before it had begun.

She had no choice but to retrace her steps, back over the mountain. The Ash must have rendered her here for a reason. The pieces of the puzzles had all been laid out for her, out there in the collective consciousness—she just had to put them together.

The World Tree was a survivor, like Iðunn. Of course, most tree specimens were hardy—possessed of a compartmentalized vascular system, they could allow parts of the whole to die while other portions thrived. And some trees defied time by sending out clones— genetically identical shoots—so that one trunk's demise didn't spell the end for the organism. The largest colonies could have thousands of individual trunks sharing the same network of roots.

The Great Ash had performed the feat over vast distances and countless millennia, seeding great forests on all the Nine Homeworlds. And somehow, she had established herself in this... Otherworld. Which was just as well; she'd need all her arboreal wiles to outlast Ragnarök.

Two roads diverged in a wood, and I, I took the one less travelled by. Words penned by another skald, a Vinlander, Róðbjartr Frosti. They offered a little consolation.

"How did you get here?" she asked, out loud, as if to the universe at large. "And how do I get home?"

"I can call you a taxi if you like," called a voice from the gate. A priest stepped adroitly through the entrance, then marched briskly along the path, swilling sweet tea to ward off the cold and the dust of a poor night's sleep. He stopped for a moment, and squinted into the rosy-fingered dawn, holding up a slice of toast over his eyes for protection. Iðunn clenched her jaws reflexively, grinding her teeth. So much for her crypsis—she must have punctured her own disguise by calling out.

"Stunning isn't it? 'It will be stormy today, for the sky is red and threatening. You know how to interpret the appearance of the sky, but you cannot interpret the signs of the times,'" the priest said. "Matthew 16:3."

Iðunn knew the quote. She'd seen plenty of Stjórn in her time—the name meant guidance—compilations of Biblical material commissioned for reading aloud, for the benefit of those who could not understand Latin. She had almost forgotten she was on hallowed ground—she might as well be genuflecting on the chamber-graves of the man's family and forefathers. She picked up her gambanteinn, and smoothed her fingers down its iron shaft, adjusting the two polyhedral knobs of bronze that fused with the black sapling wood. All Vǫlur owned a staff of office, but a taming wand was a tool used only by the highest levels of the ritual community. With it, she was able to instil near-Biblical levels of frenzied madness and uncontrollable devotion. The only real difference was her wand worked by emitting chemical cues rather than holy verses.

"Or you can come in for cup of tea. Lost souls are something of a speciality. No obligation. Either way, let me know."

She had longed to really revel in the dawn, to feast on the solitude. In all her long years, it had never seemed that time was on her side.

But the invitation was too tempting to ignore. She found she could jump readily behind the mind of the stranger and began perusing him like an open book. One of the talents of the deep-minded. The Engl-*ish*-man was stiff and starchy, but easy to read, suffering from daily crises of faith. The priest's near-naked panic when discussing the female form was easy enough to manipulate.

"To a passerby, it might seem an odd habit, talking to thin air, trying to cajole answers from the ether," she said, radiating beatific charm.

"One sometimes gets the sense that we are supposed to be embarrassed of angelic beings," the priest mooned out loud, his mind neatly divided between scripture and pleasure. There was a brief pause. "I'm sorry, I don't know why I said that," he said, suddenly as crimson as the sky. She watched him trying to shrug off the seed of ruination she had planted and rekindled her camouflage, fine-tuning the echo's resonance to mask her from any other prying eyes. Peace restored, she went back to her dawn-gazing, reflecting on her mirror world and its counterfeit sky.

The Verðandi decided to speculate with her own prayer. She was certain she could be heard, even here. The fields, forests, brooks, and fells weren't literally populated by alfar and skogsrå, dancing in the mist, but the treescape permeated everything. Yggdrasil spoke constantly if you knew how to listen, filling creation with sound, scents, and signals, connected with everything that existed. It had been an unrivalled joy dialoguing with her over the centuries, receiving her quiet wisdom.

During the time of the Travels, when the Verðandi first explored the Nine Realms, the greenseers had led a vainglorious and foolhardy search for the gods. The explorers had naming rights, and so worlds they discovered took colour from their conceits. Liminal places of legend suddenly became fixtures on maps. The Empire of the Heavens was a self-perpetuating mythology, a projection of the Norse male ego into a bubble universe.

They hadn't even had the discipline to be consistent. Her great-grandfather's own journal, the famed *Náttúra Bók*, contained tantalizing glimpses of places that he visited, including a fragment on a mythological land of "Ódáinsakr, land of the undying, that Kristinn men call the Land of Living People or Paradise." Subsequent debate over the nature, origin, and exact whereabouts of Ódáinsakr among the Vǫlur resulted in many theories but no conclusions, and Karl Lind's notes were too contradictory to lead to any clear answers.

The name didn't really matter, she supposed, but it suited the mystery. The mirror-world was here, a damn near perfect copy of Midgard, one somehow spared Surtr's blaze. This world was warmer, at least. There was snow on the ground, but nothing like the winter of discontent beyond the veil. It brought to mind another verse, from the aptly named skald.

"These woods are lovely, dark and deep, But I have promises to keep, And miles to go before I sleep, And miles to go before I sleep," she muttered.

"Ah, Robert Frost. What a joy!" the priest said, bounding back into view, like a curtain-twitcher who'd witnessed something salacious. She had to learn to stop giving herself away.

"So sorry. Me again. Reverend Riley's the name, and preaching's the game," he went on, proffering a clammy hand. "Which I appear to be very much off today," he added, apologetically. The awkwardness almost made her miss Father, but recidivism wasn't in her nature. Rendition and correctional treatments had seen to that.

She blinked at him, bashfully, hoping to quickly drench him in disruptors. The Reverend was made of sterner stuff, though, with his own shields of fellowship and faith. He stammered on undaunted. "I couldn't help noticing that fetching accent of yours. We get lots of Norwegians popping down after the Safe Sellafield conference at Whitehaven every year, looking for a bit of homeland. Used to be Greenpeace activists protesting about killer isotopes in the Irish Sea, but it's more cooperation than confrontation these days. Not that I am for the nuclear laundromat over there, right on our doorstep."

He waved his teacup in the direction of the coast, tossing the dregs onto the path, turning the snow into a discoloured arrow. This way madness lies. Iðunn felt the light drain out of her.

Nuclear power. This world had split the atom, broken their world asunder—something even the Skuld had recoiled from. It would certainly explain the dissonance in the spell song and her easily fragmented shielding. Ódáinsakr. The Undying Land, the Half-Life World. And here she was, the High Lector of the Life-wise, stuck by death's door. She was a stone's throw from the chief factory, supposed monuments of value and intellect, vaults of bogus cultural riches, its emissions and effluent poisoning the whole coastline.

Iðunn wondered if she was atoning for some form of ancestral sin. It was no longer a question of imitation, nor duplication, nor even parody: the Helvegr had led her to a world of death. She could feel the decay—scorched leaves, blighted branches, oozing lesions. The air was poison. The tree suffered incredible agony: its trunk was rotting, and oblivion gnawed beneath. All that pain, all that suffering, and still the Kristins like Riley acted like it was only the White Christ who'd been crucified.

She contorted her face into a smile of expedience, and finally clasped the vicar's extended hand. The man was almost overcome with relief.

"Anyway, if you are here for the crosses, our churchwarden knows all about them. He's rather poorly, I'm afraid. I've been besieged by a coterie of detectorists and gravediggers in his absence. All desperate to find their fortune. Who knows what old fossils they'll dig up next, eh?"

THE CHRONICLE
— OF KŒNUGARÐR —

1223

Óðinn alone knows who they are and from whence they came. Some call them Tartars and others say Taurmen, and yet more claim they are related to the Kangar, come again out from the Etrian desert between East and North.

We have written of them here for the sake of the memory of the Kings of the Rus and of the misfortune which came to them. For we have heard that the Tartar have captured many countries, slaughtered a quantity of the godless Vallanar peoples, and scattered others, for even Khagan Köten, who was the greatest among all Pale Ones, could not stand before them.

The Taurmen passed through the whole Vallanar country and came close to Garðaríki by the White Tower. Then it was that Mistileifr the Old was Grand Prince in Kœnugarðr, Mistileifr the Bold was King in Holmgarðr, Mistileifr the Brilliant in Svartrgarðr, and Markgreff Danr in Valdemarr.

And the Pale Ones ran into the Garðariki, bringing many gifts: hross and úlfaldar, visundur and girls; and they gave gifts of these to the Grand Prince, saying thus: "Our land they have taken away today; and yours will be taken tomorrow," and Köten appealed to his son-in-law, and Mistileifr the Old began to appeal to the princes of Great Svíþjóð, his brethren, saying thus: "If we, brothers, do not help these, then they will certainly surrender to them, then the strength of those will be greater." And thus having deliberated much among themselves, they were convinced: "It would be better for us to meet them on a foreign land than on ours." They made themselves ready for the journey because of both the greeting and the appeal of the Vallanar. From Kœnugarðr, they moved in the moon of Einmánuður and they began to organize their forces, each his own province, and they went, having collected the whole Garðarland against the

Tartars. They came to the river Nipr, to the island of Varangian. And all Vallanarland came there to them, and Pallteskjar came and Smaleskjar, and other lands. All these hosts crossed the Nipr—so the covered water was a bridge of boats. The Vindr Marchers went along the Nister and entered the sea. And they entered the Nipr River, and drove up to the rapids, and became near the Khortitsa River.

Then the Tartars, having learned that the Garðar were coming against them, sent envoys to the Grand Prince: "Behold, we hear that you are coming against us, having listened to the Vallanar; but we have not occupied your land, nor your towns, nor your villages, nor is it against you we have come. But we have come sent by God against our serfs, and our horse-herds, the pagan Pale Ones, and do you take peace with us. If they escape to you, drive them off thence, and take to yourselves their goods. For we have heard that to you also they have done much harm; and it is for that reason also we are fighting them."

But the Rus did not listen to this but killed all the envoys and themselves went against them, and took stand on the Nipr, this side of the Oleshye Sands. And the Tartars sent to them envoys a second time, saying thus: "Since you have listened to the Pale Ones, and have killed all our envoys, and are coming against us, come then, but we have not touched you, let God judge all." And they let go free their envoys.

When news came to the state that the Tartars had come to look at the Rus boats, Markgreff Danr, having heard it and sat down on a horse, rushed to look at the unseen army, and the crowns who were with him, and many other princes, were driven to look at an unprecedented weapon. But those came, and warriors told them to the princes, "They have arrows." And others said: "They are just ordinary people, the worst of the Khangar."

And when they arrived back, they told Mistileifr the Old about everything. And the young princes said: "Mistileifr! Do not stand! Let us go against them!"

And so all the princes crossed over. They passed the Nipr on the day of Týrsdagr. And other princes came, and they too went in the Wide Fields. And the Tartars shot the Rus regiments, but the Rus arrows defeated them, and chased them out of the field, and took their cattle, and fled the herds, so that all the troops gained full livestock.

They went after them for nine days, and passed over the Kalka river, with the Vallanar forward as outposts. There the Tartar stopped and themselves took up position and shot them, Blakkrmen and Bleikrmen alike.

And then Mistileifr the Brilliant came together with them, wishing to fight, but the Pale Ones ran away, having accomplished nothing, and in their flight they trampled the prince's men, for they had not had time to form into order against them; and they were all thrown into confusion, and there was a terrible and savage slaughter. The Svartrgarðar's body was left to the mercy of prairie scavengers.

The other Mistileifrs sat in a state without knowing this, because the Bright One did not say anything to them either—because of envy, because the great disagreement was their boundaries.

When the armies collided with each other, Danr went ahead, and Viggo of the Væringjar. They hit the Tartar regiments, and Viggo was shot down from his horse, and Danr himself was wounded in his chest. But because of youth and courage and his great strength, he did not hear the wounds that were on his body—Danr was at the age of eighteen, and he fought hard, beating the Tartars. Helgi of Smaleskja, seeing this and having thought that Danr was shot down, also rushed among them, because he was a strong man.

Danr, seeing that more and more enemies fought in the battle, the shooters shot them hard, turned his horse back to flight—because opponents rushed to him. And finally when he fled, he would drink water, and drinking, he felt a sore in his flesh that in the battle he did not notice because of the strength and courage of his age.

And Mistileifr, Grand Prince of Kœnugarðr, seeing this evil, never moved at all from his position; for he had taken stand on a hill above the river Kalka, and the place was stony, and there he set up a stockade of posts about him and fought with them from out of this stockade for three days.

And there were men in armour with the Taurmen and these warriors, having kissed the oath ring to Mistileifr the Old not to kill him, but to let them go on ransom, lied; they delivered him bound to the Tartars, and they took the stockade and slaughtered the people, and there they fell dead. And having taken the nobles they suffocated them having put them under boards, and themselves took seat on the top to have dinner. And thus the nobles ended their lives choking.

And pursuing the other princes to the Nipr they killed six more. Then Mistileifr the Bold, having previously escaped across the Nipr, cut loose the boats from the bank so the Tartars should not go after them, and himself barely escaped.

Of the rest of the troops every tenth returned to his home; some the cowardly Pale Ones killed for their horses, and others for their clothes. And thus, for our sins Óðinn put misunderstanding into us, and a countless number of people perished, and there was lamentation and weeping and grief throughout towns and villages. This evil happened in the month of Harpa. And the Tartars turned back from the river Nipr, and we know not whence they came, nor where they hid themselves again; Óðinn knows whence he fetched them against us for our sins.

THE OPUS MAJUS
— OF LECTOR MIRABILIS —

Near Lake Ilmer, Garðaveld
1237

It had all been going so well for Hróðgeirr Bakko. The dreaming spindles of Oxifjord, a seat on the King of England's council, lucubrations on alchemy and grammar published across the Commonwealth—and to top it off, an invitation to lecture at the great Pandidakterion of Miklagard. The capital school had over thirty chairs for law, philosophy, medicine, arithmetic, geometry, astronomy, music, rhetoric, and now one reserved for him in linguistics.

And still not twenty years passed since he learned his rúnamál. No wonder they called him Lector Mirabilis. The Speaker of Marvels. It was all his for the taking.

He just had to get there... which was, admittedly, something of a predicament at the present. Two thousand miles of Rus forest was impediment enough, but the gods had seen fit to throw in a ravaging Tartar horde for good measure.

One step at a time, he thought, scrutinizing the Tartar's head. Few of the Hrossmen had much of a beard, though this one had a few wisps of hair on the upper lip. They cut their hair like Kristins, shaved from one ear to the other, across the crown, although the short fringe and two long braids belied their true origin. The face was unusual, to say the least—the cheekbones stood out a good deal from the jaw, the nose was flat to the face, and the eyelids raised all the way to the eyebrows, although that might have just been the surprise of the sword blow.

The Hrossman been mid-sentence, after all.

Vilhjálmr thrashed through the fresh snow, visibly agitated. "We're fokked!" his companion cried, disappearing into the birch forest. The snowbound trees looked like a checkerboard—white against black,

Lands of the Rus

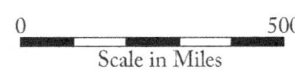

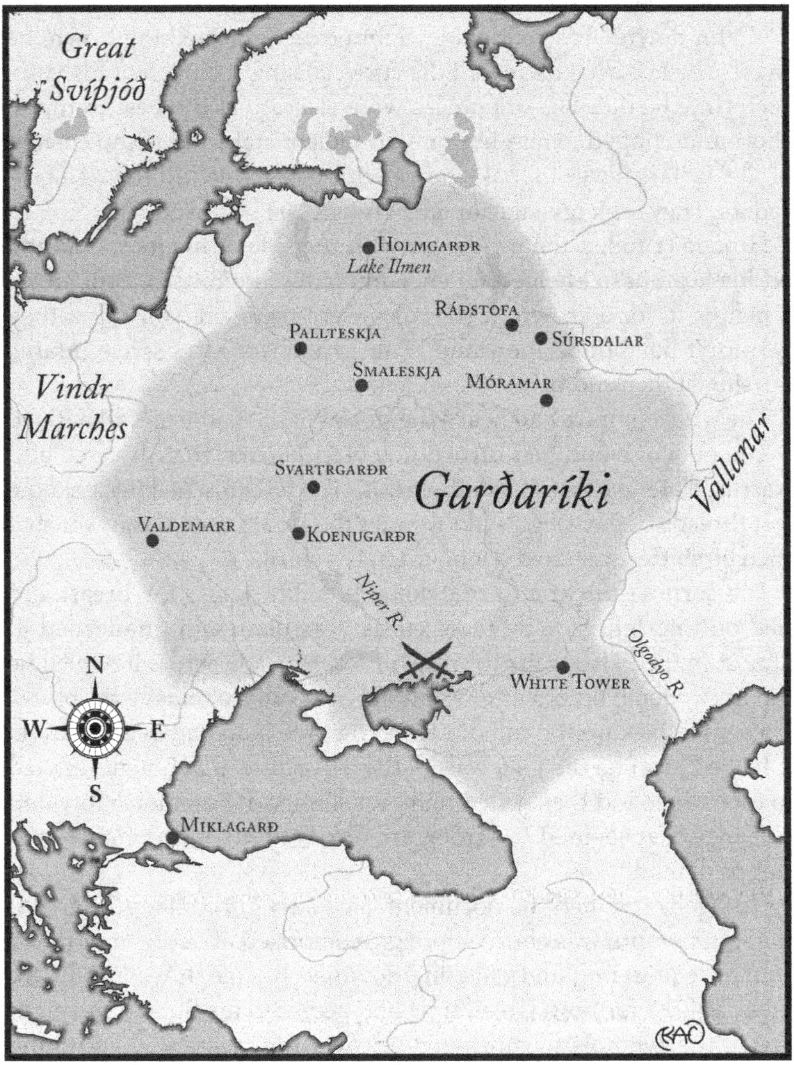

black against white—and the Kingsman confounded the eye as he hopped around like an ivory riddari.

Patterns. The whole world was a pattern, Hróðgeirr thought. Clues were everywhere, if only you could decipher them.

"Calm down," he said, when his friend re-emerged, but either Vilhjálmr wasn't listening or Hróðgeirr had mumbled the words to himself. Either were possible, he supposed—he had chest palpitations and would benefit from heeding his own advice.

"Calm down? Are you joking right now? Calm fokking down, he says." The Fríslander stressed the curse, raising the pitch of his voice each time he did. His utterances were staccato at the best of times, short and clipped, emerging now in violent stabs. "It is the custom of the Tartars never to make peace with those who kill their ambassadors. They seek revenge for such things," he bellowed.

Hróðgeirr rolled the head over with the side of his foot. "Cutting off his head hasn't helped much, admittedly," he tutted. "Still, in for a penny, in for a crown. If the roles were reversed, you think they wouldn't have done the same? The Tartar wouldn't spare infants nursing at their mothers' breasts."

The whole Empire had heard the stories of the Battle of Kalka River.

The pool of blood had turned to a black mirror, that shivered and fractured at the base of a nearby trunk. The tall, thin needles held the last threads of day's light—no wonder the local superstition was that each birch tree sheltered a long-migrated spirit.

The corpse's buckram tunic, folded double across the breast and tied on the right side by three cords, was plain and unadorned. It almost invited Hróðgeirr to wipe his sword blade across it, which he did in two long, fluid motions, one for each side, to remove the blood. He bent to pick up the roll of vellum that the man had been holding. It looked just like the geld rolls of the exchequer, parchments affixed to each other and then rolled tight, for storage. It has a formality and elegance that seemed to Hróðgeirr incongruous in the hands of a steppe nomad.

Hróðgeirr scanned the document. He had a gift for languages, but the script within was entirely foreign, comprised of oddly malformed squares squiggling and crawling down each page. It was unintelligible, at least for now. Given time and access to his library, he might match the symbols to runes and uncover the meaning. Everything had a pattern, after all.

There was a wax seal, already broken. Surprisingly, it was partially in Latin. "God in Heaven and Činggis Qayan over the Earth, the Power of God, the Seal of the Emperor of all Men." Hróðgeirr held his breath in anticipation. The scroll must be old, an ancient Kristin writing—a religious text, or a Mirror of Princes perhaps? One thing that was noticeable—the vellum was stained with tears. "He was as scared as we are," Hróðgeirr whispered. "At the end, at least."

Hróðgeirr unfurled the parchment and turned it over. There was a Latin translation on the reverse.... Ah, well then, there you have it, he thought, his hamingja was clearly making amends for the ambush. He began to read, savouring each and every word, fully aware that he was the only man in the North who might have the ability to do so.

From the King of Kings of the East and West, the Great Khan. To Danr the Ruishi, who fled to escape our swords.

Činggis Qayan and the Great Khan Ögedey have both transmitted the order of the Eternal God that all the world should be subordinated to the Mongols to be taken note of. Through the power of God, all empires from the rising of the sun to its setting have been given to us and we own them.

You have heard from both high and low what has befallen the world and its inhabitants, and what humiliation was visited upon great houses such as the Khvarazmshahs, the Saljuqs, the kings of Daylam, the Atabaks, and others through the power of the Everlasting Eternal God. You should think of what happened to other countries... and submit to us. You have heard how we have conquered a vast empire and have purified the earth of the disorders that tainted it.

We come with the power and the mission that all Christians be liberated from servitude and from tribute, from taxes and all things similar; that they be honoured and respected and that nobody lay hands on their property; that the churches that were destroyed be rebuilt, that the bells sound, and that no-one dare prevent those who adore the cross from praying for our kingdom with a tranquil and joyful heart.

Previously we have advised you, and we do so again now: refrain from rancor and obstinacy, do not attempt what you cannot do nor ignore what is manifest, for you will be sorry. Now, destroy your ramparts and fill in your moats; entrust the rule to your son, and come to us in person.

Where can you flee? What road will you use to escape us? Our horses are swift, our arrows sharp, our swords like thunderbolts, our hearts as hard as the mountains, our soldiers as numerous as the sand. Fortresses will not detain us, nor arms stop us. Your prayers to your gods will not avail against us. We are not moved by tears nor touched by lamentations. Only those who beg our protection will be safe.

Hasten your reply before the fire of war is kindled.... Resist and you will suffer the most terrible catastrophes. When I lead my army against Kyev in fury, whether you hide in the heavens or on earth, I will bring you down from the spinning spheres, and I will toss you in the air like a lion.

We will shatter your temples and reveal the weakness of your Spear-God, and then we will kill your children and your old men together.

At present you are the only enemy against whom we have to march.

Ah yes, thought Hróðgeirr. The pattern was very clear now. That kind of malice could only be preordained. Instead of the wisdom of the ages, he had uncovered an ultimatum. A death threat delivered by doom riders and night mares.

He felt quite light-headed, the birch trees suddenly even more suffocating, like a tunnel, bending towards him, burying him in branches.

"So...?" inquired Vilhjálmr. "How fokked are we?"

Hróðgeirr weighed his answer, using the question to steady himself. He extended his arm and patted his companion's shoulder amiably. Vilhjálmr of Rubekkr was a good and honest friend, one of the many Frísir he studied with. Like all Speakers, he kept his beard long, in deference the Teacher of Gods, Óðinn All Father. He'd been the first to congratulate Hróðgeirr on the news from the Pandidakterion—he'd visited Miklagard before, and offered his services as a guide, in return for recommendations when they arrived. Vilhjálmr the Elegant, they called him, his gold-hilted sword a mark of rare distinction. His family were obscenely wealthy and had practically rebuilt Oxifjord with the fortune they received at the time of the Munificence.

Of course, he reflected, they could have sailed through the Miðjarðahaf and seen the ruins of Romaborg en route. What quirk of fate made him change his mind? What made him retrace the march of history and take the Varangian route, following the trail of Botulfr the Conqueror through the rivers and portages of the Rus? The Kristins and the Musulmen might have called it a peregrination or a pilgrimage, and perhaps it was. Hróðgeirr meant not simply to visit the Great City to lecture, or to admire its treasures, but to encounter the All Father in the places where he revealed himself.

Instead, it appeared he'd found the one spot on Miðgarðr that the gods had well and truly forsaken. And so, here they were. Vagrants, beggaring belief in the riverlands of the Rus. The true horror was, there was so much of it. The treescape was endless. He'd heard the pristine monotony of the forest drew even gregarious men into silence, their companionable utterances dwindling until they could barely grunt in acknowledgement.

There was a thin groan from somewhere in the twilight, followed by the rustle of dead leaves.

"I thought you finished them all?" Hróðgeirr asked. The two men turned in unison to see a second Tartar clambering to his feet, his long, robe-like coat dark with piss, the air cloudy with foul-smelling steam.

"Be strong, because your punishment will not last long, and then at once oblivion will follow," Vilhjálmr said, striding toward him. He flashed his sword against the sky, a last sliver of light before an eclipse, and then the forest—and the envoy—was consumed by night.

Hróðgeirr nudged at the fresh corpse with his toe. This one wasn't even a Tartar by the looks of it—Mordmen or Mokshar perhaps; new vassals, their docility now tested by the Hrosslords. He wondered idly about how he might memorialize this moment, if he had to carve a stone or ink a verse. He flexed his hands in his leather gloves, trying to generate some feeling. It was a long time since he'd used a quill, and he grew anxious when his fingers went numb.

"Hlandbrenndu," he muttered, by way of elegy. May you burn from your own urine.

"Where are their horses?" he said, turning to his companion with the sudden realization. He had little hope of a worthwhile answer. Vilhjálmr was a Rúnameistar too, and though a practical man, he was used to workshops, masonry and metallurgy, not animal husbandry or tracking. The last time he'd been in a forest was presumably to fetch firewood as a boy.

Vilhjálmr duly shrugged.

Hróðgeirr tried a different approach. "Can you find your way back to the lake?"

The Frísir shook his head. "At first light perhaps, not now."

"Then, can we risk a fire?"

"Aren't you full of questions! Unfortunately for you, my friend, I have very little in the way of answers. As to the fire, I'm not sure we have a choice in the matter," came the hesitant reply. "If there are more Tartar across the lake..."

Hróðgeirr grimaced. "Would you rather freeze to death? Why don't you stop pacing and help me?"

Both men's nerves were clearly frayed. Hróðgeirr tried to focus in on the task at hand, hoping to stem the rising sense of panic. There were scattered twigs and detritus, but anything useful as kindling was buried by the recent snowfall. He dug into his pouch, and snagged a small paper gourd, containing some grey powder. Khitai snow, some of his fellow scholars called it. Essence of Thunder. He poured a small pile of the powder onto a fabric square and placed the cloth onto a nest of tinder. The powder flared up long enough to dry out the damp tinder and set it alight.

Thank Thórr, he'd perfected the formula before he left England. The priests weren't too happy to have lightning caged up in a flask, but the vote of the King's Assembly had been almost unanimous, more swords brandished at the wapentake than anyone could remember. The gods had no domain over science, they decreed, the rattling and thumping of swords and staves a passable imitation of the Thunder God himself.

He'd retained most of his possessions, despite the mayhem. His pocket watch had fallen overboard when the boat tipped over, but he was reassured that he still had his farseeing tube, the convex eyepiece mercifully unscratched.

Hróðgeirr watched his friend carefully, to see if something had snapped. The Frísir's scarlet cape and magnificent Rus hat had been torn from him in the melee, and he looked gaunt, withered even, without his finery.

"You'll catch your death," Hróðgeirr said, with as much softness as he could manage in the circumstances. "Here, try this." The Tartar hat looked warm, two flaps of sable hanging down to protect the ears.

"It stinks. Óðinn on his high seat can probably smell it in Ásgarð," his companion said, retching theatrically for emphasis. He tossed it back.

The first Tartar had worn a plush felt cone, with a turned-up rim of fur and embroidered silk. It was clearly ceremonial, rather than practical, and now boasted some more... visceral adornments, but the Englishman knew his friend well.

"This then... fit for a Kingsman," he said.

"Fit for a queen maybe," the Frísir said, inspecting it reluctantly before trying it on. He looked ludicrous, like a court fool forced to cavort and cartwheel against his will.

"Perhaps we should have kept one alive? For questioning," he mused, once he had strapped it in place.

"We have the scroll," the Englander answered, resisting the temptation to unfurl it again. That way madness lied, he thought. "Prisoners escape. Besides, we need his boots or my feet are done for."

"Charming spot, inspiring prospects," Vilhjálmr said, dolefully. "You haven't answered me—about the parchment. We must be royally fokked."

"There's no point losing heart now. Quit blathering and help me see what else they might have," Hróðgeirr deflected.

"I'm not touching them." The Frísir folded his arms and sat down, peremptorily.

"We just beheaded them!" Hróðgeirr said, incredulous.

"That was different." Vilhjálmr waved his sword for emphasis, ever the Kingsman.

"It's not a vote!" Hróðgeirr snarled, losing his temper.

"Nevertheless, I vote no," Vilhjálmr shouted back, staring in defiance.

Hróðgeirr wanted to scream at him but was worried about what might be lurking in the shadows. He set to the task himself. The Tartar had other possessions worth taking. Coats lined with fur. Underneath that, a heavy silk undershirt, that might stretch to fit either of them. Their boots were made from felt and leather, with thick fur-lined soles—though heavy, they would be comfortable and wide enough to accommodate Norse trousers, if tucked in before lacing tightly. They were heelless, though the soles were thick and lined with fur. Worn with felt socks, the feet were unlikely to get cold. There was a small mercy at last.

Hróðgeirr stripped them of what he could, then left the bodies to the snow. They divided up the clothes equally, doubling up over their own to keep warm.

"Do you remember your Hávamál?" Vilhjálmr asked, as they dressed. His friend was calmer now, more reasonable, but Hróðgeirr was still resentful. Money didn't buy manners, it seemed.

"Of course, I do. Don't start quoting me."

"I was going to suggest a translation game to pass the time till morning. Snorri Sturluson hasn't retired yet. You'll need your edge sharp in Miklagarð."

"You want to debate grammar here? Now?" Hróðgeirr said, surprised for the second time by his companion's almost child-like insouciance.

"Just passing the time till morning," the Kingsman said. "It is reason which leads us to salvation."

They lapsed into icy silence. At least in the darkness, it was easy to imagine they were somewhere else. Anywhere else.

After some time, Vilhjálmr spoke again: "What do you think they want? The Hrosslords. Why have they come again, out of the Wide Plains?"

"The Tartar mean to conquer the entire world if they can. I wonder if there is a land in the world which they have not taken, but we can be assured they are now preparing to take ours. And I think they have taken exception to the Munificence. They want the churches back..."

"The Hrosslords are fokking Kristins!?!" Vilhjálmr shrieked so the whole forest could hear him.

The Rus have a saying, that the future is written in the water. Perhaps it was a superstition borne of interminable tedium, either the slow sweep of oars across brackish water or the drudgery of subsistence, casting lines to hook bream, smelt, or pike. The fishwives took to throwing stones to the lake spirits for good luck, drawing symbols of their Vindr gods on the surface to ward off evil.

But not even the greatest spae-wife could have peered into Lake Ilmer and foreseen the confluence ahead.

Hróðgeirr had hired oars out of Nygarð, knowing full well they wouldn't make it before the snows, but hoping that Smaleskja might offer some respite from the gambling debts Rubekkr managed to accrue in the lake towns.

Lake Ilmer would take a full day to row across. The far silt-shore was low and marshy, home to a hundred fishing huts and moorings, and a dozen tributaries siphoning the water to the south. Now with the onset of winter, the water level was at its lowest, and the first ice had begun to form. There were six boatmen, who took turns warming their pernicious hearts by telling a hundred cruel tales to their visitors. The ubiquity of the Northern tongue made academic exchange easy across the Commonwealth, but other languages persisted in frozen nooks like this, and the Speaker was glad to practice his Vindr.

They spoke of the long talons of winter, poised to strangle the lakelands; about Sjöfru, the mistress of the lake, who rose to engulf the unwary in her watery embrace; about a certain land to the north, where men had human heads but the faces of dogs, a people condemned to speak only a few words of human speech before it was interspersed with barking.

"Sounds just like Oxifjord," Vilhjálmr had laughed, recalling the drunken brawls during debates at the university.

Then, the Rus's faces darkened, and they told sagas about the Vatamen, the scourge of the northern waterways, who slithered like serpents from the reeds—pirates preying on the unwary. As the afternoon wore on, the coxswain turned his stories to the Taurmen, wild beasts out of the Wide Plains who ate the flesh of the strong and drank the blood of noblemen. Each of the previous denizens of darkness had been inhuman and beastly, but the Taurmen caught Hroðgeirr's attention. They dressed in ox-hides, armed with plates of iron. They were thickset, strong, invincible, indefatigable.

To hear the oarsmen tell it, this was a land without human laws, with terrors more ferocious than lions or bears. Once maybe, when the Garðaveld was no more than a line of fortresses and earthen works at edge of the world. But these days, it was an empire of bustling burghs—Nygarð, "the New Settlement," was hundreds of years old.

Superstition and ignorance bred mournful tales. Or perhaps, they invited them. As the Frísir said, talk of the Trickster, and you step on his tail.

Hróðgeirr sifted through his memory, trying to piece together events. They'd almost crossed the lake when he saw the boats—long, thin, flat-bottomed, each carved from a single trunk. Snakes in the reeds. The Vatamen were extremely well armed and provisioned, clearly professional warriors, who'd grown rich from plundering the trade in furs. They were probably in league with the idle fisherfolk they had passed.

The first boat was carved with the figurehead of the Isbjörn, the Ice Bear, bearing thirty bloodthirsty men, outnumbering his own escort five to one. Each raider had his own sword and spear and menaced the rowers with crossbows. The irony of pirates preying on the Viking Empire was not lost on Hróðgeirr; you had to assume raiding was in the blood. But they hadn't expected to encounter them so close to Holmgarð. Evidently, neither had the pallid coxswain, who had croaked the warning about Vatamen earlier in the day. He looked dumbfounded, reduced to mouthing obscenities at his crew.

At the very same time, the travellers saw the horsemen, perhaps twenty of them, aiming to cross the river in convoy. On the far western shore of the lake was a tall, naked cliff-ledge, the Ilmer Glint. From a distance its reddish limestone rocks looked like the ruins of the fortress wall. Perhaps that's where the horsemen were headed, mistaking it for a bastion of civilization, for elsewhere, there was nothing but the faint, grey horizon, settled like a shroud on the land. The horsemen had bundled up their bags and saddles, all trussed together, into a rudimentary boat of their own, and driven their steeds into the icy water. The whole group followed, one after the other, each man on his leather vessel, tied to a horse's tail. Every warrior had two long, horn bows, three quivers full of arrows, and at least the same number of horses tied together with thick ropes.

It was an unfortunate and deadly mixture, the perfect combination of explosive elements. An accident on top of an ambush.

Hróðgeirr remembered thinking that it was unusual for hailstones to fall from a cloudless sky, and took to examining the ripples before he realized the sudden downpour was comprised of arrows, their heads exceedingly sharp, cutting both ways like a two-edged sword. Three of his oarsmen were skewered in seconds.

Vilhjálmr had the presence of mind to capsize the boat. Either that or he fell overboard in a panic and tugged at the gunwales for protection—the result was the same. The barrage continued unabated, wound wasps hitting the upturned keel. Inside, the remaining oarsmen paddled as fast they could—to those on the surface, the ship must have seemed to glide forward invisibly, as though driven by Ægir himself.

The Frísir's second act of mayhem was also inspired. He thought to hurl one of his small arsenal of thunderclap bombs—a stoppered iron gourd filled with a mix of saltpeter, sulphur, lime and willow charcoal. Upon meeting the water, it exploded with Thórr's own vitriol, the sulphur bursting into flames. The iron case rebounded and broke, scattering the lime to form a smoky fog, which blinded the eyes of men and horses alike. Some of the foemen drowned there and then, their leather boats the billows burden. Sjöfru must have been happy with her haul.

The Vatamen had fared little better. Some of the pirates were fighting bitterly in the shallows, matching blows against the wicked, curved steel of the surviving horsemen, but most boats made a hasty retreat when they saw the thunderclap. They hadn't survived the wilds without understanding when the odds were long.

Hróðgeirr gained the bank as the snow began to fall in sheets; Vilhjálmr waded after him, cursing the perfidious weather. The boatswain and his mate made the shoreline at the same time, only to fall prey to an arrow that whispered through one man's chest and shuddered into the other, leaving them both gasping their last. The snow brought an eerie, hushed quietude to their dying moments. The blinded men were an easy matter for the two Northerners to dispatch. They went purposefully among their foes, ending each life without hesitation or mercy as they stumbled across the pebbles. Within minutes, all the foes had either fallen or fled, all too easy to spot among the needles of the forest. Especially the one with the bright, pointed silk hat...

The next morning, the two fellows made their way back to the lake, climbing the escarpment to get the best view of the untrammeled wilds beyond the lake. With his farseeing glass, Hróðgeirr could see farther than Heimdall himself. The Ilmer Glint rose like a great wall, the foundations made of brick-red sediment with bands of yellow stone above, as high as any fortress. The snow shone like a silver treasure in the dawn sun, spun through with the river's golden filigree, and the trees seemed like Serkir carpet, uniformly woven from shadows, decomposing leaves and frozen bark.

Hróðgeirr had been born near the old Róm fort of Givelceastre near the Sumortūn Levels, a similar huge track of wetlands. It was remote but not insignificant: the last of King Alfred's resistance had died nearby, floundering in the swamps of Iley Oak. But, by all accounts, life had proceeded much as before—orderly and well-measured.

Ah, for those halcyon days of yore! Endless balmy afternoons, warm mead and knattleikr on the village green, spilling out onto the old Rómar road. All England's villages had a green, a place of assembly, surrounding the Thingmote. Givelceastre was no different. The elders took their seats on the hill above and proclaimed the laws and determinations of the assembled freemen, bound to keep the peace through mutual surety. His father had been both Master of the Mint and the tithingman for the Hundred—nothing like the wealth of Rubekkr, but comfortable, nonetheless. Hróðgeirr had always considered the Northern Conquest as more continuation of the past, like rekindling a lost friendship from childhood.

The Fall of Miklagarð was a different order of magnitude. The seat of the Imperial Róm for nearly a thousand years, the annexation had provided inordinate wealth for the Northern Empire. Monumental sculptures, countless artworks, and priceless jewels were all stripped away or melted down for coinage. Even the tombs of emperors were opened and their precious contents removed—furniture, doors, and marble taken away for reuse elsewhere.

Botulfr the Great had disbanded churches, monasteries, priories, convents, and abbeys in every corner of Kristindómr he conquered, appropriating their income, and redistributing the land to his thegns and thingmen. The Extirpation of the Monasteries, or simply, the Munificence as it was often recorded, particularly benefited the Frísir, who had stood vigilant for so long at the gates of the Frakkar. A whole new apparatus of state was called for. The Urðr set up Wards of Surveyance and Augmentation to dispense justice to treasonous abbots.

The most valiant húskarls were singled out for imperial favour, their houses benefitting from vast endowments. Of course, the Golden Freedoms remained, all bondsmen considered to have equal rights before the law and the elected king. But some seemed to have more equality than others.

Prizes were not reserved just for those who made the raven glad. When the fylkir threw open the Grikk Imperial Library, his skalds descended on the loggia of marble, devouring manuscripts and ancient writings that had been steadily accumulated by emperors over a millennium.

They called it the Enderborin, the rebirth.

The Varangian Hansa profited immensely too, their trading posts growing into new colonies, commerce igniting new industry from the paper mills of Hringrborg to the Arsenal at Fenney.

The Kœnugarðr Kontor and warehouse was the beating heart of all river-borne trade that crossed the great Rus plains. Textiles, wood carving, armour production, engraving, and smelting all took place at the City of Ships. The monopolization of the Nipr route ensured that the Enderborin arrived in the Garðaveld long before the rest of the Empire.

In fact, Kœnugarðr was one of the largest centers of civilization in the Commonwealth, with perhaps fifty thousand inhabitants, linked by the Nipr to the Svartahaf and from there to the Great City itself.

Hróðgeirr realized, unless they gave the city time to prepare, Enderborin or no, it would be razed to the ground by the Tartar.

From the bluff, they could see a few scattered horses, some still tied together by Tartar ropes. The lens marked them out distinctly. They were short and stocky, ranging through black to chestnut, with shaggy pelts.

"Can we catch them, do you think?" Hróðgeirr asked. He didn't intend to ride them as the Hrosslords did. In the snow, sledges were preferable to boats. With the weather turning, it was only a matter of days, hours even, before they could use the frozen rivers and marshes to make the journey south with relative speed.

"They'll be as blind as Höðr. The lime in their eyes—they are food for the blood gulls now. So, will you be if you don't put that thing away. Any road, we can't wait here until the Rus winter freezes our pricks," said Vilhjálmr, picking up the pace. "We have no choice but to retrace our steps. Winter in the Holmgarðr fortress. Ask King Halsand to send word to Uppsala."

Hróðgeirr nodded, and they began to trudge back north, debating the military applications of refracted vision to pass the time.

On the third day, they saw the boats. It looked at first like Halsand had summoned the leiðang, conscripting men and their ships to defend the city. But it soon became clear they were all moving, en masse, twenty or more, a flotilla of refugees.

There were the nimble chaikas darting ahead, broad-sailed lodyas manned with grim soldiers, and sea-faring shnek crowded from stem to stern with jagged, unkempt faces. There were even a handful of roughhewn korabls, little more than rafts, pushed along by long thin poles.

The ice was already thickening at the edge of the lake, gouging the hulls of any vessel that didn't stay in the central channel.

"Turn back, turn back!" came the cry across the water, directed at the two footsore travellers.

Soon the stream of ships became a torrent, riding a great roaring wave of fear from the north.

The alarm was soon echoed on the shore as well. First, a woman, carrying a child under each arm, stumbled past them, murmuring indistinct prayers. Then, a horse and cart drawn by a sweating black pony came trundling along, the wheels repeatedly sinking into snow-filled ruts in the path. Where the lane grew narrow by the edge of the water, a crowd was jammed behind the cart. A desperate struggle had ensued between the driver and his passengers on the one hand, and the irate mob behind them.

"Make way! Make way!" A guardsman thundered past on a piebald cockhorse, slashing his whip. Other soldiers were trying to keep order at a nearby fishing jetty, as villagers fought savagely for whatever safe passage they could find. "They're coming!" a woman shrieked. All at once, everyone was pushing at those in front, bolting blindly like a flock of sheep. In an instant, anger gave way to terror.

One man in his nightgown fell underneath the cart. The hoof missed his head by a hair's breadth, but the wheel passed over his back. He let out an ear-splitting cry then lay, writhing and screaming in the mud. The cockhorse reared and staggered sideways, tipping the guardsman into the lake. An overburdened fishing boat, violently rocked, capsized, sending more of the Rus to flounder in the water. The shoreline quickly became a quagmire.

Hróðgeirr waded into the water and hauled the spluttering guardsman to his feet. He could guess what was causing the exodus, but he wanted to hear the words.

"What is happening?" he yelled, struggling to make himself heard above the bedlam. "Who is coming?"

"The godless sons of mares have taken Móramar by storm," the guard wheezed. The man was distracted, looking around wildly for his mount. "They encircled the city and fought without surcease for five days."

"I don't understand," said Hróðgeirr, genuinely puzzled. Móramar was a border city, ten days away or more along the Olgodyo River.

"Nygarð has opened its gates freely to the Tartar, lest it suffer the same fate." the guardsman shouted over his shoulder. "I'll take my chances on the open road!"

Vilhjálmr stopped another man, and a third, fighting to keep his feet as he battled through the crowd, asking any soldiers he could find for news. Finally, he found a gore-caked priest, ringing a bell listlessly as he marched, and implored him for answers in Óðinn's name.

"There was a city of Súrsdalar, and its wealth disappeared, and its glory departed, and no blessings of it could be seen in it—only smoke, earth, and ashes. There was neither singing nor ringing in the city; instead of joy—unceasing crying." The priest stared with lusterless eyes.

Hróðgeirr fought his way to his companion, jostling and shoving until the two men could talk. "Tartar?" he yelled.

His companion nodded, earnestly. "We must get off the road. We cannot get to Holmgarð." Hróðgeirr was within inches of his friend's face, squeezed together by the maddened crowd.

"Presuming it still stands." Vilhjálmr agreed, and they turned back, joining the desperate throng on the lakeside, fully aware that they had no real choice or plan. As they trudged back the way they came, they pieced together the events of the past week from snippets of conversation and brief exchanges between the vanquished. It was difficult to determine the truth, but the story that emerged was one of utter devastation.

The Prince of Móramar had manned his walls bravely, but without relief, the town was doomed. On the dawn of the sixth day, the Hrossmen began to storm the city, with firebrands, battering rams, and countless scaling ladders. They killed all the goði and gyðja, without exception. And they burned the palace with all its beauty and wealth.... Not one man remained alive, there was not a soul to mourn the dead.

The Wind Riders next advanced in great force down the frozen rivers and streams and approached Súrsdalar with a mighty host of soldiers such as the Rus had never seen. The Tartar set up catapults for firing against the city, hurling their missiles day and night without cessation, until they breached the city's walls. Lance broke against lance, shield scraped against shield as the besiegers met the besieged in mortal combat. Then a barrage of war needles eclipsed the light of the defeated Rus. The inhabitants threw up new fortifications around the Temple of Frigg. The next day the Tartar attacked them, until all that was left was carnage and wine for the ravens. Súrsdalar, the once-great city, was destroyed like Móramar before it.

The Eastern Princes, Valdamarr and Vissivald, collected what troops they could, gathering at the timber fort on the Moskvě, but were encircled and slaughtered, the Taurmen cutting down the Rus like grass.

The lands of the Winter King had a deceptive beauty to them; the snow kept hidden the worst ravages of war.

The trees were full of plump wood grouse, feeding on the needles and buds, avoiding the cold ground. Occasionally one would whistle between branches. They were fat, ungainly fliers, sedentary and slow, easy prey for goshawks and wolves.

"The other birds have had the good sense to fly south," Vilhjálmr scowled, the symbolism not lost on either of them. "I've seen enough of the lake to last me a lifetime."

Hróðgeirr guessed the ambassador's entourage had been sent ahead to secure surrender and limit resistance—perhaps they had delivered a similar message to Nygarð before their skirmish. The whole of the Garðaveld now lay undefended, the Tartar able to strike where they chose. Not counting the marshland, there was almost literally nothing between them and Smajenksa, and beyond that, Kœnugarðr.

"Three lifetimes at least," laughed Vilhjálmr.

"Perhaps it will drive the Tartar mad and they'll turn back?"

"I doubt it. The Hrosslords are masters of the Wide Plains. Their land stretches farther than a hundred of your farseeing tubes might see. In their country there are no villages or cities, except one, and that is named Caracoron."

"Who told you that?" Hróðgeirr asked. The column of refugees might have gathered some collective knowledge, but generally couldn't see further than their noses.

"A traveller hears tales in the markets of Miklagarð. After the Fall, the People of the Book—Kristins, Gydar, Múslimar—plenty of them fled beyond the Lindibelti, poured through Yngvar's gate into the Land of Wolves. No wonder they now ride back, snapping at our heels like Freki and Geki. They have made common cause with the Taurmen, Torkmenn, and Uzes. Peoples held at bay since Sveinald Ingvarsson took the White Tower."

Hróðgeirr knew lots of Kristins at Oxifjord, some of them on reasonable terms. In the years that followed the Munificence, strenuous efforts were made to cajole Krossmenn to surrender, and, while some of them were executed, and others starved to death in prison, those of scientific temper spread their insights and understandings across the Commonwealth, commanding exorbitant wages, trading piety for extravagance. A holy war would have been anathema to them.

"One day, I hope it is possible to make a device for flying; a man might turn a crank and cause artificial wings to beat the air after the fashion of eagles' flight," Hróðgeirr said. "Anything that gets us out of here."

They didn't sleep that night, not because of the cold, but simply because they were afraid. They huddled with the gap-toothed peasants and foul-smelling fishwives, with the forlorn priests and broken soldiers. Hróðgeirr thought he recognized a Vataman in their company, leaning on his crossbow in the shadows. With the spreading ice, the whole Lakeland was sunk in ruination.

The climb to the Ilmen Glint was treacherous now. More snow had fallen in the night, although the morning proved clear and cloudless. Having gained the high ground, it was obvious that the flotilla of refugees had reached the limits of their vessels—the passage south along the Lovat river had already iced over and the illusion of escape was now ended. Hróðgeirr took up his farseeing tube, surveying the whole scene. A huge sickle-shaped crescent had formed: the larger ships at anchor, smaller vessels drawn up onto the icy shore. Some had been smashed for firewood. The rich or the well-prepared had set off with pale-eyed huskies, leaving the bedraggled and destitute to fend for themselves. They were sitting ducks, although even the ducks knew you didn't fight the Rus winter.

Hróðgeirr swung his eyepiece north and gasped in horror.

The line of Tartar was ten wide, and hundreds deep. Both man and horse wore a cuirass of leather and iron, polished and gleaming in the brightness of the morning.

Someone else on the Glint had seen the shapes on the horizon, much more dimly, but enough to recognize what they were. There was one long, full-throated cry of anguish and then hysteria erupted across the escarpment. People ran, shouting and screaming like farmyard animals, scattering in all directions, some foolhardy or desperate enough to scramble down the face of the limestone bluff. The crescent of boats below began to writhe and convulse, as the great throng slithered into the birch forest.

The Wind Racers advanced at a gallop. At the rumble of a drum, each man began nocking and releasing arrow after arrow from a still-staggering distance. Their bows were machines of laminated horn, wood, and sinew. They appeared to be riding from all directions at once, stars falling from the heavens showering the earth below.

"It will be a massacre," Hróðgeirr called.

"Worse," his companion said, watching intently. "The Hrosslords aren't shooting at people. If they intended to kill, they surely would. They mean to herd them to the next city as human shield and bridges." Hróðgeirr turned to offer him the scrying device, but Vilhjálmr was already sprinting down the hill after them, making his way down the sheer wall in bravura leaps and bounds. Hróðgeirr hastily tucked away his instrument and plummeted after him.

The Kingsman was clearly aiming to intercept a sled passing by the foot of the bluff, nearest to the shore. It stood before them on the snowbound beach, not far from where they had battled with the envoy's entourage, blocking their path. The driver had evidently been slowed by some unseen obstacles—the rigid bodies of the dead, buried by winter's thin blanket. Vilhjálmr reached him in a moment.

"This Englander," he shouted. "He must get to the Grand Prince. He has a message of the utmost importance." His eyes were ardent, shining with the darksome fire of determination. He manhandled Hróðgeirr into a nest of furs and leather sacks, staring down the complaints of the driver and his passenger. The flash of his sword hilt was enough to signify rank—and to imply the penalty for insubordination.

"Climb on," urged Hróðgeirr, clambering upright.

"No room at the inn," his friend said, winking. "Be safe, be quick. Hróðgeirr Bakko must survive these incursions; more than you know is at stake. Get the message to Kœnugarðr. Raise the defences."

"What? Where are you going?"

"Straight to Valhöll, I imagine. *Morior invictus*," he said, flashing a grin before turning once more into the flood. Vilhjálmr was immediately engulfed in the stricken tide but kept his feet and marched on. Hróðgeirr heard him roar above the din, "Men of the Rus! To me! To me!" and saw one last glimpse of his gleaming sword before the panting dogs got purchase and dragged them away.

It was said that Vilhjálmr fought so fiercely that his sword became dull, and so, taking a sword from a fallen Tartar, he would cut them down with their own blades. The Kingsman rode through the ranks of the Tartar regiments so bravely, impervious to their arrows, the Rus thought that the Valkyries had ridden to the field. Even when encircled by their best troops, he cleft their champion with one blow, through to the saddle... And finally, when the Tartar began to tire against this drengr, they set at him a multitude of tools for throwing stones and began to beat at him with rocks.

And when Vilhjálmr finally succumbed, even the Tartar king paid him homage, imagining him a winged demon, who did not know death. He gave the body to the people of the lake and ordered his regiments to let them go.

It was a story, of course, the stuff of sagas. Hróðgeirr waited, but in vain. Neither survivors nor Vilhjálmr of Rubekkr's body ever reached Kœnugarðr.

Kœnugarðr
1240

"I congratulate you on your genius, Meistar Bakko. Your... astrarium is full of artifice, created with a skill never attained by the expert hand of any mortal craftsman." The delighted Grand Prince clapped wildly, grinning through his great black bush of a beard. There was a general murmur of approval from the assembly, a few studious coughs and nods of agreement. The prince persisted in his applause until others joined in, the sound reverberating across the vaulted ceiling of the Great Hall.

Hróðgeirr took a moment to bask in the salute. It was especially gratifying coming from Grand Prince Danr, one of the only men to have fought the Tartar Horde and lived to tell the tale.

"Sovereign of All Rus, I have desired nothing so much as Your Serenity's love. I am, as ever, your vassal. Ask and you shall find me ready to do you service," he replied with a deep bow.

"Come now, Speaker of Marvels. Nothing can become a wise man less than boasting, but do not be a hnøggr with your knowledge. Tell my thegns of your accomplishment!" The Grand Prince all but hauled his guests to the central dais.

The machine stood about a metre high and consisted of a seven-sided brass frame, resting on half a dozen decorative paw-shaped feet. Admittedly, it looked like a conundrum wrapped in a puzzle—there were a variety of dials, all gilded or enameled, and a large calendar drum, showing feast days, and the position in the zodiac of Máni. There were countless wheels and pinions, some the width of a goose quill, others the thickness of a knife blade, all whirring and winding constantly. And in the middle of the whole contraption—and most confounding of all—was a brazen head, gazing mournfully back at the crowd, his long beard grown to the floor, like the King Asleep in the Mountain. The effigy wouldn't have looked out of place sheltering in a tomb.

Silent orbs spun above the head, approximating the motion of the planets—Frigg's morning star in conjunction with the baleful eye of Óðinn. Ever the antiquarian, Hróðgeirr had toyed with the idea of using the ancient Latin names, to resurrect Jupiter and Venus into the night sky, but the prelates would have none of it.

The scholar appraised the rows of reluctant faces. All the great men of the City of Ships had been summoned, and they stood, surrounding his newest invention with a mixture of polite indifference and confusion. He could almost read their minds—whatever this astrarium was, it wasn't business for a War Moot.

Each dignitary wore his finest livery—fox furs, bold yellow silks, and bright blue brocade—colours that had adorned the hall since Valdamarr gamli was the Great Konung of Kyiv. It seemed less a council of lords and more of a peacock's parade. The Prince himself wore a headdress that ballooned from his head, more akin to a Serkir turban than a Norse crown of state. Only his eyes, ridden with cunning, provided a glimpse of his true steel. They called him Danr inn óði—the Mad Dane. As a young man, he had led the frenzied charge of the Rus across the river Kalka. He had been, not surprisingly, badly wounded—his right shoulder lacerated to the bone. Twenty years later it was still a source of constant pain.

But the byname wasn't given in honour of his bravery, or in recognition of the battle. It had come to signify the prince's passion and inspiration, his championing of invention. He was possessed by the spirit of the Enderborin. There was no doubt that Hróðgeirr's scholarly ambitions had been imperiled by the war—the chair at the Pandidakterion seemed ruefully out of reach now—but he had, at least, found a patron willing to invest in his talents.

"Don't be shy," the Grand Prince said, beckoning Hróðgeirr over. "Tell them what you told me: man gains knowledge of matters of nature and alchemy through experiment. All that is Miðgarðr and the realms beneath, including the spells and wiles of conjurers and soothsayers, might be revealed in time. Think of that—we might even unmask the Urðr!"

"Your Serenity has been most gracious with his diverse gifts," Hróðgeirr acknowledged.

"Oh, I won't hear of it. You have a brilliant head on your shoulders. I am just glad to have been able to put it to use! All the great power of mathematics, built into these spheres.... In the presence of this instrument, all patterns are revealed—is that not so? All other apparatus, whether the product of wisdom or mere vulgar equipment, cease to count. I confess, the treasure of a king can scarcely merit comparison with it."

The Grand Prince was so enraptured, Hróðgeirr started to feel embarrassed.

Amongst the assorted thegns and thingmen, Hróðgeirr saw a handful of familiar faces. The boar-helmeted Markgreff Steinviðr, newly arrived from Jomsborg; Rulav, the weasel-faced Bailiff of the Kontor; Kári the Staller, sweating uncomfortably in his ceremonial carapace; and the Lord Warden of the Port, Ingjaldr, a man of very little brain, who owed his position to his imperial connections.

Hróðgeirr always thought it was something of an oddity that the City of Ships lay four hundred miles from the sea, but the majestic, swirling Nipr river could carry an armada. The river descended from the sedge bogs and uplands of Valday, until it was a mile wide as it rolled past the city—excepting the narrow gorge called the Wolf's Throat. It was a far cry from the lazy Temese river he had known as a young man, but the city had been his home, his sanctuary—and his laboratory—for the past three years.

"Raise the defenses," his friend had begged him. He could only hope he had done enough.

To some men, his invention represented the inevitable march of progress. To others, it was the enemy. Hróðgeirr expected to come under attack—unsurprisingly, it was the Markgreff who blundered into battle first. "Whose likeness is that? I do not recognize the face. It seems to me a hollow-mask—the eyes follow me across the room."

"I had modelled it on Oddgeir, the scourge of the Serkir, whose statue sits asleep in the casements of the castle," Hróðgeirr answered. "It is the metal that makes it seem a mirror—not a passive mirror of imitation but an active mirror of transformation. It invites the watcher to not mistake himself for a god, to avoid pride by knowing his limits." In truth, Hróðgeirr had based it on his memory of Vilhjálmr, but he did not want to appear sentimental in the company of the Jomsvikings. The astarium was a fitting tribute—the light of álfar, reborn from the darkness of the wolf's belly. It was a herald of a golden age to come, a rallying call to reason against the barbarism of the Tartar. Vilhjálmr would have been proud.

"Very pretty. Very hifalutin. But what does it *do*?" The Markgreff sneezed, wiping his huge nose on his embroidered sleeve.

Raise the defenses... Hróðgeirr longed to explain. He began to answer, but the prince waved him away and addressed the Markgreff directly.

"This organ, we call Mímir. Mímir the Rememberer, Mímir the Wise. With this creation, our Runemeistar has rivalled the Sons of Ivaldi, the dvergar smiths of legend. This machine has the power to hurl Mjǫllnir itself." The Grand Prince was clearly enjoying being gnomic and building suspense.

"Ingenious, I am sure. But, do tell me—how in the Nine Worlds will this... contraption... and its hammers help us defeat the Tartar who are marching on our city?!" Steinviðr thundered, suddenly unable to contain himself. His boar-crest was a beautifully stylized creature, with long slender legs and a gracefully arching back. The Markgreff himself was anything but; an aggressive snout, used to mimicking the explosive fury of a cornered beast.

"All in good time, my lord. I simply aim to whet your appetite before the real sword play begins," the Grand Prince said.

Hróðgeirr decided to let the Grand Prince defend his investment alone. He stepped discreetly to one side, and, obscured by his patron's voluminous headgear, sidled across to the window.

It was worthy of defending, he thought, gazing out into the midday sun. The view was magnificent. Hyperboreal, the ancients would have called it, a frost-rimed jewel in Skaði's frozen hall. The early settlers had seen seven majestic green hills on the steep right bank of the Nipr river, covered with kashtan trees and flowers, and built their citadel to protect themselves from nomadic tribes.

From his vantage point on the hill, he could see hundreds of angular rooftops, sheathed in shingles—steep so as best to shed the snow. The Rus were skilled wood workers, always finding ways to create strong, handsome structures—ornamental carvings displaying skills and wealth to neighbours. Below, Kœnugarðr was bustling. The air was hazy from the smoke of stoves... and the stench of dung. Even in time of peace, there was farming inside the city walls, so each stake-fenced yard seemed to contain horses, cattle, or svín in stalls and small plots for vegetables. Already overcrowded with ten thousand soldiers, the looming battle ensured the surrounding villages swarmed here like flies around a midden.

The raven banner had flown over Kœnugarðr since the age of Helgi the Seer. The Norse had united the scattered Vindr tribes and forged a great city that grew in size and strength in proportion to the predations of its warriors. The location was formidable, an imposing line of bluffs culminating in what was now Randgríd Hill, a name meaning the Shield of Peace, fifty fathoms above the river. The moniker was a misnomer, for the city was in the vanguard of wars for three centuries until the Fall of Miklagarð.

Later, Kœnugarðr's Grand Princes built their palaces and temples on Valdamarr Hill, a precipitous and wooded bank now topped by the golden domes and bell towers in imitation of the Great City to the south, while artisans and merchants settled next to the wharf on the Nipr. Here the City of Ships was protected by a shrine to Volos, the shepherd of the dead.

The Great Palace remained the dominant sight—the silver-headed thunder god, Thórr standing before the palace, flanked by the winged dog Semargl and Mokosh the Earth Mother. It was a mélange of elaborately carved white stone, the interior newly decorated with frescoes and mosaics by Grikk masters, with scores of small domes, reminiscent of Vindr temples and the Grand Mosques of the Serkir. Kœnugarðr stood at the cusp of the Empire, bordering two worlds, but there was no doubt that, in architecture at least, the marbled beauty of the south had triumphed over the warlike austerity of the north.

He turned back to the room. The discussion had quickly become fractious, with several voices raised in anger, as men who thought too highly of themselves struggled to be heard.

"He is a clockwork god..." said one man, a Keeper of the Robes if his ornamental dress was anything to go by. Hróðgeirr was used to all kinds of functionaries from his time on the King's Bench at Oxifjord, but the eastern regime was much more unorthodox.

"He? You ass! You have the temerity to trap the light of the álfar in a metal box?" said the Markgreff, turning violet with rage.

"The hunger of the álfar, rather," retorted the Staller, defending his Prince.

"In plain Norse, if you please, my lord," the Lord Warden simpered. The poor man was always last to grasp an idea, having been denied the benefits of a skaldic education.

Raise the defenses, Hróðgeirr felt like shouting. It really was that simple. This is what my friend gave his life for, you squabbling fools, he thought.

Throughout the exchange, a fourth man repeatedly rapped his staff on the stone floor, insisting on speaking—a godsman, his mantle and mitre decorated with sacral texts like a Grikk archimandrite.

"What seiðr is this? Sire, your lapdog has unmanned you with this impudence," he said, glowering. "Óðinn took the head of Mímir, embalmed it with herbs so that it would not rot, and spoke charms over it, and that was his right as the Lord of Songs. But this conjurer and his uncouth aphorisms has no such claim. It is an outrage! On whose authority?"

"A good question. I should also like to know the answer."

The voice was strident to the point of being shrill—it cut through the noise and commanded attention. The whole chamber turned as one, some men glancing over their shoulders, others spinning on their heels, issuing a collective gasp that would have been comical if they had not just as quickly taken to fawning on their knees. Hróðgeirr dropped to the ground instinctively, too, unsure if he was being obedient or obsequious.

The visitor was clearly a woman, although her face was obscured by a felt mask, held in place by a silver-embroidered silk band above her temples. She looked something like a wolf—pointed ears, a marked elongated snout with sculpted contours for nostrils, the felt brushed to give the appearance of fur. There was a large bronze key, mounted as a pendant, worn on a thread around her neckline, which plunged, open to her breasts. She held an iron rod, the bronze knob at the top gripped by the jaws of wolves, metal this time. The knob itself terminated in a ring, on which was threaded a silver hammer of Thórr. Over her dress the woman wore a woolen cloak lined and trimmed with beaver fur, fastened with two circular brooches, one bronze, one silver.

The High Urðr. Fresh as the driven snow, all the way from Miklagarð.

"My lords, you are debating whether a thousand dísir dance upon a needle's point when the Tartar will soon be hammering on your gates," the völva declaimed. Hróðgeirr wanted to cheer at that—someone with some sense at last.

She handed her cloak to servant and scanned the room to find the Grand Prince.

"Danr. My apologies for being tardy. Perhaps the Tartar intercepted my invitation?" She grinned, wolfishly. Given her garb, Hróðgeirr couldn't imagine any other suitable description. "Never mind, I am here now."

The Grand Prince offered a stifled bow. "We are grateful that the fylkir has sent us his finest," he said, with a cool politeness. Many in the assembly buried their faces in their cloaks, some drooped their heads markedly, clearly distressed, but trying not to show their fear. Silence had seized the thegns.

"Do not look to Miklagarð for further relief," the Urðr said. "The Emperor, too, is invested by the Tartar and his sómaherji vassals—a diversion, as with all things Tartar, meaning only to pin down our forces. It will take more than the Morguneyjar fleet to cause concern. Even Botulfr didn't break the walls of the Great City."

She added, with a seriousness that would brook no discussion, "I am afraid I came alone, and of my own volition. To see the war engines that you have taken such great pains to hide from the Ward of Surveyance."

The Grand Prince scowled at the slight. There was no love lost between the spymaster and the provinces. Hróðgeirr wondered if her claim to have ridden without any escort could be possibly true—any number of the Rus would dearly love to see her strangled in her sleep.

The High Urðr walked imperiously to the astrarium, her eyes hunting through the crowd as if searching for someone. Hróðgeirr kept his head down. The Priestess of the Sacrifice was bound to make an example of someone. It was said that the first of her Order had been born in the caves below the city—the Caves of Malfred, they were called, catacombs carved into the silt and sediment cast aside by the river, consecrated by the auguries of a thousand forefathers. The Urðr dwelt there still, in their covens. No man entered except bound with a chain—as an inferior acknowledging his subservience to the Fates.

"I see you have spent your electrum wisely," she guffawed. "Flying orbs! What will you do for an encore, encircle the city with a wall of brass?"

The machine emitted an effusion of vapors, as if hissing a retort.

The Grand Prince laughed. "Yes, as a matter of fact, you are quite correct, my Lady of Fate. We can always trust to you for sagacity."

Momentarily confused, the High Urðr offered her own stiff bow of thanks in return. She was clearly unaccustomed to pleasantries.

Hróðgeirr watched Danr work the room, his every utterance a rhapsody. He had never had much time for skalds, with their bloated tales of flowing blood, their fulsome flattery of the jarl of the hour. Court poets always posed as abject doting slaves, all the while continually hinting that they ought to be paid more for their lying panegyrics. But whomever had been in charge of the young prince's schooling had prepared him well—he had a fleet wit and nimble tongue.

"And so then to the order of the day. The great mountains begin to fall; pestilence rages among mankind; the peace is broken, and enmity is nourished between nations. But it is need that teaches the naked woman to spin," said the Grand Prince, deliberately baiting his adversary with a wink.

"As the Urðr say," he went on, "behind every great man is a greater woman. For what would Mímir be without his wife!" The Grand

Prince walked his guests out onto his balcony as he spoke. He thrust his armed to the heavens, then swooped low, drawing the assembly's gaze past the balustrade.

"I give you the pale nightmare, the eternal night... Sinmara herself," he declared theatrically. On the terrace below, somewhat masked by the tents of troops, were two great bulbous bottles, like hooped iron barrels turned on their sides. Each had a cluster of bolts protruding out of one end. The wind was grotesque, and none of the thegns could compete with its howling, so they stamped their feet and glowered through their whiskers as Danr went on.

"And this beauty is Gunnhild, our lady of battle." He pointed to the other ice-bound piece. "Named for my mother." He winked. "Meistar Bakko, would you please explain?"

"The bombard is lit like so," Hróðgeirr said, taking a poker from the fireplace. He tapped his forearm, and then unclenched his fist at the same time, spreading his hands to indicate an explosion. The motion didn't have quite the same grace as the Prince's mummery, but it was an effective distraction, keeping Hróðgeirr as the focus of attention.

Seconds after his cue, the bombards below boomed into life, belching fire and breathing poison across the land like the Fafnir, the terror. The noise was tremendous. Hróðgeirr imagined the whole city had stopped and puzzled, wondering what such a thunderclap could portend on a clear day.

Raise the defenses. Raze the enemy. After all, attack is the best form of defense.

"We can, with saltsteinn and other substances, artificially compose a fire that can be launched over long distances," Hróðgeirr said. "It is possible to destroy a town or an army with each bolt of this artificial lightning."

Now I am become Hellegrin, the wreck of the world, he thought. The men and women of the War Moot finally had something unarguable. They stood transfixed, humbled by the blast. Rumours of his thunderclap bombs had preceded him, but the bombards' power defied belief.

I should have warned them to stop their ears, he thought, his own still ringing.

He noticed the Urðr, fixing him with her stare. *So, you are the artificer?* she said, silently. Before he could answer, the Markgreff blustered past her question, unaware she had asked it.

"Truly, the Speaker of Marvels has a tongue of fire. I'll confess, I am impressed. But how does your cunning clock master his paramours?"

As far as most of the Commonwealth was concerned, Khitai snow was the same as Serkir naptha, or Grikk fire—it was dangerous, it was volatile, and it was foreign. "Long ways, long lies" was a familiar proverb in the minds of military men.

"Like all women, light their fuse and stand well back," some wag interjected, to the amusement of many, all the more so because of the intense irritation it provoked in the High Urðr. Hróðgeirr could see her eyes turn hostile behind the savage mask. He waited until the hilarity duly subsided, then answered the Markgreff.

"My lord, we will have time for a further demonstration soon enough. We have all seen engines of war; I have just imagined an improvement. Mímir is able to prescribe the parabola of my Gunhildr, or to lay in an elevation for Sinmara to unleash her great flood of fire. The machine is a ranging device—I call it a Dial Sight. It is shooting without seeing."

"That's a surefire way to miss the target!" Steinviðr protested.

"Draumskok!" the Grand Prince said, laughing. "The bombards will strike as surely and swiftly as Gungnir itself. That is the beauty of these dvergar devices." He smiled at the High Urðr like a lindworm feasting on a pig. "Especially now we have the Eyes of the Gods watching over us." He clearly thought he had secured the complicity of the sorceress and was delighted by his masterstroke. "And now, assuming the High Urðr is satisfied, I would like to propose that this gathering of the wise turn its attention to why we are all here. The defense of this great city."

"By all means," said the High Urðr, witheringly. "If that will provide you with solace. I have seen what I came to see."

And I can see why the Masked One chose you, she added. Hróðgeirr found that, with her mouth partially concealed, and her jewels coruscating in the light of the sun, it was difficult to see who she was talking to.

"A warning for you all. I have caused gandir to run far in the night, and I have now become wise to the movements of the Tartar," she said. "You have three days to make your plans."

With that, the woman turned and stalked towards palace servants rushing ahead of her to swing open the heavy oak doors. The assembly followed her as far as the Great Hall, thankful for being out of the biting wind.

"That—that *skoka*—is the Emperor's spymaster? I bet she doesn't see far when she has her blood in," the Lord Warden of the Port whispered as soon as the doors had closed.

"The Rus has stared at enough entrails these past three years, do you not think?" the Grand Prince said. "Where were the witch-wives at Kalka as my brothers lay slaughtered? That's what I would like to know! The Urðr can remain, festering, in their holes for all I care. The Emperor will be grateful when we deliver him from the Tartar without their help!"

"Has she gone to the caves then, with the other wenches? Her slatterns will make the vingull wet tonight!" laughed the Bailiff, inciting uproar. "Manvelar and love-spells are one thing; what do the real scouts say, Staller Kári?"

The Grand Prince nodded to Kári the Staller, who drew himself up to his full height and limped off to an antechamber. He returned with an intricately plotted map of the city, spread across a wooden shield for portability. The Staller placed it on the ground, and then as the council gathered round, he began to gesture with his sword. Hróðgeirr had heard the plans before, of course—he'd been instrumental in their design—but he was still taken by their elegance and simplicity. The preamble over, the thegns seemed relieved to be talking about battle at last, war being much more tangible than the gyrations of the astrarium.

The old marshall began, "As we know, to our cost, the Tartar fights more by cunning than by main force. They send forth troop after troop, always attempting to lure their enemy into his midst and so to surround them at a place of his choosing. So, the first rule of battle is— we must not and will not leave the safety of the great gates." He spoke with a tinge of sadness in his voice, as if weary to his bones, or already tasting the ashes of defeat. It was said he was the last of a long line of seneschals, a duty his family had borne since the days of Hvítserkr, but none of his ancestors had faced so great a threat as the Taurmen.

"Tartar scouts are always watching and devising how to practice mischief," he went on. "We gave chase to a troop of them this morning on the Smajenka Road. In days, the Tartar will attack Kœnugarð, as they must, at the wooden rampart by the Vindr gate. The rest of our walls are made of stone. They'll use the forests to screen their movements and set their catapults against us there. They will never suspect Gunhildr is trained upon their rear. We'll cast their arrows back at them!"

"And if we run out?" the godsman asked. "Of brimstone to fire his engines, I mean?"

Hróðgeirr saw a chance to interject. "I have developed a coarse powder that has pockets of air between grains, allowing fire to travel through and ignite the entire charge quickly and uniformly. The weapons have considerable range and longevity."

"And if they fail, we'll hurl granite, stones, even your miter if we have to," the Grand Prince added rousingly. The godsman half-choked, trying to maintain his dignity under the weighty bauble he wore.

The Staller looked up at him through thick-knitted eyebrows, then continued, prodding his map as if the interruption hadn't occurred.

"We will not sow the land for a long time. We have already fired the acres, which will have the consequence of leaving their horses with no forage. The Tartar need midwinter to cross the river. But they will not hold in the snows."

"We take them at the Wolf Throat and guzzle them whole. The Marksgreff and his Jomsvikings will lead a sally from the Sky Gate," the Grand Prince said, exchanging curt nods of agreement with his Vindr counterpart. "Encircle the Tartar for a change. They will flee to the river. And that is when we destroy the ice…"

That was Hróðgeirr's cue. "With more charges of thunder powder. I shall fashion fuses of wax paper for the task. As the thegn said, stand well back." The room laughed with newfound respect.

"The Kontor mariners will hold the shore. The Tartar will be trapped on the wrong side of the Nipr, or face ruin on the ice," the old warhorse finished, his gravelly tone providing suitable finality for the coup de grace.

"Let our warbands take this advice: if the enemy retreats, none are to make any long pursuit after him, lest, according to his custom, he draws them into some secret ambush," the Grand Prince said. "We'll have no repeats of Kalka. Tell your captains that both day and night they must keep their army in readiness, and not to put off their armour, but at all times to be prepared for battle. The Hrosslords will arrive within three days."

"Honoured Prince, the people know that Danr has fought many fierce battles—you have reddened the grey eagle's sharp claws in blood. I will commend your plan to the Jomsvikings… assuming we are not hoisted by our own bombards. I am sure that even Mímir cannot reconstitute the Rus from smithereens." The Markgreff grinned. His dander was up, and he was spoiling for a fight. "Just keep your guns pointed in the right direction, Englander."

"Do not be concerned, great general," Hróðgeirr said. The astrarium started to revolve in reply, its mechanism wheeling the brass orbs across the tracts of the heavens, the brazen head mouthing silently.

"My ingenious clockwork knows the will of the gods. We will not die this day."

Hróðgeirr watched the Thingmen leave, waiting until the echo of their confident footsteps and boisterous laughter grew too faint to hear. Then, with a sigh, he shuttered his machine behind lacquered wooden panels to keep it protected until it was needed. Lastly, he stepped gingerly back onto the balcony, to mentally map the defenses, replaying the Staller's ruses, stratagems, and ploys in his head. His two bombards overlooked one of the three main entrances to the walled city. The battlements that flanked the Vindr Gate were the only part of the city walls constructed of wood, and so formed a tempting target.

Hróðgeirr plucked his farseeing tube from his cloak and surveyed the horizon.

There was no sign of movement, but then the approach was masked by snow-topped forests of oak, maple, birch, and pine. While most routes to the city followed the river, there were also roads through the woods, paved with split logs to raise them above the mud. There had been discussion about razing the woodlands, but the city depended on them. Most buildings were constructed almost solely with an axe; trees were cut at this time of year and dried in the forest. He remembered his own approach, dashing through the trees, smelling wood smoke and hearing the ring of axes, long before seeing the town.

Beyond the city were the ancient Serpent Walls, earthworks fifteen feet high, fortified with redoubts at river crossings, built for the age of the Gotar King Filimer when the shining Árheimar held the waterlands. The Staller had left these unmanned, knowing that they wouldn't avail the horsemen, and being unwilling to split his forces.

The main fortifications were all the more impressive by contrast. The Golden Gate—a ceremonial arch the Rus called "the Sky Gate," as every morning the sun passed through it, seeming to rise and enter the vault of heaven—was nigh on impossible to scale or breach. From there Jarisleif's Rampart stretched across to the Gyðingr gate, encircling the whole city to the river, sixteen metres high and supported in most places by a moat. The wall itself was infested with icons and statues, its wide walled enclosures and inner cells often used to honour ancestor gods. The townsfolk fervently believed that sun and gods worked in unison to save the city from darkness and death.

Well, now they had Gundhildr and Sinmara to add to their list of saviors. *Raise the defenses, indeed,* Hróðgeirr thought, grinning. He'd raised them all the way to Ásgarð!

They came on the third day, just as the High Urðr had predicted. Word reached the palace that a Tartar ambassador stood at the Golden Gate in all his splendor, flanked by twenty horsemen. At first, the Mad Dane refused to open the gates an inch, adamant that he would never treat with excrement. Finally, after the pleas of widows on the steps of the Helgafell, he relented, his one concession to his people that he would ride out alone, taking only Hróðgeirr as a translator. After his long years of experience, he wouldn't countenance anyone else coming face to face with the fjándinn, the enemy.

Hróðgeirr was not unduly pleased to be given a second chance at diplomacy, but he strapped on his armour and rode out with the Prince, carrying his banner woven of the cleanest, whitest silk, the raven flapping its wings, beak wide open, and restless on its feet. That, at least, was a good omen, he thought.

The ambassador wore a long, silk robe decorated with sequins arranged in clearly meaningful symbols, under a voluminous fur coat. He sat on his horse, with nothing but emptiness and a hundred trampled kingdoms behind him.

"Take warning," the Hrosslord said imperiously, his nose in the air as if to avoid the stink of his enemies. "Surrender entirely to us, before the veil be taken off. For we shall have no mercy upon him that complains, nor be moved by him that weeps. We have wasted countries, we have destroyed men, we have made children orphans, and the land desolate. It is your business to run away; ours to pursue. Our horses are racers; our arrows strike home; our swords pierce like lightning; our fortifications are like mountains, and our numbers like the sand."

Hróðgeirr duly translated, the Taurmen using Latin rather than their own tongue. To his amusement, the Grand Prince simply rolled his eyes. The scholar wondered if he also found it hard to resist the urge to decapitate the envoy, to put an end to his boorish rant.

The ambassador continued, "God is against you, ye wicked wretches: we have given you fair warning, and fair warning is fair play. You have been perfidious in your treaties, you have introduced new heresies and thought it a gallant thing to commit sodomy. You take it for granted that we are infidels. We take it for granted that you are villains; and He by whose hand all things are disposed and determined hath given us the dominion over you. The greatest man you have is despicable among us; and what you call rich, is a beggar." The Prince didn't wait for any further translation. He drew up his horse and sauntered slowly back towards the city, leaving Hróðgeirr to relay his parting challenge.

"You speak too much, son of Svaðilfari. If you wish to test us, let us brandish our swords, so that they glitter in the air. This winter we have exploits to perform. With you, as with other peoples, I shall be called Fate, full of grieving songs. We shall scatter sparks among you and destroy you all from off the face of the earth."

It was an exhilarating experience, Hróðgeirr reflected, bandying words with barbarians. The Hrosslord smiled wanly, smoothing his moustaches. He clearly had the answer he had hoped for. With an almost imperceptible nod to the Englander, he wheeled his horse around and galloped away, back across the bright snow to the unseen armies of the Horde.

Hróðgeirr wasn't the least bit surprised to find the High Urðr waiting for him on his return. The whole city wanted to know what had been said out on the flood-meadows. Her powers of clairvoyance notwithstanding, the priestess would want a firsthand account, and she could hardly interrogate the city's sovereign. Besides, Danr had called the veche, eager to extol his plans to the burghers, and thousands had flocked to his princely compound near Rurik's Court for the address.

Hróðgeirr was a much easier mark, more so since Valdamarr's Hill was deserted.

What was unexpected was the manner of the greeting... it was friendly.

"Lector Mirabilis, I presume? I have been very desirous to see such a famous man," the High Urðr called.

The seiðrmistress was sitting astride one of the monstrous white marble lions in the courtyard, protected on all sides by Varangians in ceremonial armour—a dozen of them or more, giving the lie to her story that she had travelled to Kœnugarðr alone.

One of her guards came over to intercept him, taking the reins of his horse when he slowed, and inviting him to dismount with a tap of his sword. Mounted on the great beast, the High Urðr looked deceptively demure, like a bored child, trying on an air of innocence for play. Hróðgeirr was immediately wary.

Hróðgeirr knew something of the mystic arts—they involved the clouding of judgement, the freezing of the will, creating a gnawing hesitation. They also involved the summoning of spirits who could be bound to the sorcerer's will and then sent off to do her bidding, manifestations of her multiple soul. In England, practitioners of magic—cunning folk, they were called—were commonplace. There were Toad Doctors who could undo the curses of the dead, Girdle-measurers who diagnosed ailments caused by devious hulders, and a hundred other Charmers available for minor ailments like toothache or blistered feet. The Oxifjord brethren regarded them as quacks and frauds in the main, but they were mere hedge-wizards when compared to the High Urðr.

"Then my fame has given you a report that my poor studies never deserved," Hróðgeirr replied, aiming to be as deferential as possible. He wasn't sure if he was supposed to kneel, or even what the correct form of address was. It wouldn't do to insult an Imperial luminary, not if he ever wanted to lecture in the Palace Hall of Magnaura. A short conversation, then he could return to his preparations. He was sure she'd understand he had more pressing matters to attend to.

She slid down the creature's back and stood instead at the top of its pedestal. Unwilling to give up the high ground, Hróðgeirr realized. If she stepped to the floor, he would tower over her—she was not an especially tall woman, the mask being the most striking thing about her.

Like their mistress, the Miklagarðians kept their faces concealed—each wore a steel basinet with an ornate visor, shaped like a beak, perhaps to give the appearance of ravens. Next to the huge statue they looked more like pigeons, pecking at the frost-hardened ground. One of their number was busy scraping the shape of an elaborate lindworm scroll into the marble with his blade, memorializing his part in the war to come.

"Plundered from Atenborg," she said, tapping the marble statue with her rod of office. "The Grand Princes have never been much more than looters, if truth be told."

Hróðgeirr caught himself staring at the staff—he had never been this close to Miklagarð, and his curiosity got the better of him. He wondered what role it had to play in her fortune-telling. The High

Urðr followed his gaze and held up the rod for him to inspect more clearly.

"I am amazed you do not wield your own gandr, the wonders you perform," she said.

He appreciated the gesture but made light of her compliment. "Nitrate of potash, in the right quantities, that is all."

"And your scrying tube? Is it true that, with it affixed to your eye, you might count the number of grains of dust and sand at incredible distances?"

"Lenses—arranged so we can bend light to our will. Refractions and reflections. Many wise men are today ignorant of things which the common crowd of students will understand in the future. Reason is the guide of our will. It is reason that will lead us to salvation."

"Then we are in blissful accord! And my congratulations on your recent feats of diplomacy. Going head to head with the Tartar, not once but twice?"

"I have tried to learn their language as best I can, using what fragments I have," he said. "Bafflement does not translate well, and mastery is what a scholar seeks to demonstrate in a translation."

"Would it surprise you to learn that the Tartar had no writing of their own?" she asked. "They took up the script of the Huyrir, who they defeated in battle. The mongrels behave with other men in the manner of stallions. Rest assured the Urðr watch over the Empire vigilantly. We have our own ways of seeing. Just this morning, I have, in the hamr of a horse, driven them away from your Gunhildr, with the aid of the landvættir. There is an unseen war at play."

"What else have you learned?" he asked, genuinely intrigued. He had imagined he would be debriefing her and was amused to find his conjecture turned upside down.

"We know they bow to the south, as though to the Kristin God, and they make other lands who submit do the same. But their beliefs are as misbegotten as their words. They have made an idol of their first emperor: they offer horses to him, which no one dares ride as long as they live. When the spirits respond they imagine he speaking to them. And they have galdrkind among their ranks. Black saman, who run with the spirits, practicing a great deal of divination. We have sent steeds of our own against them—darkness-riders and mouth-riders—to contrive that they go astray from the home of their minds."

Shapeshifting. The infliction of insanity. Those were enviable gifts, Hróðgeirr thought. He knew that the witch-wives held their arts close—men were not admitted to their Order for some arcane and no doubt arbitrary reason. Nevertheless, he wondered if he might find them suitable patrons when he finally reached Miklagarð.

The High Urðr ended her commentary abruptly and gestured to the ramparts. "Wall-stones are wondrous until calamities crumple them," she said. "We should talk before the carrion birds choose their meat from among the men of Kœnugarðr."

As if by rung her hand, the city bells began a mournful toll. All at once, a shrill, demented wail came up from the streets below.

"You don't think the walls will hold?" Hróðgeirr said, suddenly worried. He reached nervously, fumbling for his farseeing glass. The horizon immediately leapt into focus, a black noose, slowly but surely tightening its grasp. "So soon?" he muttered.

The High Urðr gently plucked the device from his hands and tucked it into the folds of her gown. "On the contrary, I think your efforts to defend them have been exemplary. Your great bombards must be forged again and again, until they ring every city in the Commonwealth. And you, Speaker of Marvels, you must be held up for the whole Empire to see."

"I would be happy to be of service," Hróðgeirr said. "In fact, I look forward to it." He was suddenly and mortally afraid. There were other sounds now, blaring trumpets, shouts of urgency and desperation. At the base of the hill, a congregation was gathering, two unsteady priests leading the crowd to whatever sanctuary the gods offered. They chanted as they tottered forward, the plaintive orisons carried on the wind across the city like the bleating of old goats. Years of dire anticipation were reduced to this moment.

"It is a seemly thing, since a man may not himself avert his destiny, that he should suffer it willingly." The High Urðr smiled, raising her voice above the din. She seemed perfectly calm amid the oncoming storm, although her Varangians had quickly closed ranks.

Hróðgeirr saw the opportunity he had been waiting for, for once feeling confident of his prospects of escaping the clutch of circumstance. He was hungry to be teaching again, to be among scholars educated in computation and philosophy. To be far from the Tartar. "I have other designs—great ships and sea-going vessels guided by one man, vagns that move at inestimable speed. And, when the realm is secure, I wonder if I might ask you to intercede on my behalf with the Pandekterion? I had an invitation to lecture there. Other... eventualities got in the way."

The discordant bells, the drumming of hooves—he could barely think. The sense of dread was palpable, the City of Ships adrift on a sea of despair.

"The Urðr's shaping changes the world under the heavens. But there, alas, even I cannot help you. The Pandekterion has been closed for a decade. Heresy spreads amongst learned men like fire in dry grass."

"I'm sorry, I don't follow," Hróðgeirr said. He stepped back, only to find a Varangian blocking his way. "The request came four years ago at most. How is that possible?"

And so, the man and the hour have met.

Despite the horrible fracas on all sides, Hróðgeirr heard the priestess quite clearly.

You did as you were asked by the Masked One.

"It was you! The voice in my head at the War Moot!" he exclaimed, suddenly understanding what had transpired there. The woman smiled under her mask, like a macabre ventriloquist, her voice clear in his mind.

A fetch, rather, murmuring wickedness in your ear on my account.

"Who is this Masked One?" said Hróðgeirr, aghast. It was hard to focus when the maelstrom beckoned. "Respectfully, this isn't the time or the place to be playing tricks!"

By one name he has never been known, since he went among the people. You counted him your friend.

"Vilhjálmr? But... he is dead!" the scholar said, unable to make sense of the situation. "What are you suggesting?" he rasped, his voice brittle. The worshipful crowds began to sway and moan, some prostrate, grasping at whatever cold comforts the hill's graven idols could offer.

There are plenty of people so foolish that they believe nothing but what they have seen with their own eyes or heard with their own ears. Never anything unfamiliar to them. I did not count you among them.

There was a wild, headlong rush for the safety of the Palace. Hróðgeirr decided that enough was enough. This was not the time for riddles and enigmas. There was no escaping his duty. He turned... but her mind seized him, holding him like a vice.

You are fond of patterns, I think? Of understanding how the world fits together? Imagine a patterned piece of cloth, woven on a loom. The horizontal threads are woven in in layers along the vertical threads. The horizontal threads represent layers of past actions. The vertical threads represent the march of time. The colour of each horizontal thread adds to both the pattern that is established and influences the pattern that emerges. The threads already woven in cannot be changed, but the overall pattern is never fixed.

The townsfolk were streaming past now, women and children mainly, as all able-bodied men would have been pressed into manning the walls. There were screams, cries of panic—Hróðgeirr was surprised to find one of them was his. He could barely breathe.

Existing designs can be expanded into new forms. New intricacies can be added. Everything the Masked One does adds one more layer to the pattern.

Under the cover of the crowds, one of the Varangians grabbed Hróðgeirr's shoulders. The man was a mountain, blocking his sight. A hessian sack descended, and the world went dark.

Hróðgeirr dreamed through the night that covered him.

The Blood Priestess was as bare as the moon. She stood in the faintest of lights, a marsh-bloom perhaps, fungus that bathed the catacombs with a crepuscular glow.

An old, encrusted bell began to sound. The High Urðr wrenched open her jaws and yawned deeply, her voice issuing an exultant, high-pitched melody, like a herdsman calling across the valley to his flock.

"The War Sire chose you, so you could see far, and far beyond over every world." A voice fluttering close by his ear. More of the vǫlur, no doubt, the seiðwives who ruled this underworld.

Now I am become Hellegrin, the wreck of the world, he dreamed. He had found a gateway to the beyond. The Caves of Malfred, an underground city, full of twisting narrow corridors, with all their immemorial associations of terror, slaughter, and barbarous rites. A wretched den of sorrows and of torments of mind. He sucked in the air, fragrant with sweet incense, then groped about, hoping to find his way, his hands scratching through brittle bones and scraping down damp clay walls. There was a chain, cold iron manacles shackling his leg, preventing him from going further. He backed up, returning the way he came, knocking against a carved back post as he did so. A chair or a small table, judging by the way it juddered across the dirt floor.

"As man is, the gods once were. As the gods are, man may be."

A sharp-nailed finger caressing his neck. A thickening of the dark. Seconds and years pass by, the same as it ever was.

"Drink now, this draught." A third voice slid by, cradling his head. All at once, he saw the sun, a glorious golden orb. To Her, he bowed for one last time, and she rewarded him greatly. Lifting his gaze so he could see, reflections and refractions. Raising his eyes until he could count the number of grains of dust and sand.

"I am sorry for it, my friend, but clockwork is no substitute for wet work." There is and was a familiar voice, a voice full of triumph and riddles, slipped under a mask he half-recognized. The voice of a Kingsman.

"Mater artium necessitas—the great mother of all productions is grave necessity. We must all make sacrifices in war."

Time is. Time was. Time has come.

Hróðgeirr was still asleep when the assault began.

There were no war cries or trumpets. Somewhere perhaps, a signal flag had slipped to the ground. In response, the crushing weights of a mangonel had plunged downward, hauling a huge boulder into the sky, towards the city. The first shot crashed through the forest, splintering trees and cracking branches, until it fell, spent, short of the wall. Minutes later, a second barrage began, this time from multiple engines, accompanied by a storm of arrows, iron sleet, hurtling through the darkened sky.

Hróðgeirr was unconcerned. He roused himself, groggy at first, but then swift in his determinations. He could see it all now, with the Urðr guiding his vision.

Blood rains from the cloudy web
On the broad loom of slaughter.

The Tartar had massed so many men, it seemed as though Hel had disgorged its dead. The whole of the riverland was dotted with campfires, a great battle array, leagues in every direction. A mist blanketed the plain, but the size and the scale of the army was readily apparent. There must have been a thousand cloth banners, red and blue, nine tails fluttering in salute to the dawn. The symbol of this Chinghiz-khan was evidently a falcon with a crow in his claw. *How apt*, Hróðgeirr thought.

The web of man grey as armour
Is now being woven; the Valkyries
Will cross it with a crimson weft.

The whole field of battle in panorama. He saw that the Tartar had feigned numerical superiority by ordering each soldier to light half a dozen fires. Each Taurman also had more than one mount, with prisoners tied to spares, a ruse to sell their numbers to fools and cowards. He could see the siege engines. They were grouped together, targeting the Vindr gate. The third time they fired, four, five, six missiles lofted into the sky, mere pebbles, impossible to track. They seemed to blur for a brief moment, then they boomed towards the ramparts as if a troll-bride had seized a mountain top and hurled it with sudden rage.

The Tartar bows had staggering range. Flaming arrows rained onto Kœnugarðr's wooden roofs. The townsfolk dashed to and fro, drawing from wells and hauling great piles of snow, aiming to douse the flames quickly. Pots of oil came next, vessels that burst on impact, igniting wicker fences and boiling screaming livestock. Naptha was far more difficult to extinguish.

The warp is made of human entrails;
Human heads are used as heddle-weights;
The heddle rods are blood-wet spears;
The shafts are iron-bound, and arrows are the shuttles.
With swords we will weave this web of battle.

The breaching batteries were ceaseless. Manned by Khitai engineers with decades of experience, they would convert the eye of a needle into a passage for a camel. When they ran out of boulders, the mangonels fired heavy, soaked logs that churned up men and mud, shattered gables and porches. Hróðgeirr watched as the enemy launched captives, howling with terror, thudding into the walls.

The Rus garrison waited and prayed. They had been told to expect an intervention of the gods. None of them would have suspected it came in the form of a balding Englander, muttering obscenities into his beard as he wrestled with an altogether different form of engine.

Spears will shatter, shields will splinter,
Swords will gnaw like wolves through armour.
Let us now wind the web of war
Which the Black King once waged.

"Learn quickly, Mímir," he croaked desperately, his brain working tirelessly, twisting dials and turning levers, calculating azimuth and inclination.

The whole of the Chancery was at his disposal, the skalds relaying his calculations to the gunners below, as he devised plans for a dozen more discharges. Gunhildr belched fire and Sinmara roared flame. They were things of beauty, Valkyries hurtling to claim the fallen. The Tartar must have been tempted to laugh. The ruthless and deadly cannonade soared over their heads and over the tree line, not once, but again and again. The besiegers grabbed their ladders, hefted their rams, and charged—unaware that Hróðgeirr had annihilated their siege train, and the minds set against him. The two bombards were adjusted again and again, a change of elevation, a lesser charge of powder, a correction for the wind. The great encircling serpent had been decapitated, cut down the middle, but it did not yet realize it.

Let us advance and wade through the ranks,
Where friends of ours are exchanging blows.
Let us now wind the web of war
And then follow the Prince to battle

There was a deadly crack by the wooden wall near the Vindr Gate. Smoke and flames billowed.

"A dragon! The Tartar have unleashed a dragon," the guardsmen cried. But Hróðgeirr saw the truth. The Tartar had Khitai Snow too.

The enemy used stockades and human shields for protection against Rus arrows, while huge rams and ladders were brought up. The Tartar began to swarm by the moat, tossing in the bodies of their captives to form an impromptu pontoon. They carried maces, lances with a hook and snare, and curved sabres. In their vanguard rode lancers, high in their saddles, seeking to thrust home their deadly advantage. The entire broad front swept into position to storm the gap that would result.

The Hrosslords rode on, sniping any defenders unwise enough to reveal themselves. Both soldiers and horses were clad in boiled leather, the warriors protected by tunics of tightly woven silk that blunted the impact of enemy arrows; their boots were lined with sewn-in metal plates that protected the warrior's legs.

The men of Tartar will suffer a grief
That will never grow old in the minds of men.
The web is now woven and the battlefield reddened;
The news of their disaster will spread through lands.

At the Wolf's Throat, the Rus front ranks knelt behind their shields, their spear butts fixed in the earth. Behind them, the rear ranks leveled their lances over their cohorts' heads, wedging their shields in place above them. It wasn't just a shield wall—it was a ring and roof of shields, a human fortress. The thick-set grove of spears was too dense for the Tartar to charge, and impervious to their arrows. The shield troop yelled with delight as the horsemen shied away.

Abruptly, the Tartar found themselves strung out, blinded by smoke and unable to see their own face signals. They wheeled away from the city, into the killing fields. Now the city host came to the walls and threw off the ladders. Gunhildr turned her attention to reducing their siege towers to matchwood.

The mounted princes of the Rus sat astride their massive warhorses with their shiny javelins, glistening swords, white banners, and boastful liveries, until all at once, these steel riddari came thundering out of the Golden Gate, bristling with spears. They took the fleeing Tartar in the rear. The Hrosslords struck for their lives when the ranks clashed, their blows rained down on boar-crests, but the steppe warriors didn't panic. They were too disciplined for that, too fearful of the punishments that came with defeat, too eager to please their Krist-Emperor. Instead, they turned, tens of thousands moving as one, and headed for the river.

It is horrible now to look around
As a blood-red cloud darkens the sky.
The heavens are stained with the blood of men,
As the Valkyries sing their song.

Hróðgeirr smiled as he heard the explosions by the river. The mild weather had helped, but now the ice began to crack and bob under the feet of the horsemen. The Kontormen had drawn up their ships like a wooden wall, and took up positions with crossbows and wicked, hooked spears.

The trap was sprung, and victory was assured. *I am the master of my fate*, he thought, *I am the captain of my soul.*

And when the battle was over and the songs were sung, they came to him, Hróðgeirr Bakko. Deus Ex Machina, they called him, the God in the Machine. In modern warfare, the steel riddari said, artillery was god. Artillery, massive artillery decided the fate of the man.

But they came not in celebration but with downcast eyes and sorrow. They dismantled his orbs and shuttered him with lacquered boards. He could see nothing then, no corpse-strewn fields, no blasted heath, no retreating foe. In the darkness, he searched in vain for the tissue of his life.

"The war is won, Meistar, thanks to you. The Kristin scourge defeated," the Grand Prince said, from somewhere outside the ordnance crate. "We two shall now ride over the green realms of the gods in order to tell Óðinn that a great wise man is coming to see him. I am sure you will be welcome among the Æsir."

Hróðgeirr tried to protest, but only vectors, arcs, and trajectories emerged. His brazen head gazed mournfully back at the crowd, his long beard grown to the floor, like the King Asleep in the Mountain.

— ODIN'S RAVEN SONG —

**Skala Haugr Station
In the Blink of an Eye**

The old man wandered to his chair, patting the black foam arms with affection. The faux leather veneer was old, and the casters sometimes stuck, but from its immutable vantage he could watch all his creation. Sitting in the tiny control room crammed with screens and a control desk, he had plenty to keep him busy, scooting between grainy video feed on the monitors. To the uninitiated, they all showed similar rooms, littered with rubbish and smashed up bits of equipment, but there were many different ways of seeing.

He'd had many shrines and temples in his day, but this was the best of them—a veritable Hliðskjálf, perched on the cliff, looking over the Southern Isles. The Skuld regarded it warily, like a slow death-warrant; the salty, corrosive sea air playing a lethal game of kǫttr and mús with the site's aging infrastructure. He didn't mind that. They left him alone here among its labyrinth of scruffy, dilapidated rooms.

Outside the window, there was a grassy scrap of land. Seagulls would gather there and chatter, screeching loudly to make themselves heard over the constant hum of machinery, hopping over the zig-zagging pipes when they whooshed steam. They grew restless when they wanted to play. They were covetous creatures, ravenous and greedy, no replacement at all for his ravens.

The little clock sounded constantly to warn him of any breach. A tick-tock noise emitted by loudspeakers dotted throughout the facility. He'd grown so used to its chimes, he sometimes forgot it was there at all, and only later realized it had stopped working. That's when he had to go outside and check the perimeter. More often than not, it was some degenerate Imperial, more winged vermin flitting to and fro.

Tick-tock goes the clock, hanging on the wall.
Tick-tock goes the clock, telling doom for all.

He sighed and wheeled back his chair, noting that the armrest wobbled when he removed his weight. He must remember to tighten it, sooner rather than later, although he often forgot which was which.

The door opened at his word, and he shuffled outside, his walking stick leading the way, following the pipes that ran in every direction, a lattice of scaffolding that girded the sky. The countryside around was quiet, the roads deserted. Far off, unknown, scarcely remembered at all.

There were two ponds nearby, overflowing with fuel rods, riddled with cracks and rust. They consumed all things with their slow power, their green scales always glinting. The old man watched one of the gulls bobbing on the water, nodding in the direction of another innocuous-looking site on the vast complex. He decided he couldn't turn a blind eye to so obvious a portent. He paused to gather his bearings between the looming stacks of concrete monoliths, squinting at a cluster of industrial buildings, then proceeded at his usual senescent pace. After what seemed an eternity, he came clear of the cramped jumble of facilities.

Train tracks crisscrossed the ground, past the remnants of cooling towers. They reminded him of his own past. Back and forth he'd ridden, back and forth. Dasis Ravana, Ruad Rofhessa, Gestumblindi, Draugadróttinn—he had worn so many masks as he prepared for the wolf, he couldn't tell them apart.

The High Urðr had once sent sacrifices across the iron rails, to be hauled by a vast crane, its back bent with mute motion as it traced their passage into the cooling pools of water that would devour the essence. The building ahead was featureless, red and black. The last workers had called it Thorp, Thermal Oxide Reprocessing Plant, but the witch-wives had added a stave to the last letter. He had laughed at that. The Vǫlur couldn't help themselves. Since couldn't find the gods they wanted, they simply manufactured them. The great Serkir alchemists, they had understood how to bring creation out of destruction, life out of death. Had he not sacrificed himself to himself, delivered his own resurrection time after time? He was tired of eating shadows, but it'd be a warm day in Hel before he gave up any more of his secrets.

The sun rested on the cave's wide threshold, and the old man bent his grey hairs to the proud rays, sniffing the hungry wind. A moment later, he walked inside, the sound of his cane echoing, bouncing off the two-story adamantine door that blocked all further passage. Of its own accord, the gate swung open, revealing the huge interior, as bright as Glaðsheimr, all gussied up in fresh yellow paint. He tipped his hat in gratitude.

Inside, the towers of blocks were spaced so that he could walk between them. The only hint of what each box contained was a short serial number stamped on one side. A code, to be read once you nudged aside the morass of degrading plastic bottles. The ancient runes of the Ruler of Gods. Here in appointed places the Ages dwelt, with varying formulas marking their aspect. Heljarblý. Hel-metal. The very stuff of death.

The little clock sat on the wall of the near-blinding warehouse, installed when the boxes were first moved there. It was as silent as the grave. He tapped at its shell, hoping to coax a heartbeat, to feel the sap coursing through its chambers. Time passed differently for dead men, underneath the earth, near the roots of proud Yggdrasil. He could almost taste the ruin, see the coral reefs flickering out beneath plastic-infested oceans, rainforests desiccating into desert. This was a glue-scabbed world, covered in concrete and carcinogens, swallowed up by wildfires and suffocated in petrochemicals. He should never have brought the seed here in the first place. That much was certain.

He carried on, between the sprawling collection of blocks, farther into the vast breast of the cavernous hangar. He peered through thick leaded glass which gleamed with yellow-tinged fluorescence. The structure looked close to collapse—but the dvergr bots stopped it from falling. An automated dismantling machine, remote-controlled manipulator arm and crane were busy reconvening it piece by piece, starting with the concrete shield and aluminium-clad shell. It was a perversion of their original purpose, but that was true of all his innovations. Niði Bohr would have been proud.

The demolition thralls watched him warily, through sensors in their steel claws. The air inside was like unquenched fire—no one ever went in. The one-tonne BROKK-90 demolition machine smashed up sections of the poisoned lab and loaded them into plastic buckets on a conveyer belt. The buckets would be fed through an enclosed hole in the wall to a waiting EITRI master-thrall appendage, encased in a box made of steel and reinforced glass, who would repurpose them. There were smaller bots, too, able to change shape and go through small apertures into the facility. Dvergr were cunning like that.

Their forging took an age. Tongs they wrought, and tools they fashioned. An ocean of water was pumped in, and only seeming centuries later did the dvergr dissect it, dissolving the waste in acid. There, they mixed the toxic sludge with glass, placed it into a container and welded it shut. Vitrification. Windows that dissolved the soul.

The dvergr worked quietly and efficiently amid the reams of metalwork. The old man didn't bother them—he was no buzzing fly. Together, they put death in boxes in the ground, burying them in tunnels that stretched for miles. Geological disposal, the little gods had called it, before the Skuld swept them away. But even the hardest stone was just a vibration of quantum fields, a momentary interaction of forces, a process that briefly managed to keep its shape before disintegrating into dust. This was something altogether stronger: a wall of the dead, entombed beneath the roots of the worlds. One hundred and forty tonnes of destruction, the largest stockpile in the world.

If that didn't stop the wolf in its tracks, nothing would.

He went back outside. He had set up the table in the middle of the grass, buffeted by the salt spray and the howl of the wind. The opposing King had been subdued—the threat he posed had diminished over the long years. Every move the enemy had made, the old man had checked. In Miklagarð, at the Michaelion; in golden-domed Kœnugarðr; at the wide-famed well of Mimir. He had to hand it to the Taxiarch, the Kristin world knew how to fight back and fight dirty, but it was the Queen he hadn't seen coming. Plucked from the void, promoted out of nowhere, propelled through the ranks.

The old man hissed with the venting steam. Two could play at that game.

He placed his own new piece very carefully on the board, making sure it was intact, careful to avoid the gaze of the pilfering gulls. The only hope was amputation. Sever the head. Shatter the crown. Dispense with the Urðr once and for all. That had always been the intent, before the raven-thieves stole his mind.

"Your move", he said.

BOOK TWO: TIME WAS

— THE FLYTING OF MICHAELS —

**Gosforth, England
2019**

"Hoo'doo, Olaf luv?" The shrill voice pitched up the stairs. Churchwarden Michaels winced. It sounded so routine, a cheery greeting from a visitor, full of Christian virtue. Full of belonging. Perhaps that's how all invasions began, he thought. Neighbours inviting themselves into your modestly appointed semi-detached and making themselves at home. He tried to roll over onto his side, seeking an alibi in feigned sleep, but the bedframe had other ideas. It sang like a rusty canary.

Marvellous, he thought, staring irritably at the mildewed flowers that flocked down his walls.

"Co-ee. It's only me, boyo. Mrs. Jones," came the voice from somewhere below. "Are you decent?"

Behind his right eye, something shifted: something terrible. His other "unexpected guest". It always woke up just after he did, knocking against his skull. In his abject state, he could never be sure whether it was inside trying to bludgeon its way out, or outside, trying to stave a way in.

"Wakey, wakey. Rise and shine!"

Michaels didn't answer, praying that Mrs. Jones wouldn't have the temerity to come into his bedroom. Admittedly, it wasn't exactly standard liturgy, and the Lord habitually failed to heed him. But he nonetheless spent most of her visits like that, eyes clenched, as still as stone, straining to hear the click of the front door, the tiny, barely audible sound that signalled the all-clear.

He hadn't heard her coming this time, though, hadn't braced for impact. There'd been no sudden squeal of a misapplied handbrake, no measured crunch of her boots on the gravel drive. He must have been dead to the world.

To hear her tell it—and there really wasn't much choice in the matter—Mrs. Jones had purloined the spare key from the Vicarage

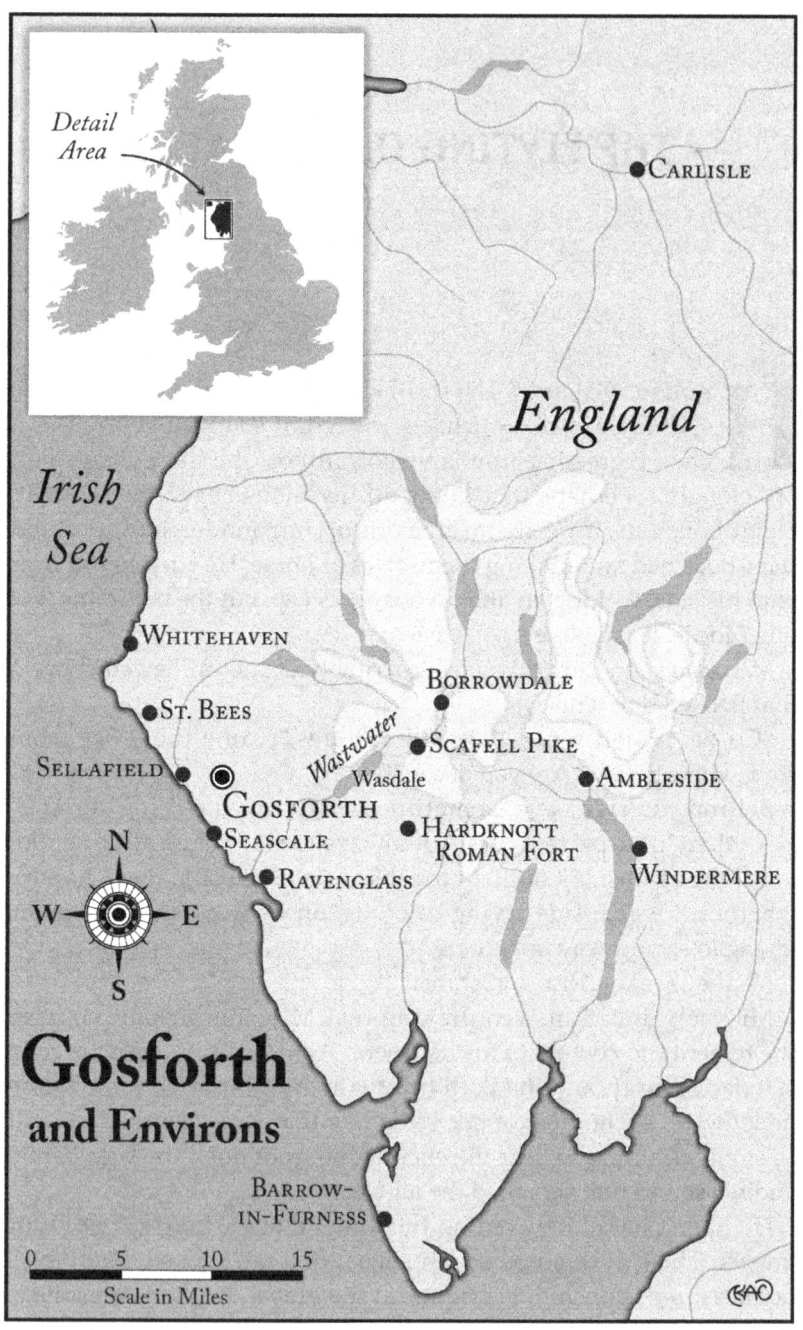

the very moment she heard he was unwell. She'd been letting herself in ever since. She knew all about migraines, she said. Suffered them herself, for years. The first visit she kept simple, delivering store-brand ibuprofen and some back-handed compliments. For most of the congregation at St. Mary's, the Bible was daily bread. For Mrs. Jones, it was more like an occasional cake. She moved quickly beyond common decency and was soon dispensing lashings of idle gossip and casual racism. She was irrepressible, like a narrow-minded Mary Poppins, offering a spoonful of saccharine to help his medicine go down.

Before Michaels knew it, she had stocked his fridge, put new batteries in his big brass kitchen clock, and even swept up the cat's mess in the pantry, all while shouting questions up at him, somehow unmuffled by the burgundy loop pile carpet and floorboards between them.

"'Olaf luv' this, 'Olaf luv' that," he mimicked, then gulped down some painkillers to dull the agony and excuse the lack of charity.

He reached to pull back the curtain. The Beast from the East had been causing the mercury to plummet of late and, consequently, the double glazing to fog. He balled up the sleeve of his cotton pajamas and wiped the condensation clear. Mid-afternoon and it was already getting dark, he grumbled. The driveway was empty, so either Mrs. Jones really did come by umbrella today or she'd walked round after Mothers & Toddlers. He wondered if anyone had put salt down by the Foodbank. Black ice could be a killer.

You could always go and check, he upbraided himself. *Migraine or no migraine, your duty is to keep God's house as your own.*

The fact was, he hadn't been to St. Mary's in weeks. He was too ashamed.

He'd been quite the village celebrity for a while. Gosforth was on the map at last, Reverend Riley had said, marked by not just one but three crosses! Centuries-old Viking crosses, to be precise, carved in red sandstone at the turn of the first millennium.

It was an amusing little joke, and not surprisingly, it got trotted out in Riley's sermons for weeks afterwards. Thankfully, the Reverend didn't mention that two of the artifacts in question had appeared overnight, just in case it made the Churchwarden look careless with the annual inventory. Or, worse still, fraudulent with the insurance forms they had filled in together over Easter.

There had been a veritable flood of national—and international—attention. He'd enjoyed it immensely at the time. Reporters from NRK and the BBC grabbing soundbites. Academics up from London. The *Times & Star* did a big feature on him and his namesake, the church of St. Olaf at Wasdale Head—the smallest church near the deepest lake and the highest mountain in England. The little church set amidst yew trees in the Viking fields of Wasdale, with roof beams made from Viking ships. The church that inspired Olaf Michaels's parents to name their son after a long-dead Northern king. Olaf Michaels, the man who seemed predestined to find two brand new Viking Age crosses, standing upright, as bold as the day they were carved, in the churchyard. The article made it all seem quite normal, no different from the Furness Hoard, a hidden Viking cache of coins and hack silver that a metal detectorist had found near Barrow a few years back.

The churchwarden didn't try to explain where the crosses came from. He couldn't even if he had wanted to—his mind went blank whenever he thought about them. Nerves, he'd imagined. A few American TV crews came by, from the Discovery Channel and whatnot. The Yanks really probed for answers, but Michaels felt uncomfortable sensationalising the mystery. Truth be told, he might have speculated if he'd been interviewed by the *Time Team*, but that show had been axed a few years back. Besides, there were plenty of other armchair archaeologists ready and willing to go on the record with outlandish theories. Instead, he took the Bishop's advice and left the explanation to the Almighty.

The headaches had started few weeks later, after the fuss had died down. The Area Dean had coaxed half of the Benefice into the church hall on Christmas Eve. Not one to move with the times, it turned out he'd recorded all the clips and burnt them onto commemorative DVDs, intending them for sale with the postcards and pamphlets they kept near the south porch. Even so, Michaels had been quite excited at the prospect. He'd been too overwhelmed to watch any of the broadcasts go out live.

The very moment the ancient projector fired up, he felt the first pang of anguish. He'd heard that the camera adds ten pounds, and so he expected to look a bit portly. But the amount he sweated under the bright lights and glare of the camera was frankly embarrassing. He looked like he was melting. Sounded like it too—whenever he was asked about the Gosforth miracle, he slurred like he'd been at the communion wine. The Reverend said he blacked out, there and then. Fainted clean away. Of course, they checked him for contusions or concussion, and he'd been well enough to walk home.

Proverbs 16:18, he sighed. Pride goeth before destruction, and a haughty spirit before a fall. He should have known better. To add insult to injury, once the Central Gosforth Scouts Group heard his given name and its background, they started calling him Snowman. The Disney Generation really knew how to crucify a man. So, no, he wasn't going out in the snow, duty or no duty. Still, for a single man of his age to be ministered to by Mrs. Jones... he dreaded to think what was being said behind closed doors. It was enough to make your blood run cold.

The *Frozen* movie soundtrack leapt out of his auditory cortex and seized subliminal centre stage. Michaels groaned in exasperation. He knew his mind was capable of playing tricks on him—the whole cross episode was proof enough of that—but he hadn't realized it could play whole concertos too. The Magic Kingdom had joined forces with his migraine to irrevocably destroy any joy he ever found in winter. He hefted onto his back again, arranging his arms across his chest briefly while he waited for the throbbing to subside. After a moment, he dropped them to his waist. This way, at least, he avoided looking like an undertaker had just arranged him for the visit.

Mrs. Jones put her head round the door. She was a spritely woman, always bustling, even in what must have been her late sixties. He kept his eyes shut and prayed fervently for deliverance. His visitor exhaled slowly and purposefully, as if creating a barrier between herself and the singular odors of a single man's bedroom.

"Oh dear, are you very badly?"

Hoo'doo. Badly. Mrs. Jones would speak perfectly proper SRP when she was with Reverend Riley, but with the laity she'd slip into conspiratorial Cumbrian speech patterns.

"I tell you what, I'll make you nice cuppa scordy. Would you like that? How about some food? Some lovely spam and baked beans?"

She cackled at her own joke. Mrs. Jones never missed the opportunity for a Monty Python reference since the crosses appeared. Dutifully, a horde of prancing, horned Vikings marched into Michaels's mind, bellowing "spa-a-a-a-a-am." He hadn't seen the show and had had to look it up on YouTube. Big mistake that was. He remembered reading that the most common method of torturing prisoners in Guantanamo was to play "I Love You" by Barney the Purple Dinosaur on repeat—then promptly wished he hadn't. A T-Rex joined the conga of Norsemen carousing through his head. The pain reverberated in time with the incessant Disney medley, pounding,

pounding, pounding. He wondered what God was saying to him through all the noise, his very own Tower of Babel.

Mrs. Jones clucked her tongue and clumped down carpeted stairs again, to clank around the kitchen, putting the din in dinner.

"Have you heard from the Vicarage?" she called up, oblivious to his suffering. She referred to the vicar's house like it was the epicentre of the world, in the same way a reporter might talk about Number Ten or the Pentagon.

"Reverend Riley popped round a few times, yes." The academics had lingered longer than the TV crews and needed shuttling around. But Michaels excused himself, and retreated to his living room and dressing gown, and then, when the migraines got worse, to his bed. Doctor Wilson's orders. At least the Vicar had the decency not to intrude.

"What was that?" the old lady yelled.

He couldn't muster the enthusiasm to repeat himself, let alone with the gusto required to be heard downstairs. Mrs. Jones harrumphed and then clattered on her way through the kitchen cupboards.

Stress, apparently, was the reason for his unexpected guest. Too much excitement by far and not anywhere near enough exercise for a man approaching forty. The headaches would go away with rest, and then the prescription was for some brisk walks. Doctor Wilson was a keen member of Active Cumbria and a fanatical rambler. What was the point of living in the Lake District if you didn't perambulate on a regular basis? he'd said.

Michaels wasn't ready for that yet, though. Frankly, if Mrs. Jones hadn't been there, he would have crawled back into the bed and tried to escape into sleep. He propped his elbows on the windowsill and tried to breathe deeply. *Count to three*, he thought.

The fields stretched away, long and level, to the coast. A snow-white patchwork quilt, criss-crossed by drystone walls, the ancient fabric of England. Doctor Wilson was right, it was something of a balm for the soul. There was a red squirrel watching him from the top of the privet hedge. *Sciurus vulgaris*. He felt a certain kinship with the poor thing. The reds were anything but common now, having to deal with their own invaders: the dreaded greys. Not to mention that it was probably just out of hibernation. All ready for spring, and then he got a dump of snow.

Michaels reached for his phone to check the time. 3:39 p.m. He glanced at the home-screen, wondering whether he had the energy to check in on the world. It was all so bloody depressing: the blackened name of the White House, the Russian cyber attacks, the endless Brexit debate, where the Mother of All Parliaments was making the mother of all messes. The last time he looked, one newspaper reported that all the trees were dying.

A loose tile fell from the roof, snapping him from his introspection. His squirrel pal had taken refuge there, no doubt, getting into the attic at the base of the old Sky satellite dish on the roof. He should've had it taken down years ago. It wasn't even connected.

"Knock yourself out, Squirrel Nutkins," he muttered. Perhaps that was the problem. The world was smaller these days, but despite all the instant communication and video on demand, people had forgotten their roots. No one belonged anywhere anymore. Even the squirrels had migrated.

There was a knock on the bedroom door, so he plopped himself back into bed. Mrs. Jones had returned with what passed for his tea.

"Ah, you look a bit better Olaf luv," she said, without looking at him, edging a tray of something microwaved and pink onto his bedside table. "Salmon. Your favourite."

She finished fussing with the cutlery, then narrowed her eyes as she focused on the phone in his hand.

"Ah, yer divvy, put that away. Obsessed with screens, you are, what with a headache an'all."

"I was just looking at the time."

"What's wrong with a watch?" she demanded, then turned and dropped a rolled-up newspaper she'd been carrying under her arm. "I brought you the papers."

They both glanced at the headline as it unfurled on the duvet. WORKERS FIRED FOR BEING BRITISH.

"Whisht! Is this what my grandfather fought in two World Wars for? Immigrants from every corner. Mrs. Haythwaite says the Germans are building another army. Can you believe it?"

Michaels tried to avoid the subject. "Is it very cold outside? I was thinking of a walk this evening. If it's warmed up a touch."

"Proper Englishmen, the old fella. Had a bit of Viking in 'em, you know, bit like you," she said proudly, obviously immune to questioning.

Michaels took a deep breath. Part of him wanted to correct her. *You can't have a bit of Viking in you,* he wanted to say. *Maybe a bit of Norwegian, if you are from around these parts. But I'm not Norwegian; my mother was from Plumstead. She just conceived me the same year they consecrated St. Olaf's and got carried away with the whimsy of Norsemen in the Lake District.*

But his head hurt, and an argument with Mrs. Jones wasn't going to fix anything. He'd had enough arguing with old codgers to last a lifetime. He wondered what happened to the cantankerous vagrant who'd accosted him in the churchyard last November and made him completely miss Pies, Peas, and Puds night. Michaels wasn't sure which of his recent visitors delivered the most torture, on a minute-for-minute basis, but the old man had seemed to linger for an eternity.

These days, Vikings had become a symbol, representing at best adventure, risk, individual spirit, and daring and at worst xenophobia, white pride, and male violence. It struck Michaels as the greatest of ironies that Vikings, once demonised as the scourge of Europe, were now a talisman for those who were mortally afraid of how the world was changing around them.

He sighed and sidled up to the windowpane, trying to stare upwards.

"You've scared away my squirrel chum," he said, a touch reproachfully. He wondered if it might be coaxed down with some salmon.

Mrs. Jones paid him no attention. "Speaking of Vikings, the Reverend asked me remind you. The Parish Council is gabbing on about the Viking Way tonight. Seven thirty. You can't keep hiding out here, like a feckless jam eater."

Was it Wednesday *already*? He'd circled the date on the kitchen calendar a while back, but he'd forgotten it in all the recent hullabaloo. It was easy to lose track of time.

The Viking Way. A planning application has been submitted to Cumbria County Council for a new bridle path that would open the fells for cyclists and walkers arriving at Seascale by rail. The name was a nod to the area's Norse heritage, filed in the days when one cross had been plenty. What with Moorforge, the new centre for Viking discovery up past Cockermouth, Cumbria would soon be competing with Denmark. The new route would run alongside the road and provide a safer crossing point over the A595. It didn't sound like much, but it would clear up a renowned accident blackspot, known locally as "Coffin Corner."

There was a lot of death in that direction. After all, this was where, in the early 1950s, the Windscale facility produced the plutonium-239 that would be used in the UK's first nuclear bomb, where Queen Elizabeth had opened Calder Hall, the world's first commercial nuclear power station. Most of his friends had gone to school at St.

Bees, just a few miles away from the iconic cooling towers. They'd huffed and puffed past it on cross-country runs, danced in its shadow at Calder girls' school, kissing the daughters of the scientists. He remembered his dad saying the nuclear men thought they were "little gods" and being embarrassed when his mum demanded that his medical records include the fact that he was schooled so close to the reactors. He'd been too young to understand the nature of the evil. How the management, profligate with money, had been criminally careless with safety and ecology, thinking nothing of trying to block Wastwater lake to get more water or trying to mine the national park for a waste dump. The plant's sheer physical isolation contributed to the local's fears. It was like a latter-day Transylvanian castle, a radioactive leper colony.

Thankfully, the long-overdue decommissioning was underway, and the government hadn't seen fit to hold up planning permission this time around. Perhaps the Viking Way would help some of the ministry men with their commute.

"Do you believe in fate, Mrs. Jones?" he asked her.

"I'm fond of a good tombola," she said, still engrossed in the newspaper.

Fate! Not fête! he almost said, exasperated, then realised he was talking to entirely the wrong person. Mrs. Jones was a paid-up member of the Conservative Party who was happiest when raising money for the RNLI or selling homemade scones at the Agricultural Show. Determinism simply wasn't something that came up in conversation in her circles.

"Well, good then. Excellent, in fact. That is welcome news. I ought to prepare some notes."

He brightened at the prospect and went so far as to attempt to corral Mrs. Jones into an awkward hug.

"Give awer yer divvy," she protested, obviously pleased despite herself. Straightening her headscarf in his mirror, she caught his eye in the reflection and winked. "Any road, I just popped in before bingo to see how you were gan. I'll be sure to tell the Vicar you are on the mend."

"Thanks for tea, Mrs. Jones. God bless you."

But Mrs. Jones was already gone.

His tea, piping hot, beckoned on the bedside table. The tablets had taken the edge off. Either that or what passed for TLC from Mrs. Jones was working its magic. He wrestled a jumper over his head and pulled on some socks, hopping back to the window to scan the horizon for chimney sweeps or flying umbrellas.

"Can't put me finger
on what lies in store
But I feel what's to happen
All happened before."

He chuckled, chuffed with his imitation of Dick Van Dyke cockney. Nothing. Just her old white Ford Fiesta reversing erratically out of the driveway. He waved, although Mrs. Jones was already busy arguing back to the Smooth Drivetime show on the radio, disturbing the whole cul-de-sac in the process. His own Vauxhall Astra VXR was carpeted in snow. It had won the Best Sporting Car from the Scottish Car of the Year in 2012. He hadn't driven it since a week last Thursday. He bit absent-mindedly into his salmon and wondered if the battery might have gone dead in the cold. He'd have to call Frank Nesbit to come and help him jump start it.

Hang on, he thought, the cars were in the driveway. Disney and déjà vu be damned! He hadn't seen them in the snow. The question was, had Mrs. Jones?

There was a dull thud outside, followed by a longer, more sustained screech of metal on hot-formed boron steel. He raced back to the window, only to find himself face to face with the squirrel.

"*Let It Go*, Snowman. It's not the end of the world," it said.

Somewhere between 5% and 28% of the general population "heard voices" that other people didn't. Michaels had read that little factoid in a Mental Health Foundation leaflet. The voices came in many and varied forms: the quiet male persona, constantly whispering death and destruction; the disconcerting screams of a woman that no one else seemed to hear; a child clapping and cheering every hour of every day. One composer claimed he'd been visited by the ghost of Schubert. Regrettably, the pamphlet had omitted mention of talking squirrels.

Something else to mention in his next check-up, he thought, trying not to succumb to the vicious circle of anxiety. Doctor Wilson had told him that he had to learn to "gradually confront feared situations." His furry friend was probably another symptom. And if it wasn't part of his condition, well, then he'd be happy to see those nice young men in their clean white coats—Mrs. Jones always said he belonged in the funny farm. It was rarer than in cases of schizophrenia, but auditory hallucinations occasionally cropped up in medical literature around migraines too. Full-scale delirium was apparently like a huge theatre, with the capacity to stage world class productions.

It took him a moment to work out where on God's green earth he was. The corner of the garage. He lay spread-eagled by the potting shed, like one of the spring crocuses struggling out the unexpected snows. Oh, good grief, he exclaimed, remembering his car. He felt dizzy, like he was falling, or rather—rotating. Vertigo. He brushed his hand against the wall to keep his balance, and when that failed to work, sat down heavily on the flower bed and closed his eyes.

A specialist had visited him last week connected to the dizziness, after Doctor Wilson had called the Cumbria Neuroscience service in Penrith.

"Diagnostically," she'd said, "headache is the easy part of a migraine. It is the surrounds of migraine—the aura, prodrome, and postdrome—that can be most challenging, and confused with other all sorts of other stuff. The borderlands are much more blurred. We must try a process of elimination. For instance, have you heard of migralepsy?"

He hadn't and didn't want to, so she put what looked like a virtual reality headset over his eyes and had him count aloud the red lights that flashed across his field of vision. Warm air blasted first into one ear and then the other. They'd been an uncomfortable pressure in his ear canal that made him feel as if he was a spinning top. He had a strong waft of her perfume. Overpowering. He'd grown nauseous, almost lost count, but the specialist had insisted that he carry on.

Suddenly, he could see himself in the kaleidoscope of colour, a young boy, running down the narrow country lanes to the village school just across the church. It was these memories that had grounded him.

"Yan, Tan, Tethera," he'd said. A sheep-counting rhyme. He used to sing-song count his way along the hedgerows and fields every day back then. He wasn't sure what prompted him to say it out loud, but playing it back in his head now, it occurred to him that his reply wasn't just childish, it was downright abnormal.

"Mr. Michaels, if you please..." she'd complained, and so he'd explained himself; it was a tradition, common in the dales of the Lake District. Yan, Tan, Tethera, Methera, Pimp. Until the Industrial Revolution, anyway. For centuries, nothing much had changed in the Lake District. That's why people visited. It was like stepping back into the past.

"Fascinating," the specialist had said, making an adjustment to her device.

"Ein, tveir, þrír," he'd said. "That's Old Norse." Perhaps he was schizophrenic? Sometimes, only lesions on the brain explained his utterances. Still, on balance, it was more likely he was showing off. The specialist was quite an attractive lady.

"I've seen you on the telly. You've got Vikings on the brain," she said, not unkindly, he thought.

Perhaps that was it. The crosses, all the attention, had overwhelmed him. He used to relish being the local expert on the Vikings. Pub quizzes at the Wheatsheaf were a doddle. But now that the crosses had multiplied, there'd been a non-stop barrage from the bloody heathens. Asatru UK would send him invitations to speak at their moot. Worse still were the ones who thought three red crosses were a badge of honour and emblazoned them on their profile. What were they thinking? The senior lay official of Gosforth parish, the longest serving local representative of the Anglican Communion in North-East Cumbria, headlining at a pagan festival? Following a fascist Facebook page?

"Did you know many Lake District names come from Norse settlers way back in the tenth century? For example, beck for stream, dale for valley, and thwaite for clearing, to name just three?" he'd asked the specialist, as she packed up.

She hadn't known, she'd said, politely, and without a glimmer of further interest. He wondered if she ever visited any local beauty spots? Five minutes later, she had gone, all retreating high heels and flushed excuses.

Personal boundaries. Spheres of expertise. No-go areas. He had no idea who made the rules anymore. No wonder he had headaches. It was like he was shadowbanned from social media, but without the slightest idea what he had done to deserve it. Plucked from his perfectly pleasant routine, without so much as a by-your-leave.

At least the land was constant. This was a special corner of England, dotted with limewashed cottages and long stretches of walls separating the fields full of hardy Herdwick sheep, reputedly brought in by the Norse to graze on the fells. Examination of the walls had revealed that each valley had a "ring garth" built by early Norse settlers in the tenth or eleventh centuries. Huge, cyclopean, rounded boulders taken from the stream bed, following the break in the slope of the valley, separating the fertile bottom land from coarse grazing on the fellside.

Not far north, the story was older and clearer still: Hadrian's Wall stretched seventy-three miles across the neck of England, dividing the civilization of Rome from the savage, painted Picts. There were no indistinct borderlands here, no fuzzy logic or shades of grey, just simple, straightforward order.

Something thudded out in the street, startling the churchwarden from his recuperation. It was immediately followed by clanging sound, the rich singing of striking metal on metal. Michaels leapt out of his skin. Hell's bells! *Not again*, his lizard brain screamed.

Seconds later, a great giant loomed out of the darkness muttering oaths, broad shoulders to the sky, smoke wreathed in his coal-grey beard. The new LED streetlights bathed the visitor in an operatic spotlight, rippling along the chains of his armour. Michaels's amygdala elided his thoughts into one fluid action. He scrabbled in the snow, his feet finding purchase on a plant pot, before flinging himself over the garage wall. The mass of hair and steel watched him go, hands held high in apology. Under the streetlight, it had the disconcerting effect of making the figure seem ready to ascend to Valhalla.

"Sorry, Olaf. I didn't mean to scare you. The Vicar sent me. I'm to collect you for the council meeting?"

"Barry," Michaels sighed. Barry Thurston-Hicks. Also known as Barry the Science Viking, an ex-high school teacher, now licensed to wield his spear in the service of STEM education. Barry organised the medieval re-enactment at Heysham Viking Festival, and often toured schools dressed as a Viking might, although he wasn't above setting up as a monk or an alchemist if the exhibitions at Muncaster Castle needed him. The kids loved him—but even so, there hadn't been much call for his unique choice of profession, so he was often away down south—or driving the local taxi.

The churchwarden stepped out from behind the wall, a little sheepishly.

"You're all dressed up, Barry," Michaels said, stating the obvious.

"Business is booming, thanks to your crosses. Funny how things come in threes. Like buses, eh?" Barry rubbed his hands together conspiratorially. He was from London originally, a place where they actually had more than two buses. It was his wife who was local. She sat on the Seascale council, the next village over.

"You are going to the meeting? Jane's poorly, so I am representing the Clan Thurston-Hicks."

"No thanks, it's not far," Michaels said, brushing himself down. He really wasn't in the mood for company right now.

"Don't be silly. I've got the van. You could arrive in style."

Michaels shrugged.

"Oooo, I see you've had a prang," Barry said, sucking in his breath as he surveyed the damage to the Astra.

The churchwarden didn't want to look. Just thinking about the insurance made him feel light-headed. There was an awkward silence for a moment or two, while both men searched for something else to say, before the churchwarden decided that the only way to stop further investigation by the local neighborhood Viking was to accept his offer.

"Where are you parked?"

"Just over the street. I had to do an emergency stop to avoid a squashing a bloody red squirrel. Don't need that on my conscience. They're on the endangered list."

"Are they? I had no idea," said Michaels, preferring to feign ignorance than think any more about his hallucinations.

They ducked into the nettles and briars to avoid a passing car, then, when it was clear, stepped into the narrow lane. The van was parked, badly, on the corner of his road. It was all gussied up with decals, a moving billboard for Barry's Viking services. There was a life-size 2D replica on the back doors, holding a longsword, hair streaming dramatically in some unseen wind.

"I've given up the taxi lark," Barry said, as if that explained why he had a van that wouldn't have looked out of place on the A-Team. "The Viking Way should be good for business too. I'm hoping they book me for the Grand Opening." He thumped his chain mailed chest in emphasis. "I've got Deathsinger in the back, in case you want to have a heft later. Eleventh century Varangian."

Michaels glanced around at all the paraphernalia Barry kept in the back of the van, worried that it wasn't properly secured. There was enough steel to outfit half a dozen re-enactors. The churchwarden had only fought alongside Barry once, during a Trivia Night at the Wheatsheaf. Ironically, for a history nut, Barry was terrible with dates. You could name any battle, even ones his beloved Vikings fought in, like Stamford Bridge or Maldon, and he'd be out by a century or more. It might have been endearing if they hadn't crashed out in the semifinal. Still, you couldn't help but admire the man's passion, even if he did play a little fast and loose with reality.

Barry turned the key and the radio blared into action... Smooth Drivetime. Michaels reflexively put his hands over his ears.

"Mind if we turn that off? I have something of a headache," he asked, raising his voice over the racket. He had no idea what made the Top 40 these days, and on the evidence presented, he didn't want to find out.

"Oh yes. I heard you'd been unwell. Well, you know what they say, music soothes the savage beast," Barry said, looking over his shoulder and reversing into the darkness.

"Breast. He wasn't a snake charmer," Michaels said, acidly.

"Pardon?" Barry spun the wheel back and accelerated.

"Music hath charms to soothe a savage breast. That's the correct quotation." He didn't like being a passenger, especially one sat so close to sharp pointed weaponry.

"Old Will Shakespeare, eh?" Barry grinned, clearly delighted to have Michaels along for the ride. The churchwarden paused before correcting him, feeling momentarily churlish.

"Congreve. Still, top marks for William."

"Anyway, we can't turn that off. This song is a classic." Barry started to sing. "*If I could save time in a bottle, the first thing that I'd like to do...*"

"I didn't know Mongolian Throat Singing was in your repertoire, Barry," Michaels said, laughing, only so he wouldn't cry.

"Jim Croce... you're the one I want to go through time with... He wrote the song for his pregnant wife, then died when his plane hit a tree at the end of the runway. The pilot didn't even try to avoid it, even though it was the only tree in the area. Eerie shit. Number one song, though."

"Oh, that is sad," Michaels acknowledged.

"It gets worse. The wife had a son, who went blind after being beaten by a stepfather—who wouldn't have existed if his dad hadn't crashed. How does that happen, eh?" Barry said, enjoying being conspiratorial.

"Some people are just born unlucky, I guess." As a member of the Church, Michaels always suspected people were somehow holding him responsible for the world's ills, the callousness of the universe.

"What was this song called again?"

"'Time in a Bottle,'" Barry said. "Growing on you, is it?"

"Your radio is a bit crackly." Michaels peered more closely at the dial. The clock display was telling the wrong time also.

"Atmospherics." Barry tapped the clock. "Big electrical storms can mess up the satellites. Probably the MSF signal too."

"What's that? The MS—?"

"Eff. It's a dedicated time broadcast that provides the source of UK civil time. Transmits from Anthorn over by Carlisle. Radio clocks pick it up."

Physics was Barry's forte. Michaels often forgot the big man's STEM credentials, but, in fairness, Science, Technology, Engineering, and Mathematics seemed incongruous when dressed snugly in chainmail.

"Like the Speaking Clock," Barry added, trying to make things as simple as possible. "With all last week's strong solar activity, maybe it's time to wear tin foil on our heads. Makes everything cuckoo."

If you only knew the half of it. Michaels smiled wryly.

They set off round Meadowview at a steady 30 mph, past the modest stucco bungalows and the ostentatious wood-cladding on the new builds, then turned onto Whitecroft. Beautifully refurbished homes in a very desirable postcode, Michaels thought mechanically. He much preferred his side of the village, where the houses had a modicum of distance from the road. Still, the new houses kept the village viable, and he was sure the Parish Council would insist on keeping a suitable green fringe around the village.

There was an unopened can of Coke between the two seats, and he was suddenly craving sugar. Or, rather, the migraine was.

"May I?" he asked.

"Knock yourself out," Barry said, graciously, his eyes still on the road ahead. Michaels took one swig, then another, and drained the rest on the third go. He was feeling as frail as glass, but the pop would help. He swilled Coke around his mouth. His teeth felt furry; they'd need a good firm brush later.

"I wonder when the special guest star is arriving?" Barry asked. "Of course, if I still had the taxi, I might have picked her up myself."

Michaels decided to be more charitable, and as chatty as his headache would allow. "What guest star is that?"

Barry snorted derisively. "What rock have you been hiding under? The Vicar said he's been emailing you. Seriously, you've not been online?"

"Not much, no. Just sleeping lots. Besides, the internet is an infuriating place, populated by morons who can't even agree what they are arguing about."

"There is that. They call it Loki's Wager."

"What now?" Michaels asked. It wasn't a term he'd seen in any of the Mindfulness & Mediation brochures.

"Loki, the trickster god. He's the bound figure carved on your Viking cross. His freeing would be a signal for the start of Ragnarok, when he would show his treachery by fighting against the gods on the side of the giants." Barry stopped briefly at a pedestrian crossing and tooted a friendly horn at some people he obviously recognised.

"Thank you, Barry, for the lesson in things I already know. I might as well be on Reddit."

"Well, smart arse, as legend has it, Loki made a bet with some dwarfs. It was agreed that the prize, should Loki lose the wager, would be his head. Loki lost the bet, and in due time the dwarfs came to collect the head which had become rightfully theirs. And Loki was beheaded, and the dwarfs were happy and there were no more problems ever in the Norse world. The end."

"That can't be right," Michaels said, suspecting something was amiss.

Barry gave a big belly laugh. "Just seeing if you were paying attention. Anyway, Loki had no problem with giving up his head, but he insisted the dwarfs had absolutely no right to take any part of his neck. Everyone concerned discussed the matter; certain parts were obviously head, and certain parts were obviously neck, but neither side could agree exactly where the one ended and the other began. As a result, Loki kept his noggin on his shoulders. Loki's Wager has become the term used for an argument that can never be decided because no-one can agree on how to define the terms."

"So, the whole internet then?" Michaels groaned. Democrats and Republicans, Brexiteers and Remoaners—the world was certainly becoming more polarised, with the only common ground being smokescreens, diversions, and stalling tactics.

"Speaking of trickster gods..." Taking one hand off the wheel, Barry rummaged in the glovebox. He triumphantly flourished a half scrunched up newspaper. "The local rag. If by local you mean sold to a U.S. media giant and printed in Glasgow, of course," he sneered, unexpectedly. There'd been a lot of bad blood when the Yanks bought the *Times & Star* after four generations of being family-owned.

Michaels took the paper and squinted at the headline. THEY DIED IN THE EAST, IN TARTARY.

"I can't really read it in this light. So, what, standards slipping?" he asked. He had no idea why an English paper would write Tartary in the twenty-first century. It was an obsolete term, for Mongolia or Siberia, the kind of thing Marco Polo would have called Central Asia.

"Here's the thing. The Ingvar Runestones is the name of a whole bunch of Swedish memorials. Hundred of men sailed east with a Viking called Ingvar the Far-Travelled. It was a fateful expedition that took place in the tenth century. Or maybe the eleventh... anyway, none of them returned. It was like the Viking version of the *Titanic*."

"Topical news then?"

"Wait till you hear the good bit. The runestones have changed. The article, it has pictures. More than twenty runestones, hundreds of kilometres apart—all of them talk about the men dying on the Mongolian Plateau."

"So?"

"Well, Vikings went nowhere near that far. And the historical record proves it. Plus, and this is the kicker, the runestones themselves changed overnight. Look at the page, side by side photos see? Old and new inscriptions. Weird, eh?"

Michaels couldn't focus clearly enough to make out much more than a page full of shadows. He shook his head slowly. "Vandals, most likely," he said, dismissively.

"Fair enough. 'The determined prankster with a chisel' theory." Barry laughed. "And this from the same august personage who had two new Viking crosses pop up in his backyard. You can't just edit a runestone. It's not a bloody word processor. Anyway, it doesn't stop there. The famous Jelling stone has also changed, and that's kept behind protective glass."

Michaels nodded. Barry had a good point.

"What does that say now?" Michaels asked, curious now. The Jelling stone, the so-called birth certificate of Denmark, had UNESCO heritage status. It was inscribed by Denmark's first Christian king, Harald Bluetooth, and featured the triumph of the Lion of Judah over the Midgard serpent.

"Don't know. Didn't get that far," Barry said, unabashed.

"Trolls then. Fake news. And since when has the *Times & Star* been printing news from Scandinavia?"

"Since you put us on the map. X marks the spot. Something's going on, mark my words. Stone stores story."

"So, who's the guest star?" Michaels asked, genuinely perplexed, although he wasn't sure whether that was because of the runestone story or the notion that a Parish Council meeting warranted a visitor from out of town.

"A professor. Danish, I think. Told you, Gosforth is all the rage these past couple of months. You should see what they dug up out by

Seascale in preparing the bridle path. Honestly, 'mind blown.' Makes the Cumwhitton dig look like child's play. Wanna go and have a look? See it with your own eyes if you don't believe me. It's not far."

They'd almost reached their destination but, instead of turning into the Village Hall, Barry suddenly sped up and headed towards the A595.

Michaels's head started pounding.

"Don't worry, we've got over an hour yet," Barry said. "I can stop at the garage and grab myself a bite. We'll be done in a jiffy. But, seriously, what with all that's been happening, you can't go into a meeting about the Viking Way without seeing this for yourself."

"If you say so," Michaels said, humouring him, much more concerned about the icy road.

Michaels resigned himself to the journey and stared off into the fields, quietly contemplative. He'd like to believe England was dreaming, under its hills, of the turn of the world and the dance of the stars, but the reality was morning papers full of EU rules and Trumpian economics. They passed the Rugby Club.

"Watch out, Barry. Construction ahead." Barry might not have been going very quickly, but Michaels didn't want Coffin Corner to live up to its name. He could see workmen up ahead, their high-visibility vests dancing in the headlights. The snowbanks by the side of the road only made the glare worse.

"Where?" Barry replied, clearly confused. "It's the middle of winter!"

"Good heavens..." Michaels said. There was something else there, by the road. Something immense, big enough to *be* the road. The night rose up, hissing, full of rippling muscles and sloughing scales. His head felt like bursting.

"Turn around! Stop the car!" he screamed, reaching over and grabbing the wheel. He twisted it violently towards him, so that the van bumped onto the kerb. The Viking gear in the back slid around freely, clattering on the panelling, as if a whole troop of re-enactors was going at it hammer and tongs.

"Bloody hell. Keep your hair on," Barry shouted, trying to get control by yanking on the handbrake.

Michaels unbuckled himself, jumped out of the van and ran back to safety of the village.

"And where are we now with that, exactly?" the official drawled. The churchwarden looked up, into the fog of faces, a maze of silvery squiggles and zigzags. He recognised the voice, even if the face was an indistinct blur. Councillor David Cornwall was speaking, the sort of man who could make time stand still with his pitch-perfect drone. It was always the faces that vanished first. They broke and scattered, like blown dandelions. A blind spot formed in the room, a small eclipse that grew as he watched, following his gaze. The creature in his skull slithered behind his eyes, skewering each person, gulping them down, swallowing first the eyes, and then the whole head.

An aura, the doctors called it.

Michaels watched with glum fascination as the Gosforth Council shrank and floated away right before his eyes. The hallucinations were getting more vivid, if the thing by the A595 was anything to go by. He should really insist on an MRI, he thought. After all, hypochondria didn't normally wriggle...

How long had he been here? He had no recollection of taking his seat. That would be the second blackout in as many hours. The churchwarden tried to focus on sounds, rather than his ailment. Cornwall was hemming and hawing through his own stack of papers, his mouth clicking as if it were dry. Through the optical haze, Michaels imagined mandibles clicking.

"I have been monitoring car park usage since we last met. As well all know, there were forty-five places in the car park; of those, five are designated restricted waiting for the bins and a further four allocated for wheelchair users."

Both the Seascale and Gosforth Parish Councils had gathered. Davids Cornwall and Quinn; Graham Hudson; Ken Mawson; Michael McKinsey; the Chair, Tyrone Reed; his deputy Christopher Baxter; and the newly installed Clerk, Jacqueline Westerman. They were already like an extended family, and the Viking Way would only strengthen the bond.

Parish Council meetings were held in the Supper Room, on the second floor of Gosforth Public Hall. The building was one ramshackle extension after another, mildew-white walls and rust-red trim on the doors and windows so that it looked damp on even the brightest of days. Even the SLOW sign painted on the cracked tarmac outside had faded and worn, as if in condemnation of council proceedings. The Supper Room itself was, if anything, even more dingy, held together by low black beams that constantly threatened to crack heads. They been recently painted, and now contrasted badly with the lemon and lime pastels on the walls and the stacks of grey office chairs that adorned them.

Ken Mawson chimed in. "One contractor in particular was seen using the car park as a Park and Ride, but other than that, there did not seem to be a huuuuuge number of spaces being used." He made his words as expansive and exaggerated as possible.

"Under the terms of our agreement, no buses or commercial vehicles were supposed to use the car park. At all. We were quite clear on the subject."

"Can I just say that the British Parking Association could offer advice here?"

Michaels reached for his phone to check the time, but the display was impossible to make out. They must have been talking for over an hour already. Worse, they didn't seem to be following any kind of agenda. The Parish Council meetings could drag on for hours, unlike the Parochial Church Council (local government was just as parochial, it was just called something different). Reverend Riley kept the quarterly PCC meetings brief and to the point, focused on refreshments for Morning Praise or the price of the laminated information sheets at the back of the church. PASEO—purpose, agenda, start on time, end on time, outcomes. It was all very clear if you stuck to the formula, Michaels thought, growing irritable.

"Excellent. Top notch idea. Will you take ownership of that, Ken? Also, Jackie, if you'd also be so kind to mention that the light on the car park was defective." The Clerk nodded that she would, indeed, report this.

The churchwarden yawned, uncontrollably. He wasn't particularly tired, but sustained yawning was another symptom of his unwelcome visitor. Combined with ineffable boredom, he didn't stand a chance. He stretched and yowled like a lonely wolf.

After a few moments, he noticed the room had gone quiet. Everyone was looking at him, clearly insulted by his gasping for oxygen.

"Sorry," he said, wincing, "perhaps a quick cup of coffee is in order?"

"Very good," someone brayed, peremptorily. Michaels stepped into the corner and reached amongst the paper cups, pouring himself some tepid coffee. He debated adding milk, in case it made it so lukewarm as to be undrinkable, but ultimately, the simple smell put him off. The meeting rolled on around him. Councillor Quinn put forward an offer from the Rotary to continue pruning work on the car park, which was gratefully accepted.

He went downstairs in search of fresh air, and stood in the doorway, looking across the tiny car park to the HSBC.

"You made it then." Barry, the Science Viking, called out from the front seat of his van. It was more of a statement than a question. Michaels heard the hesitation in his voice—Barry clearly thought the churchwarden was off his rocker. He'd chosen to sit in his van until the last minute, rather than risk further conversation upstairs.

"They ready for us yet?" Barry asked. Shorn of his usual gregariousness, he seemed small and sullen.

"Still talking about parking, as far as I know. Listen…"

Michaels started to explain himself, but confessing *I'm worried I have a brain tumour* in a car park seemed ludicrous. Thankfully, just at that moment another guest appeared at his shoulder, as if from nowhere. The aura had obviously demolished his peripheral vision too.

"Ah, Michaels. Good to see you up and about. How are the headaches?"

Hugh Bracegirdle ran the University of the Third Age. It was a small close-knit village, less than 2,000 people at the last census, but a good quarter of them were retired, and so Hugh had a solid membership list. He was a bit of a know-it-all, Michaels's bête-noire when it came to Trivia Night at the Wheatsheaf, especially in the Military History Buzzer Round.

"Migraines. I think I have one coming on now," the churchwarden said. "It starts with vision distortion."

"Oh dear, what's that like?" asked Hugh, with misplaced enthusiasm.

Michaels thought for a moment, then said, "It feels for all the world like when an IT technician remotely accesses your computer and, without you putting a finger on the mouse, moves the cursor from folder to inbox."

Hugh didn't respond to that. Michaels could only imagine the puzzled look. The old man had retired from his job at British Energy around the time of Windows 98, and probably practised for the pub quiz with a CD-ROM of Encarta.

"There are none so blind as those who cannot see," Barry chimed in, seeing fit to jump out of his van at last, given the safety of numbers.

"Will not see," Michaels corrected. "Otherwise it's a truism, Barry."

"Suit yourself. You know your Bible, I suppose," the big Viking huffed. His chainmail swished and swirled, a shoal of electric minnows. Hugh was wearing his hooded anorak, a coat that he wore constantly and without the slightest sense of irony, come rain or shine. At the end of the day, Michaels supposed, everyone wore a suit of armour.

"You here for the karate then, Barry?" Hugh enquired, sizing up the costume. The big man had brought his prize possession with him this time—the huge, two-handed replica axe he called Deathsinger.

It was Barry's turn to look bemused. "The Viking Way, Hugh. I'm not a bleedin' samurai."

"There's a new Qi-Yoga class starting up next month, Barry. Might be your sort of thing." The unsolicited advice came from Samantha Bunting, who'd just pulled up in a red blur. She ran the local Spin Studio, which, Michael realised, was a much better analogy for a migraine. Pounding music, emetic neon, and every movement a punishment.

"See?" said Michaels, seeing the opportunity to tighten the screw. "Sounds very kamikaze. Right up your alley."

"I'll put my boot right up your alley in a minute, Churchwarden, headache or no headache," Barry snapped. It was Michaels's turn to hold up his hands in apology. Barry was ordinarily a gentle giant, used to taking a tease. You couldn't really work as a Viking re-enactor without developing a thick skin. The churchwarden resolved to take him aside later and apologise properly. Hopefully, it was nothing that a free pint and a ploughman's wouldn't smooth out.

Sam Bunting leaned her head out of the driver's window. The car smelled of teenage boys, damp camping equipment and discarded gym wear. "Hello, Olaf. Should you be out and about? Not tucked up in bed?"

"I'm on the mend, thank you, Sam," he lied, backing away from the smell. He was in no state for the piquant aromas of the Scout troop.

"He has a point," said Hugh, ignoring the exchange of pleasantries. "The kamikaze literally means 'divine wind'—they were storms that are said to have saved Japan from Mongol fleets under Kublai Khan. Vikings and Mongols are two very different things."

"I *know* that, Hugh, thank you," said Michaels, thinking very unchristian thoughts.

"One in thirty-three Britons can claim direct descent from Vikings," the old man continued. "Whereas one in two hundred men globally are directly descended from Genghis Khan himself."

"Put it about a bit, did he?" Barry said, laughing.

"Penrith was revealed to have the highest concentration of Scandinavian DNA in England," Hugh Bracegirdle said. "For more than a quarter of us, it seems, our—times 40—male ancestor was from Norway."

Michaels smiled thinly, wondering whether the University of the Third Age ran courses in Unlikely Statistics and Senility.

"And half the known universe has taken some form of ancestry DNA test. It's all bogus," Michaels sniped, resentful that anyone was giving more credibility to a cotton swab Y-chromosome test than his own Norse expertise.

"Perhaps migraines are genetic?" Hugh asked, brightening at the sudden epiphany.

Sam Bunting laughed and turned off her ignition. "Triggered by stress, apparently. Last thing you should do is to turn up to a planning meeting, Olaf! Still, I hear Mrs. Jones has been doing the Lord's work? Keeping you calm?" She was either feeling neighbourly or had time to kill. It was disconcerting, Michaels realized, how much people relied on facial expressions to understand their fellow man. Eyes really were the windows of the soul.

"Oh yes," Michaels said, keeping information to a minimum just in case it led to further questions and discomfort.

"My old mam used to get them migraines," said yet another voice. Jackie the new Clerk, if the menthol stench of Marlboro Ice was anything to go by. Michaels wondered who was left upstairs in the Supper Room. The car park was like Piccadilly Circus. "She tried all sorts. Anti-inflammatories, steroids, muscle relaxants, beta blockers."

"Sounds like one of them Russian athletes," Hugh said. "Can't trust the Rooskies."

"Magic mushrooms before the school run," said Sam. "That's my secret weapon. No need to look at me like that. You take a tiny dose. You ought to try it. You don't feel high, just... better."

"Here for the meeting, Sam?" Jackie asked, somewhat icily.

"No fear. Picking up from karate."

On cue, little David Bunting ducked past the group, a flash of ginger and freckles. As he jumped into the car, Sam chirped, "Ah, here's my chubby little chipmunk!"

"Bye, Snowman!" David clucked, waving at Michaels.

Be prepared, he'd taught them. Do Your Best. Now the little buggers ambushed him with Olaf jokes every time he went near the All Saints Centre. The headlights searched their faces as the car reversed, dazzling Michaels further. The fresh air hadn't done him any good at all—his unwelcome guest really had his fangs into him tonight. On the bright side, he reflected, he had escaped without being offered a free spin class.

"Silly old witch," sneered Jackie, hidden under plumes of menthol smoke. There was obviously no love lost between the two women. Mrs. Jones had said something about an affair, but he'd done his best to ignore the more lurid details of her tittle-tattle. Village life could be very unforgiving.

"That's not very Christian," Hugh admonished, unzipping his hood slightly. "Whatever next?"

"Qi-Yoga, it would appear." Jackie laughed, sourly. "I'm sorry, but you've got to admit, Sam Bunting is a one-woman Wiccan Wave. Peddling Class A drugs from her kitchen table. Someone ought to call the police."

She looked expectantly at the group, tottering slightly on her high heels. Michaels knew better than to get involved. Even in the age of #MeToo, people liked to burn witches. Sam Bunting's feel-good hobbies, the natural convergence of self-care, green living, and new age spirituality annoyed the more conservative villagers—it just wasn't very Church of England. Besides, the Devil offered up many temptations, and Michaels had his work cut out pretending that the idea of Sam Bunting in a billowy white skirt and flip-flops, sitting cross-legged around a circle of flowers, wasn't one of them.

"What's that all about?" mouthed Hugh Bracegirdle, conspiratorially.

"Long story," moaned Michaels. "Shall we go back in?"

It took him a moment to realise that Hugh wasn't talking to him. All of them—Jackie, Hugh, Barry—were instead peering past him, up at the night sky above the bank. Sam Bunting had slammed on the brakes too and was cooing out of her window.

"What is it, Mum?" David piped up.

"The Northern Lights, Davey boy," she replied, in rapt attention. "Come quite a way south…"

Michaels almost swore under his breath. It wasn't uncommon for a burst of solar energy to send the aurora dancing across the Lake District. He'd seen them himself over the River Derwent a couple of years ago on a Scouts manoeuvre. The skies slowly cleared of clouds after sunset, the moon rose to light up the landscape, mists began to swirl around Borrowdale and just before midnight, the burst of activity in the northern sky had been… sensational. It was frustrating to be missing out this time.

"Bloody hell!" breathed Barry, snapping away with his camera-phone in one hand, and Deathsinger in the other.

"Never seen them that close before," Jackie whispered, clearly awestruck.

Michaels tilted his head and scrunched up his eyes, trying to focus. All at once, the horizon became a brilliant shade of red, clouds swept together like dust rising above a distant troop of riders. True enough, in the cloud were shapes of men and horses, each of the spectral riders carried banners, lances, spears or swords, pointed high and radiant into the sky.

And underneath it all, the scales of armour glistened like a silver gauze.

The Aurora Borealis. A geomagnetic storm. Barry had mentioned an atmospheric disturbance earlier, messing with his radio. That must have been what he'd seen, out by Coffin Corner. Not a giant, world-circling snake at all...

Vikings on the Brain, he sighed. *Bloody crosses.*

"I think I need to sit down," Michaels said. "I'm going inside."

"All in favour? Right, good, that's everyone. Let the record state it was agreed that Sellafield Ltd. be contacted in respect of amended leaflets," Councillor Michael McKinsley concluded. Then with an air of smug satisfaction, he added, "Now, I'd like to move proceedings on to the subject of the Viking Way bridle path."

There was a ragged cheer. Michaels clapped enthusiastically from the stairwell. The migraine had lifted, and as the pain subsided, so had his spirits soared. *Tumours,* he scoffed silently, nudging the bemused Barry to join in the applause.

The Northern Lights were so majestic, the Council had killed the harsh fluorescents and were content to sit in the darkness, caressed by meandering ethereal curtains of light. The dingy old Supper Room suddenly seemed a sanctuary, the thick walls, bulky filing cabinets and small windows creating a sense of security in the midst of a wild world. The strangest thing about the Northern Lights was the noise they sometimes made, like someone rustling a bag of popcorn. It was less a Council meeting than a group outing to the Gaiety Cinema in Whitehaven.

He peered in, hoping to find a spare seat, but the room was crammed, the lure of the aurora and the exodus from karate swelling the room to capacity. Reverend Riley was cheerfully topping up anyone who asked for more tea. Michaels gave him a friendly wave and sidled over, with the Science Viking barrelling after him like an enthusiastic bodyguard.

Meanwhile, McKinsley warbled on, without waiting for the excitement to die down. He was a thin, reedy man but possessed the boundless energy of the impatient. "We are thrilled to have with us a very special guest, all the way from Sweden. The heavens themselves have seen fit to welcome her. You must have put in good word, Reverend?"

"The Heavens Declare the Glory of God; and the Firmament Sheweth His Handywork," Riley intoned, obligingly.

Michaels smiled. His friend had done well since moving here—they'd rearranged the whole Benefice of Seatallen around him. He was now the priest-in-charge for Gosforth, Seascale, the Wasdales, and Beckermet. His wife often joked about the charmed "Life of Riley" he led. The diocese had long been associated with climbers, what with Scafell Pike being within its borders, she teased, affectionately.

"Psalms?" the churchwarden asked, and the priest gave him a big thumbs-up. Like the best of all teachers, he seemingly had a quote for every occasion. The two men often tried to catch each other out, just for fun.

"Is there any chance of a cup of tea? Or a seat maybe? I've had quite the turn," Michaels whispered, taking advantage of the lull. He'd meant the question for Riley, but the Chairman, Tyrone Reed, overheard him and scowled. He used to be a gravedigger, and despite now running a local machinery business, he'd retained something of the sepulchre about him.

"Oh, get up, McKinsley, and let the churchwarden have a spot at the table. Let's hope he'll stop yowling and complaining."

McKinsley reluctantly stretched, shooting the churchwarden an annoyed glance as Riley passed him one of the bone china cups of tea. Michaels accepted with a smile, but before he took a sip, he raised his cup in a toast: "Blessings upon all the Council! Glad I can join this Christian fellowship today!" He was feeling unusually full of himself. Cocksure, like an inmate unexpectedly reprieved from Death Row.

"Well, if you are quite finished..." McKinsley muttered, before addressing the room at large. "May I present Professor von Linné from the University of Lund?"

Michaels's eyes turned to the special guest, tucked away in the corner. It was a relief to be able to see clearly again, even if the lighting was more atmospheric than practical. How long she had been there, he didn't know, but he didn't think that the Council would be so cruel as to subject her to their whole agenda. She must have snuck in through the back door.

"Thank you for having me," the woman said, calmly looking around the table, making solid—and, Michaels thought, slightly intimidating—eye contact with those around the table. Her accent was almost neutral, although he wasn't surprised by that—the Swedes were often named as the best speakers of English as a second language in the world. Not just because of their schools, or business savvy—at root, the languages were very similar.

The professor wore a sombre polo neck jumper, in a poorly disguised attempt to hide some extensive inkwork on her neck. She was youthful, although somewhat haggard—the Lord knew it wasn't an easy journey from Stockholm; the person who designed Manchester Airport had allegedly had a hand in devising the Labyrinth at Knossos—but there was something hard-bitten about her. She wouldn't have been out of place as a lead in a Nordic noir show—one of the bleak crime procedurals that dominated TV these days. Not so long ago, the BBC was content to give its viewers recycled period dramas headlined by Victorian—or Belgian—detectives, but now the schedule teemed with gruesome murders, sordid local government conspiracies, and ominous shots of fjords bathed in the midnight sun. They'd proven Sweden's biggest export since Abba or Volvo.

When she turned her attention to his side of the room, the professor nodded, curtly, and Michaels was overcome with a nervous urge to snigger. Perhaps McKinsley had laced his tea with booze and given him the wrong cup? Sneaky bastard. Barry Thurston-Hicks stood at the back of his chair, grinning down at him like the cat that got the cream. He was far too excited for a meeting about mere planning permission.

"This is going to be good," he said, stroking his beard in anticipation.

Meanwhile, Councillor McKinsley, never one to stand on ceremonies, wasted no time launching into the debate. "Let me start by saying, while I respect the desire of the two communities to forge closer links..." he began, beginning to pace as best he could in the confined space.

"And cut down my commute," interjected Hugh Bracegirdle almost immediately, felling the councillor in mid-sentence.

"And cut down Mr. Bracegirdle's commute." McKinsley feigned amusement before ploughing on. "I think now is the perfect time to apply for an archeological grant from the Department of Portable Antiquities & Treasure. The dig is just too important..."

"Told you!" whispered Barry, emphatically in Michaels's ear, distracting him completely.

"You haven't told me a thing yet!" Michaels hissed back, aware that the councillors wouldn't be keen on yet another disruption to proceedings. He felt for all the world like one of his more errant Scouts, all attention deficit disorder and pent-up energy. It was an oddly childlike position for a supposed pillar of the community.

"I was trying to show you!" Barry said, rolling his eyes. Michaels racked his brain, tried to guess what all the fuss was about. The Victorians had once found a ninth century silver-gilt relic in the area, called the Ormside Bowl. That was part of a touring collection now. The Furness Hoard had been ninety or so silver coins, some of them Arabic. Nothing that would stop planning permission, though. The British Museum was obviously getting involved, so it must be something big—perhaps another Viking Age cemetery like the graves at Cumwhitton?

"Excuse me, Mister...?" the Swedish professor inquired politely.

To add to the embarrassment, Reverend Riley was staring at him with raised eyebrows. Michaels shrugged apologetically. Of course, they were making a racket, but Michaels couldn't help wondering if Barry's medieval garb drew extra unnecessary attention. The great pole-axe tucked under the table was doubtless a Council first.

"That's Olaf Michaels. The churchwarden at St. Mary's," clicked David Cornwall.

"AKA, the Runestone Cowboy," some wag added. Michaels suspected it was Deputy Baxter, but he was too busy blushing shades of beetroot to search out the culprit.

"Who!?" Reed asked, before spotting the joke. "Ah, Glen Campbell is it? That's a good one." He laughed like a drain as he mentally rode out into a star-spangled rodeo.

The professor smiled at the churchwarden, ignoring the commentary from the peanut gallery. Michaels was warming to her already. What with the sounds of chomping popcorn from the aurora, Michaels was finding it almost impossible to concentrate, but she was the epitome of cool and calm, keeping her head when all around were losing theirs. He was impressed with her resolve.

"Boundary stones," von Linné said, matter-of-factly. "We found boundary stones."

"A boundary for what?" Michaels asked.

"For whom, rather. An early burial custom, characteristically Scandinavian but also found across Europe. Graves were often surrounded by stones in the outline of a ship," she said. "I have sketches. If you'd like to see?"

For a moment, Michaels wondered if she was joking. Then he realized: *Of course you do.* Very Scandi-noir. What was it with these Scandinavians, he thought, using pictures books and doodles when there were perfectly good camera-phones? Hadn't the University of Lund *invented* Bluetooth technology?

She reached into her case.

"Of course, I'd be delighted to look," Michaels said, genuinely intrigued. "But what makes you think they are Norse? There are plenty of stone circles in the Faerie Hills of Cumbria. Castlerigg, Long Meg, Elva Plain. They were here thousands of years before the Vikings landed."

It was true. Over the centuries, Cumbria had been a fertile ground for myths and legends, with its remote landscape of mountains, forests and woods. Stories had been passed down by the generations for a thousand years. There were a dozen spooky spots where he'd take the Scouts camping—the coastal village of Ravenglass, just five minutes away in the Astra, claimed to be home of King Eveling, faerie ruler of the Rath, cursed by Merlin to haunt the Fellside. His Rath—or stronghold—was actually Mediobogdum, the ruins of a Roman fort located on the hair-raising Hardknott Pass between Eskdale and the central Lake District, but locals hadn't let actual facts get in the way of a good yarn. The conjunction of fairy stories and Arthurian myths remained compelling even now, combining magic and mystery with a promise of redemption and restoration. The Once and Future King would return from Faery to assist the Britons in their greatest struggle. In some far distant future, Mrs. Jones's descendants would probably tell stories of how King Arthur defeated an evil giant named Brexit in this very spot.

"Scarce images of life, one here, one there, Lay vast and edgeways; like a dismal cirque, Of Druid stones, upon a forlorn moor," Riley quoted, moving round to peer over his shoulder.

"Keats?" Michaels ventured, earning his second thumbs-up of the evening.

"You're like one of those calendars. A Poem-A-Day," Barry guffawed in his ear.

The professor placed a sketchbook on the table in front of Michaels, spinning it round to face him. There were twenty stones, maybe more, all of varying sizes. The illusion of a ship had been reinforced by larger stones at either end.

Michaels scanned the image, then flicked over a page to where there was a pencil rubbing, designed to show the imprint in the rock beneath. The characters certainly looked like they were part of a runic alphabet rather than any Roman graffiti. It read:

ᛖ=ᛖᚲ²

"Can you translate the runes?" the professor said, her eyes tunneling into him.

Michaels reached for a pencil and scratched for meaning, cycling through letters in his head. "He doesn't know? What rock has he been under?" Graham Hudson asked the room, his pitch rising with his incredulity, hoping to get cheap laughs. Perhaps they'd all been drinking—Hudson was almost swaying with intoxicated abandon, his face blotched, lined with the broken blood vessels of the almost-alcoholic. The whole room was watching the exchange intently, egging them on, the local expert pitted against international renown. Somehow, Michaels didn't feel he had home turf advantage.

"$E=mc^2$?"

"See!" squealed Barry. "E equals MC squared. It's the world's most famous equation. And the Norse worked it out before Einstein!"

Michaels looked round the room, incredulous. "Oh. Dear. Me. Okay—where is the hidden camera? Joke's on me."

He was surprised to see every face was deadly serious. As sombre as stone, you might say. Perhaps he was the only one not in on the joke. Either that, or this was a practice run for the World's Biggest Liar competition. Every November at Santon Bridge, competitors had five minutes to tell the biggest and most convincing lie they could without any script or props. Last year, the winning story claimed that many Cumbrians were four per cent badger. This runic-whopper would be right up there.

"Come off it. Reverend?" he implored his friend.

"Exciting, isn't it, Olaf? Even bigger than the crosses! I knew you'd want to see for yourself."

Michaels wasn't excited. *Fool me once, shame on you. Fool me twice, shame on me*, he thought. The Gosforth cross was one thing—the original depicted various characters and incidents from the Norse tale of the end of the world. It was a simple, primeval story, good versus evil, showing how the old Norse beliefs passed away, superseded by Christian truth. But this—he didn't even know what it meant. $E=mc^2$. Something to do with relativity and the speed of light?

Barry must have read his mind. "Energy equals mass times the speed of light squared. On the most basic level, the equation says that energy and mass are interchangeable; they are different forms of the same thing. Now, we don't see them that way—how can that aurora and a walnut, say, be different forms of the same thing?—but Nature does."

Barry was breathless with excitement, and paused to stir and slurp his tea, hastily gathering his thoughts. He grabbed his spoon and wielded it with renewed inspiration.

"Say you could turn every one of the atoms in this teaspoon into pure energy—leaving no mass whatsoever—the spoon would yield twenty kilotons of TNT. That's roughly the size of the bomb that destroyed Hiroshima in 1955!"

Someone at the back of the room saluted Barry with a wolf-whistle. The big man gave a little bow of appreciation.

"And this is related to the changes in the other runestones, is it? The ones in Sweden and whatnot?" Chairman Reed asked.

"That's what I am here to find out," the professor said.

Michaels was dumbfounded. He couldn't be accused of being a natural skeptic: not so long ago, he'd been on the other side of the fence, trying to defend the sudden appearance of two medieval crosses to TV journalists. But there was a clear difference—the ornate patterns on the crosses, the interwoven carvings were fashioned by craftsmen. There was even a name for the style they used: Jellinge. Antiquarians could attest that they had existed in the past—Michaels couldn't explain how they appeared or who put them there, but it was as if someone had simply stood them up again. He was fairly sure that the main body of maths came to the West from medieval Islamic scholars and knew for a fact that the equals sign was devised by a Welshman. You didn't forget that kind of trophy-winning trivia.

"Look, I'm sorry. This is ludicrous. Something doesn't add up. I mean, that's modern maths alongside, what? Fifth century runes? By the time the Vikings settled in Cumbria, they used a wholly different script, the Younger Futhark. I'm more inclined to go with—what did you call it, Barry?—the determined prankster with a chisel theory."

He was tempted to reach for his phone and call forth the gods of Google, but there was a loud grumble from amongst the councillors. It was getting late, and even the aurora was losing its lustre. He stared hard at von Linné and pressed on. If it wasn't an elaborate practical joke, perhaps it was wishful thinking. Or pure greed. The whole village was high on the hog.

"At the risk of being unpopular, let me tell you about the Heavener Runestone. In Oklahoma, of all places. Experts from all over the world examined it, even the Smithsonian. It took another Swedish professor to debunk the whole thing. It was a nineteenth century hoax, carved by a Scandinavian immigrant during the Viking revival. There are a lot of similar stories and they are all, I'm sorry to say, simply untrue, because the Vikings didn't travel to Oklahoma. Same as they never dabbled in physics."

"What did the runes say?" asked Hugh Bracegirdle.

"Gobbledygook. There were eight runes, some Elder Futhark, some Younger, some back-to-front. The stone's most charitable translation is 'Gnome Dale,'" he said, dismissively.

"But there is evidence for Viking colonization all over Vinland, isn't there?" Hugh persisted. The old wolf clearly thought he had scented prey and was determined to make a meal of it.

Michaels brushed him aside. "There are plenty of tall tales and clever hoaxes—the Maine Penny, Beardmore Relics, the Kensington Runestone, even the lost city of Norumbega. It's just wishful thinking that falls apart under analysis. Look, I get it. We'd have another fifteen minutes of fame. Tourist revenue would go up next summer. Barry would have another banner year. But it's not real. I'm sure the Heavener Chamber of Commerce didn't like their bubble being burst either, but you can't hide from the truth."

The professor smiled, still holding his gaze. "Very well observed, Churchwarden. Many valuable truths are hidden in plain sight."

Michaels wasn't sure what she meant. It almost sounded like a threat, or a warning. Bloody gnomic Swedes and their cliff-hangers, he thought. She carried on watching him through the kaleidoscope of lights, drumming her forefingers on her sketch paper, drawing his attention back to her drawing.

"My point is this," she said. "The Norse believed the stone ship would equip the dead with everything he had in life. But the world is not so much made of stones as of fleeting sounds, or of waves moving through the sea. Trust me when I say this—I don't think the passage is one way."

"Oh, I think it rather has to be," Michaels argued. "That's pretty much the definition of death. 'An undiscovered country whose bourne no travellers return.' *Hamlet*. Perhaps you know it? He was a Dane, I suppose, but close enough. I'm sorry, what did you say you were a professor of?"

"I didn't." The professor laughed. Michaels had started the day thinking he was going mad. Now he was beginning to wonder if he wasn't the only sane person in the room. Von Linné had clearly decided to dig in her hiking boots and continue to argue her point. "Let me take on the burden of proof."

"I hope it's better than your spurious faery circle," Michaels said, groaning. "I'm afraid the church rather frowns on the testimony of leprechauns, boggles, and elves."

Michaels wondered if she was baiting him or whether she was entirely deranged. Clearly, the Wiccan Wave had reached Scandinavia. Either that, or the Lutherans had become even more radical. That was the problem with Christianity—there were all kinds of splinters, needling into the skin of the Church. "I don't understand. You've come all this way to tell us think you've found a gateway to the underworld? Is there anyone in this room, over the age of nine, and halfway sane, who believes in the existence of actual ghosts and goblins?" Michaels spluttered. He wondered if Riley, or Barry—or anyone—might intervene, but he didn't dare break the professor's gaze. Her stare had him riveted in his seat, locked into their debate.

"It doesn't matter. The boundary is crossed," she said, her eyes boring into his. "The equation proves that there is... intent... behind its creation."

Well, doesn't that just take the biscuit, Michaels thought. He tore his eyes away and looked at the stupefied room, all as silent as shadows in a magic lantern. Today was turning out to be entirely miserable. If the literal headaches weren't enough, he was stuck in *A Midsummer Night's Dream* as directed by Ingmar Bergman. He should have stayed firmly in his bed.

"Well, there you have it, gentlemen," he said, witheringly. "There is a fine dividing line between seeking the limelight and inviting a Doomsday Cult into Council chambers at the taxpayers' expense, but you've managed to cross it. I hope you bought her return ticket." He noticed he was sweating profusely, damp stains ringing his armpits, his hands cold and clammy.

"Why do we care what the snowflake thinks?" Baxter spat, suddenly roaring back into action.

"Snowman," Michaels corrected, instinctively. That was it, he thought. Enough turning the other cheek. He decided he'd had altogether enough of the councillor's snide remarks. He looked round for Reverend Riley, hoping to give him fair warning that he was about to blow his top. "Keep that up and I'll knock your block off. Best you stick to cowering in your tedious parking rules and regulations." Michaels surprised himself with how venomous he sounded. He heard Barry draw a long, slow breath. He was shaking with cold fury.

Baxter glowered, popping open the button on his right cuff, and rolling up the sleeve. The councillor had all manner of sigils and staves cut deep into his skin, a web of purple welts and electric ink. "You want to take it outside?"

Michaels hadn't ever been challenged to a fist fight before, at least, not since he was a child. He laughed, despite himself. "Oho! Baxter the Benchwarmer has found his courage, has he? Come on then. Give it your best shot!"

Michaels stuck out his chin, tapping it with his finger in case Baxter needed lessons in accuracy. He was dimly aware that the whole room was charged, glowing like a grotesque Saturday morning cartoon, kernels of popcorn whistling and popping round their ears.

Jacqueline Westerman spoke up through the chaos. "Gentlemen, please calm down. Remember where you are. We have guests!" she pleaded, nervously gathering up the crockery as a precaution.

Michaels hissed, dripping with rage and perspiration. He felt fully in his element, finally free of his prim and proper skin. It was clear to him that the meek weren't blessed in any way, shape or form.

"Oh, shut up, Jackie. How many of this lot have you spread your legs for? I wonder whether it was worth straddling Reed's flaccid cock for those cheap trinkets?"

The secretary almost burst into tears. "Fuck off, Snowman!"

"Brrr, cold indeed," he quipped, relishing the witticism. "You were a great deal warmer when you used to beckon me into your bed. Since we're in the middle of baring everyone's faults and misdeeds, we might as well mention that."

McKinsley had spent most of the past few minutes quietly banging his forehead on the table. When he looked up, his glasses were comically askew. "Oh, come now. There's no harm in ladies having a few lovers on the side," he said.

Michaels's dander was up. He wasn't going to be lectured by a jumped-up security guard with ideas above his station. "Piss off, McKinsley. You might think you have our respect, but I've heard things about you too. The kinky stuff with Eileen Eastwood's daughters. When those ladies have to pee, I hear there is no end to the water sports at your house."

McKinsley growled back across the table. "Have a care and hold your tongue, mischief maker, or we'll call the police. They'll throw the book at you."

The room strobed in silence. Finally, at long last, Reverend Riley stood up, pressing together his palms in a prayer for calm, a restoration of sanity. "Faþer vár es ert í himenríki, verði nafn þitt hæilagt."

There was a high-pitched whine in Michaels's ears, like a microwave overheating. Someone was screaming.

"Gef oss í dag brauð vort dagligt," Riley chimed at almost the same frequency. And there was a third noise, the hum of reverberating metal. Barry had planted Deathsinger in Tyrone Reed's skull and was standing triumphantly over the still-warm corpse of the Council Chair.

"All this glittering wealth, gold gleaming like fire... let true flames flicker over it all!" the big man yelled.

The professor tapped Michaels gently on the shoulder. She looked entirely unmoved by the bedlam unfurling around her. The whole room had descended into a brawl.

"Do you know why I am certain the boundary has been breached?" she said, with a gentle sigh. "Because I crossed over myself."

Michaels vomited, a technicolour yawn to match the undulating skies.

It was still dark when the churchwarden woke up, but his surroundings were reassuringly familiar. Somehow, he had found his way to his church. It looked different at nighttime, the long rows of tombstones stretching like rows of blackened teeth, the grass corroded by patches of lamp light.

Across from him, the embers of a fire glowered at the base of a tombstone. He clutched at a handful of ivy to reveal the hand and heart motif of the "Grand United Order of Oddfellows," still half-masked by lichen. Something meaty... leathery... had been cooking in the fire, the smell so thick and rich that it was almost a taste. He retched, dry heaving on his knees onto the grave, strands of drool mixing with the half-frozen soil.

Blackouts, hallucinations, voices in his head. He wasn't sure if any of it was real. He propped himself against the church wall, hoping to borrow from its sheer solidity. There was a sanctity to the old Norman church, a reverence that could quieten the mind. At least the aurora had disappeared, returning the night sky to the usual matte, mundane dreariness.

Pull yourself together. Think, god damnit.

"Sorry," he added out loud, hoping that the man upstairs might overlook the sentiment. Given the circumstances, a bit of blaspheming seemed the least of his worries.

He remembered the last time there was a murder in Gosforth. The day had begun in sunshine. The streets were filling up with families enjoying half-term, and the village was bright with the promise of summer. Then the first shots rang out. A father of two, shot dead while working in the fields outside Gosforth, a random victim of a crazed man's rampage. Village life came to a standstill, as Gosforth's three pubs, bank, smattering of shops, and café had all closed as a mark of respect.

The killer had been a local taxi driver. By the time police recovered his body ten miles away in the Hardknott Pass, the death toll had reached a dozen. His victims included several pensioners out shopping, most of them shot at point-blank range with a shotgun. At the height of the manhunt the nuclear power station at Sellafield was locked down for the first time in its history, while Cumbria police deployed all their armed teams along with helicopters and dozens of vehicles to give chase.

It was a day that shocked them all to the core. How could it not? This wasn't London. For years before that, the worst thing the Cumbria Constabulary had to contend with was a scuffle at closing time.

Around two hundred people had been here, in the chapel, with hundreds more spilling out into the church grounds, mourners listening to the service broadcast on a PA system. Michaels had joined in with a hymn popular in the countryside, "We Plough the Fields and Scatter."

He crawled closer to the fire and dusted himself down. Somewhere over his shoulder, he could hear diners leaving the Gosforth Inn. He waited, holding his breath, straining to hear the slam of car doors. If he had his keys, he might have gone inside St. Mary's, to seek comfort and offer up a prayer. He was mildly surprised there had been no sirens. At some point, once he had caught his breath, he'd go back into town and deal with the insanity. For now, since the Almighty had seen fit to deposit him here, he'd just enjoy the quiet. It might be the last peace he got for a while.

St. Mary's was a keeper of ancient tales, a conduit to England's green hills and forests and what lay beneath. There was something in the very fabric of the building, buried deep in the centuries-old stone. There had been churchwardens here since 1600, not long after the plague claimed a third of the souls in the parish. He wondered what plagued him now. There had been a church here since the eighth century, and Christianity was in the northwest of England long before that—Roman soldiers had spread the faith, and left traces when their armies were withdrawn. Wandering saints and preachers came up the Irish Sea from Rome, such as the man later venerated as St. Patrick or Bega of St. Bees, bringing their religion to the Anglo-Saxons who settled there.

The Celtic monastic culture of the area provided a network of patronage for craftsmen, who carved high crosses for the abbots. When the Vikings came, the influx of colonists were absorbed without any undue trouble. But the new Norse patrons wanted to record their traditions and styles of art, using novel themes and motifs. The crosses fixed in stone the very moment when Norse pagans and Anglo-Saxon Christianity fused together. The theology was a little unexpected, but it well illustrated the contemporary church policy of "taking over" and interpreting pagan beliefs, breathing Christian life into them.

The three crosses stared down at him.

He knew every inch of them, and familiarity bred contempt. Especially the swastikas at the top—once a sacred symbol in pre-Christian religions, representing the sun, now they were weaponised, like a neo-Nazi North Star. Arduus ad solem—"striving towards the sun." Ironically, it had been his university motto.

One of the sun circles had toppled off, and where in the past it had been frivolously recast as the rectory sundial, these days it was kept under lock and key in case troublemakers took advantage. The other two kept watch, focusing the rusted light from the Wasdale road into malevolent stares.

"What are you looking at?" he spat. "You've caused me enough trouble."

"Oh, I think your troubles have barely begun, Warden," came a voice from the ether.

Michaels looked wildly around the empty graveyard, scanning the path from the gabled porch to the lychgate. There was not a soul to be seen, except for a squirrel scampering across the tombstones. It was hard to be sure in the stuttering streetlight, but Michaels had the unnerving feeling that it was watching him. Intently. Behind the two, dark lustreless pools was a keen intelligence.

"Hello," the squirrel said. "Small world, isn't it?"

Instinct propelled Michaels into action before he could register shock. He fled, as fast as his feet would carry him, slipping and sliding across the hard-crusted snow. Rounding the north side of the chancery, he lost his left shoe, but he continued headlong nonetheless, puffing and panting with the exertion. He pounced onto the wall by the old cork tree. Surely, if he could flag down a car at the Gosforth Inn, or perhaps use the phone behind the bar, someone could call Doctor Wilson. Or the Dane Garth Mental Health Unit. He was past caring.

He scrunched up his left sock, conscious that the gravel would hurt if he landed awkwardly, then, after gathering his somewhat precarious balance, he judged his hop to freedom...

And landed straight back into the graveyard. The three crosses, that by rights should have been behind him and retreating at pace, loomed *above him* again. The squirrel was right there, too, near the potting shed, warming itself by the fire. It had even gone so far as to retrieve his shoe.

"And getting smaller all the time," the squirrel snickered. Michaels realized it wasn't vocalizing; he wasn't sure that would be anatomically possible for a squirrel. The voices were in his head, racing through his misfiring synapses.

"I'd stop running if I were you. It's not worth the effort," it "said," more with quiet resignation than ill temper.

Michaels froze, eyeing the creature cautiously. There'd been a rabid squirrel in the Big Apple a couple of years ago that had made the nightly news. The year before that, a squirrel ravaged a retirement home in Florida, attacking the elderly patrons quietly playing chess, doing puzzles, and reading books. And it wasn't just the overactive imaginations of Americans —he distinctly remembered the *Flesh-eating squirrel stalks streets of Knutsford* headline about the time he was at college. The School of Dentistry had kept its vicious little incisors on display. He was certain of it: quirky little stories like that made the world go around.

"Let me ask you this: if you were me, would you stop and talk to a squirrel?" he asked.

"Depends on whether you want answers, I suppose," the rodent offered.

"What the merry fuck is going on?" Michaels was exhausted. He slumped down, almost exactly back where he had regained consciousness.

"I'm keeping you on a tight leash. You don't want to go back to the village—I would have thought that much is obvious," the squirrel seemed to say.

"Oh, yes. Obvious," Michaels deadpanned. He reached tentatively for his size nine brogue and dragged it back onto his foot. "Where did you come from?"

The squirrel gestured, inasmuch as a squirrel could gesture, to the crosses. Viking art, to a large extent, consisted in turning the everyday and mundane into the fantastic and grotesque. Real and imaginary animals, taken to imaginative extremes. At the bottom was a rather rolled-up dragon, and above it a serpent that seemed to have plaited itself. Above that was a wolf and another writhing serpent, then came a gagged wolf, chasing another serpent, this time with ears. It was quite the menagerie.

But it was immediately apparent what the squirrel was focused on. The bases of all three were round, like tree trunks, carved to represent the evergreen ash tree, Yggdrasil, the Norse World Tree that embraced heaven and hell with its branches and roots. The original cross had told the tale of Ragnarok, depicting various characters and incidents from the Norse end of the world—but the other two carvings wove different stories. On the second, near the stone roots were unmoving fountains, from which the Norns, the sisters of past, present, and future, kept the tree watered. An eagle, four stags, and a squirrel inhabited its branches: Norse mythology named the squirrel as Ratatoskr, who ran up and down, trading insults between the eagle and Nidhogg, a huge, hideous serpent who lay deep below. The tree nourished all these creatures—the tree of life, of knowledge and time, bearing the trials and troubles of the world.

"Ratatoskr?" the churchwarden guessed, warily. "You've come to life from a stone carving!"

"Of course not," the creature replied, reclining on its haunches. "Don't be preposterous."

Professor von Linné stepped into view as the squirrel dissipated into the smoke of the fire, her brow furrowed in a scowl.

"Christ on a bike!" Michaels exclaimed, sharply, driven by a mix of surprise and sheer bewilderment. It was very genteel as battle cries went, hardly likely to strike terror into the heart of his enemy, but it did help steel his nerves.

Okay. This is the job, he told himself, resisting the temptation to turn on his heels a second time. Defending sacred ground was what he had signed up for. The Canons of the Church of England made it clear that he was a guardian, his role to maintain order and decency in the church and churchyard.

The problem was, they didn't make provision for dealing with a bona fide witch. He briefly regretted not paying attention when Sam Bunting had talked to him about the different types of incense she used.

He mulled over his options. In times past, the residents of Cumbria tied bunches of rowan onto their front doors to ward off the ne'er-do-wells at Halloween. Michaels preferred the police-issued poster on his door: "No trick or treat," but it didn't matter because he had neither to hand. King James' exhortation "Thou shalt not suffer a witch to live" seemed a bit over the top in this day and age, long since replaced by ecumenical dialogue and interfaith outreach. Even the label stuck in his craw: at a time when misogyny was rampant, and women's rights were on shaky ground, "witch" didn't seem an awfully PC term. Besides, he didn't have the authority to rebuke demons—even Reverend Riley couldn't perform an exorcism without permission from the Diocesan bishop. The churchwarden was left with reciting scripture or braving a hymn. The Psalms of David perhaps?

If in doubt, sing, he thought.

"Let God arise, and let his enemies be scattered, let them also that hate him flee before him," he ventured, trying his best to be rousing.

Von Linné snorted in derision and sat down, cross-legged next to the fire. "I'm intrigued, has that ever worked?" she said, obviously amused. "I think you are a little out of tune. Off key." She looked taut, muscular, sinewy—much more like Disney's Maleficent than the traditional old crone. Her hard, angular face possessed a mesmeric beauty. "No wonder your doors of perception remain firmly locked." She smiled. Her eyes were deep wells; Michaels struggled lest he get drawn in.

"Stay back. I refuse to be seduced by the Devil and his legion of demons."

"Has it occurred to you that perhaps you're just afraid of women? A witch, after all, is just a woman with power and independence. I'm not sure I have either of those things anymore," von Linné said ruefully.

Michaels sneezed, repeatedly, suddenly enveloped in smoke from the fire, missing half of what the woman said. He didn't dare ask her to repeat it. "I should give you fair warning: in England, churchwardens have specific powers to keep the peace in churchyards." His eyes were streaming.

He'd seen his fair share of drunks and would-be vandals. There was even the odd pagan, keen to cavort naked around the cross. Under the Ecclesiastical Courts Jurisdiction Act of 1860, he could apprehend offenders and take them before a magistrate. Of course, in practice, it meant affecting a citizen's arrest and waiting for the police to arrive. Most of the time, the constable would just issue a warning and move people on, citing lack of evidence. CCTV was only used in the bigger towns, in Whitehaven and Barrow. It was all down to budget cuts. Austerity. The usual suspects.

"Sounds ominous. Should I be concerned?" von Linné said, staring into the fire.

"The law is quite clear. Molesting, disturbing, vexing, troubling, or by any other unlawful means disquieting or misusing any clergyman in holy orders is punishable with a two hundred pound fine. Causing the Reverend Riley to speak in Old Norse seems to qualify. Not to mention provoking Barry to murder the Council. You may as well throw in fire safety issues."

"You realise that until your Church of England decided to stamp out an inconvenient rival, belief in the Otherworld was commonplace and universal," von Linné said. "Huldufólk and Álfar. The Norse settlers had the álfar, the Irish slaves had the hill fairies or the Good People. Over time, they became two different beings, but they both stem from a deep reverence for the land. Time was that almost every cottage would have a Bible, and the histories of giants, fairies, witches, and apparitions, occupying the same shelf and, equally, sharing the belief and engaging the attention of their readers. Your clergy got going with primary schools in the nineteenth century, ripping out folklore root and stem, before it could take hold in young minds."

Michaels was rapidly losing patience. "Quite right, too. I don't know how you do it in Sweden, but functional skills of literacy, numeracy, and ICT are the bedrock of the British education system. If you were landing at Manchester airport, would you rather depend on what can be gleaned from the Brothers Grimm, or the science of aeronautics?"

"If your Church needed belief in faeries for governing the populace, motivating them to war, or any other such purpose useful to rulers, there would today be sacred groves, a High Urðr in Canterbury, and daily readings of the Konungsbók in schools. It's how all religion works; it doesn't matter how you decide to dress it up," she said, with more than a hint of reproach.

He reached into his pocket, to fish out his phone. The device was his lifeline, his only connection to the outside world. Distressingly, there was still no signal, despite his having upgraded the router in the Church office over Christmas. He thumbed 999 for an emergency, but there were no signal bars. He had the distinct feeling of déjà vu.

"I plead not guilty by reason of electromagnetic disruption," the woman said. She glanced up, registering Michaels's confused expression.

"The pineal gland in our brains is affected by the electromagnetic activity. The aurora can desynchronize your sleep-wake cycle—your biological clock. The psychological effects are typically short-lived but chaotic or confused thinking—erratic behaviors—often result."

"You are saying the Northern Lights drove people to murder?" Michaels asked, dumbfounded by the thought. Barry had mentioned that, with strong solar activity, it was time to wear tin foil on their heads. Michaels had never dreamed the effects could be this drastic.

The woman continued, somewhat reluctantly, "I admit, I might have miscalculated. I imagined the psilocybin would be subperceptual, but who knew you people drank so much tea?"

"For Heaven's sake... You drugged us?!" Michaels's mind was reeling under the onslaught. Psilocybin was the active ingredient in magic mushrooms. It sounded horrendously plausible. Not only was this "professor" clearly part of some kind of Wiccan witch-cult, she had literally made them drink the Kool-Aid.

"The hope was to reconnect you to what you have closed off," von Linné explained. "To find out why I am here."

"Because you come from the spirit realm?" he spluttered, his allergies making it hard for him to seem anything less than incredulous.

"Exactly. I'm glad you've been paying attention." The woman stoked the embers of the fire with a long metal rod. She seemed to have conjured it from nowhere, a mistress of legerdemain. On closer inspection, she had changed her clothing too—the severe polo neck replaced by a tightly woven shawl and sleeveless tank top, her arms festooned with so many interlaced patterns, she seemed to be an extension of the ivy that crept over the tombstone behind her. Michaels shivered, realising that he'd left his own coat at home, when he'd been all but bundled into Barry's van. He was too numb to think straight.

"Perhaps I should I call Ghostbusters?" he asked, witheringly. "Oh no, I can't, can I? Because this fucking thing never fucking works when you need it to!"

Michaels wasn't usually given to being potty mouthed, unless it was swearing by Almighty God. Parishioners had been shocked when Reverend Riley had driven around with sticker "WTFWJD" on the back of his Subaru, a play on the motto "What would Jesus do?" By Riley's reckoning, it wasn't a blasphemy but a vulgarity—an Old English word. He'd even told Mrs. Jones she should "get out a little more." Christ came to save us, not put a stick up our backsides, he'd said—thankfully, in private.

It struck the churchwarden now as the perfect question. "What the fuck would Jesus do?" he screamed in desperation. He weighed the phone in his hand, momentarily considering hurling it into the darkness. It looked back at him, his face a flickering reflection on the darkened glass, the mirrored eyes pitiful and scared. It was little more use than a slim black brick, yet somehow Michaels felt sorry for it. Who would have thought that a heap of aluminium, iron, and copper could engender such devotion? He decided on a stay of execution. Besides, it was out of warranty with the Carphone Warehouse and he couldn't abide cracked screens.

"Give me your tölva," von Linné instructed, holding out her hand.

Michaels stared at her blankly.

"The prophetess of numbers? The farspeaker? The device you were going to throw?"

"You mean my *phone*?" he asked, flabbergasted.

"Yes. I must make sure of the correct words," she explained.

"Really? Your English is flawless."

"To a point. The explanation is complicated and there is a divergence around modern terminology and recent events," she said, somehow summoning power and connectivity. Her face bathed in the glow of the screen, like the moon gliding between clouds. "Ah— tölva is computer. Different linguistic roots, you see. This 'phone,' for instance, we'd call a *sími*—which translates to thread in your tongue."

Michaels was momentarily wowed. The word was both poetic and decidedly apt, and she clearly had more than a BTech in Computer Science. Perhaps the woman was a hacktivist, an eco-warrior prowling the Darknets—overlay networks that required specific software, configurations, or authorization to access, the territory of trolls and phishers, traders in pharma and extortion. She could have rigged all the news articles about runestones, baited most of the isolated villagers in one place, then killed everyone to harvest their organs. He'd seen less gruesome and convoluted plots on Nordic Noir thrillers. *The Professor with the Dragon Tattoo*.

"And how do you explain your bushy-tailed minion? Drone technology? Drugs?" Michaels guessed, trying to rationalise recent events.

"I suppose. Any sufficiently advanced galdrar is indistinguishable from technology. One of Arnþórr C. Klakkr's laws. The creature is a *fylgja*. Think of it as the 'mind-given-shape,' an emissary, which may be sent forth to perform various tasks. I choose a form that is dear to me."

A familiar. A totem spirit, a gateway to unseen worlds. Michaels knew enough about the Norse sagas to recognise the term. In the story of Hárvarðar the Halt, the hero had a dream about eighteen wolves running towards him with a vixen as their leader. As it turns out, the dream presaged an attack by an army with a sorcerer at the front.

"I thought black cats were de rigueur among the coven classes. What else do you have up your sleeves? A magic mirror? A crystal ball?"

Von Linné ignored him, clearly elsewhere. "Let me ask you this," she said, still staring at the device. "When you were a boy, would you have believed anyone who told you that there would one day exist an object that would fit in your palm, able to hold the contents of all the world's libraries, that would be able to compute the density of a star?"

"No, I suppose not," Michaels admitted. He was still mildly aggrieved that his Scouts knew nothing of the experiences he'd found formative as a youth. Things like programming the VCR, or, heaven forfend, remembering an actual telephone number. Tasks that were essential when he was a boy were now just drudgery and inconvenience.

"And yet, you take all of its wonders for granted." She handed back the phone. "This, my friend, is a slice of seiðr."

The word was unfamiliar. "Say-the?" Michaels repeated.

"A way to see geographically or temporally distant events. Your device now resonates with the Evergreen."

"The Evergreen? Is that what you call the 5G network in Sweden?" Michaels hazarded. He'd heard Telia and Ericsson were primed to spearhead the rollout of the latest technology across the Nordic region but didn't want to sound clueless.

"I'm not sure whether to find it charmingly naïve or downright obtuse that you are still clinging to the belief that I am from Sweden after all you have seen. Your faith is a stubborn one. My home is in the Járnviðr—the Iron-wood. My name is Iðunn Lind. I am the head of a holy order known as the Verðandi, keepers of the greenways and guardians of the World Tree. I am what you might call a *hægtesse*, a peace-weaver, able to step across the divide. Or at least I was..."

"What divide? The North Sea?" Michaels swallowed the air in surprise. Despite himself, he found her softness quite disarming.

"We share a common ancestry. And I know these lands. Hvithafn, Vatnsá lake, Skalli Fjall, Borgardalr. My people didn't just settle and farm. The Kings of the North fought and died in these hills and valleys and cut your faith from their realm. I do not know the reason why, but I have fallen from Yggdrasil and am now confined here in this Otherworld. I am, if you will, *Aðaliz Through the Looking Glass*."

"Am I the Hatter or the March Hare?" Michaels wailed, noting that most of Lewis Carroll's supporting characters were mad. He was starting to get the hang of von Linné's odd turns of phrase, though. He wondered if he was in his right mind. Or if he was in someone else's wrong mind.

"Look, you are searching for an understanding. So am I. Perhaps we can help each other. I need you to answer some questions for me."

"Or what? You'll turn me into a toad? What is going on?" The last remnants of his confidence were disintegrating. Migraines, hallucinations, unnatural lights in the sky, bizarre equations—it was all a bit much. "How do I know what's real and what's not?" he howled. He shuffled past her, sitting down by the fire and shutting his eyes. It would all be a lot clearer come morning, he thought. He'd just wait it out, let the drugs leave his system. He'd tried smoking some skunk in Amsterdam once. That hadn't been fun either—it was like speaking in a tunnel of treacle. He'd had to lie down in Schiphol airport—missed his connecting flight, of course, but the fuzziness had passed.

"Olaf, I told you. I can help you, if you'll let me," she said, gently placing a hand on his shoulder.

Michaels kept his eyes firmly shut. Perhaps he was susceptible to feminine wiles, or simply starved of attention, but he felt a compelling need to hug her. *Disgusting*, he instantly reprimanded himself, *you're no better than a prepubescent schoolboy, all tumult and misplaced libido*. He tried to concentrate on his breathing. Regulation, that was what he needed. Moderation in all things.

Alternate realities could wait for tomorrow.

"When was the last time you left the village?" she asked.

"What has that got to do with the price of tea in China?" the churchwarden scoffed, half sitting.

"Humour me," von Linné said, casting her shadow directly over him. There was a sudden frost in her voice, an air of cold command that cracked Michaels's reserve. He ransacked his memory, happy to be in sunnier climes, sifting through mental images of his recent trips round the Lake District. Of course, they were all neatly categorized into albums on his phone. He'd been up to St. Ives… no, that was last autumn. The scout camp at the Rath? The Derwent Pencil Museum maybe? On reflection, he hadn't been anywhere recently, not since the crosses appeared.

"Before Christmas. I've been unwell."

"Ah yes, your inconvenient headaches," the woman said, with what he thought was a hint of skepticism. She returned to the crosses, her fingers lingering on the intricate carvings. She continued to speak, somewhere in the comforting darkness. "I know something of your faith. There are those who kneel before the rood cross among my order. But something has been lost from this place. It is as if consciousness has been dismissed, and magic banished. Your philosophers and scientists have stripped their crafts of anything that might seem mystical, forgetting that the universe is a living, breathing entity. What is left is inert, mechanistic. Unthinking. Unfeeling. The Norsemen who made these crosses were trying to keep that understanding alive. Did you never wonder how they appeared overnight? Or why there are three of them?"

"What do you mean? I didn't decide to put them up," Michaels answered, instinctively parroting the Bishop's advice. "God moves in mysterious ways."

"Does he indeed? People don't normally leave an archaeological trail. Not unless they go out of their way to. Is there definitive physical or archaeological evidence of the existence of your Jesus?"

Michaels half opened a curious eye. The "professor" was milling in between the crosses, a shadow in the streetlight. He decided he preferred to think of her as von Linné, despite her revelations.

"I don't think that's a reasonable expectation give the past two thousand years in the Middle East," he said. "Hardly a case of one careful owner."

"Few nations have been so poor as to have but one god. Gods are made so easily, and the raw material costs so little. Where is the fylfot?" she probed.

"The sunwheel?" Fylfot was an old name, used mainly by antiquarians and experts in heraldry, but it had come into use again to allow people to carefully avoid the word *swastika*. "It's never stayed on. The stone is cracked at the top. It's beyond repair." "The everglow steps to her divine sanctuary with brightness; then descends the good light of grey-clad moon. The diurnal rotation of the skies. The universe seems to turn around us, wheeling above our heads. It took us centuries to realise that the heavens don't revolve at all. It is we who turn. And the sagas carved here—how well do you know them?" the professor asked. "The Norse believe the end of all things is inevitable, the way of its coming fixed and inescapable..."

Michaels tutted, fervently wishing people would stop telling him what he already knew. He'd looked after the original cross for donkey's years and written every permutation of information pamphlet possible on the subject.

"Good will be overwhelmed by evil, but at the same time, evil will be fought to a standstill in a final battle for heaven. Odin, chief of the gods, will perish, but others will rise in his stead, to herald the new world." Michaels hastened through the description, with a supercilious air born of endless repetition.

"Interesting," said the professor, without meaning it in the slightest. "Myths give us a blueprint for triumph or tragedy. You can build with it, carve whole civilizations from stone and wood. Or destroy with it. Demonise your enemy. Make whole cultures that much easier to disinfect. That which destroys the old becomes the new, like a snake devouring its tail. And so, the cycle repeats."

Michaels was happy to let her monologue. It would help pass the time until morning, and he enjoyed people encountering the church for the first time. He shifted his weight, trying to get comfortable. *Move along, nothing to see here.*

St. Mary's was a hodgepodge of history. It was recorded in the National Heritage List for England as a designated Grade I listed building. Even the tool shed, built of stones from the original church, was now a listed building. Most people knew about the Hogback tombs and the crosses, but there was plenty more to marvel at. There were cannon balls, forged in the Dardanelles, made for the Crimean war. The old Chinese bell—captured in 1841, during the First Opium War. When the bell came to Gosforth, a local blacksmith made a clapper for it and hung it in the bell tower. However, Chinese bells were designed to be struck from the outside so at the first ringing with the clapper, the bell cracked and had to be taken down. Typically

English—no regard for anything foreign. But it was amazing—all these relics of Empire in such a far-removed place. The thought was quite stirring. The empire on which the sun never sets. There was something clichéd in that, but also something bucolic, something bountiful. It was easy to see why, here in the North, amidst the refuse of the industrial system, people would vote Leave. They wanted to turn back the clock, to time before the dark, satanic mills blighted the landscape and imperilled the planet.

"What the fuck would Jesus do?" he chuckled to himself. He began to hum, contentedly. *And did those feet in ancient time, Walk upon England's mountains green.* "Jerusalem" was an old patriotic song and a church favourite.

"The sculptor arrives at his end by taking away what is superfluous," the professor said, gently, turning back to the third cross and caressing its side.

Michaels was half-minded to argue but decided to turn the other cheek. There was nothing like a good hymn to restore your faith. He'd been right after all—if in doubt, sing!

And was the holy Lamb of God, On England's pleasant pastures seen?

"You might be right. I wonder," she said, suddenly inspired, "if we aren't being watched. Someone following our every move, from the very beginning..."

Michaels looked around, wondering what she meant. There weren't any good vantage points to spy on them, at least not without being seen.

Perversely, the professor seemed to have taken up the verse as well. For a brief moment, Michaels wondered if he'd made a convert. She was suddenly squawking a bizarre parody of the tune, almost in a falsetto, her eyes rolling back into their deep-sunken sockets. Her mouth opened wider and wider, like her jaw was unhinged. The sound was at once ghastly and eerie—it was as if she was harmonising with the stone spindles.

Michaels tried to scrabble away, but she lunged for him, grabbing his ankle. He kicked at her arm with his free leg, trying to dislodge her, but her grip was freakishly strong. Under the shadows of the tombstones, all he could see was the whites of her eyes, as blank as the snowfall. So much for his inadvertent proselyting and boyish infatuation, he scolded—the lion and the lamb may sometimes lie down together; but if you pay attention, when the lion gets up, the lamb is generally missing.

"A hall I see standing remote from the sun, on the Corpse Shore," she hissed. Michaels tried to extricate himself again, but she started to clamber up his legs, placing her knees firmly on his shoulders, her voice booming out a hideous bedtime story, a nightmare from the recesses of his memory. As a boy he'd seen the West End farce *No Sex Please, We're British*. A young couple innocently sent an order off for some Scandinavian glassware, but what came back was pure Scandinavian smut, engulfing everyone involved in veritable floods of pornography, photographs, books, films—and eventually, nubile, scantily clad girls. That had been another formative experience. Come to think of it, it was probably the reason he'd learned to programme the VCR.

"There fell drops of venom, in through the roof vent. The hall is woven of serpents' spines. I there see wading, onerous streams, men perjured and wolfish murderers and workers of ill with the wives of men."

"Really madam, I must insist you unhand me!" Michaels shouted, trying to dislodge his arms. He felt giddy and drowsy and completely turned on, struggling on the brink of an embarrassment that he'd never live down. RIP Olaf Michaels—died of erotic asphyxiation defending church property.

"There Malice Striker sucks the marrow of the dead, the wolf tears men. Do you still seek to know more?" She leaned in, suffocating him in her odour. Her face luminous, invigorated—Michaels couldn't help picturing a cigarette dangling from her lips, imagining a post-coital glow, and felt wretched for doing so.

Michaels wanted to point out that he hadn't sought to know anything in the first place, and that, if it was all the same to her, he'd pass on the extra information. But before he could, he saw something writhing in her hands, something sinuous, coiling around her arms and neck in a deadly embrace.

He recognised it at once: his unwelcome visitor. The viper in his mind, jaundiced yellow and netted with purple veins. The churchwarden let out a slow, undulating moan. In a flash, it all came back to him. The old pagan, reeking of piss and vinegar. He'd mistaken him for an actor at first, perhaps one of Barry's cohorts. It was an easy mistake to make—there were plenty of re-enactors out there—Regia Anglorum, the Norse Film and Pageant Society, the Society for Creative Anachronism—and they were all drawn to the cross like proverbial flies.

The raised spear. The hideous, shrieking ravens. The glimpse of other worlds. He had squashed down the whole traumatic, terrible incident into someplace dark and tiny and the woman had dived in and retrieved it. His memory felt jagged, like a shattered mirror—the most horrific images leapt unbidden into mind. Not whole sequences, just impressions—of velocity, of ancient fury. An emptiness, too, a void swirling with the gnawing urge to end it all.

He ripped the serpent from the witch's hands, dashing it on the ivy and granite, over and over, his hands slick with blood, his face dissolved into snot and spittle.

And when it was over, he slumped down in the snow and fluids and wept.

— IÐUNN'S HEL-RIDE —

Gæslingfjord, England
2019

H*elvíti drullukunta!* Iðunn panted as she steadied herself, gripping the cold, crumbling masonry on the side of the church for support. *Trollskap.* Dark magic. Someone had literally hijacked Michaels's nervous system, changing his reality. Gróa alone knew how they did it or why, and she wasn't sure she wanted to find out. The same reaving was unbalancing her own galdrar, coercing her spells-songs. The Vǫlur were not used to being manipulated.

There was constant fluctuation in the night sky, blue strobing lights framing the towers and chimneys of the Baleworks beyond, the Gap alive with vibrations of energy. There were the now-familiar long, threnodial whistles, as if clouds were a bustling waystation, full of passengers to-ing and fro-ing under the frown of petulant conductors. She had no doubt that something else lurked out there, among the tumbling becks and tawny bracken. A mind forever voyaging through strange seas of thought. It was time to leave, time to be far away from the nuclear plant and its rivers of clanging weapons.

The warden was asleep now, crumpled untidily in the gabled porch of his charge. She could only imagine what he had seen—consciousness was a bitch at the best of times, but he had been spectacularly ill-equipped for the combination of pharmacology and pheromones she'd unleashed to jailbreak him. She watched the slow rise and fall of his chest, his wobbly chin and sagging jowls, his protruding "Adam's Apple," envying the man his repose. The Verðandi were all fastidious with their own sleep hygiene and the protective cloak it gave them. All of the Hinterworlds had varying solar cycles—if you merrily persisted in Midgardian light-dark habits, you'd quickly succumb to chronic fatigue. Travellers often required a modicum of entraining to remain functional.

She picked up her gambanteinn, twirling it like a black baton. It had been a vital tool in conducting the village moot, even if the melody had ultimately been led astray. It was equally useful for prodding people into action.

"Come on, soldier, up and at 'em. Draum-Njörun has you in thrall," she barked, poking him with the business end. The churchwarden groaned, then began mumbling incoherently, his unconscious mind replaying the past, searching for rhyme and reason.

Iðunn peered past him, winnowing into corners of his mind, consolidating what understanding she could. She wasn't impressed with what she found. Men like Michaels lived in a memory, his whole world obsessed with history. You didn't have to be a mind reader to see it: the inhabitants were backward looking, their culture debilitated, in decline. It was as if a great Empire created a map that was so detailed and so large, it outgrew the Empire itself. A map of conceit and hubris, that expanded as the Empire conquered territory. When the Empire collapsed, all that was left was the map, and the people went on living in it, perfecting each and every detail in their imagination while the reality itself crumbled away from disuse. The skalds might say she was behind the veil of tears. Perhaps this world was a twin to hers, separated at birth.

Michaels rolled over and began snoring quietly. *Scratch that*, she thought. If it was a twin, this one had been raised by eldhúsfífl. The churchwarden had been an easy mark for whoever had caged him.

She tapped him again with the rod, nudging him until his eyes startled open.

"What just happened?" the churchwarden wheezed. He gagged a little, although whether it was a reflex or something of genuine concern, she couldn't tell. The man's thoughts felt calloused, his reasoning brittle. He dusted himself down, freeing himself of the crusted snow that had clung to his coat during the tussle, but his knees and back were sodden. Iðunn saw him wince with pain as his shoulder twinged, clearly not used to sudden exertion.

"Difficult to explain. Come. It's time to leave," she snapped, gathering what few belongings she had from the fireside. She was moving with purpose, at once concerned and irritated by the unexpected new threat, hoping that momentum would calm her own nerves. The churchwarden kept his eyes downcast, barely noticed her bustling around him.

"Really!" she insisted, shining him her best kjálkagálkn smile.

The man looked up at her, his face puffy with misery and exhaustion. His voice was as plaintive as the sirens in the sky. "Go where? I tried that already."

Iðunn took a moment to realise what he meant. "You can move freely now," she said, with as much sympathy as she could muster. "How did you do... that? Whatever it was. With your magic wand?" Michaels pointed at her gambanteinn.

She smiled genuinely at that. Notwithstanding its unfortunate Kristin connotations of party tricks and story-book wizards, that's exactly what it was. A vöndr. She used it to point insistently to the road beyond the low brick wall, shifting her stance to suggest that he should follow.

Michaels paused for a moment, as if tongue-tied or struggling to explain himself. "And the snake?" he whispered, as if he dreaded saying the words. *So, he'd visualised snakes during his ordeal—that made sense*, Iðunn thought. Snakes were used across the North to decorate the houses of the dead. They formed the boundary between life and death. This whole area of Lakeland was a pit of vipers.

"It was just like the ones on the hogbacks," the man muttered.

Iðunn was keeping time with a tapping foot, trying to limit his scope for chatter. But her companion's agitation was infectious, and she felt compelled to ask: "Hogbacks?"

"I'd show you, if only I had my key. Everyone assumed they were tombstones—grave markers," the churchwarden said, gloomily. "But I think they are something else.... There are other examples all round Cumbria, their roofs gripped by muzzled bears. Except our ones. At Gosforth, we have rather a lot of serpents instead..."

He trailed off into his private desolation. The man obviously found comfort playing tour guide, reciting his facts like a cherished catechism. For a moment, she considered dialing up the exocrines. She needed him moving. Iðunn reached down, intending to tug his sleeve, to drag him out of his inertia. But even as she stooped, she realised his question was perfectly valid. Where could they go?

She was stuck listening to stultifying detail about tombs, in a moribund world. It was dead-end in every sense of the phrase. She crouched down to his level, breathing in his despondency.

"You've lived here your whole life?" she asked, trying a change of tack.

The churchwarden seemed to rouse himself at that, remembering where he was at last. He began rolling his shoulders like a prize-fighter who'd gone to seed, trying to rub the disbelief out of his eyes with his bloodied knuckles.

"I'm so sorry, what did you say your name was?" the man asked, ponderously, as if he cultivated reserve.

"Iðunn Lind—remember?" In fact, his question caught her off-guard, and she searched him quickly for signs of amnesia, or other degeneration. It didn't occur to her that he was simply being polite. Gentility wasn't in the Norse lexicon.

"That's an, um, unusual name. The Norse goddess of youth?" he said, speculating. "The one with the apples?"

"It's a name of the álfkunnr, the elf-kindred. You would rather my parents had named me Eve, or Hesperia?" she said, more question than statement, hoping that the explanation might help him connect to their previous conversations. He didn't bat an eyelid, although she got the distinct impression that he was fixated on her ears.

"People associate 'north' with up and 'south' with down, but only because the Grikks drew the first maps that way round." She sighed.

"I'm not sure I follow," the churchwarden said.

"As soon as you label someone, you change how people perceive them. The passage of the sun, the rejuvenation of spring—all of these things are deeply rooted in my culture. My family name was coined from the great warden tree in my family homestead, Linnagard, when my ancestors first clasped the branch of the life-wise. The trees brought the first men and women to life—and the gods too. Odin's mother, Bestla, is a wife of the bark; Loki Laufeyjarson was born from the womb of a tree goddess. But the alfar are not dainty fairies frolicking among the bluebells and our gardens are not quite so ornamental as your church estates. The tree is life and it is death; there is beauty and there is terror in her boughs."

"Yggdrasil—that's the tree you mean? It's not just a myth?"

"The hoar-tree is as real to me as your cross is to you. It is the shelter and salvation of every child of the North."

Iðunn had given lectures on the Great Ash once: her breakout thesis, ahead of its time in many respects, certainly impactful enough to antagonise the Urðr. Now wasn't the time to discuss comparative theology, but there were parallels in parallel worlds—and she needed something to put a spring in Michaels's step. She paused in her preaching, looking around at the church and its towering windows of Victorian stained glass, the bright coloured scenes leeched leaden grey by the night.

"The White Christ. He was crucified, died, and rose again in radiance. That is the central pillar of your faith—that the son of god died to atone for your sins. He is the gatekeeper to everlasting life."

"And your point is?" The churchwarden shuffled round to share her view. Iðunn held up her vöndr for him to see more closely, to see the spirals of the sapling wood and feel their power.

"Our All Father sacrificed himself for knowledge. For magic staves, keys to the Tree of Life itself. Then, as soon as he had them, he flung open the doors and let his offspring find their own path to eternity. Yggdrasil was his own road—the name itself means Odin's horse. A steed for the ages."

The rod trembled in her hands, invisibly connected to the vines and branches of the arboreal sentience. The whole horizon began to dance with delight.

"How are you doing that?" the churchwarden said, with a reluctant half-smile.

"Skuggsjá, er, quantum. Róteind and nifteind, root-particles and sister-particles." Once you understood the intimacies of photosynthesis and the migration of birds, the intricacies of quantum biology were simple, but she didn't have the language to explain the galdr in Michaels's plain English. The demonstration would have to suffice to engender a little trust.

"Words are living things, you know, inasmuch as they are our interface with reality. It stands to reason that the words we choose as labels have power. Your own name, Michaels—a popular name, from what I can gather, so common as to be innocuous. In the past, it had altogether much more impact. It was the name of an archangel, the marshall of the armies of God, the Prince of the last and lowest choir, the trumpeter who heralds the second coming. When Miklagard fell, there were no less than fifteen churches dedicated to the warrior saint. But change it to Mikjáll or Miguel or any of its variants, and it sounds alien. Off-putting. A rós by any other name would still smell as sweet, but still you insist on only seeing the þorn. Michaels is an upright member of the local parish, Miguel is..."

"I see your point," said Michaels, looking squeamish.

"What you, Herra Michaels, call magic is no more than persuasion. Convincing people to think how you want them to think, to see what you want them to see. Enchanters unveil the choices ahead, the charmed suppose they are choosing of their own volition. Names deliver that power instantly."

Iðunn stabbed at a loose plastic bag that had billeted in the doorway, holding it aloft with the end of her wand. A drifter, roving unwanted and unloved, over the hills and downs. SPAR, blazed the logo, ringed by a small green fir tree. "Binding and branding. One and the same," she seethed, appalled at the corruption. "Someone was keeping you right where they wanted you." She was reminded of their predicament. "Frozen out, trapped in the doldrums of Vindrskali. Do you have any idea why?"

"Windscale, you mean? Sinister bloody name. It's not called that anymore. They changed it years back, to the much more hopeful Sellafield, as if that would clean up the nuclear dustbin of the world."

Either the man hadn't heard her, or he had chosen not to. He seemed content to sit and wait, a contradictory bundle of neurosis and staunch indifference. She probed a little deeper, unpacking the residence of his mind, rooting through his untidy neurons. Round and round she went, feeling his knotted stomach and ransacked self-regard, the fragments of mental fortitude. Iðunn realized she'd have to tread lightly to get sense out of him.

There was a startling bang, an ominous, rolling thunder in defiance of the clear sky, accompanied by the strident squeal of horses. Iðunn heard the commotion before the warden and took a couple of hesitant steps toward the lych-gate before he looked up. She could see better past the treeline to the road from the new vantage, and watched a while, half expecting to see Hermóðr riding Sleipnir across the golden Gjöll bridge. Seconds later, a large metal wain roared into view, emblazoned with Einherjar recruitment propaganda, a bearded warrior yelling furiously from its window. It sped up to the gate, then squealed to a sudden and abrupt halt.

"What are you doing? Get in!" the man screamed, his face coronary red. The wain's rear doors flew open, thumping heavily against the fleet markings on its side.

The churchwarden apparently needed no further explanation. He was hotfooting it like a bandy-legged funafugl, suddenly, inexplicably, rejuvenated. Iðunn started after him, puzzled and cautious at first, then quicker, compelled by the insistent honking noise. The machine belched and fumed, visibly blackening the clumped snow piled at the side of the road. She could feel the hedgerow choking.

"Barry!" Michaels shouted, with obvious delight. "Aren't you a sight for sore eyes!"

Iðunn recognised the big warrior from the village moot—the man was the living embodiment of a wapentake, evidently still testing his decibel range by gargling with rage. There was a third man, cloaked and hooded like a Skuld meistari. He wore a white name tag, on which was scrawled "HUGH" in uniform letters. She clambered into the back of the wagon, following the churchwarden. It was obviously military issue, although the weapons in the racks seemed oddly antiquated or else purely ceremonial. There were two flip-up jump seats bolted onto the bare metal. Oil spread in a prismatic puddle near her feet, making her gag with its acrid smell.

Barry put two mailed hands on the steering wheel and began impatiently cycling the engine. "Put your bloody seatbelt on! Sauntering out of the church without a care in the world. Never mind the bloody whole world has gone to hell in a handbag!" he glowered, accusingly.

"Give me a second, why don't you!" Michaels retorted, flustered. Iðunn watched him fighting to put a large axe into its binding before the vehicle sped off. Dealing with one of the Gæslingfjord men had been challenging enough. She wasn't relishing contending with three of them in cramped quarters. Both the driver and the passenger were constantly craning round or checking their mirrors.

Barry's eyes were frantic goggles. "Hugh, can you see it?" he said, switching gears.

The older man shook his head, then swivelled in his chair to properly scrutinise the churchyard. Michaels finally fastened the axe into place with a relieved sigh. He still looked as surprised as Barry was distracted. The wagon began to careen down the village lane at speed.

"Are the police after you? I thought I heard sirens," the churchwarden said, glancing quickly at Hugh for confirmation. Barry was busy ranting, throwing barbs over his shoulder in between gunning the controls. The Verðandi decided there was nothing she could or should add to the maelstrom.

The ant-like Hugh scuttled up, his head rotating up from the cover of the passenger seat. "I think you've shook it. Hello, Professor," he said, remembering his manners and Iðunn's existence at the same time.

"Where is everybody else?" Michaels asked.

Barry looked momentarily grim, then shook his head slowly, continuing his commentary as if nothing had been mentioned.

"It was like déjà vu, but in reverse. That feeling when you're waiting at home for the missus and hear a door open—see a shadow, even—only to realize that no-one is there. I could feel it in my bones.

Minutes later, this black shape appeared out of thin air. Went straight for the boys in blue. Hugh, back me up here?"

"I'd have said you were still three sheets to the wind if I hadn't seen it myself," Hugh said, shivering.

Iðunn scratched through their minds for answers. The churchwarden was as incoherent as a stalled cipher, the Skuld inhabited a bizarre, baroque world full of useless ornaments, and the big Viking's memories were adrift on a sea of alcohol-snapped synapses. None of the men had the precognition talents of the Vǫlur—she would sense them, even if dormant. It was possible that their perceptional fields were still being distorted by the drugs, their neurological signals delayed or misfiring. But that wasn't it. Something else had crossed over. The impossible beast was dangerously real.

Barry emitted a surprised yelp, instinctively and deftly hammering his pedals and shifting gears. "Fuck! It's back. What do you think it is, Prof? Something to do with that boundary of yours?"

She stared out of the frosted glass panels in the rear door. Her dual fovea implants magnified the pursuer far more adroitly than the machine's mirrors, an enormous black form lurching after them.

She recognised it at once for what it was. A hunter—sent to track her down. Trumba certainly had long arms, to reach across the betweenness opening around them. The Verðandi decided to maintain her conceit with the newcomers; folklore and superstition were a convenient mask for the true terror stalking them. There was nothing she could do but offer a distraction.

"An Utburd," she said, naming her fears. A creature birthed from the soil of a shallow grave and a mother's shame. They'd been a common enough horror among Kristins, after the Extirpation of the Monasteries. It seemed horribly appropriate: a reflection, designed to mock her, a travesty of the Children she had birthed.

"You say that as if it is an everyday occurrence. Jesus, Mary, and Joseph! What happened to good old-fashioned English beasties like the Tizzy-Wizzy?"

Barry's tirade smouldered in the coals of his beard. He drove the engine harder, padding fiercely at the sweat beading on his forehead with an old T-shirt. Michaels filled the silence that followed, quoting whatever he had found on his phone. "A restless dead-child. Children born out of wedlock or to parents who lacked the means to care for them were left to die unbaptised."

"Using your phone is cheating," Hugh admonished.

"I've never heard of anything so cruel," Michaels said.

"Because no one spoke of it. She has been denied acceptance, and she'll find no salvation now," Iðunn answered the unspoken question, confronting the shards of her past, present and future.

Iðunn watched as the thing thrashed through one hedgerow and scrabbled for purchase on the road. Of course, it hadn't just appeared unbidden. You had to manufacture nightmares and set them loose— just as she had designed the Jötnar in a lab. She could picture the required shaping—it wasn't pretty to play around with corpses, but it could be done.

"Well, it's gaining on us," Barry said, changing gears again, then swearing as the engine developed a worrying clack-clacking sound. The creature behind them swam up the road, moving with hideous speed. Then, with a bound, it thudded onto the roof. The wagon groaned and slowed under the weight.

The big man wrestled with the wheel, the controls sluggish, trying to shake it loose on the narrow lane. "Any ideas?" he yelled.

"How did you even get yours working? I've lost all reception," Hugh said, trying to snatch Michaels's phone. The Skuld was apoplectic, as if he had been victim of a ruinous insult. His voice was rasping with what Iðunn assumed was jealousy. She could have sworn the two men were trying to score points off each other, oblivious to the danger lurking overhead.

"We've got a man of the cloth here! Sprinkle some holy water on it," Barry insisted.

"I'm not ordained, Barry," came the strained reply. "Besides, baptism's a bit more complicated than that. It's about becoming one with the Body of Christ, a testimony to our commitment to the Church. It's symbol of the resurrection."

"It looks pretty fucking resurrected to me," Barry wailed, trying to ignore the rhythmic thumping on the roof.

"Why is it after us?" Hugh screamed back.

Iðunn struggled to answer, fighting her own rising sense of panic. The life-wise had been messing around with the warm, wet world of cells for years, tinkering with heredity, using the enigma of enzymes to accelerate biochemical reactions. They had learnt to capture tiny packets of sunlight and hop them unerringly through a forest of chlorophyll molecules, sampling all possible routes at once to find the quickest way. They had even built chemical compasses in the proteins of the eye, sensitive to the orientation of Midgard's magnetic field. The patterns of paired DNA could be used to tune the flow of electricity as smoothly through the genetic code as through a metal wire, the tethered strands of DNA acting like circuit boards. The hunter would certainly be immune to anything she might throw at it. Adaption was a key part of any custom design. The Outsider would be attuned to her and her alone.

Glancing outside, she thought she recognised the road. It was the old Waingate that ran from Hrafnóss to Ámelsætr, through the Harthrknutr Pass. It was a steep and narrow pathway, winding between the fells, famed as one of the most treacherous in the North. The snowfall was deeper here, obscuring the asphalt altogether. A tall wooden sign slipped into view, confirming her guess. *Hardknott R. Fort*, it read. *Ancient Monument.* The other passengers had also noticed the heart-stopping bends.

"Barry, this is no good. Too much ice on the road," Michaels whispered, his eyes fixed on the alarming hairpins ahead.

"Difficult going west, cruel coming east," Hugh, added, as if quoting from a local guide. Both men clutched the sides of their seats as Barry screeched first one way, then the other, trying to shake the interloper loose, each emitting a low fluctuating moan as they rolled into each turn.

"Go left. To the fort," Iðunn instructed the driver. She had the beginnings of a plan. If they could scramble up the precipitous rise, she would try use the structure to amplify a protective field—her very own boundary stones. She had a hunch that, whoever it was pulling the strings in Ódáinsakr, they weren't about to let her fall at the first hurdle.

"The Rath? Why?" Michaels asked.

"The fort predates the advent of Kristindómr. It may provide protection," she said.

"Have you seen the walls? They are two feet high. It's a ruin—it couldn't protect a cubs' away-day," the churchwarden howled in derision.

"Walls can be more than stone," she said, her answer punctuated by hammering on the roof. "I should hurry. Our friend will only become more enraged, until she slices through the metal."

Barry grinned with relief. "Stone stores story all right!" he roared triumphantly, thumping the roof. Iðunn was briefly concerned he might be goading the creature, and held out her hand to steady him, but the big man was unrepentant. He rolled the steering wheel round and scrunched across the ice and gravel into the tiny parking lot.

"Do we make a run for it?" Michaels whispered, still apparently hanging on for dear life despite the vehicle having already shuddered to standstill. Barry reached past him, pawing in the darkness until he grasped the handle of his long axe. All four remained silent, still-life models for an unfinished frieze.

"Er... no need. It's buggered off," Hugh whispered. "Least, as far as I can tell."

Iðunn cast her mind out, above the vehicle, to see for herself. Hugh was right—the Utburd had given up the ghost.

The Rómar fort was perched like an eyrie, high on a rocky spur. Its dark slate walls dominated the bleak plateau, spreading over what must have been three acres. To the east of the ruin was the remains of a circular bath house, and two heavily buttressed walls that might once have been granaries. Beyond them, an artificially levelled parade ground, where the first light of morning now practiced its manoeuvres with the sheep who dotted the ridge. The woolly generals commanded a spectacular view of the pass below: the scene as stunning as it was remote.

The Rómar had come this far north and sought to defend their borders. It was more built up than Iðunn remembered, reconstituted from the collapsed rubble by the local government perhaps. It seemed somehow fitting that she was penned up here, haunted by her mistakes. On her Midgard, the parallel structure had crumbled away to near nothingness, a reminder of the fate of failed empires. It occurred to her that Útgarð would face a similar end, left to weather on a mountaintop, a memorial to her folly. She searched the horizon for signs of the revenant, wondering what other secrets Trumba had unearthed from the citadel.

Behind her, the three Gæslingfjord men were bickering about whether to call the police again and whose fault it was that they had no video evidence. After a few minutes, the large man signalled some kind of resolution by simply walking away, stomping over the long grass to where she was standing.

"Chin up, Prof! Might never happen," said Barry, threatening to invade her space with his outsized, outstretched arms. She sidestepped what she could only imagine was a hug, thankful that he'd left his mail brynja in his wagon. "It's gone then. Your Outbird?" he said, conspiratorially.

"Our nightmares tend to vanish in the cold light of day," she said, without having the slightest suspicion that it was true. The only reason their assailant would have left is if they were just where it wanted them. She feared the fort was little more than a trap.

"Well, I'm still living mine. I think I'm going to drive down to Barrow Police Station. Take the Wrynose Pass. Nothing else for it. It might make sense if we all went together. Borrow a little of your prescience, so to speak. Can I offer you a ride in Skíðblaðnir?"

Iðunn eyed him suspiciously.

"My van. Just a little joke. It's big enough for my whole clan to travel aboard with all their war gear and weapons in tow and gets us just where we need to be. It was sold to me by young David Trotter, and he's only about yay big. So pretty much a dwarf. Of course, it can't be folded up like cloth and placed in your pocket, but you never know. One day technology might catch up."

"One day you might not power it with decomposing plants," Iðunn said, horrified by the whole inefficient mess the vehicle made. The Norse had heat engines, of course, but nothing that required gouging Mother Jörð.

"Hark at Greta Thunberg. Quite right, though. Can't be helped—have you seen the price of the Ford Transit hybrid? What do you drive, over in Sweden?"

"I don't." Iðunn smiled as sweetly as she could manage and tried to step past the man. The last thing she wanted was to tangle with the Lakeland authorities.

"Solar power then, is it? It's just a problem of energy density, I suppose. A trickle of electrons will work wonders if you can turn on the taps." He grinned. "So, what do you think? Strange runestones, Northern Lights, people going berserk, Scandinavian demons chasing us out of churchyards. Have you put it together yet?"

"Herra..." she paused, realizing she hadn't any clue what his surname was, let alone why she was talking to him. "Barry, I'd benefit from some peace and quiet."

"Ah, I see. Well, you were the one the Council invited. It's a bloody mystery and no mistaking." The large man sniffed and rubbed his hands together to kept warm, then started to stride down the hillside towards the parking lot, bounding from boulder to boulder, yodeling as he went. "Hey, Olaf, fancy a sing-song? Keep the spirits up, eh?" he bellowed. *"I love to go a-wandering, Along the mountain track, And as I go, I love to sing, My knapsack on my back."*

The noise was horrendous, so Iðunn walked in the opposite direction, pretending to be admiring the view. She wasn't sure whether it was a national trait or a religious quirk, but these people seemed to sing whenever there was a crisis. They'd understood the power of the galdar once—they still had words like En-chant-ment and Nightin-gale in their tongue. Trace memories, perhaps, of a time when their Ænglisc was closer to the dansk tunga.

It was then that she realized what had been cooing in her ear all this time. The key to remove Michaels's binding had been a Kristin song, hiding in plain sight. Who knew what else the mysterious galdr smith had threaded together for them to find?

The churchwarden had taken to lying flat on his back, sheltering from the wind in much the same way as the huddled sheep, fussing over his phone with the older man.

"The song you were singing in the churchyard. How does the rest of it go? Quickly, now," she urged.

"Jerusalem? Well, it was a poem first, by William Blake—and only set to music during World War I."

Iðunn gave him a look that clearly imparted just how much she cared, and rather than tempt fate, Michaels began to skip-sing through the words to the hymn.

And did those feet in ancient time,
Walk upon England's mountains green?
And was the holy Lamb of God,
On England's pleasant pastures seen?

And did the Countenance Divine
Shine forth upon our clouded hills?
And was Jerusalem builded here
Among those dark Satanic mills?

"And then? What else?" Iðunn began pacing furiously, conducting the churchwarden's solo performance with frantic gestures.

Michaels's head rolled from left to right as he scanned a mental lyric sheet. Hugh joined him, finishing some of the lines and repeating others. It was like a lyrical car-crash.

Bring me my bow of burning gold:
Bring me my arrows of desire:
Bring me my spear: O clouds, unfold!
Bring me my chariot of fire.

I will not cease from mental fight,
Nor shall my sword sleep in my hand
Till we have built Jerusalem
In England's green and pleasant land.

Iðunn barely waited for him to finish. She reeled away as if she had been shot. "Of course. Hvað þú ert mikið rassgat!" she swore violently. "The dream of paradise regained." She was certain now, as certain as if she had carved the charm herself. Michaels looked at her blankly.

"Galdrar are songs, at root. Frequencies and vibrations that form keys. Your gaoler is telling us exactly what he is doing and why. What is the song about?" she asked excitedly, happy to find a key to her own confinement. She'd never had much of an understanding of the Kristin Devil and his own fall from grace, but having spent several days in this benighted world, she had started to discover all kinds of sympathy for him.

"The poem's theme is linked to the Book of Revelation. The Second Coming. Jesus creating heaven, here in England." Michaels babbled, preferring to stick to his own safe and secure frames of reference than entertain more Otherworldly thoughts.

"A New Jerusalem," Hugh added, eager to be helpful.

Now do I see the earth anew, Rise all green from the waves again. Iðunn could picture Angeyja, hear her tremulous cry, standing in the Grove. Her words echoed those of Trumba and her vision of a rebirth. The answer was snared somewhere within the spell-song, she just had to prise it loose. She stepped up to Michaels and seized his shoulders, shrouding their conversation from the ever-curious old Skuld. She wasn't particularly surprised when the warden failed to register any protest at all.

"I need you to think. Focus. There must have been others who crossed over, before me. Someone who came to your crosses."

"He was interested in the cross and the hogback tombs. He said there were markers—anchors. I'm sorry, my memory is still... foggy. Why is it important?" Michaels prevaricated.

Iðunn could sense she was close to the heart of the mystery. Michaels was a witness; he had seen her fellow traveller on the Raven Roads, someone well acquainted with death.

"On my world, people look up at a molten sky. A whole hemisphere irradiated beyond repair. The Northern Lights are less a shimmering curtain and more a funeral pall."

"Wow. I mean, how?!" Michaels wheezed, awestruck.

"A *hvellrisi*. A supernova. Someone blew up a star. Not *the* sun—Sol—but enough to lance the atmosphere. The sun was his weapon."

"Well, look, I am sorry and all that, but isn't that an Act of God?"

"Spoken like a true believer. No, this had agency. Intention. Your friend with the axe was right about the explosive power of the equation. $E=mc^2$ explains why stars shine, how the trees capture starsong, what transpires inside black holes." Iðunn couldn't prove that the gods didn't exist, but science made them entirely unnecessary.

Michaels's eyes and mouth hung open; his face deflated and wrinkled like an old balloon. "And that's why you came here? From your Vikingverse?" The end of the world was clearly a lot to digest.

"I didn't choose to. I'm beginning to think I was summoned. And that the equation on the boundary is an epigram—a calling card left by the summoner."

Iðunn was convinced of it. Ironically, Michaels had been right all along. The determined prankster with the chisel—someone had carved the runes knowing they would be found. That was the whole point of a grave marker, to commemorate the journey into other lands. But whoever had engraved the equation had wanted it to be discovered, like a thief who couldn't help but taunt his victims, or an anonymous street artist basking in his own cleverness.

"We should join Barry," she said, letting go her grip and plotting the quickest path down to the waiting wain. She started to walk down the bluff, the two men scrabbling at her heels.

"Are you sure we won't get accosted by trolls or giants?" Michaels said, peeping over her shoulder into the bleak dales beyond.

"If we encounter a mob, I'll hit them with manvelar. Love spells…" she said, realising that she enjoyed tormenting the Englishman. He probably imagined her whole world was a riot of sex, drugs, and spindles.

"You can do that?" Michaels's eyes bulged; his whole demeanour was tumescent with concern.

"Wouldn't you like to know?" She winked, sighing through him on the breeze. She wasn't too old to have fun after all. She felt quite exhilarated by her swift unravelling of the mystery. Forcing the conversation was helping matters.

"Barry's going to drive down the Wrynose Pass. Completely the wrong direction," Hugh interjected. "The pass of the raven. Ravn hals became Wrynose over the years. The English language is funny like that."

"What did you…?" Iðunn said. The sentence stalled as realisation crept up on her. "Focus harder. You are the only witness who can identify the *vargdropi*," she insisted.

"Mr.… Chandler?" Michaels asked, feeling cautiously for the name on his lips.

She could see him now, a portrait in Michaels's memory. Indistinct, but clearly a person, somewhere in the wind, rustling through the leaves.

"He had a spear, if I recall correctly," Michaels offered, meekly. "He looked quite authentic."

"Gungnir. Made by the Sons of Ivaldi. It never misses its target," Barry offered, his voice carrying easily, despite the distance between them. He had grabbed a suitable prop out of the back of his van, which he plucked from the ground as they approached. He twirled the spear around his head as if it were as light as Iðunn's wand.

"Odin began every battle by hurling his spear over the enemy host and crying, 'Óðinn á yðr alla!—Odin owns all of you!' The Norse repeated this gesture before every battle, gifting the opposing army to the All Father, in hopes that the sacrifice of the slain would lead to their victory." The burly Viking strode up to them, a shit-eating grin beaming under his beard.

Iðunn stared at him in disbelief.

"Looks like things have moved on. Sacrificing whole worlds eh? So, instead of Professor Plum in the Dining Room with the Candlestick— it's Odin in Proxima Centauri with the Gamma Ray Burst," Barry said.

For a brief moment his form slipped away, a mummer's guise cast off at the end of a play, revealing the greasepaint and glue underneath. The man underneath was older and leaner, with a hungry glint in his eye. Iðunn sucked in her breath, impressed by the boundless depth of the disguise. She hadn't even had a glimpse of what lay underneath the muddled antics. The costume was a stroke of genius, the perfect concealment. She noticed that Michaels had instantly stuttered back up the hill in a blind panic born of recognition. He was already vaulting the fort wall, far, far away from his "Mr. Chandler." Hugh had been less circumspect, and was now simply inactive, paused mid-motion like a store mannequin, the creases of his face pursing around the unrequited question on his lips.

"Smells like a setup to me. The whole reason to lodge here was to escape Ragnarök, not trigger it," the warrior said, tapping his nose.

"Who are you?" Iðunn asked, terrified that she already knew the answer.

The old bear tossed the spear back into his wagon and clanged the doors shut.

"Who am I indeed? I have dispensed with names. Are we not just histories of ourselves, memories soldered together, scattered across time? I am the soils of my farm, the strings of my harp, the scent of tallow, the curse of the Skuld. I am the one who planted the seed, and the reason for the raven's flight."

The man was as old as ice and flint, and as brilliant as the new dawn. Iðunn could barely watch as he strode toward her. Her faculties lulled into ancient sleep, she tottered on the edge of drowsiness. He reached out a long, slow forefinger and touched her head. His voice was the mead of poetry, drenched with honey.

"We are stories, contained within the twenty complicated centimetres behind our eyes. But you know that better than most, álfadóttir. Reality is formed only by memory. You have helped restore mine."

The Kristin song, the rescue from the Grove—why? Iðunn asked, probing at the ineffable only to be immediately repulsed. She was as powerless as if struck with sleep-thorn.

"Accustomed to a more pleasant abode? The World Tree needs a world-class surgeon. You wanted evidence, did you not? You wanted to hold someone to account?"

Iðunn didn't reply. She found she could no longer utter a word. Tears trickled from her eyes as she struggled to come to terms with what she was witnessing. The man watched her face, scrutinizing her as if she were a half-finished statue, and he was holding his chisel aloft, planning his next subtraction from her form.

"No need for tears. We are all prisoners of our own artifice, caged by our own plans. I had a dream of power, of glory, and of wisdom. And I could make people believe in my dreams. All too well, it would appear. I have been both jailed and jailer in this, my starry mound. I can see the Urðr have a lot to answer for," he said. He walked back to his wagon and climbed into the driver's seat. Iðunn noticed the engine had been idling all this time.

"Night is the time for new counsels. Have a care for Old Worm's Bane," he said, gesturing towards the retreating churchwarden. "He might well prove your star witness."

The wain stretched and skewed, as if in a loom for folding the sea. The radio began to blare through the open windows. The old man waved, one hand high, as the vehicle rolled onto the Raven Roads and vanished from sight.

Iðunn regained the use of her limbs—and her vocal cords. She was just about to swear, when she noticed the whole empire had assembled the parade ground and was marching straight toward her.

— TRUMBA'S NEW TESTAMENT —

Ravn Hals
2019

"Iðunn Lind, as I live and breathe. The forbidden fruit herself," Trumba purred with delight, like the kattakyn that got the cream. "How long has it been? I'm tempted to say you haven't aged a day, but of course, you know that." She glanced round, making sure the Propagation Men were vying for the best shot. It was important that her embrace looked warm and giving, playing to the imagers that buzzed like stungumý above her head. Trumba intended to make sure this moment was the cynosure of all Imperial eyes: it wasn't every day that she ushered in a golden, new dawn.

The Verðandi looked obligingly shell-shocked. She had barely moved a muscle since the *Ormr inn Langi* flitted into dock, a skvader in the headlights, immobilised by the enormity of the moment. To be fair, the flagship was both vast and scaldingly bright, but then making an entrance really was the whole point of owning a drakkar.

Trumba watched the exile from behind a veiled mask, a hood of lace and black leather, somewhere between fairytale princess and bondage vixen. The flits were quite draining, and she didn't want anyone to see the ravages of time. Elsewhere, she had gone to such lengths to adorn herself that she had almost become her clothes. Her outfit was contoured with a strangling lattice-work corset, all that restraint designed to harness the hypersexuality of the troops. Hammered metal bars caged her bust, her breasts visible under the translucent chiffon beneath. Of course, Iðunn hadn't dressed for the occasion. Her rags almost matched the dusty ruin she'd been found in, but thankfully she still managed to carry off a kind of timeless chic. The Vǫlur had standards to project.

"You look surprised, my dear. I'm sorry, did you think the hel-road was your sole preserve? The Urðr have been speaking with the dead for as long as the world has turned," Trumba went on, taking her by the arm. The Thought and Memory drive had proven a real boundary buster, flitting between the here-and-now, the been-and-gone and the never-should-have-been. Tunnelling between realities was almost instantaneous. It was simply a question of finding the right co-pilot—and it turned out dead men and dökkálfar were eager dance partners, desperate not to fade from view. The rest had been a question of strapping on hel-shoes and dancing the blues.

There was still no answer from the exile, which wouldn't play well with karls or the prince-electors. They'd be expecting some kind of drama. Fight, flight, or freeze: trust a Verðandi to choose the most soporific response to trauma. Perhaps the old Djöfull was addicted to analgesics? Trumba knew from bitter experience that self-medicating was an all-too-delicious pursuit.

The Empress walked round the tumbledown walls, sizing up the surrounding barrens. At least the setting was suitably mythic. She'd insisted on a backdrop that would really resonate with the displaced. Something that would leverage the refugee's homesickness. The fort sat on the landscape in a diamond, with one corner and its tower almost directly north, one to the south and the other two to the east and west. She'd been told that the four towers in the corners of the fort were aligned so the rising and setting sun's rays shone nearly exactly through the gates: her great dragon looked like a black lizard basking on a golden rock.

The flagship was unfurling a full complement of guardsmen down its ramps, serrated teeth on a morphic tongue. The soldiers were drawn from the whole empire: there were long-faced Varangians, gowned in their grey executioners' garb, disgruntled Jomsvikings dragging their spindled heels, even a snatch of Dain-riders sitting on muzzled Brunnmigi. This was how pomp and patriotism should be done.

"Urth. What a delectable morsel. This ruin is Rómar, I take it? I wonder what happened to their gods. Jupiter, Mars. Sol Invictus, the unconquered sun. What an enduring ideal! Which reminds me, Iðunn, did you find what you were looking for? I certainly did."

Trumba's bewitching sweetness underscored the show of force.

Trumba looked toward past her flagship towards the aurora above, lifting her visor slightly to see the unalloyed sky. The blue strobing reflected off the snow, scampering along the road even in daylight, the draw-down from the Thought and Memory incision point. The dragon itself crackled with broadcasts of biological noise, music shimmering from root to canopy, reaching out to the remote fleet with symphonies, drones, rhythms, and songs. Trumba caught her quarry glancing up at the halo also. Finally, something had seized Iðunn's attention!

"You were hoping to stamp a return ticket?" the Empress said. "I'll happily be your conductor—I have so much to show you in my Brave New Worlds."

She beckoned a Varangian from amongst the ranks, with the same delicacy as if they had been at a cocktail party. The man shuffled to her side, his uniform immaculate, ornamented by an array of Polar Stars.

"You remember my good friend, Perfect Váli Heidumhær?"

"Delighted to see you, Lector." The Perfect spoke with casual civility, but in an utterly dead tone, as if the meeting were a pointless inconvenience. Trumba thought it one of his most endearing traits. Váli was a new breed of assassin, withering his victim's good name until they were as scorned as a nithing pole. It was almost as if he had been born to do it.

"You are a long way from home," the exile said. She clearly recognised the Perfect at once, startling like she had seen a ghost. A whole fright of Vættir, in fact: Váli wasn't the only Perfect on parade. Trumba had assembled an army from the residue of Jötunheim. Víðarr, Móði, and Magni, all birthed in the very same vats the Ljósmóðir had used. The doppelsöldner had the stuff of stars in their veins, coils of DNA designed for reaving. A new race of gods—manufactured from the moulds of myth. She'd always been taught it was important to recycle.

"What are you doing here?" Iðunn asked. Trumba silently rejoiced: introducing the Perfect had been a masterstroke. The woman, jolted out of her torpor, was the perfect blinkbait, a sure-fire ratings winner. A fallen foe, battered and broken, rescued from the Wolf-Dales. Everyone loved a family reunion.

"Hah! Have you any understanding at all of where you are?" Trumba wondered. She'd be very surprised if she did. Trumba had access to the best minds in the Níu Heimar, and it had taken her decades to fully grasp the twisted ladder of the conjoined world. Of course, now she had scaled to unimaginable new heights, her Vǫlur able to place the rails with incredible accuracy. Trumba could walk through walls, walk on water. Under her direction, the Norse had mapped the turbulent motion of trillions of randomly moving particles. She was like the captain who harnesses gusts and squalls to maintain her ship upright and on course. The weirdness welling up from the quantum undercurrent of reality was the creed of the new Urðr. Life itself was her weaving loom.

"I call it Ódáinsakr," Iðunn blustered.

Her host could barely suppress her laughter. "Ódáinsakr. Oh, that is choice. Well, you Verðandi always did like naming things. I'll give you that as my gift. *The Undying Lands*. So… antique and yet so very, very incorrect." Trumba was overjoyed at her rival's threadbare ineptitude.

"You know this place?" Iðunn said.

Trumba signaled for a handmaid to bring her a drink. Talking to this sanctimonious old hag was going to be a slog, so she decided to take the edge off in advance.

"Know it? I practically originated it," she cackled. "The Völuspá made mention of it. It was just a matter of finding it, out here, tucked away in the greenways." The Urðr had always been staunch adherents of the Æsir. Shaping narratives was second nature to them, and the very best prophets cited the actual course of events as proof that they were right from the very beginning. The cloud of imagers would do the rest, seeding her vision far and wide over the worlds of man.

Ertu að djóka? The Verðandi wasn't impressed. Her wrinkled her nose and folded arms radiated disdain. She really was a godsend: the perfect straight-woman for the job at hand.

"I'm deadly serious. The sacred texts call it Andlàngr, the everlasting, where the good and righteous will dwell for ages. MIM helped of course, with the quadrangulation." Trumba winked. Self-fulfilling prophecies were the best kind. She'd always said, if you want something done, do it yourself. The real power of the High Urðr wasn't the armies or the fleet. It was the predictive modelling, the infallible plans of the matchless MIM, the Midgardian Instancing Marvel.

Andlàngr was a good story, a wonderful way to sluice out interest in claims. The showcase would seal any number of contracts with the Kontors. Who didn't want to own a little slice of heaven?

In reality, the mirror world was a wasteland: a brutalist monstrosity, suffocated by concrete slabs and throttled by copper wire. The denizens had smashed the atom, and then flung its constituent parts around mountains like a quantum holmgang. It was like taking a hammer to the sun and calling the darkness progress. Their broadcasts didn't relay information or deliver bulletins, but instead groomed its audience, telling them how to think, what to think, as if they'd looked at the way electrons arrange themselves and used them to build cages. The system had created such a proliferation of fear and panic, each misrepresenting and masking the others so well that they threatened to undermine reality. Not to mention they were obsessed with their tölvas—a kind of portable memory bank—giving them the false impression that they knew everything, which perversely meant you could tell them anything and they'd believe it. Everyone isolated in a web of one, discoursing in an echo chamber. No wonder the infiltration had been so easy for MIM to optimise.

"There comes on high, all power to hold, a mighty lord, all lands he rules," Iðunn mumbled, darkly. The last line of the Völuspá. There was a shadow of reluctance on the exile's face, as if she was trying to blanket her thoughts. Trumba instantly divined why.

"You didn't know I'd rebuilt the Rememberer? Oh, we've been sewing together Skuld parts for decades. We couldn't do without the Mighty MIM. Always keep your files backed up." Trumba smiled, looking straight into the array of lenses, so as to directly connect with the audiences at home.

"What do you mean, decades?" Iðunn hissed, unable to hide her dismay. For all her longevity, she looked like a recalcitrant schoolgirl, caught playing truant.

Still, that *was* interesting, Trumba thought, glimpsing just how out of the loop the Lector was. Live broadcasts could be so unexpected, she was enjoying the frisson of danger. She could almost imagine the unscrupulous jarls, glued to their visors, desperate for a taste of the original Apples. Hungry for a return to immortality. You couldn't put a price on eternity, but she'd be damned if she wouldn't make her Bailiffs try. She reached out to put her arm around the Verðandi, partly out of showmanship but mostly to shield her aside.

"The hel-roads weren't designed for excursions. You didn't just take a little day-trip to the fjords. Generally speaking, conveyance requires you to be deceased. It has taken you the best part of fifty years to resurface."

Frankly, she was surprised Iðunn had been found at all. Unless someone had fished her out...

"The fool on the hill. He spoke to you, I take it," Trumba surmised, distinctly unimpressed.

Sá gamli. The bloody Birdman of Valaskjálf. Even with his wings clipped, the mordant old fucker still managed his flights of fancy. According to the annals, he was some malicious experiment in longevity, royally fucked by a Skuld sorcerer and his probing spirit-penis. Trumba's predecessors had aided and abetted the old vagrant while he flapped around, sticking his beak in where it wasn't wanted, croaking his huge raven laugh.

Well, they couldn't transmit this. The last thing her subjects needed was a reliquary to fawn over. She began motioning to the Propagation Men to kill the feed, resorting to a private message when they failed to recognize her swift cutting motion. When there was no immediate response on her visor, she almost screamed. She seized her imperial gambanteinn and began hammering it like a gavel.

It had been high time to cut off the loose ends and start afresh. Any weaver would understand. A dropped stitch falls off your needle and unravels what you are working on. As soon as she grasped hold of the High Urðr rod of office, she shoved Old Longchin in a derelict reactor and went thermonuclear on his bony arse. As far as she was concerned, he just another resource for extraction—she strip-mined his nucleotides to see what made him tick. The breakthrough in Thought and Memory Drive had come shortly thereafter. You had to hand it to the Skulds, they really did know how to bend someone double and fuck them over repeatedly.

"Doesn't ring any bells?" Trumba probed. "The ornithologist. Axe to grind with the Skuld? Quite immune to radiation, so we've made him caretaker over the Álfröðull. All the older generation is fit for. A bit of broom work and feeding the gullible."

Gods were like a speck of a lens of a telescope, like a magnifying glass. The image you got depended on how far you hold the lens away from you. All fathers are gods to their children until the kids grow up, until they realise they are just men. Errant, self-obsessed men. Her own father had been the same, unable to protect anyone, least of all his flesh and blood. Seen close up, the old man was simply a tinkerer, playing with his toys. It was a damnable inconvenience that he'd slipped his guards and escaped her gene-tempered trackers.

Iðunn still didn't answer, keeping her own infuriating counsel. Trumba watched her, calculating how best to drag her onside.

For a moment, the Empress forgot that she was the Oak Queen, the Lady of Always Summer, the scion of the sightbands. Her voice rattled in her throat, her mask almost dropping. She reached, wondering if she could swat the moskitóes herself. Thankfully, one of the Perfects chose that moment to lumber over. Magni, perhaps, judging from his height. She could barely tell the difference between them without their insignia, such were their anodynes. The Perfects were able to effortlessly deaden even her heightened senses. Outside the doll, inside the plague, as the old saying went.

"We caught these two on the fjalls, ma'am," the Varangian stated, proffering some local prisoners—somewhat surprising, given their remoteness. She'd been assured the bridgehead was far from prying eyes.

"I'm sorry, who are these people? Pet Kristins?" She sighed. "Iðunn, you really shouldn't feed the wildlife."

There were two men: one a Grœnland whaler, buttressed in his annoraaq; the other, a puffy boar-faced man whose flushed cheeks matched the gammon colour of the morning sky. One of the Jomsvikings pushed the prisoner's snout directly into the feed, so the whole Empire could see straight up his nostrils. It was part examination, part advertisement.

"Who on God's green earth are you people?" the man-swine wailed. He swelled up further when he saw Trumba's salacious garb, stinking of rectitude.

Trumba smiled. Respite at last! It had been hours since she'd had quality torture time.

"You dare to speak without my permission. Take him away and sew his mouth shut," she instructed with practised efficiency. The man squealed like the stuck piggy he was, until one of the soldiers trotted him mercifully out of earshot.

"And this?" she asked, turning to the other prisoner.

She pointed to the gaunt old man, scuttling like an ant transfixed under a magnifying glass, desperate to avoid the sun's lethal stare. He looked like a Skuld, deeply hooded and clutching his prophetic wand with entitlement.

"Hugh Bracegirdle, your Majesty," he dribbled.

"Hugh? And what is it you do, Hugh?" she said, regally. Before he could answer, she continued swiftly on. "Don't bother to answer. Force of habit when presented with commoners, I really don't care," she whispered in his ear.

She turned to the waiting soldiers and waved the prisoner away. "Take him for dissection. We might be able to extract something worthwhile from his marrow."

Iðunn twitched as they bundled Hugh to the floor, transparently thinking about the cost of resistance, even though it was now far too late. Old habits died hard in religious orders. Trumba had to hand it to herself, she had a keen nose for treachery. She hoped the imagers had captured her profile in all its magisterial glory.

"*Hugh knew* this could be such fun?! Oh, don't be upset. I'll have the Treasury issue wergild," she said, ignoring Iðunn's childish pout. Trumba had decided long ago that, if you were judge, jury, and executioner, you couldn't very well be swayed by poetic notions like justice. She tapped her vöndr, adjourning her one-woman court.

"That goes double for any would-be prospectors watching. Stake a claim and seize a Speglar thrall or two to help you," she said, addressing the imagers, before turning back to Iðunn, ever the gracious host. "Do you like it? *Speglar*. I made it up myself, rooted in the old tongue. It means 'mirror-people.'"

It was a splendid description as far as she was concerned. In her limited experience, the people of Andlàngr were myopic, navel-gazing, self-absorbed. The only trouble was the warranty. The Speglar were still struggling with the science of aging. They weren't averse to infusing blood, drinking chemical cocktails, or freezing themselves like the ice-cold stone of Uth. An understanding of telomere shortening, senescence, and the principles of Hrvatska's clock were only just coming to the fore, decades after the Verðandi had cracked the secrets of immortality. People in this world died a straw death, or in the vernacular, they "passed away peacefully, after short illnesses"— and gods forbid that anyone should try and engage with the spirit afterwards.

Trumba was all too aware that Iðunn wasn't answering her questions, but she was limited by the broadcast, cognizant of the attention span of the adoring public.

"The Álfröðull? You mentioned it before. What do you mean?" Iðunn said, no doubt curious about the mention of her heritage. Either that, or the mirror world had addled her mind. Her incessant questioning was insufferable, like the twaddle of a bantling.

"Yes, the glory of the alfar, a chariot of fire. Didn't I mention? I've been building a new sun," Trumba said, trying to sound nonchalant.

The Skuld had finally redeemed themselves. It had taken an inordinate amount of time, but the Order's remnants had learned enough from the rejuvenation of Svalinn to stabilise plasma for use in fusion. Their dvergr would soon bring the new technology online, transforming the old Speglar reactor. She could only imagine how many votes that would guarantee. She might be able to get rid of the Electoral College and the Serene Buttresses altogether. Some malcontents complained that Ruler for life used to mean something different, back when she was a girl, before Iðunn's Apples paved the way for her Platinum Jubilee, and that the constitution should be changed. Trumba's lawspeakers argued the Empress could hardly be blamed for out-evolving the aging process.

LOKI'S WAGER • 241

Of course, the rassragar always had ants in their pants about something. Now the Skuld were filing reports, claiming an increase in flits would tear reality. They made comments about increased auroral conjugacy and the extended flanks of the magnetotail, but Trumba knew that it was just coded smut. She'd torn them a new one instead, told them not to bring her inconvenient truths. The most successful nornir exhibited wilful blindness, conveniently filtering out whatever unsettled them. It saved them from enforced adaption—cognitive correction drugs and perception filters played havoc with the libido.

Iðunn clearly had no such qualms, daring to smirk in the royal presence.

"I'd like to see the blueprints for a castle in the clouds," the exile chuckled, apparently oblivious to just how much pain Trumba could inflict on her.

"Your mind, Iðunn, is brilliant, but it has an amazing aptitude for pattern-matching and self-deception," Trumba said, filling the air with feigned friendship. She was tapdancing for time. Finally, mercifully, the hovering lenses were turned elsewhere, and Trumba was able to vent. She felt discomforted, oddly compelled to defend her vision against the old relic.

"You think that is funny?" Trumba raged. "Don't you see? We can have best of both worlds. Quite literally, heaven on earth. Ragnarök was our chance to wipe the slate clean! More than a rebirth, a resurrection! It really is the most optimal approach. I told you we could be gods, before you ever stole into the Grove of Thórr."

She remembered the conversation as if it were yesterday, recognizing that for Iðunn it probably was.

"What happened to my children?" Iðunn asked pointedly. Trumba could see that Iðunn had inwardly snapped. There were too many soldiers for her to go far, so the woman simply milled around the edge of the stone wall. For the second time that morning, Trumba wondered who was really captive and who was audience.

"You are the great greenseer. You tell me. Let's pretend for a moment that you were queen—what would the best strategy to ensure the long-term survival of your lineage?"

"I'm not sure I benefit from your good breeding," the Verðandi snorted. She really was the most ungrateful wretch.

"Ah, and there you have it. I have had plenty of time to think about it. All that talk of splicing and grafts and hybrid vigour from the war. Our cells age and decay, they become wizened and ornery."

The Empress was assaulted by images of her own, undisguised reflection, the fractured skull beneath the mask, but she denied them all, thrust them back into the furthest compartments of her mind. She wasn't interested in weakness, only the vigour of her own great works.

"I plan to take leaf from Yggdrasil itself," Trumba went on. "Take two cells and call one the princess, and the other—oh, let's say the thrall. The mother cell accumulates all kinds of clutter over its lifetime and then gives it to the thrall clone, but nothing to the other offspring, the princess cell. Those cells then replicate, and by the time they divide, they too have their fair share of detritus. The two cells follow the same pattern, they divide and dump all their garbage on one of their children. Now, consider this next generation: one cell is an abominable wreck, another is a mere mouth-breather, but two cells are beautiful princesses. Half your progeny! Half of your descendants become more and more decrepit as they fill up with bleak and useless genetic junk, while the others are kept pristine and perfect. That's how the Apples work, isn't it? They divide and delete, turning back the clock of aging. It's the ultimate form of sacrifice, cleansing all that source data."

Iðunn grew more hostile still, her eyes cloudy with anger. "I'm not sure that counts as any kind of sacrifice at all. Nothing that a real mother would recognise. Who decides what's pure and what isn't? You?"

"Whoever hold the molecular scissors. They are the ones who get to snip. To cut the strands of DNA. Isn't that how you created the Jötnar? If you could imagine it, you could engineer it," Trumba insisted.

"It takes years to perfect broods, to make these changes. There isn't a laboratory big enough," the Verðandi said, secure in her expertise.

"You know better than that. Why is it that religions outlast their worshippers? Because we experience the world as speakers and shapers. We carve the runes to preserve our stories, to pass them down to the next generation. Why? Because it confers a benefit. Because the stories help us survive! We encode our beliefs into our very DNA, just as surely as the Norse came out of the trees."

"You bend people to your will. Condition the herd. Tell me something I don't know," the Life-wise tutted.

"Yggdrasil, what does it mean? Not that old claptrap about Odin and his horse." Trumba paused for effect. "Yggr means terror. That is what I am doing. Terror-forming. The Great Ash is my laboratory. This world is my Arboretum."

That comment knocked the wind out of the exile's sails. She rocked back on her heels, almost toppling over the side of the wall. "You *kúkalabbi*! What are you thinking?" she gasped.

Trumba was bone-tired, both of the hypocrisy of the woman and her ridicule. "As if you have the right to complain about dragooning fellow citizens into some grotesque experiment, after you overturned your dustbin full of accidents on us all. You left us no choice, sister. Where were your precious Apples when the lifeblood of the empire was thinnest? Fifty years! Fifty years you have been gone. I'm taking the best parts of your Undying Land. Harvesting this world. Minerals, wealth, and thralls."

"Our rebellion was a fight for freedom. It was nothing like this," the Verðandi said, quietly.

"No, your rebellion was a war for the heavens. For who was fit to rule."

"I must have missed the memo," Iðunn said, spitting. A globule of dissent rolled onto the Empress's leather boot.

"The fact is that civilisation requires thralls. Unless there are lower castes, manacled to the ugly, tedious work, refinement becomes impossible. I will not trust to the Skuld, or the thralldom of the machine. That is not where he future of our world lies. For nearly a thousand years the Norse have been striving to civilize the world, and with what result? In Affrikar and Asaland, did we not teach the Blue man the worship of the Red God, so he might acquire strength for the battle of life? Our system commits no violation of Heimdall's laws. When Man is alive, he stands still. It is only when he is dead that he swings. It is the creed of the Lord of the Hanged."

Trumba hadn't argued like this in a long time. She had almost forgotten how. She switched tactics, tapping into her nootropic reserve, her demeanour shifting, issuing chemical cavalry to cover her retreat. But the exile had grown practised at forming squares, she knew to defend against the charge.

"Would to the Æsir we were all such prophets. I don't know what part you expect me to play in this. I'll not be a handmaid to your disaster."

"And yet, you made such divine children. The beauty Jötnar, handsome Risi, terrible Thurs. They were the best of us," Trumba simpered. "They were my inspiration."

"And you murdered them. Murdered everyone who stood in your way! Did you think you wouldn't be found out? Ragnarök was staged. You triggered the whole unspeakable thing. I can see clearly now, your greasy fingers smeared all over the mirror. You detonated a star, so you can build the world you actually want out of the ashes and dirt. You already knew about this place. You knew you'd have the building blocks to recover."

Iðunn looked like she might go supernova herself. She was incandescent with rage, her entire being broiling with accusation. Trumba was speechless. Old Frú Mærrpill had worked it all out, *The Mirror Cracked from Side to Side.*

Still, she wasn't about to be harangued in front of all her general staff, no matter how complicit they all were. The Verðandi's temerity knew no bounds! As if she had been appointed Óðrerir's keeper! The Empress clicked first her tongue, then her fingers, urgently, repetitively, until she sparked some attention from her guardsmen. She rounded on her sister, glad to be free of the shackles of pretense.

"Sometimes history needs a push. I mean, have you ever been to the Fringes!? Disgusting places, packed squalid floor to swollen sky with lesser races. Not god-fearing at all. *Now do I see the earth anew, rise all green from the waves again.* I plan to create Iðavǫllr, named in honour of you and I, women of eternity. The plain of the Idisi. It is all right there, in all the holy prophecies. Golden-roofed Gimlé, the most beautiful homestead in the celestial regions, still standing when both heaven and earth have passed away."

"And what of this world?" Iðunn protested, her faced swollen with sorrow.

"Does a shadow complain when it is seared out of existence? When our warriors have finished with it, when we have built great Gimlé, we'll ignite the Álfröðull. Sol Invictus reborn! The Ljósálfar of Víðbláin installed in the heavens!"

Trumba waved her away. The bonds of sorority only went so far, and if you weren't part of the solution, you were part of the problem. It wasn't as if many of the Verðandi had outlived the purges.

"The Kristin God planned to remake this world, to raise all people to new life in it. That is the promise of his gospel, his New Jerusalem. I just happened to beat him to the punch." She grinned. "It's easier to rule an empty room than a house of potential traitors. I'm bored of you now. You may go. I don't much care where."

Trumba flounced towards her ship, the men crawling after her like an armoured train, leaving Iðunn swallowed in the press, unheeded and unnecessary. The gangplanks scowled under the weight of so many men at once, then stiffened to accommodate the tide. The

Empress began to sweep through orders, exorcising her irritation. The time for pontificating was over.

"Váli, assemble the Reginthing. Call forth the prince-electors. Make sure everyone has a prospectus."

And sá gamli? What about him? Váli crowed, his message directed straight at her visor. It was accompanied by an array of imagery, like a rogues' gallery comprised of only one villain, pictures ranging from age-old stones and golden bracteates to silent reels from siege of Útgarð.

"Bolt the greenways again, but nothing more. I won't waste gunpowder on dead crows. He can't go far."

The heralds saluted up as she stepped past them, blasting long, sonorous notes from their immense luðr. The Wolf Dales rang with their warning. Trumba always enjoyed their music. It was a good day to be alive.

BOOK THREE: TIME IS PAST

— HRAFNAGALDUR ÓÐINS —

Örgöö, wandering monastery-town, Wide Fields
2019

In the middle of a clearing she stood, surrounded by a low wall made of stacked teacakes, tall, white, and leafless. Eej Mod, the Mother Tree, was bright with colourful scarves. They wrapped around her trunk, swirled from her branches, and lay humbled near her roots. Some of the scarves were stiff and sour, doused with offerings of days-old milk by opportunistic hands. On other branches, travellers had hung rubber tires and engine parts, hoping to be granted safe travels, seeing no irony in their vehicular abandon.

The Zunghar held that she was once a woman, promised by her father to a rich foreigner. The woman did not want to marry the old stranger, and so she ran away. The old man, of course, sent his soldiers after her, but before they could catch up, she turned into a tree. And there she stayed, the most kind, most special tree, and so the forest people named her Eej Mod and began to make offerings to her.

Of course, it wasn't true. Nearby the swathe of scarves, a low building had been constructed around the root of the previous Mother Tree, obscuring it from view. That particular incarnation had perished in a fire started by a soldier's cigarette years ago. Allegedly, anyway. The shaman remembered the blaze well, and the story his uncle had concocted to cover it up. The negligent constable had been quietly reassigned; everyone spared the wider conflagration of truth so soon after Ragnarök. The shack was a testament to short memories.

The shaman was a stout man in his early seventies, with grey hair pulled back in a thinning ponytail. He was already dressed, even though it was dark outside: the rites began at dawn, as they did every year on the first morning of the spring, in this dusty copse. There were thousands of dilapidated tents around the Khan's palace-yurt. They had all seen better days. When he was a boy, the monastery-town had moved every few years, as supplies and the demands of merchants dictated, drifting between various sacred sites along the Selenge, Orkhon, and Tuul rivers. But that was before the Children of Ülgen fell from the Eternal Blue Sky. Before Ragnarök. The Termagant said the Sleeping Lands had borne the brunt of the starburst. The steppe wouldn't awaken any time soon.

Every year, he arrived early to visit the low building and the ossuary within. When he closed his eyes tightly enough, he could still see the truth. The woman imprinted there, at the base of the tree. Of course, there was no bringing the girl back from the flames. The shaman had tried, countless times, calling on Tengri-Thórr until there were no more of her scarlet locks to offer him. She had been his first greeting. Perhaps that is why she had lingered long after all of the other lights of his life had faded.

He resigned himself to his fold-out chair, drinking milk tea with a vodka chaser. It was never too early for vodka. He cast some juniper twigs into his cast-iron stove, to call the spirits. Beyond the white tree, there was nothing but steppe and sky. It was a harsh land, where bad weather could break a herder, and where the gods were cruel. Vodka helped him make his peace with leaving his goats behind. Today, ravens were perched amongst the Mother Tree's branches, representatives of spirits come to parley. The shaman was glad of that. He could claim that only the greatest shamans could command such allegiance. He might mention that the ravens had come to heal Eej Mod at last. It had been a long time since he had told that story.

Soon, there were scores of other shamans, doling out advice or dancing around fires in reindeer-skin boots, and innumerable worshippers circling the Mother Tree, praying, muttering, and tossing milk and vodka at it. They stuffed sweets and banknotes into the bark, as payment for their salvation.

In the field they used for parking, vendors sold succulent marmot organs from the backs of wains, and nomads peddled trinkets and squirrelskin coats. One ger, the domed fur tent used by his people for millennia, doubled as a kindergarten, ringed by children playing in the parched grass. Clouds of gnats and the smell of boiled mutton hung in the air. A sheep had been ceremonially slaughtered and quartered and was simmering away in a massive pot.

By the hour of the horse, hundreds of faithful had gathered. The shaman roused himself and donned his plumes of eagle feathers, before he began to channel the spirit of the tree into his body. It was a practised performance. His headdress was like a warrior's helmet, and his face was a painted shadow. He walked slowly at first, mechanically, his breathing laboured. To invoke the other world, he twanged a mouth harp with his fingers, while a young assistant held a microphone to his lips to capture the eerie sound. The onlookers held their palms up and cried "Hree! Hree!"—come! come!—as the shaman banged his large sheepskin drum.

His eyes were closed, his voice was rough and the melody repetitive, like an ancient ballad: "Oh, great blue sky, which is my blanket, come to me."

He slowly drew the drum up and over his face, dancing as he went into his trance. The crowd pressed in, a sea of expectant visors, as keen as he was to hear from the spirit world. The first sign of his gift had been a yellow snake that came into the ger where he was born. He began receiving spirits as an adolescent, with the guidance of his uncle, who was zaarin before him. He had performed this ritual every year since.

Once the spirit was in him, the shaman seemed transformed. He certainly had the rapt attention of the spectators. The spirit spoke in a throaty voice, but its first utterance fell short of the supernatural. The audience, it said, should stop falling for such obvious blinkbait. Then it cackled like a sightband villain, downed a shallow bowl of vodka and smoked a cigarette through a long, thin pipe, surveying the acolytes.

"In the summer there will be a deluge," the spirit predicted. "Malignant winds that will not cease. The world will sink towards Ginnung's abyss. We suffer time because we must lose what we have. Perhaps the gods have many more seasons in store for us, or perhaps this is to be the last winter." The shaman sucked the gaps in his teeth.

And that was it. The shaman banged his drum again to exit the trance, and as the spirit left his body he blinked and jerked his head, as if returning to consciousness. The crowd immediately mobbed him, a formless queue snaking to receive his blessing. The assistant grabbed the sounder and yelled at them until they stopped shoving.

And that was that, for another year. All that was left was to watch the fires slowly burn out, the shamans and believers to wander back to their horses. The shaman paid his assistant well, then said goodbye, happy to relax in his chair and watch as the spirits retreated to their higher plane.

Except, not all of them had left.

"You are lost, great sky," he said to the darkness.

He reached for a nearby bottle and, finding it empty, stood and lurched in search of another. The ger where he slept was rich with the symbols of his people. Behind his fur-lined throne was a large relief of two fierce wolves and a portrait of the Great Khan; in the middle of the tent was a tasselled helmet perched on a pole, black yak hair flowing down from it—an ancient war banner. And inside that, his hidden stash of vodka.

His eyes refocused on the table, to the taped-over menu of services it held. It cost twenty thousand tukgrik for a first consultation, ranging all the way up to 300,000 tukgrik for Fire Worship and Vodka Curing. The shaman wondered if his laggardly spirit might take offence. He slid the tasselled helmet to hide it from view.

"Sky of the wolf, please help me. I am man in need, with a heart of peace," he moaned.

He took a generous swig, then turned the bottle sideways, holding it to the corner of his eye. He recognised him at once—the impossible old man, Boru, the sky god who rode with the wolf and the raven. His uncle had mentioned him, and the duty his family owed to this great Wayfinder. The shaman dipped his fingers into the clear liquid, flicking a few drops into the air and then toward the ground for good measure. The last moisture, he daubed on his crinkled forehead. It was an auspicious moment, after all.

"You have come to the right place," he said, nervously. "I am glad you found me. You cannot throw a rock in Örgöö these days without hitting a shaman, who will probably tell you the rock has a spirit in it. Did you know, we even have a Corporate Union? Of shamans. Who ever did hear of such a thing?"

The shaman sank heavily into his chair, sour sweat gathering in the folds of his neck. He combed at his beard with a greasy hand, then began rummaging in his coat for his snuff box. Suitably invigorated, he slouched behind a man-sized tripod of wood and reached for another of his totems: a round oak shield, glazed with colours, well preserved with charms and oils. All of the mortal realms were there, in bands of red, green, and blue. The script was Norse, although neither the shaman nor his uncle had ever deciphered it. His family had been told to keep it hidden. The old man Boru took it, scrutinising it in the light of the fire, and smiled.

The shaman was glad the spirit was contented.

"My uncle says it saved us, when the sunspear fell. The Shield of the World. Right where you left it."

He searched behind the frame again and drew out a square of yew wood, dotted with holes, and ornamented around the edges with carved panels. There was another relic too, an exquisite six-stringed khuur, that his guest embraced like long-lost family. There was no disguising his delight.

"Heim again, heim again," the old man said, dancing a veritable jig. "The Second Coming of Óðinn. Has a nice ring to it, don't you think?"

GLOSSARY

As you read through the novels of the Vikingverse, you will no doubt stumble upon many words that are unfamiliar or difficult to pronounce. Old English, also known as Anglo-Saxon, was a language spoken by the Angles and the Saxons, Germanic tribes who settled the British Isles—a language that forms the basis for the *Angle-ish* we speak today. It shares a common ancestry with the tongues of other tribes of northern Europe. Old Norse was one of those related languages.

The journey towards modern English began with the Norman invasion of 1066, which brought a new elite of French speakers to English shores. The church added to this development, introducing words with Latin or Greek origin. But, in the worlds of the Vikingverse, this progression is interrupted. By removing or marginalizing the effect of Christianity, northern Europe is left with a Germanic linguistic foundation for a lot longer.

Even today, when you know where to look, the Old Norse rót is still apparent among the tangle of Anglo-Saxon, French and Latin branches. The language of the Vikings may have become subdued over the centuries but make no mistake about it—from byrðr(birth) until we deyja (die)—the raw energy of the Norse shapes many of our words. Just look at a Viking the rangr way, and he might þrysta a knifr into your skulle. Even the word Kindle comes from the Norse kynda!

Eth (uppercase: Ð, lowercase: ð) is a letter used in Old and Middle English, as well as Icelandic, Faroese and Elfdalian. It was also used in Scandinavia during the Middle Ages but was subsequently replaced with dh and later d. It is often transliterated as d, although in Icelandic, ð is the same as the *th* in English that. For example, Iðunn is anglicized as Idunn or Ithun, so choose whichever pronunciation works best for you!

Thorn or þorn (Þ, þ) is a letter in the Old English, Gothic, Old Norse, Old Swedish, and modern Icelandic alphabets, as well as some dialects of Middle English. The letter originated from the rune Þ in the Elder Fuþark and was called thorn or thurs in the Scandinavian rune poems. In modern Icelandic, it is pronounced similar to *th* in the English word thick.

Æ (æ) is a letter in the alphabets of some languages, including Danish, Norwegian, Icelandic, and Faroese. As a letter of the Old English Latin alphabet, it was called æsc («ash tree») after the Anglo-Saxon futhorc rune ᚫ; its traditional name in English is still ash. It was also used in Old Swedish before being changed to ä. Today, the International Phonetic Alphabet uses it to represent a short «a» sound (as in «cat»).

Aðaliz – Old Norse form of the name Alice.

Ægir's daughters – in Norse mythology, the goddess Rán and the jötunn Ægir both personify the sea, and together they have nine daughters who personify waves.

Alfadóttir – elf daughter.

Ālim – in Islam, the ulama, singular Ālim, are scholars, literally "the learned ones," guardians, transmitters, and interpreters of religious knowledge.

Alpandill – elephant.

Arshimīdis – Arabic name for Archimedes, a Greek mathematician, physicist, engineer, inventor, and astronomer.

Bandruí – woman-druid.

Banū Mūsa – "Sons of Moses," pre-eminent scholars who worked in astronomical observatories established in Baghdad.

Baṭlumyus – the Arabic name for Claudius Ptolemy, a Greek mathematician, astronomer, geographer, and astrologer.

Bilād Fāris – Lands of Persia.

Boru – Qormusata Tngri "King of the Gods," the Mongolian sky god with the crow and the wolf as his "faithful agents."

Brynja – mail shirt, armour.

Butescarls – a professional soldier, but one who fought on a ship, as marines did in the 18th century English navy.

Chenoo – Skraeling term for person possessed by an evil spirit or who committed a terrible crime.

Dellingr – (Old Norse "the dayspring") is a god in Norse mythology, a personification of a dawn.

Dhimma contract – the notional contract that governs relations with Christians in classical Islamic law.

Dhira – an Arabic unit of measurement, approximately 60 cm or 24 inches.

Doppelsöldner – "double-mercenaries" or "double-pay men"; originally Landsknechte in 16th-century Germany who volunteered to fight in the front line, taking on extra risk, in exchange for double payment.

Dreki – dragon.

Drengskapr – bravery, manliness.

Einmánuður – the sixth month of the year in the old Nordic calendar and the last winter month.

Eldjötnar – a particularly ruthless race of fire giant who lived in Muspelheim.

Englismaðr – Englander.

Félagi – Old Norseword for fellow, partner, companion, comrade.

Franj – Arabic term for Franks.

Frísir – a native of Frísland, modern day Netherlands.

From Fehu to Othala – phrase meaning from "A to B," using the Futhark instead of the Latin alphabet.

Funafugl – flamingo.

Furðustrandir – the Wonderstrands, a stretch of coastline mentioned in the Icelandic Eiríks saga, located on the coast of Labrador.

Galdrkind – "magical creatures," composed from spell songs.

Gambanteinn – a "magic" wand, staff of office.

Garðariki/Garðaveld – Old Norse term used in medieval times for the states of Kievan Rus.

Grikkir – people of Greek descent.

Gulrstein Caldera – Yellowstone Caldera, a volcanic caldera and supervolcano.

Gyðingar – people of Jewish descent.

Hādīth – the record of the words, actions, and the silent approval of the Islamic prophet Muhammad.

Hājib – court title for chamberlain.

Hálogi – "High Flame," a fire giant, the personification of fire.

Hamingja – a guardian spirit, the personification of the good fortune or luck of an individual or family.

Hamr – form or appearance, that which others perceive through sensory observation.

Haugbui and kattakyn – mound-dwellers and demons.

Helhest – a three-legged horse associated with death and illness in folklore.

Heljarblý – Plutonium, named after the Nordic equivalent of the name Pluto

Hjúki and Bil – a brother and sister pair of children who follow the personified moon, Máni, across the heavens, akin to Jack and Jill from the English nursery rhyme.

Hrafn – raven.

Hrímfaxi – the horse of Night.

Huldufólk – hidden folk.

Hvalros – walrus.

Imārat Qurṭuba – Emirate of Cordoba.

Islendingr – native of Iceland.

Karkadann – the "Lord of the Desert," a mythical creature said to have lived on the grassy plains of India and Persia.

Khalīfah – leader of a Caliphate.

Khitai – Chinese.

Kjálkagálkn – crocodile.

Knattleikr – an ancient ball game played in Iceland.

Kornbretaland – Cornwall.

Kvaðrilljón – a large number, millions.

Læknir – doctor.

Landvaettir – spirits of the land in Norse mythology that protect and promote the flourishing of the specific places where they live, which can be as small as a rock or a corner of a field, or as large as a section of a country.

Líf and Lífthrasir – two humans who are foretold to survive the events of Ragnarök.

Ljósmóðir – literally Lightmother, in modern Icelandic used to refer to a midwife.

Madīnat as-Salām – the City of Peace, Baghdad.

Mother Jörð – in Norse myth, mother of the thunder god Thor, and the personification of earth.

Muhatasibs – a supervisor of bazaars and trade in the medieval Islamic countries.

Majūsiyya – a female pagan/queen.

Mordvargr – murderers.

Morguneyjar – Japanese (literally "morning isles").

Morior invictus – a Latin phrase that means "Death before defeat"; the literal translation is "I die undefeated."

Mundilfari – in Norse mythology, the father of Sól, the sun.

Mushrik – an idolater, a heathen.

Muwalladan – Neo-Muslims of Spanish origin.

Muya-hidīn – the term for one engaged in Jihad (literally, "struggle"), used in the period to mean the faithful of Islam.

Namsborg – Nantes.

Nasrani – Arabic name for Christians.

Ormr inn Langi – the Long Serpent; the original 10th century ship was built for the Norwegian King Olav Tryggvason and was the largest and most powerful longship of its day.

Ortug – unit of measurement, an ounce.

Qarāqīr – a type of boat, precursor to the carrack.

Qarlush bin Ludhwig – Arabic name for Charles the Bald, King of the Franks.

Qays'r al-Rûm – Roman Emperor.

Rudhmīr of Jiliqiyya – Ramiro II, Christian King of Galicia in northern Spain.

Rúðu – Roeun.

Rúnamál – runic alphabet.

Sækonungrs – sea-kings.

Sætumálmur – Norse form of chemical element Beryllium. Beryllium-10 is a radioactive isotope.

Sá gamli – the Old Man.

Sahir – witch, black magician.

Seidrkona – witch.

Seimgalir – Semigallians, a Baltic people living in the region of modern Latvia.

Sēnou – River Shannon.

Serkir – people of Arabic descent.

Sessrúmnir – a field where the goddess Freyja receives half of those who die in battle.

Shatranj – Arabic variant of chess.

Shayāṭīn – comparable to demons or devils in Islamic theology.

Skalli Fjall – Sca Fell Pike, the highest mountain in England.

Skjaldborg – shield wall.

Sómaherji – samurai.

Stari – starlings.

Svaðilfari – in Norse mythology, the stallion that fathered the eight-legged horse Sleipnir with Loki.

Sviar – Swedes.

Þráðriða – thread riders, specifically members of the three holy orders.

Þrǫstr – thrush.

Thurse – a giant, a Jötunn.

Til árs ok friðar – a toast, for a good year and frith (peace).

Trelleborg – Viking ring fortress.

Ugla – owl.

Ulfr – wolf.

Ülgen – a Turkic and Mongolian creator-deity, usually distinct from Tengri but sometimes identified with him in the same manner as Helios and Apollo.

Vafþrúðnir – "mighty weaver," a wise jötunn in Norse mythology.

Vargdropi – outlaw, miscreant; literally "wolf dropping."

Vesturljós – Western Lights.

Vingull – a horse's male organ, used in some rituals.

Vísdómsmaðr – sage, soothsayer or prophet.

Visundur – bison.

Vǫlur – collective term for members of the holy orders.

Wazaghah – a type of lizard.

Ya Sharmouta – insult meaning "you bitch."

Ýmirs eistna – an exclamation: "the testicles of the progenitor giant!"

Zunghar – "the left hand," one of major tribes of the Mongolian steppe.

NOTE OF THANKS

Thank you for taking the time to read *Loki's Wager*. If you enjoyed it, please tell your friends—and if you hated it, tell your enemies. Word of mouth is an author's best friend and much appreciated.

ABOUT THE AUTHOR

Ian Stuart Sharpe (Ión Stívarður Skarpi) was born in London, UK, and now lives in British Columbia, Canada. Having worked for the BBC, IMG, Atari and Electronic Arts, he is now CEO of a tech start up. As a child he discovered his love of books, sci-fi and sagas: devouring the works of Douglas Adams, J.R.R. Tolkien, Terry Pratchett, and George MacDonald Fraser alongside Snorri Sturluson and Sigvat the Skald. He once won a prize at school for Outstanding Progress and chose a dictionary as his reward, secretly wishing it had been an Old Norse phrasebook. *Loki's Wager* is his second novel, a continuation of the Vikingverse sagas.

He can be found here:
Website: www.vikingverse.com
Facebook: www.facebook.com/vikingverse
Twitter: @vikingverse
Instagram: @vikingverse